The Sea Stone Sisters

After a haphazard early career that took her around the world, **Eleanor Buchanan** settled in York and began writing award-winning romance, historical and time-slip novels under various pseudonyms. She has now turned her hand to a brand-new series of enthralling stories that combine her passion for travel, her belief in the power of evocative love stories and her enduring fascination with the relationship between the past and the present.

The Sea Stone Sisters

ELEANOR BUCHANAN

REVIEW

Copyright © Headline Publishing Group 2026

The right of Eleanor Buchanan to be identified as the
Author of the Work has been asserted by her in accordance
with the Copyright, Designs and Patents Act 1988.

First published in 2026 by Headline Review
An imprint of Headline Publishing Group Limited

1

Apart from any use permitted under UK copyright law, this publication may
only be reproduced, stored, or transmitted, in any form, or by any means, with prior
permission in writing of the publishers or, in the case of reprographic production,
in accordance with the terms of licences issued by the Copyright Licensing Agency.

Cataloguing in Publication Data is available from the British Library

Hardback ISBN 978 1 0354 2595 2
Trade Paperback ISBN 978 1 0354 2597 6

Typeset in Janson by CC Book Production

Inside Illustration © TimPetersDesign.co.uk 2025

Printed and bound in Great Britain by Clays Ltd, Elcograf S.p.A.

Headline's policy is to use papers that are natural, renewable and
recyclable products and made from wood grown in sustainable forests.
The logging and manufacturing processes are expected to conform to
the environmental regulations of the country of origin.

Headline Publishing Group Limited
An Hachette UK Company
Carmelite House
50 Victoria Embankment
London EC4Y 0DZ

The authorised representative in the EEA is Hachette Ireland,
8 Castlecourt Centre, Dublin 15, D15 XTP3, Ireland
(email: info@hbgi.ie)

www.headline.co.uk
www.hachette.co.uk

*Four great stones once stood on a remote Scottish headland –
the Sisters of Skara.
Legend has it they were raised by a grieving father,
to guide his abducted daughters home.
A curse was placed on anyone who laid the stones low:
their family, too, would be scattered to the winds,
never to find their way home.*

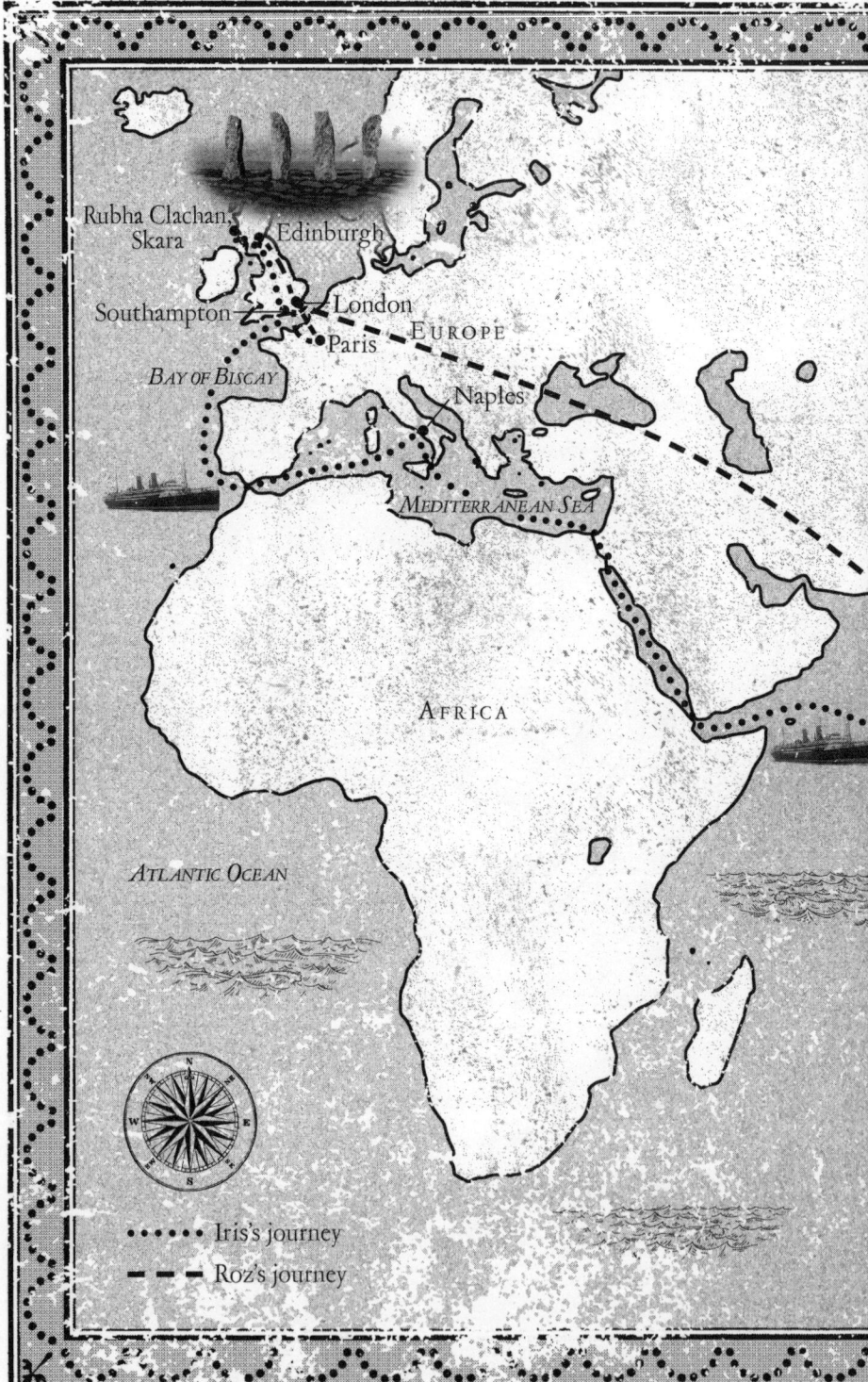

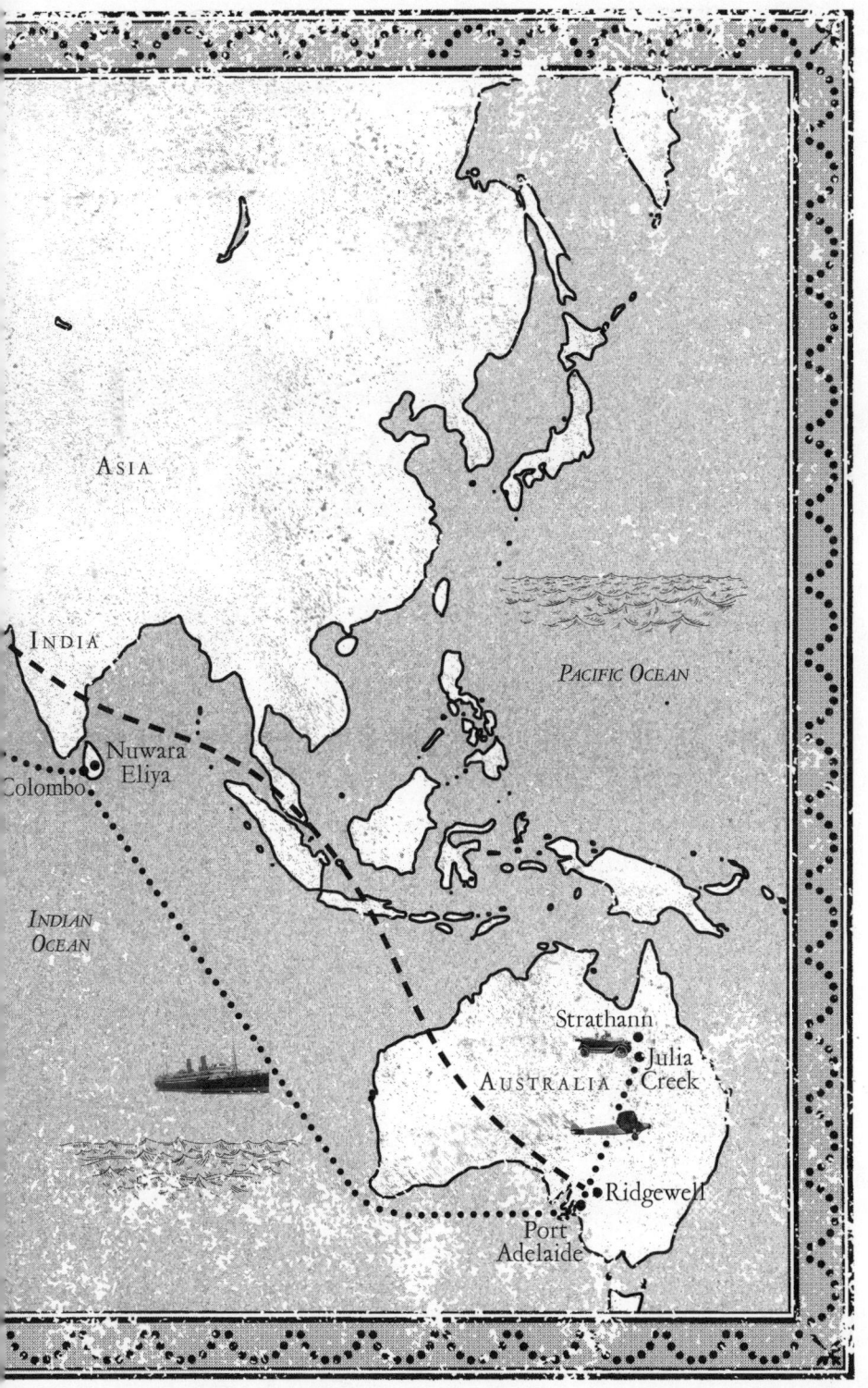

For Caroline Shelton, with love and respect

For Caroline Sheldon, with love and gratitude

PROLOGUE

Skara, c. 2800 BC

He had got back just in time, he thought, dragging his boat up onto the beach. On sunny days, the sand was a glaring white against the blue sea, but that day the water was choppy, dark and restless, the waves slapping warningly against the shore. Black clouds roiled behind the hills, and a growl of thunder announced the first stinging drops of rain. He was lucky not to have been caught out at sea in the storm.

Later, he would remember thinking that, thinking that he had been lucky.

He would need to secure the boat in the dunes quickly, before the wind picked up too. The keel scraped laboriously over the sand as he hauled it upwards, his breath rasping with effort. His two youngest daughters usually ran to help him. They chattered and teased and squabbled gaily, words tumbling out of them, their nimble hands freeing the net, or gutting the fish with practised strokes of the flint, or, like now, helping pull the boat ashore.

By the time he reached the dunes, the rain was already a torrent, and still he did not realise.

He convinced himself that the younger girls were sheltering with their sisters. The eldest was sensible, even if they were not. She would have seen the storm coming and would have told them to stay in the hut. His second daughter, quick-tempered and fiery, would be there too. He pictured them taking the fish from him, settling him by the fire. He would watch them as they moved around in the purposeful way of women, would listen to the rise and fall of their voices, that undercurrent of gurgling laughter as warming as the burning peat.

Other men pitied him for having no sons, but he did not care. Why would he need sons when he had his daughters, all long-limbed and strong? He was proud of the way they walked with a straight back, of how they looked strangers fearlessly in the eye. Each was different in her own way, but laughter came easily to all four. They ran along the sand, their hair blowing free, and their voices rang through the seagrass in the dunes and danced over the heather. When they were small, they had giggled when he tickled them, and now they loved him still, hanging their arms around his neck and pressing their cheeks against his.

He had secured the boat at last and was dragging out the fish when, out of the corner of his eye, he saw the shoe.

Soft leather, laced with a trailing thong and oozing the dried grass his daughters used to keep their feet warm. It lay discarded on the sand, with drag marks on either side.

Ice balled in his stomach. He was not in time at all, he understood instantly. He was much, much too late.

'No!' Too late, but he ran anyway. Discarding the fish, he stumbled up through the dunes and the clumps of spiky grass. The wind took the names he called and tossed them contemptuously out to sea, unheard.

By the time he reached the hut, the rain was slicing down, slicking his hair to his head and already obliterating the signs of struggle. He spun helplessly in the storm, shouting for his daughters, his precious girls, with their bright laughter and their warm chatter, while the wind screamed, uncaring, and the sky was splintered with lightning and the thunder crashed an accompaniment to his despair.

The hut was empty. The peat still smoked sullenly. There was a broken pot on the floor. A storage jar had been knocked over, spilling grain.

'No, no, no ...' His tongue was so knotted with sorrow and shock that that was all he could utter. 'No, no, no ...'

He had told them they would be safe here. They had a home at last, he had promised them. This was their place and they would never have to leave it.

Why, *why* had he not turned for home earlier? Had they cried out for him when they were taken? How could he have kept fishing when his world was ending? He should have known.

Heedless of the sluicing rain and the savage spears of lightning, he stumbled back outside. He shook his fist at the sky and cursed the gods who had let his daughters be taken. Tortured with grief and rage, he fell to his knees in the mud. Where were his girls now? Were they cowering in a boat, or had they been dragged ashore? His mind screamed at the thought of what might be happening to them. He must find them! They were strong, he tried to reassure himself. They would find a way home if they could, if he could not find them first.

The next morning, the villagers crept over the hill in shame. The sea fret had come in fast, the way it sometimes did, bringing the sea wolves with it. Only when the mist had cleared had they seen the boats thrusting through the water, heading far out to sea. They had heard the savage yells, seen his daughters roped together, but they had done nothing. There was nothing they *could* do, they told him.

'You will never find them,' they said. 'They will never find a way home. They are lost to you.'

He would not listen. He would find them, he vowed, or die trying. Home he had promised them and home they must have, whether he was here or not.

Before he left, he raised four great stones, one for each of his daughters, to stand there always to guide his girls back to the island. The villagers, afraid of the madness of his sorrow, helped him haul up the stones, tall and slender like his daughters, the rock speckled with bright shards that glinted in the sunlight. One, two, three, four, they set them on the point looking out over the sea to the islands and mountains beyond.

He imagined his daughters on a boat, scanning the shore for a landmark, imagined them exclaiming and pointing at the stones. 'Look!' they would cry. 'There is home at last.'

A curse on anyone who lays them low, he cried when the stones were set. Their family would be broken as his had been, their children dispersed across the seas, never to have a home, until all his daughters were together and home once more.

The villagers were charged to care for the stones while he

was gone, and seeing the depths of his despair, fearing the gods, they agreed. A curse on any who let this place be changed, he warned, sweeping an arm to encompass them all.

And then he took the shoe he had found and set off in search of his daughters, leaving the four great stones standing to guide them back to where they belonged.

1

Iris

Skara, April 1931

When it was all over, and the cups and saucers were being washed up by Mrs Grierson with much aggrieved clattering, they went down to the stones.

Once, the four stones, the Four Sisters, had stood tall on the headland, but Iris had only known them as they lay tumbled on their sides, arranged in a rough semicircle facing the sea. This was their special place, the place the four Blackmore sisters came in their turn, to dream and to plan, to whisper secrets and to sulk, to laugh and to rage.

Sometimes Iris sat here alone, too, with her sketchbook. She drew the view out over the spiky seagrass to the curve of white sand, out across the sea to the islands beyond, a scene unchanged for aeons. She often thought about the four sisters of legend, and imagined how they must have gazed out at the same hills, the same sea. Had they loved this place as much as she did?

Rubha Clachan, headland of stones, clung to the very end

of Skara, a peninsula narrowly attached to the west coast of Scotland. To the west lay the distant blue hills of Harris and Lewis and, on a clear day, North Uist. The looming mountains of the mainland jutted into the sea to the north, while the northerly finger of Skye pointed from the south.

At other times, Iris drew the bay itself, with Dundonan Castle standing doughtily on the other headland, its ancient towers and turrets a contrast to the starkly modern house Charles Blackmore had built at Rubha Clachan.

But she wouldn't look at Dundonan now.

She kept her eyes fixed on the hills across the sea instead. She loved the view when it was like this, the sea kicked up by a brisk breeze into a dancing, glittering turquoise, the mountains seeming so close and clear that she could almost reach out and touch them.

She loved it, too, when the water was calm, pale and milky in the still light, ruffled every now and then by a cat's paw of breeze, and the hills rolled away in soft, subtle shades of blue. Or when the evening sun struck the hillsides purple and gold. Even when the water heaved grey and sullen and the rain swept across the bay like curtains being drawn and the mountains were smothered in cloud, emerging ghostly through the mist for a brief moment before submerging into obscurity once more.

She had drawn it in all its moods and loved all of them. This was Rubha Clachan, this was home.

And she had to leave.

The thought of it sat like a boulder on her chest.

She didn't want to go.

She had to go.

Usually, the sisters sat on the stone each considered her own, but today they huddled close together for comfort. Daisy leant against Iris, Rose had her arm around Lily, the two older sisters bookending the younger ones. At twelve, Daisy was growing up fast, but Iris would for ever think of her as the baby. Lily, now fifteen, had always been quick and clever. Iris remembered her at three, pointing out the obvious way that she and Rose should build a sandcastle for the fairies on the beach.

And then there was Rose. Iris could not remember a time when her sister had not been there. Barely fifteen months between them, they might have been twins had they not been so different in character. Iris was twenty now, Rose just nineteen. She should have been the eldest, Iris always thought. She was bright and brave, eager to explore, to take a chance, while Iris herself was gentle like their mother, and more cautious.

Now Rose leapt to her feet, unable to sit still. 'There *must* be some other way,' she said, pacing in front of the stones.

'There isn't.' Iris twisted the ring on her finger, thinking of the promise she had made her mother. *I'll find him. I'll make sure we stay together. We'll be all right.*

'But . . . Ceylon! It's so far away,' said Lily. 'Iris, you'll hate it.'

She would, Iris was sure of it. The idea of Ceylon made her shudder. For Rose, the thought was exciting, but for Iris, it conjured up images of strangeness and snakes, of heat and tangled jungles, when the only place she had ever wanted to be was here on Skara, with the sea and the sky and the soft Scottish light. She was anchored here, she thought. The very stone she sat on seemed to thrum its agreement. *This* was her place.

The ring on her hand felt uncomfortable in a way Iris couldn't explain. She had promised her mother she would never take it off, but it made her uneasy. Something about the weight of it on her finger, the coldness of its blue flash.

They each had a ring, made from four exquisite blue stones, each unique, all perfectly matched. A shimmering opal, a glowing moonstone, a mysterious sandstone and a glittering sapphire. Their father had had them laced with sparkling diamonds and made into a necklace for their mother when they had first moved to Rubha Clachan. Iris had been eight, Daisy just a baby.

'A stone for each beautiful daughter, my darling,' Charles had boomed, fastening the necklace around Amelia's throat, and it might have been that, but even then Iris had suspected it was as much a peace offering as a celebration.

She remembered how proudly her father had shown them round the house he had built for his adored wife. 'Every modern convenience!' he boasted. There was electric light. There was a telephone in the hall. A refrigerator and a gramophone. There were bathrooms attached to every bedroom. There were spacious rooms and a curved staircase sweeping up to a wide landing.

But when Charles flung open the door to the drawing room, with its huge rounded windows looking out to sea, Amelia stilled. Rose and Lily scampered ahead, but Iris, holding the baby, had heard her mother's sharp intake of breath.

'Where are the Four Sisters?' she asked in a strange, tight voice.

'The stones? They were interrupting the view, so I had them taken down and laid flat. Now don't worry,' Charles hurried on, holding up his hands as he caught sight of his wife's face. 'They're still here. They'll make a perfect place to sit on a nice evening.'

'Oh Charles, what have you done?' Amelia said faintly.

'You're not thinking about that ridiculous curse, surely?' He clicked his tongue in frustration. 'My darling, it's 1919! The twentieth century! We need to embrace the future, not be tied to the past by hocus pocus and superstitious nonsense. It's not as if I broke the stones. They're still here, but they can't get in the way of progress.'

That was when he had produced the necklace. 'For you, my love. To mark our new life here. Do you like it?' he asked eagerly, as Amelia opened the flat box.

'It's beautiful,' she said obediently.

Iris hadn't understood her mother's stricken expression, not then. To her, the house at Rubhan Clachan was a home of their very own at last, a happy place, all space and light. Then there had been servants aplenty, rolling their eyes affectionately at Charles Blackmore's modern innovations. She and her sisters had a pony each, and party dresses, and later, new hats. There were flowers in every room. There was a white piano in the drawing room, and dancing to the gramophone, and champagne and laughter and a fire in the library on cold winter nights.

Now there were bare patches on the walls where valuable paintings had hung. The garden was untended, the silver unpolished. Only the Griersons laboured on, for love of Amelia, without even a parlourmaid to help. Charles's beloved Bugatti sat rusting in the garage.

Amelia had broken the necklace into four stones and had them made into rings for each of her daughters, so that they could wear them in memory of her.

Or perhaps so that Charles couldn't sell the necklace, or

gamble it away. Loyal to the end, she hadn't said as much, but Iris thought that might be it.

Daisy, the youngest, had the sapphire, Lily the moonstone. Amelia gave the sandstone to Rose, and to Iris, the opal, with its glimmering blue depths, set in a simple gold bar.

Iris turned it now on her finger, remembering the sadness in her mother's smile, and that strange jolt as Amelia pressed the ring into her palm and closed her fingers around it. 'For you, dearest Iris.'

Iris recognised the stone at once when she uncurled her hand. 'But Mummy, your beautiful necklace . . . !'

'The necklace is no use to me now, Iris, and I wanted you all to have something of me. I will give your sisters their own rings, but this one is for you.' Amelia's smile was painful. 'The opal has always reminded me of you, so clear and simple at first glance, but so much more colourful and interesting when you look closely. Wear it and take my love with you wherever you go.'

'I'm not going anywhere.' The words knotted in Iris's throat, and she rested her forehead on the side of her mother's bed so that Amelia wouldn't see her tears. 'I won't leave you.'

'My darling girl, you must. I am dying.' Amelia stroked Iris's hair. 'I wish I didn't have to ask this of you, but I need you to find Ralph and look after your sisters. I know you won't want to go, but I'm afraid that your father . . .' Her voice faltered, faded.

Choking down her grief, Iris lifted her head. She wouldn't make her mother say the words. 'Don't worry about Papa. I'll find Uncle Ralph,' she promised. She pushed the ring onto her finger. It seemed to tingle a warning, but she ignored it. Somehow, she found a wavering smile. 'I'll always wear this and think of you, Mummy. Always.'

Now her gentle mother was gone. Only that morning, they had laid her in a grave on that comfortless hillside, the last and worst of the losses they had endured over the past two years.

The stock-market crash had been only the beginning. A patent applied for too late, a rival firm snatching victory from under Charles's nose. Bankruptcy and a court case.

'Bad luck,' Charles said, as the losses turned from a trickle to a flood.

'Damned bad luck,' when he gambled the last of his fortune and lost, and then borrowed to gamble some more.

'My cursed luck,' he said, emptying the whisky bottle into his glass, unable to afford a doctor for his dying wife.

Perhaps he had been unlucky, but Iris remembered overhearing old Nessa talking to Mrs Grierson once. Her voice shook with fury.

He threw down the stones. He'll pay for that.

Daisy spoke as if she knew what Iris was thinking. 'This is all Papa's fault! If he hadn't knocked these stones down, he wouldn't be drinking, Mummy would be alive and you and Ian ...' She broke off as Iris flinched. 'You wouldn't have to go to Ceylon or anywhere else,' she amended.

'Now, Daisy, you know that's just a superstition,' Iris managed.

'Do I?' Daisy stuck out her chin. Her eyes were overbright and Iris knew that she was struggling not to cry. 'It's funny that it's all happening exactly as the legend said.'

'I've always thought it would be unfair for the curse to be

taken out on us anyway,' Lily put in. 'Why should we suffer because of something Papa did without asking us?'

Iris drew a steadying breath. They were all upset. 'Even if we *did* believe in the curse, which we don't, it says that the whole family will be scattered,' she said. 'But it's just me that's going. The rest of you will stay here until I can get back, so there will be no scattering.' She tried a reassuring smile.

Daisy tucked her hand into Iris's. 'I don't want you to go,' she said, her voice wobbling. 'I don't want to be here without Mummy or you.'

'I know, darling,' said Iris. 'I don't want to go either, but I need to find Uncle Ralph. I promised Mummy I'd do that. I'll come straight home, though.'

'Can't we all go?' said Lily. She held out her hand, and the moonstone in her ring flashed blue in the light. 'Mummy told me that she gave us these rings so we could always be together, like the stones were on the necklace. If you go away on your own . . . it feels wrong.'

'I wish we could go together, but we can't afford it. I'm lucky Lady Carsington wants a companion and will pay for my passage, otherwise I wouldn't be able to get to Ceylon at all.'

'Why does she *need* a companion?' Rose, so practical and independent, was unimpressed by the whole idea. 'It can't be that difficult to sit on a ship, surely?'

'I don't know,' said Iris. 'Apparently she's a friend of a friend of Lady Malcolm.' She kept her voice carefully neutral when talking about Ian's mother, who had avoided her eye at the funeral but done what she could to help. 'I presume she's an elderly lady who needs someone to deal with porters or sit and talk to her.'

'I bet she's a monster,' said Rose. 'She'll be making you run and fetch all day. I *wish* you didn't have to do it, Iris.'

'What else can I do, Rose?' Iris said patiently. Rose did understand, but they were all feeling raw from the funeral and Iris didn't want to snap back at her sister. 'I can't afford the fare and we must get hold of Uncle Ralph somehow.'

'Perhaps we could ask if she'd like all of us as her companions?' Lily suggested to break the tension. 'I'd play bezique with her, and Rose would organise trips ashore, and she could pat Daisy's cheek and tell her she was a sweet child.'

'And all I'd have to do was sort out the porters?' said Iris, smiling gratefully at Lily. 'It would be fun, wouldn't it? But I don't think Lady Carsington will pay for four of us, sadly. Besides, I need you to say here and help Rose deal with Papa.'

It made Iris's heart crack to think of their father, swaying at the graveside that morning. They had loved him so much when they were younger.

'My, you girls are the prettiest bunch of flowers I have ever seen!' he would cry, holding open his arms whenever he came home, loud and boisterous, full of enthusiasm for some new project, and he would scoop them up and spin them round until they squealed and giggled. Iris could still remember the scratch of tweed against her cheek, the comforting smell of tobacco and the sense of utter trust.

She could trust him no longer. It was far too late for that. Now her beloved father was a problem to be dealt with.

She had faith in Rose to do that. Rose had always been Charles's favourite. She had all the boisterous confidence that Iris lacked. Lily was bright and Daisy enchanting, but Rose would be able to handle him best. Iris had already hidden away the rest of their mother's jewellery and the better paintings.

'Sell what you need to pay Mrs Grierson and the household bills,' she had said, giving Rose the key. 'Try not to let Papa know. If he finds out there's any money at all . . .'

'He'll gamble it away,' said Rose. 'I know. I'll be careful.'

'I don't want you to go,' Daisy said again. 'I won't be able to *bear* it!'

'It won't be for ever,' Iris said. She could see Daisy's mouth wobbling, and she hugged her little sister to her as she glanced at Lily to forestall any sharp retort about Daisy's tendency to over-dramatise. But today Lily's lips were pressed fiercely together and she said nothing.

'I'll be as quick as I can. People go to Ceylon all the time,' Iris went on, trying to convince herself as much as her sisters. 'I've just got to find Uncle Ralph, and then everything will be fine.'

2
Iris

'What if he won't help us?' asked Lily. 'Aunt Edith said he was a "scapegrace", although I daresay that means he's a lot worse than that,' she added with a look that belonged to someone a lot older than fifteen.

'He will,' said Iris, stiffening her voice. 'It's a debt of honour. Mummy lent him the money to buy his tea plantation years ago.' Before all the money had gone. 'She said he promised to pay it back, and even if he can't do that, he'll look after us somehow.'

'He hasn't replied to any of her letters,' Lily pointed out.

Iris had wondered about that too. 'I don't think that means much,' she said, more confidently than she felt. 'Mummy said he was always terrible at keeping in touch, even though she was closer to him than to any of her sisters. She told me that he was the naughtiest boy, but so charming he could get away with anything. I get the impression that he's rather selfish and spoiled, but deep down he's … well, he's a gentleman. He'll keep his word.'

She hoped.

'In the meantime, we'll have to keep Aunt Edith at bay,' said Rose. 'She's full of plans for splitting us up among various relatives, although I notice *she*'s not offering to give any of us a home.'

'I wouldn't want to go and live with her anyway,' said Lily. 'What a bossy boots!'

'Lily,' said Iris with a reproving look.

'Well, she *is*.'

'She means well,' said Iris, remembering the conversation with her mother's blunt-spoken sister.

'This is a bad business.' Formidable in a black astrakhan coat and hat, Aunt Edith had shaken her head at how few guests had come back to the house after the funeral. 'Poor Amelia, she deserved a better send-off than this.'

Graciously accepting a cup of tea from a red-eyed Mrs Grierson, she turned back to Iris. 'One minute Charles is cock of the walk with his millions and his modern house and his modern conveniences and his new-fangled ideas, and the next the money has all gone, Amelia's in her grave, and judging by the state of your father, he's drinking.'

She cast a disapproving glance at where Charles Blackmore stood swaying in the corner, clutching a glass of whisky.

'We did warn her,' she remembered with a sigh. 'She *would* marry your father, though. For a girl who would never say boo to a goose when she was growing up, Amelia could be quite headstrong when she wanted. She threatened to run away if she didn't get permission to marry Charles. I thought our father would have an apoplexy!'

She shook her head again and turned back to Iris. 'I suppose you'll have to postpone your wedding now, too?'

Iris had known this moment would come, but it was still an effort to unstiffen her face and muster a smile.

'Oh, didn't you hear? There isn't going to be a wedding,' she said lightly.

'What? I thought you and young Malcolm had an understanding?' Aunt Edith's brows shot up and then snapped together. 'Bottled it, has he? The bounder. It's not your fault your father's been a fool and gambled away his fortune.'

The cup and saucer trembled in Iris's hand as her throat closed. *I mustn't cry. I mustn't cry.* 'We . . .' Her voice was high and painful, and she coughed to lower it. 'We agreed we did not suit,' she managed.

Aunt Edith snorted. 'It didn't suit him to have a penniless wife, no doubt. Well, I can't say I'm surprised. Your father is . . . not quite out of the top drawer, shall we say? I daresay the Malcolms were ready to overlook that when he had his millions to throw around, but it's a different story now. You won't mind me speaking frankly, I know.'

But I *do* mind, Iris thought rebelliously. Why was it that speaking frankly always meant saying things that only hurt the person on the receiving end of the frankness?

Rose or Lily would have answered back and been accused of being rude. Daisy would have let her great blue eyes fill with tears and made Aunt Edith apologise for making her cry. But Iris was the eldest, the responsible one, the one who got on with it and made everything right, so she said nothing.

Aunt Edith was still talking in any case. 'Well, I'm sorry for it, Iris, but there's no use crying over spilt milk.' She looked around the drawing room, stripped of the best paintings but still boasting its magnificent view across the bay. 'What are you going to do? You can't carry on like this.'

Why is it up to me to decide? Why must I always be the one who has to sort out the mess? But of course she didn't say that either.

'I know.' Iris swallowed, steadied her voice. 'That's why I'm going to Ceylon to find Uncle Ralph.'

'Ralph!' echoed Aunt Edith with all an older sister's scorn. 'Ralph never had two pennies to rub together. I wouldn't rely on *him*!'

But Iris had nobody else to rely on. Amelia had been adamant that her younger brother would help, and Iris had promised to find him.

Now she made herself smile reassuringly at her sisters. 'I know Aunt Edith can be a bit much, but at least she's here and she's got our best interests at heart. I've told her there's no question of splitting you up. I won't be away long. I'll be home before you know it.'

And what then? Iris wondered later, when Rose had taken Lily and Daisy inside and she could be alone at last. She sat on while the sun sank behind the hills and the sky flushed a pale apricot. There was an iron band around her chest, tightening, tightening, until she could hardly breathe.

If only their father hadn't made that foolish investment. He had always been so astute. How could he have made such a terrible mistake? Iris couldn't understand it.

If only Amelia hadn't fallen ill. If only they could have afforded a doctor.

If only Lord Malcolm hadn't gambled away what was left of his fortune all those years ago. Then Ian wouldn't have needed a rich wife.

But then Charles wouldn't have been able to buy the land at Rubha Clachan from the Dundonan estate. She wouldn't have had those years with Ian, riding and sailing and walking in the hills.

Their mothers were school friends, so they might have met, Iris supposed, but it wouldn't have been the same. She had loved Ian from the moment he had taught her how to skim stones on the sea when it lay still between the hills and lapped creamily at the shore. She had been ten, he a year older. From then on, they had done everything together. Ian-and-Iris, everyone called them, or 'the two I's'. *Where are the I's?* people would ask. *What are the I's doing?*

Iris looked across the bay at the castle that seemed to grow out of the opposite headland. She had never doubted that she and Ian would marry one day. They didn't even discuss it. It was simply taken for granted. They loved each other, not in a silly, simpering way, but truly, bone-deep. They *knew* each other. When they were apart, they both felt as if things were faintly askew, but the moment they took each other's hand again, the world clicked into place and righted itself.

But then had come the great recession and the catastrophic failure of her father's luck at one venture after another. As his fortunes changed, so did he. Iris's ebullient father had turned surly and then morose. His love for his wife and his daughters faded before his desire, his need, for whisky.

Iris and Ian worried. 'We should marry now,' Ian said. 'We should just go away and get married and you can all come and live at Dundonan. So what if there's no money? We'll manage.'

Yes, Iris wanted to say. *Yes, I'll marry you now.* 'I can't,' she said instead. 'Not yet. Mummy's so unwell and someone has to look after the girls. And I'm only twenty. They would never let us do it.'

One day, not long before Amelia died, Ian's mother invited Iris to tea. Iris loved Dundonan. Her father's house at Rubha Clachan was striking, with its stark angles and light rooms, the exact opposite of Dundonan, which dated back to the thirteenth century and was all turrets and towers and stone battlements, all twisty corridors and odd steps. Inside, the castle was comfortable. It had a traditional drawing room, whose thick red velvet curtains could be drawn against winter nights, and a great hall lined with gloomy ancestral portraits and stags' heads.

Most of all, Iris loved Lady Malcolm's sunny sitting room at the rear of the castle. Her windows overlooked the delightful gardens, walled to keep out the sea wind. Iris had thought those rooms would be hers one day. The light was perfect for painting. She had often pictured herself there, looking up from her easel to watch her sturdy children playing in the garden, smiling up at Ian as he came in to drop a kiss on the top of her head.

Isobel Malcolm and Amelia had been at school together in Edinburgh. Amelia had fallen in love with Rubha Clachan when visiting Dundonan before her marriage, and the two friends had regarded the romance between their children indulgently over the years. So when the invitation came, Iris ran eagerly over to the castle. Lady Malcolm would know what to do, she was sure. She was a practical woman, but kind.

'Ian's not here?' she asked in surprise when she was shown into the sitting room and had kissed Lady Malcolm on the cheek.

'No, I thought you and I should have a chat on our own.' There was something off about Ian's mother's smile, and although she had returned the kiss with warmth, her eyes didn't quite meet Iris's.

'Let's have some tea,' she said brightly as she rang the bell. 'How is your mother?'

'Not well.' Reminded of her greatest worry, Iris bit her lip. 'I want to call a doctor, but Papa says we can't afford it.'

'Oh, my dear.' Isobel sighed. 'I know only too well what it is to have to make economies. Your poor mama. It's so very, very unfortunate that your papa's affairs have taken such a turn for the worse.'

She flitted around the room, unable to settle, until Iris began to feel uncomfortable. 'Is something wrong?' she asked at last.

'Well ... Ah, here's the tea!' Isobel greeted the appearance of the parlourmaid with relief. 'Thank you, Elspeth. Leave the tray on the table. I'll pour.'

'Very good, milady.'

Iris smiled at the maid, but Elspeth only gave her a sour look. She was from Acheravie, and since the stones had been taken down, the villagers refused to work at Rubha Clachan. The place was cursed, they said. They would have nothing to do with it. All the Blackmore servants had come from the mainland, drawn by the excellent wages Charles offered. They were long gone now, of course.

Tea was poured, milk and sugar offered, and they sipped in awkward silence until Isobel set down her cup and saucer with an air of resolution.

'I wanted to tell you that we have decided to invite a few young people from London.'

Iris nodded slowly, unsure where this was going.

'We feel that we should have done this before,' Isobel ploughed on. 'I know what good friends you and Ian are, but it's not healthy for him to have such a small social circle.'

A tiny tremor started in the pit of Iris's stomach.

'You're a sensible girl, so I'm sure you agree.' Isobel paused hopefully, but Iris could only clutch her cup and saucer and feel the tremor spread.

Isobel swallowed. 'Your father's situation has changed things for us. The truth is that we simply cannot afford to keep Dundonan unless Ian is practical when it comes to choosing a bride. I know how fond you are of each other, but there's never been a formal engagement, has there?'

'No.' Iris barely moved her lips.

'I can only feel blessed that Ian was too young to have had to fight in that awful, awful war, but much as we might like to pretend that all is better now, it's simply not.' Isobel twisted her pearls fretfully. 'One can't manage with the cost of everything nowadays. You have no idea of the upkeep on a castle like this...' She petered out and gazed miserably at Iris.

Iris had the strangest feeling that she was watching herself. Inside, the tremor had become a quake, but she was able to put down her cup and saucer quite steadily.

'You want Ian to marry someone rich.'

'It sounds so hard-hearted, I know, but James is threatening to sell up completely. You know how much Ian loves Dundonan. What would he do with himself if we sold it? Where would he go?' Isobel's voice trembled with distress. 'Can you imagine him in Edinburgh?'

No, Iris couldn't. Ian belonged here in the hills, with the sea.

'We did hope that your father would recover his fortune and then we could all have been happy,' Isobel said, 'but it seems that isn't going to happen, and we have to face up to how life is, not how we would like it to be. It is women who have to do that, Iris, as you will learn. Look at your father, drowning his sorrows in drink, or James, making wild threats that he won't be able to carry out instead of understanding that there is only one solution. Ian must marry money.'

Iris drew a breath, and then another. She steadied her voice. 'Would you like me to talk to Ian?'

'Please.' Isobel's lips wobbled. 'You are such a dear girl, Iris. I am so sorry. I wish it could be different.'

'I do too,' said Iris quietly as she got to her feet.

Ian raged, refused to let her break their engagement. It would be her or no one, he vowed, but Lord Malcolm, like many weak men when pushed, dug in his heels. He swore that he would make good on his threat.

'You can't let him sell Dundonan, Ian,' said Iris. 'Imagine life away from Skara. *Think* of it.'

Iris loved Skara, but Ian was *part* of it. For generations, the Malcolms had walked the hills here, had put out to sea and fought for the land. Dundonan was the warp and Ian the weft; they were woven together into a single fabric. Iris had seen him when he returned at the end of every school term, seen how he lifted his face to the breeze and gulped in the air as if only then could he breathe properly. He had refused to go to university.

'I just want to be here with you,' he'd told Iris.

Now she saw the flicker in Ian's eyes as she forced him to picture a life elsewhere.

'I can change,' he said, setting his jaw. 'We can be happy in another place. It doesn't have to be Dundonan. My father seems to be able to consider living somewhere else,' he added bitterly. 'He doesn't care where he is as long as he can gamble his life away.'

'You're not your father,' Iris said gently. 'I'm not sure I could bear to see you anywhere else, Ian. You would be wretched, and I would be wretched, too. Imagine what would happen to Dundonan and the people who work here,' she added. 'Imagine if it was sold to someone who didn't care for it as you do. Someone who might knock down walls and modernise it and put a tennis court in the garden.'

Someone like her father.

Iris saw Ian flinch at the thought.

'They might get rid of the servants and bring in outsiders and, I don't know, turn it into a hotel or something awful.'

'Don't,' said Ian. 'I can't bear the thought of it.'

'I know,' she said. 'And that's why you must marry a girl who can bring some money to Dundonan. You have to face up to it.'

'But I *love* you, Iris,' he cried. 'I need you.'

'And I love you,' she said, 'but you need Dundonan more. We will have to be dear friends. That will have to be enough.'

But it was not enough. It was too hard to be together but not be able to kiss or to lay her head on his shoulder. To be snarled up with yearning.

'I can't do this,' Ian said desperately.

'I know,' said Iris. 'My mother is dying,' she said at last. 'Don't come. Don't write. If I see you when I'm walking, I will turn and walk the other way.'

Ian had been at Amelia's funeral that morning. Iris stood at the graveside clutching her sisters' hands, Lily on one side and Daisy on the other. She had felt his eyes on her, but she couldn't look at him. If she had, she would have thrown herself into his arms and begged him to hold her, to never let her go. Instead, she had squeezed Lily and Daisy's hands so tightly it must have hurt them. Neither of them said a word.

The wind had dropped now, and Iris could hear the sea sighing against the shore, echoing her own sighs. Her father should never have taken down the stones.

He'll pay for that, Nessa had said. But Charles wasn't paying. Iris let the bitter thought creep into mind. She was.

There had been so many goodbyes lately. Her dear old pony, Blossom. One by one the servants had left. Nanny, Mrs Grierson's great rival, had gone tearfully back to Edinburgh.

Ian.

Her mother.

And now she must say goodbye to her sisters too.

Iris felt as if her chest was folding in on itself, but she made herself square her shoulders, lift her chin. She remembered what Lady Malcolm had said. *We have to face up to how life is, not how we would like it to be.*

She must find her uncle so that she could support her sisters. That was all there was to it.

She set her hands flat against the stone beneath her, anchoring herself. It was almost warm, almost *tingling.* She was safe here, part of the stone, part of the landscape.

She wanted to sit there for ever, watching the hills as the light faded from the sky, but she forced herself to her feet and smoothed down her skirt. She drew in a breath, smelt the heather on the hills tangling with the scent of the sea, and then with one last look at her stone, she turned and walked back towards the house. She needed to pack for her voyage to Ceylon.

3
Roz

Ridgewell, South Australia, present day

A butterfly was fluttering in desperation against the window. Roz cupped her hands gently around it and carried it to the door that opened onto the veranda. She could feel its wings brushing frenziedly against her palms as she stepped outside into the heat and opened her hands, smiling as it flew into the sunlight in a flash of orange.

She stood for a moment in the shade of the veranda. If she narrowed her eyes, it was like looking out at an abstract painting, all blocks of grey and green, fractured shade, and blobs of yellow in the lemon tree. Once there had been bougainvillea scrambling over the back fence, a raft of agapanthus, and, in the shade, the shrub roses her father had tended so carefully in memory of his home in England.

The bougainvillea had been too messy for Richard, though. That had been cut back, while John Chatton's roses were dug up and discarded.

Don't think of him, Roz told herself. It's over.

Her father had loved his garden. He would have hated how neglected it looked now, the coarse grass dusty and unkempt, the wattle overgrown, the ground beneath it carpeted with its cheery yellow pompom flowers.

She should get someone in to tidy it all up. Roz added another job to her mental list. In the long months since her mother had died – nearly two years now, she realised with a shock – she had done her best to pretend that nothing had changed. She had gone back to Sydney, gone back to Pete and her job, and put all thoughts of the investigation and the trial and the grinding legal process in a mental compartment marked 'only open if absolutely necessary'. Roz was good at compartmentalising.

But now Richard had been convicted, the law had confirmed that the house was hers to sell, and she had come home to clear it at last.

No, not home. Ridgewell hadn't been home for a long time.

She shook the thought away and closed the door behind her as she stepped back into the welcome cool of the living room, now strewn with clothes and sacks full of tightly packed garments.

'This is the last of it.'

Bronwen staggered in with a black case. She dropped it by the sofa and stood back, swiping wisps of blonde hair from her face with the back of her arm. 'I found this on top of the wardrobe.'

'Thanks, Bron.' Roz smiled gratefully at her old schoolfriend. 'I don't know what I'd have done without you.'

'Hey, it's a nice change from wrangling the twins.' Bronwen cleared a space between the piles of clothes and dropped onto the sofa. She looked around her. 'Who would have guessed that your mum would have so many clothes?'

'She always did like to be well groomed,' said Roz. Appearance was everything for her mother.

Bronwen looked at her more closely. 'How are you doing?'

'Fine. To be honest, I'm embarrassed that you've had to do all the hard work today. It's just ... I can't face going into Mum's room yet.'

'Roz, it's okay,' Bronwen said kindly. 'I don't blame you. It's hard enough clearing out a house at any time, let alone under these circumstances.'

Roz sighed. 'I feel so *stupid*. I can get to her bedroom door and then I can't go any further.' She had tried it several times, but it was like walking into an invisible wall. Her legs refused to move. She got as far as reaching for the handle, only to be swamped by sickening waves of dread that made her fall back.

'Honestly, I'm surprised you can bear to come into the house at all,' said Bronwen. 'I wouldn't have been able to do it.'

'I made myself come back. If I hadn't, it would have been like letting Richard win.'

But it had been hard.

She hadn't had to deal with it in Sydney. She had closed the door firmly on thoughts of Ridgewell. The trial had taken place in Adelaide, so there had been no need to come back until the previous week.

The first time she came to the house, Roz hadn't made it past the front door. She stood on the veranda, her heart racing, in turns hot and cold, before she admitted defeat and went back to the car and sat sweating with anxiety.

But she refused to give up. Stubborn, her mother had called her, though she hadn't meant it as a compliment, Roz knew.

The next time, she managed to open the door. The time after that, she walked down the long hallway with its polished jarrah floor, her footsteps muffled by the Persian runner, past the traditional Australian landscapes on the wall. Through the front door, down the hall, stopped and came back. That was enough for the third time.

On her fourth visit, she made herself look into the living room, the dining room, the kitchen, just as she had done that day.

On her fifth visit, she told herself that she was ready. She climbed out of the car and stood in the crushing heat, unease uncoiling slow and serpent-like inside her. She let herself smell again the citrusy scent of dried gum leaves on the nature strip. She walked up the steps and hesitated at the door.

That day, she remembered, it had been ajar. Not enough to be noticeable from the street, but a warning. It had needed only a slight push to swing open.

She went inside. The house smelt different now, the familiar scent of polished wood now overlaid by dust and emptiness and the throat-tightening smell of chemical forensic cleaning, which lingered like a bitter memory. Roz tried to block it out as she re-created her movements. 'Mum?' she had called out. 'Mum, are you here?' Her voice sounded tight and high.

She had looked in the living room, in the kitchen, out to the empty garden, before heading back towards the bedrooms. Outside her mother's room, she had stopped. Through the oppressive silence came the relentless drip, drip, drip of a tap from the en suite bathroom.

The sound had put her already frayed nerves on edge. 'Mum?' she tried again as she pushed open the door to the bedroom. The room was empty, and she felt a rush of relief. Her mother must be outside after all. She would turn off the annoyingly dripping tap and then go and find her.

Her mother hadn't been outside. She had been in the en suite.

Roz's counsellor had suggested putting the memories of that room in a mental box, shutting them away and letting herself look at them one by one. Roz was more than capable of putting bad memories away, but she was less keen on confronting them. At her counsellor's urging, she had tried opening the lid once or twice, but the memories leapt out, shrieking, terrifying, uncontrollable: her mother's mouth hanging open, lipstick smeared; the angle of her head; the terrible twist of her arm.

Roz could slam the lid shut on the memories, but she still couldn't go into her mother's room and see the bathroom door.

Which was why she had had to ask Bronwen to spend most of the afternoon emptying the wardrobe and chest of drawers and carrying her mother's clothes through to the living room, where Roz was packing them into bags to be taken to the op shop and sold for charity.

'No more phone calls or messages?' Bronwen probed, clearly unconvinced that all was as well as Roz insisted.

'Nope.' Roz shook her head. For months she had been inundated with anonymous phone calls, sometimes silent, sometimes abusive, and texts accusing her of being a liar.

The messages had gone into another mental compartment. They had nothing to do with her life in Sydney, with getting the ferry to work, going to the beach with Pete. It was only now that she was back in Ridgewell that her nerves had tightened with the conviction that she was being watched. In shops, her neck would prickle and she would glance over her shoulder, but the other shoppers would be absorbed in their trolleys. Or she would think that she heard a hissed insult in the street, only to be met by blank looks if she swung round.

'I still think you should have gone to the police,' Bronwen said. 'Anonymous messages are nasty.'

Richard *was* the police, Roz thought. He had been a popular officer. Most of Ridgewell's police force probably thought she deserved everything she got. At his trial, it had come down to whether the jury believed his reputation as an upstanding cop or her evidence as the flaky, estranged, jealous daughter.

There had been moments during the trial when she thought he was going to get away with it, too.

It's over, she reminded herself.

'I changed my phone number and there's been nothing since,' she told Bronwen. 'But I have to admit I feel safer knowing Richard's in prison. Anyway, let's have a glass of wine and forget about him,' she went on briskly. 'You deserve it after all your hard work.'

She retrieved a bottle of Pinot Grigio from the otherwise empty fridge and found the two glasses she had brought over. Pouring the wine, and handing Bronwen a glass, she toasted her friend.

'Thank you, Bron, for everything.'

Bronwen chinked glasses. 'What are friends for?'

'I just need to take this lot to the op shop tomorrow and then that's it. I can put the house on the market and get on with my life.'

'I'll drink to that,' said Bronwen. 'Will you go back to Sydney?'

'Actually, I was thinking of heading to the UK for a bit. Mum said something the last time I spoke to her.' Roz looked down into her glass, remembering. 'She mentioned a trip to London that we had been planning before Dad died. It wasn't like her. She never used to talk about that time. I said maybe we should think about going together one day – just casually – and she closed the conversation down as if I'd spooked her, but I wish now I'd pressed her about it.'

'You always think you're going to have the time to ask,' Bronwen said sympathetically, and Roz nodded.

'Anyway, I thought I'd go to London the way the two of us might have done if things had been different. Dad was British, so I've got a passport. I might get a job there, see a bit of Europe. I fancy drifting for a while.'

'What about Pete? I thought you were getting serious?'

'You know me, I don't do serious.' Roz jumped to her feet before Bronwen could comment. What her friend saw as a fear of commitment, Roz considered a sensible approach to relationships. Keeping it light on both sides meant that no one got hurt.

'You drink your wine,' she said. 'I'm going to finish sorting this stuff.'

She looked at the case Bronwen had carried in last. It stood in the middle of the rug by the coffee table, squat and black and somehow menacing. No, not menacing, she decided. Portentous.

Bronwen followed her gaze. 'It was stuffed right at the back of the wardrobe. I nearly missed it altogether. Aren't you going to open it?' she asked, when Roz didn't move.

'Sure.' Roz pulled herself together. It was just a suitcase.

Shaking off the feeling, she stepped over to the case, laid it on its side and unclipped it.

She found herself looking at a plastic bag that contained what looked like a tweedy jacket and a pair of men's shoes.

Bronwen had leant forward, but now she sat back, unimpressed. 'Doesn't look like anything exciting.'

'It's Dad's stuff.' Roz's voice sounded odd, as if it was coming from somewhere outside her. Crouching down, she touched the tips of her fingers gently against the shoes, and then pulled the jacket out of the plastic covering. 'They must have been sent back from the hospital after he died.'

She lifted the jacket to her face, hoping that it would still smell of her beloved father, but there was nothing: just the mustiness of old, slightly scratchy fabric. Grief clogged her throat.

'I remember Dad wearing this,' she said. She straightened so that she could shrug on the jacket. It was inexpressibly comforting, and for a moment she could almost imagine him settling a steadying arm about her shoulders.

'It looks good on you,' Bronwen said. 'You always could carry off the vintage look.'

Anxious to banish the sadness, Roz put her hands in the pockets and peacocked for her friend's benefit. 'Perhaps I'll keep it— Oh!' A strange jolt ran through her as her fingers closed over a small box. She drew it out. 'There's something in the pocket.'

'Ooh, a jewellery box!' Bronwen leant closer. 'Open it!'

Roz hesitated as unease stirred again inside her. But it was just a box. There was no reason not to open it.

Almost reluctantly, she lifted the lid.

Inside was a ring, nestled into a bed of satin stained with age.

Bronwen peered over her shoulder to see. 'Is that an opal? What a beauty!'

'I think so.' Momentary unease forgotten, Roz lifted the ring from the box and turned it to catch the light. The opal was oval, almost a rectangle, and set as a band across the finger. Its blue depths were clear, fractured into a myriad facets, each with a different shade of blue. It seemed a living thing, glowing, pulsing.

'Put it on,' Bronwen said in a low voice.

'Okay,' Roz said, equally quiet as she slipped the ring onto the third finger of her right hand. It fitted perfectly. She glanced at her friend. 'Why are we whispering?'

'I don't know,' Bronwen admitted. 'It just feels... momentous.'

Roz knew what she meant. She had the oddest sense that her life to date had been arrowing to this point and that she had somehow made a choice by putting on the ring.

She was sure that she could feel it warming on her finger. How could that be? All at once her heart was beating hard. She looked down at the ring where it glowed and, yes, *tingled* on her hand.

'I know this ring,' she said slowly. 'Mum inherited it from her mother, and it didn't fit. She was determined to have it adjusted and she badgered Dad until he took it to a jeweller. I remember all the fuss she made. And then Dad was due to take me to a netball match, but Mum said she'd had a message that the ring was ready and she insisted that he go and pick it up instead. I don't remember how I got to the match, but I remember feeling really cross about it. I got a lift with a friend, probably, but when I got back, there was a police car outside.'

She stopped. She remembered hearing her mother howling like an animal and covering her ears. She had stood on the veranda in the dark, not wanting to go in, not wanting to hear what was making her mother cry and cry and cry. Not wanting to know. Roz could still smell the jasmine that twisted around the veranda rail, still see the scuff marks on the floor.

A police officer had come out in the end and found her. 'What are you doing out here, love?' she had said.

Roz looked up then. 'I want my dad,' she said. 'Where's my dad?'

She had been eleven.

And now it appeared that the ring her mother had made such a fuss about had been forgotten, tossed into a case with her father's things. Roz realised that her hands were balled, and she flexed her fingers, studying the glimmer of the opal. She had forgotten about the ring that had cost her father his life. If he hadn't been on the road then, at the moment the other car swerved, if he had taken her to netball after all instead of giving in to her mother's nagging, he might still be alive. And so might her mother.

Her mother had never worn the ring. But Roz would.

4
Finn

Edinburgh, present day

'Ah, Findlay, come in . . . come in.' James Kingan, senior partner in Kingan, Kingan & McVean, beckoned to him from behind his vast desk. 'Settling in all right?' he asked as Finn took the chair opposite.

There was only one answer to that. 'Very well, thank you, sir.' Finn winced inwardly as he heard himself. He'd been told to call the senior partner James on several occasions, but the man put him so forcibly in mind of his old headmaster that the 'sir' kept popping out.

Kingan, Kingan & McVean was an almost laughably traditional firm of solicitors. Founded in 1923, the firm occupied a large Georgian house in Edinburgh's New Town and enjoyed a reputation for unrivalled discretion and sound legal advice. Finn knew that he was lucky to have been taken on as an associate solicitor. The musty-looking books in James Kingan's study, the polished desk and green leather chairs could hardly be more different from his previous office in an industrial estate outside Dumfries.

'Everyone has been very friendly and welcoming,' he added, although Faiza, the office manager, and the two legal secretaries in reception terrified him. That morning he had paused outside the imposing sandstone house with its sash windows and fanlight over the grand black front door. The brass plaque was polished daily, shiny enough for Finn to see his nervous face reflected as he climbed the steps, still pinching himself to believe that he was actually there, wee Findlay Drummond from Glenussie, a scattered collection of houses high in the hills, on his way to becoming a criminal defence solicitor in the nation's capital.

Or at least to gaining his father's approval at last.

'Good, good.' Pleasantries over, James Kingan sat back in his seat and steepled his fingers together over his substantial stomach. 'Now, I've been thinking how best to introduce you to the way we do things here at Kingan, Kingan & McVean.'

'I was hoping to get some experience of working on criminal cases,' said Finn, resisting the urge the check the knot in his tie. 'As we discussed at the interview,' he added.

Angus had shaken the dust of Glenussie from his feet a long time ago, and was a barrister in London, dealing with complex financial cases. Finn knew there was no point in trying to match the achievements of his brilliant older brother, but he could make a name for himself in the Scottish criminal courts.

He hoped.

'Yes, of course, but you'll need to understand how we work here first,' James said firmly. 'One of the issues we face is shortage of space, and we have a number of open cases from the past that it would be beneficial to close. It occurs to me that going through some of these old files would give you a good sense of our methods. It would be very helpful if we could get rid of some of them.'

Ignoring Finn's unenthusiastic expression, he pushed a bulging box file across the desk. 'You could make a start with the Blackmore Trust. It's been gathering dust since before the war. Have a read through, see what the situation is, and whether we can close this.'

So much for his dreams of arguing the finer points of Scottish law in the High Court of Justiciary. Finn sighed inwardly as he took the file. Working through a dusty folder was a far cry from strutting around a courtroom, but he supposed he had to start somewhere.

'I'll get right on it,' he said.

5
Roz

Ridgewell, South Australia, present day

For the first few months after John Chatton's death, Roz had struggled through a numbing haze of misery and disbelief. In the moments before she opened her eyes in the mornings, she let herself believe that she had just had a bad dream. She strained to hear her father whistling in the kitchen. Keeping her eyes screwed shut, she persuaded herself that she could still pad barefoot along the corridor and he would be there, mug of coffee in hand, gazing out at his beloved garden. That he would turn and smile and say, 'Sleep well, pet?' the way he always did.

John Chatton was a scientist who had come out from England to Adelaide, where he had met and married Millie, and then taken up a position at the government's research institute at Ridgewell. He was a clever, quietly witty man and Roz adored him.

It was her father who had taken her to netball, who had taught her to swim and to ride a bike, who had comforted her when she fell over and listened to her involved stories of who had said what at school. It was he who did most of the cooking, too. Millie was always 'exhausted' at the end of the day.

'You have *no idea* what it takes to run a house,' she would sigh, drooping on the sofa while Roz helped her father in the kitchen. 'You two are thick as thieves,' she used to complain. 'I'm always the outsider.'

Millie was felled by her husband's death. She couldn't eat, she couldn't sleep. Ridgewell was a small town, and friends and neighbours were kind. They brought casseroles and held her hand. They put their arms round her and told her to cry, to let it all out. And she did. She sobbed and wailed and howled, clinging to anyone who was there, or sat slumped with glazed eyes. Sometimes she refused to wash, and lay in the frowsty bedroom clutching an old shirt of her husband's.

'First my mother, and now John,' she would say tearfully, though Roz was puzzled by the reference to her grandmother. Millie had been embarrassed by her mother. She called her a disgusting old hippy and refused to invite her to stay. Roz didn't understand why she was grieving for her now.

'I can't bear it! I don't know how I can go on . . . I want to die too!'

'You've still got your daughter.' Sometimes people would remember Roz's existence, and then they would scout her out, frown at finding her silent and hollow-eyed. They told her she must do more to help her mother. Roz took over the cooking as best she could, though as often as not Millie refused to eat.

'Do what you can to comfort her,' people said. 'You're all she's got.'

But Millie would take no comforting. Her grief ballooned to

consume all the air in the house. She wrapped herself in so much tragedy and distress that nobody noticed Roz unless it was to tell her to be a good girl. 'Your poor mum, she's beside herself with grief,' they said.

There was no space in the house for Roz to breathe, but if she went out to see Bronwen, people would shake their heads. 'Shouldn't you be with your mum?' or 'Your mum needs you.' Others were more tolerant. 'She's young,' they would say. 'She doesn't understand.'

It was true, Roz didn't understand. She couldn't understand her mother's extravagant displays when she herself was terrified of the grief inside her. She thought of it as a dragon with raking claws, ripping at her entrails until she thought she would literally die of pain. If she were to wail and weep like her mother, she was certain that the dragon would rouse itself. It would lash its tail and roar and devour her. She learnt to hold herself very still so as not to disturb it. She boxed it away deep inside her and locked it where she could keep it under control.

Richard Heissen was the police officer who investigated the crash that had killed John Chatton. He came to the house often, though at first Roz was too scared of the dragon inside her to notice much. He brought news of the investigation, which never seemed to go anywhere, and would offer to change a light bulb or fix a dripping tap. 'I'll just mow the grass for you while I'm here,' he would say.

'He's been so kind,' Millie told Roz. 'It's such a comfort to have a man around.'

At first Roz was relieved that Richard's presence was pulling Millie out of her grief. She started fluffing up her hair and putting on lipstick whenever he came round, but as months passed and the investigation closed and Richard was still there, Roz began to resent his constant presence.

She didn't like him. She didn't like the angry clench of his jaw, the chill of his eyes. She didn't like his meaty fists or the way he sat with his legs spread wide, taking up all the space. He didn't like her either, she understood that.

When Roz was twelve, she came home to find Richard Heissen sitting on the back veranda with a beer. When he saw her with her school bag, he drained the bottle. Without taking his eyes off her, he called into the kitchen, 'Millie, get us another beer, willya?'

'Coming up!' Her mother's girlish call floated out from the kitchen, and the next moment she was hurrying outside, beer in hand. Richard took it wordlessly, handing her the empty bottle in return, staring triumphantly into Roz's accusing gaze.

And just like that, Roz knew that she would be living with an enemy.

Scowling, she swept past him, letting the screen door bang behind her, and dropped her bag onto the kitchen counter with a thump.

'Why is he always here?' she demanded hotly.

'Shh, he'll hear you!'

'I don't care. I don't like him!'

'That's a very silly thing to say, Rose.'

'He wants to come here and take over.'

Sure enough, it wasn't long before all reminders of her father were put away and Richard moved in.

When Millie broke the news that she was marrying him, Roz was horrified.

'It's barely a year since Dad died!'

'You don't need to remind me of that, Rose. I'm the one who has been grieving while you've just got on with your life. Sometimes I think you have no feelings at all. You're cold, just like your father.'

The sleeping dragon inside Roz stirred and twitched its tail. Its flaming breath scorched her heart and its claws slashed at her entrails, and for a moment she couldn't breathe with wanting her father. But she said nothing. She would never win in a battle of emotions with her mother. Let Millie think that she was cold. It was safer than letting the dragon loose.

'I don't trust him,' she said.

'That's ridiculous! He's a police officer. Of course you can trust him. And you're to be polite to him,' Millie warned. 'No more of your silly sullen looks. Richard is going to be your stepfather and you're to respect him. If nothing else, you might at least make an effort to be happy for me after all I've suffered!'

Roz ignored that. 'But how well do you really know him, Mum?'

'I know that he's a good man and he'll be a good provider.'

'Really? I notice he's not providing his own beer!'

'Don't be sarcastic. It doesn't suit you.' Millie smoothed her hair. 'One of these days you'll realise how important it is to have a man about the house.'

She punished Roz for her truculence by making her wear a frilly pink dress to the wedding. The only upside was that Roz was allowed to stay with Bronwen while Millie and Richard honeymooned in Noosa.

Things changed again the moment they got home. Now the

house had to be immaculately clean and ordered at all times. A cushion left askew was met with a curt demand to straighten it. Glasses had to be washed, dried and put away instantly. Anything going into the dishwasher had to be rinsed.

'This is stupid,' said Roz. 'What's the point of washing them before they go into the dishwasher? Quite apart from anything else, it's a waste of water.'

'Just do as he says,' Millie whispered when Richard's face darkened. 'Why must you antagonise him?'

'Why do we have to do everything he says?'

'Because he's the head of the household.'

'You do know this is the twenty-first century, Mum?'

'Please don't be impertinent, Rose. Richard is very well respected.'

Which was sadly true. In the town, he was widely admired. Once promoted, he boasted that he ran a tight ship in Ridgewell. He clamped down hard on petty crime, and was always genial – unless crossed, of course. Roz and Millie learnt that he was obsessed with neatness. He got rid of John Chatton's flower beds and the plants that softened the stark lines of the fence. He covered most of the lawn with paving and bought himself a massive gas barbecue, although they rarely entertained as it meant too much mess.

Roz was still expected to do most of the cooking. 'Your mother needs to rest,' Richard would bark. 'She's not strong.'

To the outside world, Roz was fortunate, she knew. True, she had lost her father, but she had a beautiful, if fragile, mother and her stepfather held a position of power and influence in the town. They lived in a lovely old bluestone villa. She had clothes to wear and enough to eat, and although she sensed that he was often tempted, she couldn't say that Richard ever raised a hand to her. There were times when he seized her arm so that he could frogmarch her to her room and lock her in, but those were the only bruises she could show. She couldn't run to anyone and say that she was in danger, and anyway, who would she run to? The police department under his command?

Millie always made excuses for him or turned it round to make it Roz's fault that he punished her. *Why do you provoke him? He's very stressed. Don't be insolent. Don't antagonise him.*

Roz knew with bitter certainty that her mother would choose Richard over her daughter every time. In the end, she kept her eyes lowered so he wouldn't read the hate in them. The house that had once been so happy was now silent and rigid with tension. With the help of Bronwen, Roz set her teeth and waited out the years until she could leave.

'I'm going to Sydney,' she announced the day school finished.

'To do what, may I ask?' Richard sneered.

'I want to go to art college.'

'Art? What good is art? Art won't get you a job.'

John Chatton had left money for Roz's education, and while she sensed that Richard hated to give up control, he was also glad to see the back of her.

After college, she got a job as a graphic designer and threw herself into Sydney life. She would never need a man the way her mother did. She kept her relationships light, undemanding.

When Bronwen asked her to be her chief bridesmaid, Roz couldn't put off returning to Ridgewell. She steeled herself to call her mother. When she explained about the wedding, there was silence at the other end of the phone.

'Will you be staying with Bronwen?' Millie asked eventually.

Roz drew a breath. So much for the fatted calf. 'If that would be easier for you,' she said.

'Well, it would.' Millie couldn't hide her relief. 'Richard made your old room into his office and he doesn't like having his things disturbed.'

Heaven forbid he should have to move a few papers so that Roz could stay in her own home.

Not that it was home any more. It hadn't been home since her father died.

She was glad not to have to go back to that frigid atmosphere, which had none of the cheerful clutter and chaos of the house she shared with Pete. There, wetsuits hung over the veranda rail and there were always surfboards propped against the wall, and nobody dug too hard into what you were feeling or why. The height of the waves mattered more than a buried sense of longing for a home that was lost.

'Perhaps I could come over and see you when I'm back?' she said instead.

'I'd have to ask Richard...'

'Mum, do I *really* need to make an appointment to visit?' Roz thought she was entitled to feel exasperated.

'Don't be silly. It's not that, it's just that this is a very stressful time for him. He's under a lot of pressure at work.'

Roz sighed. 'All right, Mum, let's leave it that you'll give me a call if you've got time to meet me when I'm there.'

They arranged to have coffee the day before Bronwen's

wedding, but at the last minute, Millie cancelled. 'Richard's not very well,' she said.

Roz told herself that she didn't care. She danced and sang at the wedding, then went back to Sydney and got on with her life. She worked hard during the week, and at the weekends she and Pete went to the beach.

Pete was a mad keen surfer. He had wanted her to try, and she did a couple of times, but she hated the crashing waves, the sensation of being dragged around by the monstrous ocean. She preferred to stay in control, the sea at a distance. Her perfect Sunday morning involved sitting in the shade with a book and an iced latte.

She was happy to watch the waves rear and roll relentlessly towards the shore before collapsing in a froth of white. It appealed to the designer in her. How could you better the boldness of nature's design for an Australian beach? The abstract blocks of blue sky, blue sea, the perfect curls of white, the yellow sand dotted with human figures and beach umbrellas making blobs of bright colour.

One day she found herself sitting near a mother and daughter chatting animatedly together. They were so clearly affectionate and enjoying each other's company that the dragon of grief stirred and shook off its sleep. Roz actually flinched as its talons raked the lid of the box she had it trapped in. She had lost her father, but she had lost her mother too, she realised.

Except that she hadn't lost her. Millie was still there. Roz let the book drop to her lap as she stared out to the ocean. She had let herself be pushed away, but perhaps she was at fault too. She could have tried harder with her mother instead of resenting her, she thought honestly. Millie's occasional phone calls were stilted affairs, but how often did Roz call *her*?

On an impulse, she got out her phone.

Millie sounded breathless when she answered. 'Rose!' She was the only one who ever called Roz that.

'Hi, Mum. Just thought I'd give you a call to see how you were.'

'Oh. I'm fine. Fine.'

She didn't sound fine. Her voice was thin and her breath short, as if she were in pain. Roz frowned.

'Is everything okay, Mum?'

'Yes, of course. Well, I fell over and hurt myself a bit. Stupid of me, but I'm fine now.'

Roz sat up straight in the rattan chair. 'What happened?'

'Nothing. It was just a silly accident. Don't make a fuss, Rose.'

'Okay.' What else could she say?

There was an awkward pause. Bronwen could chat to her mum for hours, but Roz and Millie had never had that easy relationship. So Roz was surprised when her mother broke the silence.

'Do you remember how your father talked about taking us to London?'

'Of course.' Roz was puzzled. Since marrying Richard, her mother hardly ever mentioned her life with John Chatton, and it felt as if an olive branch had been offered. 'We never did get that trip,' she continued. 'Maybe we should go together one day?' she added lightly.

'No, no, I didn't mean . . .' Millie sounded almost panicky.

'Okay,' Roz said again soothingly. 'But I was thinking I should come and see you. Especially if you've had an accident.'

'There's no need for that.'

'I'd like to come.'

She could almost hear her mother thinking. 'Richard's very busy at the moment,' she said at last, and Roz's frown deepened.

'Mum, are you sure everything's okay?'

'Yes, of course. It's just that he doesn't really like having guests when he's working at home. It's so hard for him to concentrate.'

'I'm sure I could stay with Bron and you and I could meet up—'

'It's really not a good idea, Rose,' Millie interrupted her. 'Please don't worry about me. I'm absolutely fine. I just need to take it easy for a few days. You enjoy your weekend.'

She hung up, and Roz was left staring at her cell phone. Something was wrong. She knew it. Her mother was often brittle and nervous, but there had been something else in her voice.

Roz was afraid that it was fear.

'I'm going to Ridgewell tomorrow,' she said to Pete when he came out of the sea at last, his face white with sunblock. Salt encrusted his skin and his hair stuck up in damp spikes.

'Okay,' he said easily. 'What for?'

'I'm worried about my mum. I'm going to take a few days off work.'

'I didn't think you and your mum got on?'

'We don't,' said Roz. 'I've just got a bad feeling.'

She flew to Adelaide, hired a car and drove up to Ridgewell, through the broad, familiar streets lined with jacaranda where the houses were set back from the road behind high fences. When she turned into her mother's street, she saw Richard closing the gate behind him and pulled into the kerb so that she didn't have to meet him. She saw him glance around, get into his car and drive off.

She had been glad. She had thought it meant that she could catch her mother on her own.

Parking by the nature strip, she stepped out into the crushing heat and stretched after the long drive. She tucked her phone into the pocket of her jeans and smelt the citrusy scent of crushed wattle and dried gum leaves. She even stopped in the driveway to admire the elegant turned veranda with its original lace ironwork. Her father had loved those details. 'That's why we bought this house,' he used to tell her. 'I hope it will be yours one day and you'll love it the way I do.'

And then she had gone in search of her mother and the nightmare had begun.

6
Finn

Edinburgh, present day

'I've taken a look at that file, sir... James,' Finn corrected himself hurriedly. He had bumped into James Kingan a couple of days later, after reading through the file in detail. 'As far as I can tell, the Blackmore Trust was set up by Charles Blackmore in 1936. He had a large house on Skara – that's a peninsula on the west coast—'

'I know where Skara is, thank you, Findlay,' said James in his crisp Edinburgh voice. Finn himself had a soft Highland accent, and to him Edinburgh folk all sounded as if they were exasperated. 'We're quite well acquainted with our country here in Edinburgh. It *is* the capital.'

'Oh. Yes, of course.' Finn tugged at his tie, cleared his throat. 'Anyway, Blackmore left the house and all its contents in trust for his four daughters or their female descendants. All the daughters appear to have gone overseas before Blackmore's death and it's clear from his will that he had lost touch with them. It's possible they were estranged, but certainly he wasn't able to provide any addresses when it came to rewriting his will.'

'What happened when the house was sold?'

'That's the thing. I can't find any record of that happening. There were bequests to a couple called Grierson, and those were paid. Clearly we had the will here and got probate, but after that, nothing.'

'Did we do anything to find the daughters?'

'We put an announcement in the papers, that kind of thing, but no response. It's as if they all vanished. Charles Blackmore had a brother, Percival, who was an archaeologist, and a letter was sent to him in Egypt, but it's hard to know if it ever reached him. There was no response, anyway.'

'Oh, well, Egypt,' said James, as if that explained everything.

'And then I suppose everyone was caught up in the war, and tracking them down wasn't a priority.'

'The law is always a priority, Findlay,' said James disapprovingly. He stuck his thumbs in his waistcoat and considered. 'What about the house? If it was never sold, is it still there?'

'It's possible.'

'I think you'd better go and find out.'

Disconcerted, Finn stared at his boss. 'You want me to go to Skara? But I've only just arrived in Edinburgh,' he pointed out.

'Good timing, then. You're not distracted by other cases. You may as well sort this out and find out what's what. Perhaps there'll be some indication in the house of where to look for the missing daughters, if the place is still standing.'

'That would be helpful,' Finn agreed. 'When would you like me to go?'

'Sooner the better, don't you think?'

7
Iris

Southampton, April 1931

Below Iris's feet, the deck throbbed in warning as the great propellers churned up the water and smoke began to pour out of the funnels overhead. Three deafening blasts of the ship's horn made her jump, and she gripped the rail with her gloved hands.

Her fellow passengers crowded beside her, waving and tossing streamers and calling to their friends and family far below, though Iris couldn't see how they could possibly recognise anyone in the crush. There was no reason for her to search the upturned faces. The only people she wanted to see were her sisters, at home in Skara.

And Ian.

Don't think of Ian.

Don't think of home.

Her throat closed with longing. She was so homesick already, she could barely breathe. Iris couldn't bear to remember those awful goodbyes, how the sisters had clung together on the platform at Acheravie. 'I'll write,' she had promised, leaning out of the carriage window while steam from the engine billowed in the air and the brakes hissed and the train drew remorselessly away. 'I'll come home soon.'

She mustn't cry. To distract herself, she planned in her head how she would sketch the scene below to include with her next letter home. How would she show the scale of the great ship looming over the dock? She could draw the crowds on the dockside cheering and whistling to wish *RMS Orphea* luck on her maiden voyage; the band playing 'I Got Rhythm', the jaunty tune barely audible over the noise.

Beside her, Lady Carsington moved her elegant shoulders in time to the music, careless of who might be watching.

Iris had met her new employer for tea at the Ritz the previous day. Expecting a gaunt dowager or a frail old lady, she had discovered instead that Ariadne Carsington was barely forty, a glamorous woman in a chic green afternoon dress and *the most delicious little cloche hat*, as Iris had written to her sisters that night. *I will leave you to imagine how I felt in my darned stockings, sensible shoes and serviceable coat*, she had added.

'I have to say, I thought you would be older,' Lady Carsington had commented, studying Iris across the tea table with eyes as green as a cat's. 'You look very young.'

Iris refrained from saying that she had thought exactly the same thing. This woman would have no need to send her running up and down to fetch a lorgnette or an ear trumpet as Lily had predicted. 'I'm twenty.'

The pencilled brows rose. 'Really? You don't look it. Are you out?'

'No.' In the full flush of his fortune, Charles had been keen to show off his daughter, but Iris hadn't wanted to be a debutante. Why would she want to spend a season in London looking for a husband when she already knew that she would be marrying Ian? 'No, I stayed in Scotland.'

'That explains the unspoilt look, I suppose.' Ariadne selected a fish-paste sandwich from the stand and bit into it with relish as her gaze swept over Iris's dress.

Iris was uncomfortably aware that the drop waist and flower print that had seemed so charming when it was new in 1928 now looked hopelessly outdated next to Lady Carsington's fashionable outfit.

Ariadne clearly agreed. She sighed. 'I do think Moira might have warned me.'

'Moira?'

'Moira Bannister. She recommended you to me.'

'Oh.' Moira must be the friend of Lady Malcolm. Iris could feel the interview slipping away from her. She cleared her throat. 'I am more sensible than I look. I've helped bring up three younger sisters.'

'I'm not a child. I don't need someone to wipe my nose for me.'

A flush was creeping up Iris's neck. 'Still, I hope I can be of some use to you. Perhaps help with porters and ... and that kind of thing.'

'I've got a maid to do that. Baxter deals with everything.' Ariadne considered the selection on the cake stand and selected a chocolate eclair. 'My husband is old-fashioned,' she explained. 'He the governor's second-in-command in Colombo, and he's ridiculously keen on appearances. He doesn't like me to travel on my own, so I've started hiring a companion just to keep him quiet. Last time I went out, I employed some ghastly missionary who quoted the Bible at me the entire voyage and disapproved of me even more than my husband does. So this time I thought I would try someone younger and more . . . fun.'

'Oh, I see.' Iris felt crushed. It was clear Lady Carsington was looking for someone more sophisticated. What if she told her to go home because she wasn't amusing enough?

There was a part of Iris that would have given anything to run home to Skara, but what would happen to her sisters then? They would be back to square one.

'I play bridge,' she offered, but Ariadne was unimpressed.

'Do you drink?'

'Not much.'

'Smoke?'

'No.'

Iris could see Lady Carsington getting ready to dismiss her. 'Please,' she said. 'I know I'm not very sophisticated or amusing, but I really do need to get to Ceylon. I'll do whatever you need me to if you'll just take me with you.'

Ariadne narrowed her eyes. 'You sound desperate, darling, and desperation is *so* unattractive.'

'I *am* desperate,' said Iris frankly. 'I need to find my uncle. He owns a tea plantation there. My sisters are counting on me.' She met Lady Carsington's gaze. 'I can't afford to pay for my own passage. The only way I can get to Ceylon is as your companion. *Please* take me.'

'Well, you're honest at least. I suppose that's quite refreshing.'

Ariadne slotted a cigarette into its holder. Lifting an eyebrow was enough to summon a waiter to light it for her. She sat back and blew a cloud of smoke up to the ceiling.

'No tedious moralising?'

'No, of course not,' said Iris, her eyes stinging from the smoke.

'No complaining?'

She shook her head.

'No being shocked?'

Iris paused at that. She had a feeling that Ariadne Carsington would enjoy shocking her. 'I'll try not to show it if I am,' she said cautiously.

Ariadne laughed. 'Very well, then. Iris Blackmore, consider yourself appointed.'

That morning, Iris had travelled with Lady Carsington on the boat train from London. Since then, she had been swept up in a whirl of porters and luggage, and had pushed, flustered, through crowds towards the gangway, trotting to keep up with her employer.

It had been Lady Carsington's maid, Baxter, who had quietly dealt with the enormous number of trunks that Ariadne Carsington had judged necessary to bring. She sorted them into those that would not be wanted on the voyage and those that would be taken to the cabin.

Iris had already made a quick sketch to show her single battered suitcase sitting meekly to one side.

To embark, Lady Carsington had dressed in an elegant blue matching skirt and jacket with a fur swathed casually over her shoulders. Her mouth was lipsticked a bright red, her chic little hat set at the perfect angle. Iris had seen the critical look her employer had cast at her own tweed suit and sturdy shoes. Like everything else she owned, they dated back to the years before Charles Blackmore had lost his fortune. The tweed was the best quality, but it had been designed for walking in the Scottish hills and not for elegance.

'Is that the only hat you've got?' Ariadne had asked, with a pained look at the rather battered felt hat Iris had worn to the Ritz.

'I'm afraid so. At least, I do have another, but it's just like it.'

'Good Lord,' said Ariadne and turned away.

Now, as the great ship eased away from the dock, Iris felt as if she were being ripped away from home, a snail being torn from its shell. *Stop!* she wanted to cry. *Stop the ship! I've changed my mind. I want to get off.*

But there was no way *Orphea* was stopping now. Her huge bulk was moving surprisingly smoothly through the water, looming over the bustling tug boats that guided her.

Ariadne tilted her face to the brisk breeze and held on to her hat. 'I love this moment when it's too late to change your mind,' she said, almost as if she had read Iris's thoughts. 'It's always so exciting, don't you think?'

Iris hesitated. She was petrified rather than excited, but she didn't think saying so would impress her glamorous employer.

'It's all very new to me,' she admitted.

'There's nothing like an ocean liner,' said Ariadne, adjusting the fur around her neck. 'For a few weeks you can be whoever you want to be, and nobody on board will know any different.'

Iris just wanted to be herself. Or at least the person she had been before her mother died. Before she and Ian had said goodbye. Before her innocent dreams for the future had been blown apart.

Swallowing hard, she fingered her mother's ring through her glove and pressed her lips firmly together. She was doing what needed to be done. Focus on that, she told herself.

The land was fast receding, but seagulls still wheeled above them. Iris held on to her despised felt hat and squinted at the wind blowing into her face. It brought the comforting scent of the sea, though the water here was noisy and a metallic grey, tinged with an oily mechanical sheen.

'Now, we must find ourselves someone to flirt with on the voyage.' Unaware or uncaring of Iris's sadness, Ariadne turned to lean back against the rail and study their fellow passengers, who were already starting to mill around the decks, farewells over. 'What have I said?' she added at Iris's jolt of surprise.

'Oh, nothing,' said Iris, flustered. 'It's just . . . perhaps I misunderstood. I thought you were going out to join your husband?'

'I am.' Ariadne touched the pearls at her throat with a complacent expression. 'Johnny doesn't mind what I do as long as I'm discreet.' She laughed at Iris's expression. 'Good Lord, you are a little country mouse, aren't you?'

Mortified, Iris flushed. 'I'm afraid I've led a very sheltered life.'

'Well, a sea voyage should be eye-opening for you at least. Are you saving yourself for some sweetheart at home?'

'No.' Iris hoped her voice wasn't as bleak as her heart.

'Well, then, this is the perfect opportunity to find someone to enjoy yourself with,' Ariadne said languidly.

'Oh, I really don't think so,' Iris said, disconcerted. 'I've never known how to flirt.' Which was true. She had never needed to play silly games with Ian. She had just been herself.

But look where had that got her. She sighed inwardly.

'Then you should practise,' said Ariadne. 'It's a useful skill for life – and it's fun!'

Turning her attention back to the other passengers, she began a running commentary on the gentlemen going past, making no attempt to lower her voice and apparently unconcerned by the possibility that she might be overheard.

'Dull ... too fat ... too thin ... he looks worthy,' she sighed, with a roll of her beautiful eyes.

Iris suspected that Ariadne was enjoying the fact that her innocent companion was squirming with embarrassment. Mindful of her promise not to seem shocked, she tried to keep her expression neutral.

'Dull again ... duller ... too pleased with himself ... ugh,' Ariadne went on remorselessly. 'Too awkward ... too married, his wife's a clinger ... too old ... ah! Now *he* looks interesting! What do you think, Iris?' she demanded with a malicious smile.

Reluctantly Iris followed Lady Carsington's unabashed gaze to where a dark-haired, hard-mouthed man was leaning on the rail, glowering out to sea. As she watched, he turned his head without warning, and she found herself staring into a pair of piercing eyes. She jerked hers away, feeling oddly jolted.

'Interesting.' Ariadne drew out the word in a drawl, looking between Iris and the stranger. 'It's the captain's cocktail party tonight. I must try and bump into him and introduce myself. You must admit that he's very attractive?'

Iris couldn't agree. The man seemed sinister to her, with those cold eyes and that rigid mouth. 'I think he looks dangerous,' she said, and Ariadne's gaze went back to the stranger, who was now ignoring them completely.

'A challenge,' she said with a feline smile. 'Even better.'

8

Iris

RMS Orphea, English Channel, May 1931

When Iris discovered that she would be sharing a cabin with another young woman, she hoped to find a friend for the voyage, but Geraldine Woolstone looked up from her unpacking and greeted her with a cool nod that did not suggest she would be welcoming girlish confidences.

She was a teacher, she admitted, returning to her school in Trincomalee, and an old Ceylon hand. When she learnt that Iris was companion to Lady Carsington, she looked down her nose.

'Her! I don't know why Johnny Carsington puts up with her. He's been in Ceylon for years and is respected by everyone in the country. His first wife was marvellous. We were all so sorry when she died,' she said. 'Goodness knows what he was thinking remarrying someone like Ariadne French-Fiske! She's only ever in Colombo when she needs to get away from one scandal or another.'

'She's been extremely kind to me,' said Iris stiffly. It was not quite true, but she was certainly not going to gossip about her employer.

She looked around the cabin instead. There wasn't a lot of room, with two single beds separated by a bedside table, a dressing table with a chair, and a neat chest of drawers each, but it was comfortable enough. Through the porthole, the sea stretched greyly to the horizon.

Disappointed that Geraldine seemed so determined to be unfriendly, Iris lifted her suitcase onto the other bed – bunk, she corrected herself – and began to unpack in silence. It would have been nice to have someone to talk to in place of her sisters. She could have admitted how disconcerting she found Ariadne Carsington, who was by turns sharp and amusing, malicious and embarrassingly frank. Iris didn't know what to make of her.

She could have confessed how horribly homesick she was, or asked advice on what she should wear that evening.

'Are you going to the captain's cocktail party?' She broke the silence at last.

'No,' said Geraldine shortly. 'It's always ghastly. Just a lot of silly people squawking at each other and showing off.'

That was not what Ariadne had said. She had told Iris that the party for the first-class passengers was the highlight of the voyage, and that it was important to make a good impression. 'Wear your best evening gown,' had been her parting words.

But which was her best? Iris pulled the two evening gowns that she had brought with her out of the suitcase and regarded them dubiously. They were both sadly creased.

A flutter caught her eye as she shook out the gowns, and she bent to find an envelope on the carpet. As she leant down, two more dislodged from the folds of the silky material and slithered onto the floor

Her sisters had known how lonely she would be and had written to her.

Fighting back the tears, Iris lowered herself to her bunk. The first envelope had her name on the front, illustrated with swirls and flowers. That would be Daisy's.

She opened the envelope and pulled out the sheet.

Darling Iris, Daisy had written in her large, loopy handwriting, liberally sprinkled with exclamation marks. *It was Lily's idea to write to you so that we could pretend to be there to advise you on what to wear for your first night on board ship! I do wish we really could be there! I would tell you to wear the blue satin. The colour brings out the blue in your eyes and the bias cut is very flattering. Wear Mummy's pearls with it and dress your hair the way I showed you!*

Iris's smile wavered. Dear Daisy! Her youngest sister had always had a flair for fashion. Even as a very small girl, she had worn her tweed skirt and jumpers with a kind of style that had always eluded Iris. Daisy was the baby of the family and its undisputed star. Her eyes were blue and bright, and when Iris thought of her, it was in constant movement. Daisy singing, Daisy dancing, Daisy twirling along the beach or up and down the stairs at Rubha Clachan. Her little sister brought the sunshine into the room with her on the gloomiest of days, cajoling them into letting her fix up their hair or direct them in plays that she wrote and starred in herself. Their roles were always supporting ones, Iris remembered affectionately. Mind, Daisy was no saint. She had a famous temper that could erupt without warning and for the most trivial of reasons.

Daisy had signed her letter with extravagant swirling and expressions of love. *PS*, she had added. *Don't forget your evening gloves!*

Iris opened Lily's letter next. It was characteristically neater than Daisy's. Lily was the sister who looked most like Iris. Like their mother, they had dark hair and eyes the dusky blue of the hills at twilight, while golden-haired Rose and Daisy took after their father, their eyes the sparkling blue of the sea on a sunny day.

Lily was a crisper, cleverer version of Iris, Iris always thought humbly. Iris had hated being sent away to school – Charles was a great believer in female education – but Lily had loved it until their straitened circumstances had meant there was no more money for school fees. No money for university either, although Iris knew Lily had dreamt of that.

I wonder where you will be when you read this? Lily had written. *I hope you are safely on board the ship and have escaped for a moment from the fearsome Lady Carsington's demands for a shawl or her ear trumpet. I am picturing you collapsed on your bed with a wet flannel over your brow. Have you hung up your gowns yet to let the creases drop out? You must have unpacked if you are reading this, and I know you will be missing us as much as we are missing you. But you are braver than you think, dear Iris. I know you will put on a gown –* I *think the sea green more elegant myself, though I know Daisy favours the blue! – and square your shoulders and do what you always do, which is the right thing. You are such an example to us all, Iris. I could not wish for a better sister. Your affectionate sister, Lily.*

Iris laid Lily's letter aside with a crooked smile. She could almost hear her sister's dry voice and picture the gleaming amusement in her expression.

The last letter was from Rose, Rose with her lion's heart and her boundless appetite for adventure.

Please do try not to worry about us, Iris. You always think about other people, but perhaps this is a chance to think about yourself for a change and enjoy the voyage. Imagine, you will get a chance to see Pompeii! I so wish I could go with you! Please write from there and tell me what it is like. Do not stay on board and run around after old Lady Carsington anyway. You must go!

Daisy is pestering me to tell you to wear the blue gown, and Lily the sea-green (doubtless just to annoy Daisy, as I cannot imagine that she cares), but really, I don't suppose it matters. Wear whichever makes you feel most courageous!

Iris laughed quietly to herself. Her sisters had quite the wrong impression of Lady Carsington! But oh, how she missed them all!

Swallowing past the constriction in her throat, she stood up and hung up both gowns in the hope that at least some of the creases would drop out.

Wear whichever makes you feel most courageous. Her mouth twisted. Brave was the last thing she felt, but in the end, she chose the blue, which would please Daisy. It was Lily's advice she took later, though, straightening her shoulders when she tapped on the door of Ariadne Carsington's cabin.

Her tentative knock was answered by Baxter, the maid, who offered her a sympathetic smile before stepping aside. This cabin was on a much grander scale than the one Iris shared with Geraldine. It was easily twice the size. The carpet was thicker, the upholstery more sumptuous, the fittings more luxurious. The walls were panelled in wood and hung with pictures. If not for the faint thrumming from the engines and the view through the portholes, they might have been in an upmarket hotel on land.

Ariadne stood in the middle of the cabin, pulling on long evening gloves. She was strikingly dressed as usual, this time in a yellow crêpe georgette gown patterned with bold black flowers. She looked pained when she saw Iris in her plain blue satin gown, her only jewellery Amelia's pearls and the ring she always wore on her right hand.

'*That*'s your best evening gown?' Not waiting for Iris's reply, Ariadne turned to her maid. 'Baxter, can you do something with her hair?'

'I think so, milady. Just sit down there a minute, miss,' said Baxter, gently pushing a crushed Iris down onto a stool in front of the dressing table.

'Do it for me,' Ariadne told Iris, fixing a cigarette into a long holder. 'Think of my reputation.'

Iris hung her head. 'I'm sorry,' she said. She had done her best, as Daisy had instructed, but it was clearly not enough.

She and Rose had had a maid for a while, but since the precipitous decline in the Blackmore fortunes, they had had to let her go. Since then, they had got used to helping each other with their hair and clothes, usually with Daisy's advice, but they were nowhere near as skilled as Lady Carsington's maid.

Under Baxter's deft fingers, Iris's hair was miraculously transformed into a simple but elegant style. In place of the plain rolled bun, it was swept round and over the top and secured with a jewelled and feathery hair ornament Baxter had found on the dressing table.

'Gosh,' was all Iris could say as she studied her reflection.

'You've got lovely hair, miss, and a natural curl to it. It's a shame not to make the best of it.'

'Yes, well done, Baxter,' said Ariadne, looking on approvingly. 'That's better. And now the plain dress is the perfect foil for the hairstyle.'

Iris smoothed down her gown as she got to her feet. 'Thank you, Baxter.'

'Enjoy the party, miss. And you, milady.'

They could hear the party long before they reached it, a babble of voices and laughter that rang along the corridors and spilt out onto the promenade deck. Overwhelmed, Iris baulked at the entrance, but Ariadne moved with assurance into the throng and Iris had little choice but to follow, smiling nervously, pushing her way through what seemed an impenetrable wall of backs. The air was thick with smoke and perfume. It shimmered with colourful fabrics, georgette, crêpe, satin and silk. The women were all wearing floor-length evening gowns, jewels glittering at their throats and ears, while the men made a contrast in their severe tuxedos. All of them seemed to be talking at the top of their voices.

Ariadne accepted a cocktail from a passing steward, and Iris did the same. She didn't usually drink, but she didn't want to appear any more provincial than she already did. Her mother hadn't approved of ladies drinking or wearing cosmetics. Iris was fairly sure that Amelia wouldn't have approved of Lady Carsington at all, and she sent her mother a mental apology. *It's the only way I can find Uncle Ralph, Mummy.*

'Ariadne Carsington!' Iris was taking a cautious sip of her

martini when a screech from across the room made Ariadne turn, missing Iris's spluttering cough and watering eyes.

'Oh dear,' she sighed under her breath. 'Daphne Leadbetter. Ghastly woman, but impossible to avoid.' She fixed on a smile as Mrs Leadbetter thrust her way through the crowd towards them. 'Daphne! I didn't know you'd be on board.'

'It's marvellous that you're here too! We can have a proper catch-up. I haven't seen you for an *age*. Where have you been?'

'Here and there,' said Ariadne vaguely. 'I've been staying with the Fawcetts on the Riviera.' Graciously she allowed a passing gentleman to light her cigarette and rewarded him with a dazzling smile of thanks. Blowing out a cloud of smoke, she turned to Iris, clearly hoping to foist the unwelcome Mrs Leadbetter onto her. 'Let me introduce you. Daphne, this is Iris Blackmore, who is keeping me company on my way to Colombo. Or, as Johnny hopes, keeping me in check.'

'How do you do,' said Iris politely.

To her dismay, Daphne Leadbetter appeared to be one of those people who could never rest until they found a connection. After a lengthy inquisition about whether Iris was related to the Shropshire Blackmores and where exactly in Scotland she lived, Daphne was delighted to find a point of contact.

'Skara! Oh, then you must know the Malcolms?'

Iris flinched inwardly, but kept her face composed. 'I do, yes.'

'We were shooting there three or four years ago.'

Iris had thought the woman's long face and avid eyes had looked vaguely familiar. That would explain it. She took a gulp of the martini.

'Isn't Dundonan magical? *Such* a romantic castle!'

'It is beautiful,' Iris agreed, feeling as if a rusty ball of barbed wire was rolling raggedly around inside her.

'Falling to pieces, of course, Those old places are hellishly expensive to keep up.' Daphne turned to Ariadne. 'Did you ever know Isobel Jardine, Ariadne?'

'Before my time, I think.'

'Ah yes, probably. Anyway, she was thought to have done well landing Lord Malcolm, and they had a big society wedding, but James Malcolm turned out to be a gambler. Poor Isobel's had the devil of a time with him, I hear.'

'Sounds like they need to marry the son and heir off to an American heiress,' said Ariadne, without much interest. 'All the best families are doing it.'

'I *did* hear that they've invited Margaret Ricci up for the shooting this year.'

'Is she that fabulously wealthy girl? Daughter of some New York industrialist?'

Daphne nodded. 'They'd be lucky to get her, but if the boy's got a bit of charm and she likes the idea of a draughty castle, it could work.' She remembered Iris, whose knuckles were white around the glass she was holding. 'You probably know more than we do, Miss Blackmore, if you're neighbours.'

'I don't, I'm afraid.' From somewhere, Iris summoned a smile. She had to get out or she would faint. 'Excuse me,' she managed. 'It's a little hot in here.'

9
Iris

Without waiting for a reply, Iris fumbled her glass onto the nearest surface and blundered towards the exit, barely aware of someone holding the door for her as she burst out onto the deck and gulped in the gloriously cool, clear air. The contrast was so great that she put a hand to her spinning head.

The next moment, a firm hand was pushing her down onto a wooden lounger. 'Put your head between your knees,' a brusque voice advised.

She dropped her head as instructed and closed her eyes while the heat and the smoke and the memories of Ian and Dundonan spun and swirled in her brain and Daphne Leadbetter's crystalline tones echoed endlessly. *Fabulously wealthy . . . lucky to get her . . .* Iris's heart clenched. *Ian, oh Ian . . .*

'Are you unwell? Should I get a doctor?' The abrupt voice above her made Iris lift her head. She found herself staring at the dark and dangerous-looking stranger she and Ariadne had seen on deck as they left Southampton. Somehow he seemed even more menacing in a dinner jacket.

'No, I . . . I'm sorry, it was just the heat,' she managed, moistening her lips. 'I don't need any help. Honestly. Please, don't let me keep you.'

'I'm glad to be out of it, to be honest.' He sat on the edge of the lounger next to hers and lit a cigarette before remembering to offer her one. When Iris shook her head, he took a deep pull and blew out a cloud of smoke that was instantly snatched away by the wind.

'I can't stand those affairs, with people yabbering at each other,' he said. 'They don't want to talk to you. They just want to know who you know so that they can pigeonhole you. You have to have someone in common before you can be accepted.'

'Why did you go to the party if you dislike it so much?' said Iris, unaccountably riled, given that that was exactly her opinion.

'Oh, why do any of us go?' He shrugged. 'Captain's cocktail party and all that. It seemed the thing to do. Why did *you* go? I could tell you were hating every minute of it.'

Iris stiffened. 'Were you watching me?'

'I *noticed* you,' he corrected. 'Everyone else was dressed up to the nines and you stood out.'

Doubtless because of her shabby dress, Iris thought, mortified.

'There's something . . . refreshing about you,' he said. 'In a roomful of champagne and cocktails, you're like a cool drink of water.'

Iris flushed, unsure whether that was meant as a compliment.

'I saw you go pale and rush for the door,' he went on. 'I wondered if you were ill, so I thought I would make sure you were all right.'

'Oh. Well, thank you. I'm fine, though.'

He didn't take the hint to go. Instead, he sat and smoked, apparently content with silence.

Iris studied him under her lashes. He had a saturnine face and he smoked his cigarette with a kind of controlled rage. He was angry about something. She was just glad that rage didn't seem to be directed at her.

After a moment, she sat back on the lounger. It was cold on deck and she was still getting used to the movement of the ship, but it was restful not having to explain herself, not having to pretend that she wasn't sick with longing for home, for Ian, for happier times.

'You never get cross,' Rose had said once, exasperated. 'You never complain. You just *accept* things, Iris.'

'What can I do? Getting cross won't change anything.'

'But it's always you that has to take responsibility and sort things out. It's not fair! Don't you want to stamp your feet and have a tantrum like Daisy sometimes?'

Iris's mouth softened thinking about the legendary tantrums her little sister had been prone to when she was a toddler. Rose used to mock her by pretending to have an even bigger one, throwing herself on the floor and drumming her heels until Daisy's big blue eyes had brimmed with a mixture of rage and puzzlement that almost always dissolved into gurgling laughter.

What would it be like to burst into tears in front of a stranger? To scream and shout and raise her fists to the sky? To wail that it wasn't fair, none of it was fair?

The man sitting beside her so calmly smoking his cigarette would be horrified, and the thought of his expression made her smile.

'What's so funny?' He must have been watching her more closely than she thought.

'Oh ... nothing.' It was cool out there and she rubbed her bare arms.

'Cold? Have my jacket.' The offer was abrupt. He seemed unbothered by social niceties. There was a suppressed fierceness about him that for some reason made Iris acutely aware of her own body, of the air leaking out of her lungs, of the beat of the blood in her veins.

'There's really no need.' She got to her feet, hugging her arms together. 'I must go back to the party.'

'Must you?'

'Yes. I'm Lady Carsington's companion. She's expecting me to be there.'

'If Lady Carsington is who I think she is, she seems to be more than capable of looking after herself.'

Iris was betrayed into a smile. 'Still, I'd better get back. Thank you for rescuing me, Mr ... ?'

'Henderson. Guy Henderson.'

'I'm Iris Blackmore.'

'Perhaps we'll meet again,' he said. 'The ship's not that big.'

Iris hoped not as she smoothed down her gown and escaped inside. Escape? Was it fair to feel like that when he had been nothing but kind? But something about that saturnine face and those strange, piercing eyes made her nervous.

Guy Henderson was Ian's opposite. He was dark where Ian was fair, alarming where Ian was steady and loving. Oh, how Iris wished Ian were there now! She would give anything – anything! – to be able to lean against his strong chest and feel his arms close around her. To rest her face against his neck and breathe in the dear smell of him.

I can't bear it. I can't bear it. I CAN'T.

Staggering under the weight of longing, Iris put her hand out to brace herself against the wall. She made herself take a breath, then another. Angrily she brushed the trickle of tears from her cheeks.

She must bear it. She had no choice.

She found herself standing at the top of a great wooden staircase that curved up through the centre of the ship. There was wood panelling everywhere and huge chandeliers glittered over the stairwell. The cocktail party was still in full swing in the first-class lounge on the right. In the dining room on the left, Iris could see white-jacketed stewards laying tables. The babble of voices competed with the subtle chink of cutlery and the faint thrum of the engines.

The thought of going back into the party made her head ache, and for a moment she was tempted to return to the cabin, before remembering that Geraldine would be there. She would get no sympathy from her room-mate.

Stop being so wet, she told herself. What was it Lily had said? *Square your shoulders and do what you always do.* Fixing a smile to her face, she plunged back into the party.

It was some time before she found Ariadne, and when she did, her employer was flirting very obviously with Guy Henderson of all people. Impossible to tell whether he was enjoying the attention. His expression was unreadable, Iris thought, just as he looked across the room and their eyes met with another of those uncomfortable jolts.

Flushing, she looked away, but was annoyed to find herself sneaking looks at him as he moved away from Ariadne. She had to admit that he stood out in the crowd. It wasn't so much his dark dinner jacket, which contrasted with the colourful evening gowns worn by the women, as that was true of all the male passengers. It was more the guarded expression and sense of unsmiling focus.

Ariadne put her arm through Iris's as they made their way into dinner at last. 'I met the dark stranger,' she murmured in her ear. 'Guy Henderson.'

It was on the tip of Iris's tongue to say that she knew, but then she would have to explain how she had met him, and it would all get too complicated.

'He's an interesting man,' Ariadne said. 'I've asked the purser to put him on our table.'

Iris was dismayed. 'Can you do that?'

'Darling, I don't see why I should be trapped with a bore for the entire voyage when there's an interesting, attractive man available to keep me company.'

The dining room rang with noise as everyone introduced themselves. When Ariadne and Iris found their table, they discovered a ponderous young man with faintly bulbous eyes talking to Daphne Leadbetter, who, it turned out, had also been harassing the purser. 'I got him to put us on your table.'

Ariadne didn't look entirely pleased – Colonel Leadbetter was as taciturn as his wife was talkative – but Iris guessed she could hardly complain. 'Lovely,' she said, with an insincere smile. 'You on your way back already, Bertie?' she went on, turning to the young man, who flushed an unattractive brick red and eyed her as he might a dangerous beast. 'I thought you'd just gone on leave?'

She introduced him to Iris as Bertram Spencer, a district officer in the Ceylon colonial service. Iris felt a little sorry for him, but was relieved to be sitting next to him and not Guy Henderson, who nodded brusquely around the table before taking his seat.

He was really very rude, Iris thought. Ariadne didn't seem to mind, though. Guy must be a good ten years younger than her, but she flirted with him outrageously. It was hard to tell what he thought about it. His lean, dark face gave little away.

Aware that Guy's eyes rested on her from time to time, Iris turned brightly to Bertram.

'Your work must be so interesting, Mr Spencer.'

'Oh, call me Bertie, please. Whenever anyone says Mr Spencer, I look around for my father. And he's been dead for ten years.' He brayed with nervous laughter.

Iris managed a smile. 'How long have you been in Ceylon?'

'Five years now,' he told her. 'I'm on my fourth posting. They like to move us chaps around.'

'Do you get home on leave often?'

'No, not often,' he said. 'This was only the second time. I've been staying with my mother and sisters in Pinner.'

'That must have been nice for you. How many sisters do you have?'

'Three, Emily, Sophia and Cath. They're all older than me.'

'I have three sisters too,' Iris told him. 'Though mine are younger than me, and we all used to wish that we had a brother. Did your sisters spoil you rotten?'

'They did rather.' Bertie was relaxing. 'Of course, it's different now I'm grown up. Still,' he added with wistful look, 'it's jolly hard to say goodbye.'

'I know,' said Iris sadly.

They fell silent, lost in their memories.

Daphne Leadbetter leant across the table. 'What about you, Mr Henderson? What takes you to Ceylon?'

'Business,' he said.

'Oh, what kind of business?'

'Family business,' he said, with a smile that effectively shut down further questioning.

Mrs Leadbetter bridled at the obvious snub and Iris turned hastily to Bertie. 'Where are you posted now?'

'In Nuwara Eliya, in the hills,' he said, clearly also picking up on the strained atmosphere. 'The climate is much cooler there. Where I was before, in Haldummulla, the heat was quite crushing. You must visit while you're in Ceylon. It's really a very nice place, is it not, Lady Carsington?'

'We go up sometimes when the races are on,' Ariadne agreed. 'People say it's like being at home, but I wouldn't go quite that far.'

'You can visit a plantation and see how the tea is plucked and packaged,' Bertie added eagerly. 'I would be very happy to arrange a tour if you're interested, Miss Blackmore.'

The mention of tea plantations had Iris sitting straighter. 'I wonder, Mr Spencer – Bertie – if you know my uncle? Ralph Davidson? He owns a plantation.'

To her surprise, she saw out of the corner of her eye that Guy Henderson had stiffened, and his hand was clenched around the stem of his wine glass.

'I don't recognise the name,' said Bertie apologetically, just as Guy leant across the table. 'Where is your uncle's plantation, Miss Blackmore?'

'That's the thing,' said Iris, embarrassed. 'I don't know. We've always written to him *poste restante*.'

Guy sat back but kept his eyes on Iris's face. Beside him, Ariadne lit a cigarette and looked from him to Iris, her eyes narrowed through the smoke.

'Have you ever heard of a Ralph Davidson, darling?' Daphne asked her husband.

'No, but then I don't have much to do with tea planters,' Colonel Leadbetter said shortly.

'That's true,' Ariadne put in. 'If your uncle was in the service, we would definitely know him. As it is, some of the planters are rather a law unto themselves.'

'I can certainly ask around for you,' said Bertie, eager to help.

Iris smiled at him and tried to ignore the fact that Guy Henderson's unnerving gaze was fixed on her. 'Thank you so much, Bertie. That would be marvellous.'

10
Roz

London, present day

'Hey, Roz, can you take this out to table six?'

Joe finished lighting the last candle on the cake and handed it gingerly to Roz. 'It's the mum's sixtieth birthday and they want a big fuss. Make like you're thrilled.'

'Got it.' Roz plastered on a smile and steadied the huge cake between her hands before pushing her hip against the kitchen door and swivelling out into the restaurant.

She had been working at Cork & Candle as a waitress for three weeks now. The bistro had wooden floors and tables and a lively atmosphere, and she liked to be busy. It was a change from her old job as a graphic designer. She would get back to that eventually, but just then, she wanted something mindless.

She had done too much thinking over the past couple of years, she reckoned. Too much regretting. Too much wondering if her last conversation with her mother had somehow triggered

Richard's attack. Too much fearing that no one would believe her and that Richard wouldn't be convicted.

That he would come for her if he wasn't. *I'll find you. You'll pay for what you did.*

She had a new phone now, registered in the UK. Richard would have no friends in the police here, she hoped. He shouldn't be able to track her down even if he weren't in prison. Only Bronwen and her solicitor had her number, she reminded herself constantly.

It had been March before she was able to leave Australia. The house was empty and for sale, the last boxes stuffed into Bronwen's garage. There had been little, in the end, that Roz had wanted to keep. The paintings that Bronwen insisted should not be given away, some family papers, old birth certificates and the like, and, most consoling of all, a letter that Millie had started but never finished. It was dated the day before Roz had found her mother's body.

Dear Rose, it had begun. *I thought about sending you an email, but somehow it feels better to write a letter. Or easier. I wish I'd been able to talk to you properly on the phone today. You took me by surprise and I wasn't ready.*

Ready for what? Roz wondered.

I have been thinking a lot about your father lately. We never did have that trip to London he promised us, did he? Perhaps—

And there it stopped.

'We'll go to London first.' Roz could hear her father's voice still. 'Do the Tower of London, Buckingham Palace, the lot.'

In the aftermath of his death, she had forgotten those few excited weeks when the three of them had planned the trip to the UK. Her father had talked about taking them north to see where he had grown up, but Millie and Roz had been united for once in wanting to see London.

Roz had found the letter shoved at the back of a drawer in the bureau. She had smoothed it out, picturing her mother sitting down and reaching for a pen, only to be interrupted. Had it been Richard coming home? Was that why she had pushed the letter hastily out of sight?

What would she have said if she had finished it? Would she have taken Roz up on her suggestion that they go to London together? Roz wanted to believe that was it, that Millie would have insisted that Richard stay behind and that she spend some time alone with her daughter. In the end, though, it didn't matter. What mattered was that her mother had thought of her, and whenever Roz had faltered, whenever it had all seemed too hard, she had taken the letter out and read it, feeling closer to her mother than she ever had when she was alive.

She had left Millie's jewellery in a safe deposit box. She kept only the unfinished letter and the opal ring that she had found in her father's jacket pocket. It fitted so comfortably on her finger and felt so oddly *right* there that she wore it every day.

She would take that long-postponed trip, Roz had decided. She would go to London just as she and her mother had planned so long ago.

Arriving in England had been the contrast she craved: the air was murky and damp, the light dimmer than in Adelaide, where everything was so sharply outlined in the brilliant light you had to squint at it. The streets of London were crowded and noisy, but Roz didn't mind that. It was silent houses that made her heart race now, that made her sweaty and panicky.

She had found a flat near Ladbroke Grove, on the top floor of a tall stucco-fronted house, which she shared with two other girls. Her roommates seemed nice enough. One, Sasha, was a fellow waitress and a fellow Australian, and Keeley was a Brit who worked for an accountancy firm.

Roz kept herself to herself for the most part. The parting with Pete had been amicable, and in a way it had been harder to say goodbye to Bronwen, who had been such a good friend to her. But Bronwen had a husband and children and all the ties that made Roz recoil. She didn't need Roz making life awkward for her in Ridgewell, even if Roz had wanted to stay. There were still plenty of people in the town who believed that Richard was an innocent victim of his stepdaughter's vendetta. Roz was afraid that Bronwen had suffered for her loyalty to her friend. Easier all round to avoid any kind of relationships, she had decided. It was enough to look after herself.

Not that she needed looking after. The box of terrible memories in her head stayed firmly closed, but it was always there, squatting in the middle of her mind so that every thought she had was forced to dodge around it. It was exhausting, but apart from that, she was fine.

The candle flames wavered as she carried the cake across the restaurant, but they stayed alight as she presented it at the table to many oohs and aahs. They seemed to be a nice family party: the mother, her husband, three grown children with partners, a couple of sisters or friends. Roz couldn't help feeling envious of how easy and affectionate they were with each other. The daughter stood behind her mother, chin on her mum's hair and arms draped over her shoulders, both of them smiling widely at the phones being pointed their way as Roz approached.

She had never had that kind of loving relationship with her own mother. Roz smiled and took photos of the whole family together and tried to push down the jumble of conflicting feelings that surfaced whenever she thought about Millie: guilt, regret, remembered horror . . . oh, and there she was, tiptoeing around that bloody box again.

She had lost her mother in the most horrible way, but sadder to Roz was the sense that she had never really had the mother she wanted at all. Millie had been a man's woman. Roz had been a rival for John Chatton's attention, a complication for Millie's relationship with Richard. She had never just been a daughter.

But maybe, right at the end, there had been a chance for them to be closer. They could have planned that trip to London together. They could have talked without Richard looming in the background.

Until Richard had put an end to it all.

Enough, Roz told herself, handing out plates for the cake. Getting on a plane to London was meant to be drawing a line. She had thought this would be a fresh start, but she still felt as if she were suspended in time, untethered. It was as if she was waiting for something to happen, but she wasn't sure what. Still, coming to London had been a good move. There were no gum leaves here to crunch beneath her feet, no scents of crushing heat and eucalyptus. No still houses where the sound of the air conditioner was broken only by the slow drip, drip of a tap.

Yes, definitely a good move. For now, Roz was content to tread water. Waitressing was hard on the feet, but as most of her shifts were in the evenings, it left the day free to explore London. She loved the babble of different languages, and the parks, and the secret thrill of walking past signs pointing to Buckingham Palace or Piccadilly Circus or the Tower of London. Sometimes she imagined Millie by her side, exclaiming at how old everything seemed after Ridgewell, or pursing her lips at the weather. She pictured the two of them sitting in a coffee shop, poking around Camden Market, or spilling out of a theatre after a show.

But what she liked most about London was the anonymity. In Ridgewell, she had been exposed, aware of hostile eyes on her. There were too many people who believed that upstanding police officer Richard Heissen was innocent, too many people who fell for the wide smile and never noticed the meaty fists and bitter mouth.

Richard had been convicted, Roz reassured herself constantly. He was in prison now. Her solicitor had warned her that he would appeal his sentence, but there was no reason to suppose he would be successful. There was no way her stepfather could suddenly appear, no way he could find her, surely, not here in this sprawling city. In London, no one was interested in her at all. Alone in the crowds, she felt safe.

For once, it wasn't raining when she woke the next morning. Through the small attic window in her bedroom she could see that the sky was a pale watery blue. In the three weeks she had been in London, this was the first time Roz had seen the sun. It had come out like a gift and the city was transformed. The trees in the parks were covered in a zingy green haze, so different from the dusty, silvery greens she knew in Australia. The sunlight softened the creamy stone facades and made Londoners less rigid, less huddled into their coats. Their steps slowed, their heads lifted.

With no particular plan in mind, Roz wandered along to Notting Hill Gate. She liked the back streets, the neat houses with their painted doors and tidy front gardens and the contrast with the bustle of Portobello Road. She sat with a coffee for a while, and then crossed the road and headed down Kensington Church Street.

There were more inviting side streets to explore here. In spite of the sunshine, it was much colder than she was used to, and she kept her hands in her pockets as she walked. She should get some gloves, she thought, vaguely aware that she was fiddling with the opal ring with her thumb. Odd. Usually, it was so comfortable she didn't feel it at all.

Still fiddling, not really concentrating, she hesitated at a crossroads. Right or left? To the right lay an attractive street, to the left a glimpse of a row of shops, some awnings, an elegant pot at a door. She turned left.

The awnings seemed to belong to antique shops of one kind or another. One sold fabulous carpets, another glossy brown furniture and huge Chinese pots. There was a jeweller, a couple of art dealers and, a little less polished than the others, a shop that seemed to sell a little of everything: antiquarian books and prints, old maps, paintings and curios. The shopfront was painted green, the name *Ballantyne's* picked out in gold.

Roz wasn't even looking. She glanced idly at the window as she had at the others and was already wondering what the next shop would be when she saw it.

Propped on an easel, in an unpretentious frame, it showed four standing stones on some sort of headland, with misty hills in the distance. She didn't recognise the scene, but something about the painting called to her. It was the strangest thing, and obviously she must have been imagining it, but she could swear that the opal ring throbbed on her finger. Without making a conscious decision, she pushed open the door and stepped into the shop.

Inside, it was a mess. There were shelves jammed with books, and more books piled on the floor and on the steps of a staircase leading up to the next floor. Prints and pictures were stacked against the wall. Bric-a-brac cluttered a random assortment of tables, and odd bits of furniture were shoved on top of each other. At the back, a harassed-looking man with a horseshoe of tufty grey hair and the kind of checked shirt and cardigan Roz had only ever seen in movies was standing behind a desk on which teetered piles of papers and yet more books. He was holding the phone away from his ear and pulling faces at the tirade of abuse that was clearly being delivered.

She offered a sympathetic grimace and indicated that she would look around until he was finished. There was no way to get at the window to look more closely at the picture that had so intrigued her, so she poked around and flicked through the stacks of prints, most of which seemed to be of old maps. Her fingers itched to straighten everything up.

At the end of what was clearly an increasingly fraught conversation, the shop owner says goodbye with exquisite courtesy, dropped the phone onto the desk and swore loudly before belatedly remembering that Roz was still in the shop.

'I do beg your pardon,' he said hastily. 'That was quite unnecessary language.'

Roz laughed. 'Having a bad day?'

'Oh, just dealing with one of my esteemed clients who wants the impossible done by yesterday,' he said with a sigh. 'My computer is on a go-slow and last week my barely adequate assistant left without notice, so I'm not really on top of things.' He took off his glasses, pinched the bridge of his nose then put them back on. 'My apologies again. I'm Hugo Ballantyne. Can I help you?'

'Could I have a closer look at one of the pictures in the window?'

'Of course. Which one?'

'It's a landscape. With some kind of standing stones?'

'Ah, yes, charming, isn't it?' He struggled through various bits of furniture to reach into the window and lifted the painting from its stand. Turning it over in his hands, he read out the label on the back. '*Four Sisters*, by Amelia Blackmore.'

Roz had the strangest sensation that her ring was actually pulsing. 'Oh!' she said, looking down at her hand.

He glanced up at her involuntary exclamation. 'Do you know the artist?'

'No. Sorry, I was just … No, I've never heard of Amelia Blackmore,' she managed. 'Is she famous?'

'I wouldn't say famous exactly. Like many late-Victorian and early-twentieth-century artists, she wasn't well known during her lifetime, but since some of her works have started emerging, she's grown in popularity. She's very well regarded nowadays.'

Roz liked the way he talked, his rounded, almost plummy voice so different from laconic Australians.

He held out the picture. 'Do you want to have a closer look?'

'Could I?' She took it gingerly. This was weird. Her ring was definitely throbbing. 'Where is it?'

'Now, that I don't know,' he confessed. 'It looks very like Scotland, don't you think?'

'I wouldn't know,' said Roz. 'I've just arrived in the UK. I haven't made it out of London yet.'

'Oh, you must go up to Scotland while you're here. I believe Amelia Blackmore was from the west coast somewhere. Certainly, the standing stones look a little like the ones on Lewis... the Calanais stones, I think they're called. Really remarkable, I believe.' He peered at the picture again. 'Yes, it's an interesting little picture. Atmospheric. Do you like it?'

'I do,' said Roz slowly. 'I don't know why. It's not my usual kind of thing at all.'

'You've got a good eye.'

'How much is it?' she asked on an impulse.

'I'd need to check.' He rummaged around on his chaotic desk, jabbed at his computer a few times and eventually emerged with a piece of paper. 'Here it is. Five hundred and forty pounds.' Catching sight of Roz's dismayed expression, he added, 'But I could let you have it for five hundred.'

'Thank you, but it's still out of my budget. I'm being silly anyway,' she said resolutely. 'I'm travelling. What would I do with a painting?' And yet she was curiously reluctant to give the picture back to Hugo Ballantyne.

He smiled kindly as he took it from her. 'Well, you know where it is if you change your mind.'

11

Finn

Skara, present day

The road was familiar as far as the turn-off. Finn squashed the feeling of guilt as he passed the sign to Glenussie without slowing down. It was barely two weeks since he had been to see his parents. They wouldn't expect him at the manse again so soon.

Anyway, they would only be disappointed that Angus hadn't come back instead.

And he was working, he reminded himself.

The weather had been predictably dreich since he had set off from Edinburgh that morning, but as he drove over the narrow stretch that connected Skara to the mainland, the sullen grey clouds broke up without warning, leaving the sky flushed with pink and gold, while purple mountains emerged from the murk like huge, silent beasts. The road shrank to a single track as it followed the coast, and he drove past empty white-sand beaches where the tranquil silver water lapped at the shore.

It felt very remote, but then Finn was used to remote. Skara was not so very far from Glenussie, the scattered parish where his father had served as minister, but it felt like a different country, a gentler, fairy-tale world compared to the houses and farms clinging grimly to the mountainsides where Finn had grown up. Glenussie had its own grandeur, but he could understand why city types like Aileen found the landscape daunting.

Not that she had admitted to being intimidated. 'You didn't tell me it was like this. There's just nothing here,' she had said, looking out at a magnificent mountain view. Then she had leant over to Finn, so close that he could smell the exotic perfume she wore, and smiled the wicked little smile that made his head spin. 'Your dad's a bit grim, isn't he?' she murmured.

'He's not well.' He found himself excusing his father, as always.

Finn was tired by the time he finally drove into Acheravie, the main settlement on Skara, which boasted the peninsula's only two hotels. Sadly, his budget didn't extend to a stay at the five-star Dundonan Castle, and he had booked instead at the Anchor Inn, an austere whitewashed building with little in the way of frills, inside or out. A sensible-looking woman with a name badge reading *Morag* gave him the key to a plain but functional room with a spectacular view across the sea to distant blue hills, and reminded him that last orders for food was 7.30.

The bar was as functional as the rest of the hotel. The wood-panelled walls were lined with padded benches, with square tables and uncomfortable upright chairs ranged opposite. Finn would have welcomed an easy chair after his long drive, but he stood at the bar and ordered a pint. He had come straight from the office and felt out of place in his suit, but at least he had thrown his walking boots and some outdoor gear into the car that morning.

Morag appeared to double up as barmaid. 'So, what brings you to Acheravie?' she asked. 'You're not here for the walking,' she observed. 'Not in that suit.'

'No, I'm here on business.' He took a sip of his beer. He might as well start work now. 'Do you know of a house that once belonged to Charles Blackmore? It would have been in the 1930s.'

Her face changed. 'I do. Rubha Clachan.' She gave a quick shudder.

Well, that was easier than Finn had expected.

'Is it still standing?'

'Aye, on the headland.' She tilted her head to indicate the direction. 'But nobody ever goes there now.'

'Why not?'

'It's cursed,' she said, matter-of-fact.

'Cursed?' Finn repeated carefully.

'No need to look down your nose at me,' Morag said, wiping down the bar. 'Ask anyone round here.'

'Right.' He made an effort to keep his voice expressionless but clearly didn't manage it, as she scowled at him.

'Why are you interested in the house anyway?'

Finn hesitated, unsure of how much he should say. 'I represent the Blackmore Trust.'

'The Blackmores brought nothing but trouble to Skara,' said Morag. 'If you're representing that family, you can tell them now that they're not welcome here.'

'You'll appreciate that I'm not in a position to discuss confidential matters,' he said, uncomfortably aware of how pompous he sounded. He finished his beer and set the glass on the bar. 'But I do need to get into the house. Do you know anyone who might have a key?'

'I doubt it's locked.' She shuddered again. 'Like I say, no one round here would set foot in it. And if I were you, I wouldn't either. You'll regret it.'

12

Roz

London, present day

What was I thinking? Roz asked herself as she wandered on. What would she do with a five-hundred quid painting? She couldn't believe that she had gone into the shop at all. Her taste had always been for the modern, for space and clean lines, not dusty old bric-a-brac and faded paintings.

But she couldn't shake the image of those four stones on the headland. The sense of recognition nagged at her, tugging at her mind. That night she dreamt: of sea and wind, of fear, of loss, and the opal glowing a terrifying blue. Her dreams left her restless and uneasy.

Somehow she found herself back at the shop the next afternoon, staring again at the picture in the window. She wouldn't go in. She just wanted to look at it.

She stood outside, staring so hard at the painting that she could almost swear she could hear the wind blowing over the tufty seagrass, bringing the seaweedy tang of the ocean to the quiet Kensington street. And yet it was just a painting of some stones. There weren't even any people in it. Her ring was tingling, growing warm.

Abruptly she turned and walked away.

Over the next few days, Roz was exasperated to find herself back outside the shop, peering into the window at the picture of a place she didn't know but somehow recognised. Every time, she set off determinedly to explore a part of London in the other direction, but there was always a bus heading homewards via Kensington, or she would be on the Tube, following the stops, and there was High Street Kensington, and why not walk back to the flat from there? Looking at the picture was a craving, like yearning for something sweet and knowing there was a bar of chocolate in the fridge. The shop appeared to be closed for a lot of the time, and she wondered how it could do any business.

One day, the painting wasn't there.

Roz didn't stop to think. The old-fashioned bell above the door jangled as she pushed open the door in a panic.

Hugo Ballantyne was behind his desk, having apparently made no progress tidying up. He looked up, seemingly unsurprised to see her.

'Hello, are you back for another look?'

'Yes, I ... Have you still got that picture? The one of the stones?'

'Somewhere here.' He looked around vaguely as he got to his feet.

'I thought you'd sold it.' Her voice was taut with anxiety as she watched him look through some paintings propped against the desk. 'It's not in the window.'

'I was planning to rearrange everything, but then I got distracted. I must have brought the painting in as a start and put it somewhere... Ah, here it is!'

He lifted the picture out of the pile and Roz's muscles went limp with relief as he handed it to her.

The scene was just as she had remembered it: the restless sea, the watching stones that seem to be poised as if waiting. The soft grey-blue light and the hills across the water.

She let out a breath she hadn't realised she had been holding, then looked down again at the painting between her hands. Was it her imagination, or could she really hear the wind that bent the seagrass and ruffled the surface of the water? That carried an echo of voices too faint to understand, voices that lightened into laughter at times and at others edged abruptly into horror?

'I've been dreaming about this picture,' she blurted out, but he didn't seem to find anything strange about her confession.

'Some paintings will do that to you,' he said. 'I'm like that with old maps. My speciality. There's always one that just won't let you go.'

Roz smiled at him. 'It's kind of you not to make me feel weird.'

'Nothing weird about it,' he said stoutly. 'It's a pleasure to meet someone who reacts to a painting on a visceral level rather than just looking for one that blends with their decor.'

She made herself give the picture back to him. 'I'm sorry. I don't want to waste your time. I can't afford to buy it. In a few months, maybe,' she added, thinking of her mother's house. When it was sold and the estate finally settled, she would have the money, but for now, she was living off her meagre savings and her earnings as a waitress, and in a city like London, that didn't go far. 'I just wanted to look at it again.'

'No need to apologise,' Hugo said with a smile. 'Come back any time.'

The next time Roz went back to look at the picture, the window was empty, and inside, the shop was even more chaotic than usual. Hugo was struggling to shift a table.

'Let me help you with that,' she said, taking one end.

'Oh, thank you. I just decided to move one thing, and somehow that has meant turning the entire shop upside down. I wish I'd never started it now,' he confessed.

When the table was in place, Roz picked up a Chinese vase that had been plonked precariously on top of a teetering pile of old books. 'Where do you want this? Here?' she added as Hugo dithered, setting the vase on a rather dusty bookshelf.

'That looks fine,' he said gratefully.

'What else are you moving?'

'Well, I was thinking that armchair would look good in the window . . .'

'Let's do it,' said Roz, brushing the dust off her hands.

'Oh, I mustn't take advantage of you,' he protested. 'I'm sure you have much better things to do.'

'I'd like to help,' she said. 'I don't start work until six and you've been so kind letting me come back and look at the painting. I think it's made me a bit crazy, to be honest.'

'Nonsense, a response to art is never "crazy", as you put it.' He let her take the other side of the chair and they lifted it towards the window.

'Hang on,' said Roz, eyeing the state of the display area. 'Let me have a sweep first. Got a dustpan and brush?'

'Well, yes, somewhere, but . . .'

Roz had already found a brush under his desk. She set about clearing out the dust and cobwebs, and for good measure found a cloth and wiped all the surfaces.

'Right, let's get that chair in.'

They stood back and admired their efforts. 'It needs something else,' Hugo decided.

'Why don't you put the other armchair in there, and a table between them with some books? So it looks inviting, like the kind of place you'd sit down and read or have a chat?'

'And a lamp perhaps?' He was getting into the spirit of it.

'Yes, and pictures on the wall behind,' said Roz, helping him lift in the second armchair. 'What about this table here?'

By the time they had finished, they had created a cosy scene. 'Let's put your picture up on the side wall too,' Hugo suggested, picking it up. 'That way if I'm away at auction and the shop is closed, you'll always be able to see it.'

Roz pulled a face. 'What if someone else sees it and wants to buy it, though?'

'Somehow I don't think they will.' He hung it as part of the display and stood back to consider it. 'There's obviously a connection between you and that painting.'

'That's how it feels,' she agreed, her eyes on the scene. 'I can't explain it. I mean, it doesn't make sense. I'm an Aussie. I've never been to the UK before, let alone Scotland.'

'Does your family come from Scotland?'

'Not that I know of. Dad was from Newcastle, but Mum was

born in Australia and her mother before her, I'm sure. I never heard her mention Scotland.'

'Intriguing,' said Hugo.

Roz almost told him about the ring and how it seemed to tingle in front of the painting, but that really did sound crazy. She looked around the shop instead. How on earth did Hugo find anything in here?

'Still no assistant?' she asked.

'I'm afraid not.' He took off his glasses and hunted around for a handkerchief to polish them. 'Dev, my last assistant, used to deal with all the invoices and cataloguing, but he was an actor and he always had one foot out the door. Working here fitted in with auditions, and the moment he had a part, he was off.'

The glasses went back on, not quite straight. 'Not that I begrudge the dear boy his success – we all have to follow our dreams, after all – but I haven't found anyone to replace him and everything is getting rather out of control.' He looked sadly around the room.

'I could come in and help you sometimes if you like,' Roz said impulsively.

'Really?' His voice lifted in hope. 'But didn't you say you were working?'

'I'm waitressing at the moment, but I'm just doing evening shifts.' She was surprised at how eager she was to work there. 'I could easily come and give you a hand for a few hours a day.'

'That would be marvellous,' he said. 'Are you *sure*?' He hesitated. 'It's too dull for most young people, and I'm afraid I can't offer much in the way of pay either. That's why it's been so difficult to replace Dev.'

'I don't mind.' Roz pointed at the painting. 'I'll work for that.'

'No, no, if you are going to work here, we must be above board and dot the i's and cross the t's. In any case, the painting is clearly yours. We'll put a sold sign on it until you're ready to take it away.'

He rubbed his hands together, delighted. 'I don't suppose you know anything about computers?'

Roz looked at him. 'I'm twenty-eight,' she said.

'Then of course you do. One forgets that you young people have grown up with them.'

'I'm a graphic designer in the real world. I work on computers all the time. I design a lot of maps, funnily enough. Street plans, that kind of thing,' she added hurriedly. 'Nothing like the maps here.'

'That sounds very clever,' said Hugo. 'I'd have thought there would be lots of call for a skill like that.'

'I could probably get a design job if I tried,' Roz admitted. 'I just fancied a change.'

And she would be harder to find if Richard came looking. He knew what she did. It wouldn't be that difficult to track down a graphic designer, but waitresses were ten a penny in London.

'Working here will certainly be a change for you,' Hugo said with a disarming roll of his eyes. 'If you know how to navigate a computer screen, you'll be doing better than me. I'm over eighty now,' he said. 'My generation just missed computers being a fact of life – or I did, anyway – and I've never got the hang of that thing.'

'I can't say that I know anything about old books or paintings, but I can certainly help with the admin,' said Roz. 'And I can tidy up and answer the phone, that kind of thing.'

'That sounds perfect.'

'I'm Roz, by the way,' she said, holding out her hand. 'Roz Chatton.'

'Well, Roz, I'd be absolutely delighted if you could spare some time to come in and help,' said Hugo, as he shook her hand formally.

'Thank you!'

'No, thank *you*,' he said. 'I was starting to wonder how I was going to manage.' He looked around the shop with a rueful expression. 'To be honest, it's all getting a bit much for me, but when I think about not being here, well, I can't bear it. So I keep muddling on.'

He brushed his hands on his trousers. 'I suppose we'll have to sort out a bit of paperwork, but let's have a cup of tea first.'

Roz couldn't help laughing. 'That's very British of you!'

'You'd better get used to drinking tea if you work here,' Hugo said agreeably, vanishing into a room at the back. 'Won't be a tick.'

Smiling, Roz took down the painting she thought of as hers and studied it. She was glad she had come in today. She didn't need the second job, but it would be fun to work in such a charmingly eccentric place.

'Sit down and make yourself at home,' Hugo called out from the kitchen, and the ring on her finger gave a warning pulse.

Home.

She stilled as the picture between her hands seemed to echo the word. She could hear it fading out over the painted sea, towards the far painted hills: *home, home, home* . . .

When Hugo came back holding two mugs of tea, she was still staring at the picture, frowning a little.

'Everything okay?' he asked.

'Yes.' She couldn't tell him that the painting was literally talking to her now. She put down the painting and smiled brightly as she took a mug from him. 'Yes, of course. Thanks, Hugo. Everything's great. I can't wait to start.'

13

Finn

Skara, present day

Finn slept badly but woke to a fresh morning. It had rained overnight, and the air was soft and damp. A watery sun was trying to break through the clouds and glimmering in patches on the silvery sea. He pushed open his window and breathed in the smell of salt and damp grass. It was very quiet, just the gentle shush of the sea and a sheep bleating somewhere on the hillside. He felt as if he was on the edge of the world.

It was a beautiful place, and he wanted someone to share it with. Perhaps he could bring Aileen here one day, he thought, but then sighed.

Who was he trying to kid? Aileen was never going to see him as anything more than a friend. When he had rung to tell her, oh-so-casually, that he had got a job at Kingan, Kingan & McVean and would be moving to Edinburgh, she had whistled, impressed. Aileen had been in Edinburgh since graduating. She was a commercial lawyer, her expensively shod feet already on the ladder of success.

'Your father must be pleased,' she said. She had known Finn long enough to know how hard he worked for his father's approval.

'He is,' said Finn, although his father had just grunted. Nothing Finn ever did could compare with his brilliant brother.

Aileen wouldn't be so impressed when she found out that he was just dealing with cold cases and reading through dusty folders, he thought glumly.

They had been students together in Glasgow, Finn allowed to tag along at the edges of a group that had Aileen always at its centre. She was funny and bright, and he was thrilled just to be in her orbit. It was soon obvious that his role was to be a dependable friend, someone who would pick her up at odd hours, who could check her tyre pressure and provide a broad shoulder for her to cry on when the latest relationship crashed and burnt. 'What would I do without you?' she would sob.

'Don't you get tired of being taken for granted?' another member of the extended group had asked Finn one day, but he didn't mind. He had no illusions about himself, and why should Aileen think of him as more than a friend? She didn't owe him anything. He was steady and stocky and sandy-haired, and he had early on accepted that she was out of his league. He knew that she was fond of him, and having her friendship was better than nothing.

At breakfast, Morag reluctantly gave him directions to the house. It wasn't far, she admitted. Finn drove cautiously up the narrow road, past the single shop with a fuel pump outside, past a woman who was hanging out washing and who stopped and stared suspiciously at him as he went by. The road wound its way up to the headland, where he glimpsed an imposing castle, and then round a bay with a pristine white beach to the headland on the far side, where he reached two stone gateposts. Between them, old iron gates hung dejectedly open. He stopped the car and got out. This was literally the end of the road. But he was in the right place. Walking over to the posts, he peered at the worn lettering and could just decipher the words *Rubha Clachan*.

Finn put the car back into gear and drove cautiously between the gateposts and up the long drive. After a while, it became so overgrown that he had to stop and get out. At least he was prepared. If growing up in the hills taught you anything, it was to always make sure you had decent boots on.

It wasn't long before he came in sight of the house itself. He wasn't sure what he had expected – some baronial mansion, perhaps? – but it certainly wasn't a square, striking house built in the art deco style. Originally white, it was now badly in need of a new coat of paint, but nothing could disguise the large windows and stark lines, or detract from the spectacular setting on the headland.

Glad of his waterproof trousers, he waded through the long grass to the front of the house, which faced out to sea. There had been a terrace here once, though the slabs were now broken and choked with weeds. There seemed to be a kind of seating area further towards the cliff edge. Finn ploughed on and discovered that the seats had been created by four great stones, which had been laid on their sides. He turned to look back at the house, with its flat roof and those huge windows with curved sides. It would be a great setting for one of those Agatha Christie adaptations his mother liked to watch on the telly, he thought.

Back at the terrace, he cupped his hands to peer through the windows. Morag had been right. The house appeared to have been abandoned, its furniture still in place, as if the family had walked out one day and never come back. There was a glass door leading out to the terrace. Finn tried the handle. It was stiff, but opened after a bit of wiggling. He went in, feeling eerily as if he were stepping into the past.

Inside, dust lay thickly over every surface, while spiders' webs festooned the corners.

He was standing in what must once have been a grand entrance hall, evidently decorated in the very latest style in the 1920s. A dramatically curved staircase led up to a great porthole window on the landing and then disappeared into shadows.

On the hall table stood a black Bakelite telephone with a round dial and a heavy receiver. Finn eyed it with the uneasy sense that it might be about to ring. Which was ridiculous, he chastised himself. It had clearly been disconnected long ago. Still, he couldn't shake the idea that it was waiting, that at any moment it would shrill, and if he picked up the receiver, he would hear someone asking for Charles Blackmore or one of his daughters.

The silence was thick, dense, almost suffocating. Finn found that he was holding his breath, and when something flickered at the edge of his vision, he turned sharply, his heart jerking.

A bird flying past a window, he told himself firmly. The house was empty, that was obvious. It had been empty for nearly a century, and yet when he looked up the stairs, he almost expected to see a young girl leaning over the banister, beckoning him up into the shadows. He even put a foot on the bottom step, only to shake himself back to reality. What was he thinking? This place was a health-and-safety nightmare. Only an idiot would waltz up unknown stairs in search of... what?

Clearing his throat, Finn crossed the hall and pushed open double doors into a huge drawing room with a spectacular view out to sea. Everything had been left as if the Blackmores had simply gone out for a walk. There was a gramophone in one corner, a messy pile of records next to it. The piano had its lid up, with sheet music on the stand. Books were tumbled on the coffee table and a newspaper had been abandoned on one of the sofas.

Finn picked it up gingerly and grimaced as he shook off the dust so that he could read the date: Monday, 13 July 1936.

Behind him, something shifted, and he dropped the paper in a flurry of dust that made him cough. Embarrassed to find an empty room when he spun round, he made a big show of brushing his hands together. He was not a believer in the supernatural, but there was something very creepy about this house. It had just been abandoned. Nobody had ever closed the place up. It was waiting for the family to come back. He couldn't help feeling that if he closed his eyes, he would hear the gramophone playing, that if he turned very, very slowly, he would find men in two-tone shoes and baggy trousers lighting cigarettes and pouring martinis for women in cloche hats and dropped-waist dresses.

He pulled a face at himself. Never mind his mum. He must have been watching too much Agatha Christie as well.

Come on, he told himself. He had a job to do. He wasn't

sure exactly what he was looking for, but there must be some indication here of what had happened to Charles Blackmore's family. Closing the door of the drawing room very carefully, he retraced the trail of his boots across the hall. He found a dining room with a long table and chairs in art deco style. There was no abandoned meal on the table, but this room, too, was ready for the Blackmore girls to come in, chattering gaily as they sat down.

There was a small sitting room, doubtless belonging to Charles Blackmore's wife, Amelia, which looked across the headland to Dundonan Castle. Under the dust, Finn found an embroidery panel, half finished, and more books. One had a bookmark between the pages, ready to be picked up once more. He brushed off the cobwebs to see the title: *The Five Red Herrings* by Dorothy L. Sayers. Someone in the house had liked a mystery. He wondered if they had known that they would be part of one themselves one day.

A door opened into a corridor leading to the kitchen. He peered in, then made his way back to the hall, ignoring the prickle at the back of his neck. There was nobody watching him. There was nobody there. The house was not cursed. It was just... empty.

Opening another door, he found himself in what must have been Charles's study, judging by the book-lined walls and the art deco armchairs on either side of the fireplace. Finn looked around in dismay. It was a mess. The cupboards were bulging with papers and there were empty whisky bottles everywhere.

In the bay window stood a desk, with two framed photographs poking through the piles of papers that covered it. One showed Charles Blackmore and his wife on their wedding day.

They were stiffly posed and unsmiling, but it was possible to see Charles's chest puffed with pride, and the sweetness in Amelia's eyes.

When Finn blew the dust off the second photograph, he saw that it was of four girls. They were smiling at the camera, their arms around each other. One of them was laughing as she held on to her hat.

These must be Charles Blackmore's daughters. Finn's throat was oddly tight. What had happened to them? Where had they gone? How could a family that had once looked so close vanish, apparently leaving their father alone? Finn had looked through all the papers and it was clear that Charles Blackmore had died on his own. There was a sadness in the wording of his will, as if he realised that he had left it too late to find his daughters and make his peace with them.

Coughing at the dust, he pulled the desk chair back with a screech that had him looking nervously over his shoulder. But no one came to see what the noise was about – of course they didn't! – and he sat down cautiously. Feeling like a thief, he pulled open the desk drawers. There must be something useful in here, surely? In the third drawer down, he found a pile of letters, still in their original envelopes.

Fastidiously, he fished out a handkerchief and cleaned his hands as best he could before reaching in and lifting the letters out onto the top of the desk. He slid a sheet of paper out of the first envelope. The letter was dated 15 April 1931, and was written from the Ritz hotel in London. *My dearest sisters*, it began.

An unexpected shaft of sunlight laid a stripe across the desk. Finn paused, abruptly aware of the sound of his own breathing.

In the distance, he could hear the mesmerising suck and sigh of the sea, but the house itself was completely still and silent, waiting. Finn was not a fanciful man, but he couldn't help feeling as if the place was tiptoeing up behind him to read the letter over his shoulder. The feeling was so strong that he glanced back uneasily, only to feel foolish when the room was, of course, empty.

Quickly he scanned the letter. It seemed to describe an interview, and as he turned the sheet over, he found a vivid little sketch, almost a cartoon, of a glamorous woman sitting at a tea table, while heading towards her was a dowdy-looking girl in a frumpy hat, wearing a comically dismayed expression. It was cleverly done, he thought with a smile. There was a signature at the bottom of the page.

Iris.

14
Iris

Orphea, Bay of Biscay, April 1931

The *Orphea*'s dining room, with its white tablecloths, silverware and magnificent chandeliers, had been so like a grand hotel on land that Iris had almost forgotten that they were on a ship. But overnight a storm blew up, and when she woke the next morning, there was no doubt that they were at sea. *Orphea* was ploughing through great waves in a corkscrew motion, pitching forwards and backwards and rolling sickeningly from side to side while heavy rain splattered against the porthole like gunfire.

There was a dreadful groaning sound filling the cabin, and it took a moment for Iris to realise that it came from the other bunk.

'Geraldine?' Without thinking, she threw back the bedclothes and swung her feet to the floor. 'Geraldine? Are you all right?'

'Go away!'

Iris hesitated. Surely she couldn't just ignore the fact that her room-mate was so obviously suffering. 'There must be something

I can do to help,' she tried, but Geraldine only turned her face to the wall, her voice muffled.

'I *said*, go away!'

Getting dressed was a challenge given the way the ship was tilting first one way, then another. Iris hopped around, grasping at the furniture. She could now understand why it was all screwed into place. There was a rail around the top of the chest of drawers to stop things falling off, but the hairbrushes and combs and one of Iris's lipsticks were making so much noise rolling around that she grabbed them and shoved them into a drawer.

Lurching from side to side in the gangway, she made it down to the steward's station. He was surprised to see her. 'You up and about, miss? You must have your sea legs already.'

'Miss Woolstone is very unwell,' Iris said. 'I'm worried about her.'

'I daresay she'll feel she's dying, but she's just seasick. She'll be right as rain in a day or two.' He reached into a cupboard and produced a basin. 'She might be glad of this, though.'

Iris took it and returned to the cabin, where Geraldine snatched it out of her hands without a word of thanks and retched into it.

'I'll ... er ... leave you to it,' Iris muttered.

It seemed tactful to check on Lady Carsington too. She tapped on the cabin door and was met with a querulous 'Come in.'

Ariadne was in bed, looking wan and bedraggled and barely recognisable as the sophisticate who could summon gentlemen to light her cigarette with the mere raise of an eyebrow. She lifted herself up on her elbows and stared blearily at Iris.

'Ugh ... What are you doing up?'

'I just came to see if you needed anything.'

'I think I'm dying!' She flopped back onto her pillow. 'Where's Baxter?' she moaned.

'I suspect she may be seasick too. There's hardly anyone around. I think everyone is in their cabins, feeling ill.'

Ariadne eyed her with suspicion. 'Why aren't you seasick?'

'I think I must be lucky.'

'I hate you,' she said, closing her eyes.

'I'll go and check on Baxter,' said Iris, feeling for once at an advantage.

Sure enough, Ariadne's maid was prone in the cabin she shared with another lady's maid, neither of them able to lift their heads from the pillow. Iris made sure that they had basins and water, and took another basin back to Ariadne's cabin.

'Just in case,' she said, setting it on the bedside table. 'I don't think Baxter will be able to help you much today,' she added, as she headed for the door.

'Where are you going?'

'I thought I'd try and find some breakfast.'

Ariadne reached for the basin and turned her face away. 'Ugh ...' She swallowed a retch. 'Go away and leave me to die in peace!'

Iris suppressed a smile. 'I'll come back later and see how you are.'

The breakfast room was eerily empty. Iris had coffee, a boiled egg and some toast, then, relieved of her responsibilities, went back to her cabin to put on her coat and hat. Tiptoeing in, she found Geraldine still retching helplessly. She paused. The other girl had made it clear enough that she didn't want any help, but what if one of her sisters was alone on a ship and feeling this unwell?

She went back to the steward, found a clean basin and slipped it into Geraldine's shaking hands as she deftly removed the other.

In the bathroom at the end of the gangway, she disposed of the contents with a grimace and wetted the flannel she had found in Geraldine's toiletry bag.

'I know you don't want any help, but you'll feel better if you at least wipe your face and hands,' she told her. She held out the flannel, but Geraldine just slumped back onto her pillow, turning her face away to hide tears of weakness.

'Here, I'll do it for you,' said Iris. Gently she wiped Geraldine's face and hands. 'I've left some water on the table here if you're able to drink something. I'm going out, so you can have the cabin to yourself.'

Geraldine's face twisted, but when Iris had found her hat and coat and was at the cabin door, she heard her croak, 'Iris?'

'Yes?' Iris turned.

'Thank you.'

Outside, the weather was atrocious, but it was no worse than a wild winter's day on Skara. Cautiously Iris pushed open the heavy door and stepped out onto the deck. She was greeted by a buffet of wind that flung rain at her face, making her gasp and stagger.

Between the gale and the wild rolling of the ship, she struggled to stay upright, but she was reluctant to go back inside. The air was blissfully fresh and free from the fustiness and the faint but pervading smell of vomit inside, and after the close confines of the cabin, she was exhilarated by the cold and stinging wet.

She lurched along from bollard to lifebelt locker, from bulkhead to the heavy cleats set into the ship's solid metal rail. Sometimes she tried walking into the wind, leaning forward, and then with the gale behind her, threatening at every moment to blow her off her feet – if her ungainly progress could be called walking.

Ten times round the ship, she told herself, but she had barely rounded the deck below the bridge when she bumped into something solid. As she recoiled, the wind snatched at her hat and took it tumbling out over the Bay of Biscay.

'Oh, my hat!'

Turning to follow its progress, she was instantly drenched by the spray from a rogue wave. Blinking the water from her eyes, she found herself facing Guy Henderson.

'What in God's name are you doing out in this?' he demanded.

'What are *you* doing?' she countered.

They both had to raise their voices to be heard above the wind and the spatter of spray as the waves crashed against the ship. Iris turned up the collar of her coat, but could do nothing now about the drenching rain.

'I wanted some air.'

'I did too.'

'You're soaked,' Guy pointed out. He offered her his hat, but she shook her head.

'There's no point in both of us getting wet.'

'Come round here, it's more sheltered,' he shouted, pointing, and without waiting for her reply, he took her arm and led her to a covered area under the stairs up to the bridge where there was a metal locker they could boost themselves up onto and sit watching the wild weather, safe from the driving rain.

Iris wasn't sure that she wanted to be alone with Guy Henderson, but she wasn't ready to go inside yet. It wasn't that she felt unsafe. It was more the way he made her skin prickle with awareness. Still, at least he didn't seem to expect or want polite conversation. She tipped back her head so that she could take deep breaths of the cold air.

If she closed her eyes, she could imagine herself back on the beach at Skara, or on the stones outside Rubha Clachan. She could picture it all so vividly: the seagrass flattened by the wind, the white crests of the waves being driven towards the rocks below Dundonan, bringing with them the smell of the sea. Could almost hear the crunch of her boots on the crushed seashells that covered the beach as she walked back from seeing Ian. She would be able to look up and see the windows of Rubha Clachan lit against the afternoon darkness. Inside, Daisy would be dancing, dipping and swaying to the gramophone, while Lily had her nose in a book and Rose pored over an atlas. In her vision, her mother was there, smiling fondly, and Papa too, magically restored to the man he had been, expounding on some new invention. The door would open and Mrs Grierson would bring in a tray with tea and scones. 'One of you girls go and call in Miss Iris,' she would say. 'She'll catch her death out there.' And Iris would go in, shaking worst of the rain from her coat and hat, and it would be warm inside, and safe.

It was all so clear. She could practically smell the fire, practically taste the scones. Her chest was too tight to breathe, and she didn't want to open her eyes in case the picture disappeared.

'What's the matter?' a rough voice beside her asked.

'Nothing!' Startled out of her dream, Iris brushed the tears frantically from her cheeks.

'You're crying.'

She turned her face away. 'It's just the rain.'

'If you say so.' Guy shrugged. 'It's not the weather for a walk,' he said, making it sound like an accusation.

'You're walking,' she pointed out.

'True.'

Iris wanted to preserve a chilly silence but found herself saying, 'I had to get out.'

'In this weather?'

She smiled faintly. 'You haven't been to Scotland, have you?'

'Is that where you're from?'

'Yes, a wild westerly part of it.' She knew that longing coloured her voice, but she couldn't help it. 'I'm used to weather like this and my cabin mate is horribly seasick, so ...' She spread her hands to encompass the stormy deck below them.

'Mine too,' said Guy. 'It's not pleasant, is it?'

'You're sharing a cabin?' Iris was surprised. He seemed so solitary.

'I wanted to get out to Colombo as soon as possible, and a shared cabin was the best I could get.'

'Have you got urgent business there?'

'Urgent to me.'

His expression was so grim that Iris shivered.

'Cold?' he asked.

Those penetrating eyes reminded her of a hawk, sharp and focused and missing nothing.

'A little,' she said, shaking off the feeling, 'but I don't mind. I like it cold. I'm not sure how I'm going to manage in Ceylon,' she confessed. 'Do you think it will be very hot?'

'Yes,' he said in his abrupt way. 'Not that I've been to Ceylon before, but I grew up in Malaya and I imagine the climate is not dissimilar.'

'What's Malaya like?'

'Probably about as different from your wild Scotland as you could get,' he said. 'It's lush, and green, and languid. The people are graceful. The coconut palms bend in the breeze and the air is hot and smells of spices. At dusk, you can sit on the veranda and the tropical night comes alive with the sound of insects and the scent of frangipani.' He stopped abruptly.

Iris had no idea what frangipani was or what it smelt like, but she recognised homesickness.

'It sounds like you miss it,' she said.

'I haven't been there since I was fourteen. I had to go back to school in England at the end of the summer holidays. I remember saying goodbye to my father that day.' A muscle jerked in his cheek. 'I never saw him or Malaya again.'

'I'm sorry.' Iris couldn't think of anything else to say.

'Exactly half my life ago,' Guy said as if to himself.

Iris would have put him at older than twenty-eight. The lines of bitterness in his face were more ageing than grey hairs.

'Couldn't you go back now?' she asked tentatively.

'There are too many bad memories there.' His voice was curt to the point of rudeness.

There was a pause while they watched a wave rear up and smack against the side of the ship, sending spray high over the deck.

'So you're on your way to Ceylon instead?'

That forbidding look was back on his face again. 'Yes.'

Iris decided not to ask any more. She didn't want to be snubbed the way Daphne Leadbetter had been the night before, and anyway, she hadn't come out here to make conversation. Guy was the one who had steered her to this sheltered spot. Let him fill the awkward silence.

She stared out at the heaving, frothing sea and tried not to notice the hard angle of his cheek at the edge of her vision.

'What about you?' he asked at last. 'It doesn't sound like you're keen to get to Ceylon if you don't like tropical heat. You must be the only person on board who actually prefers this,' he said, gesturing at the driving rain.

'I hope it won't be for too long.'

'I think you said you were hoping to meet your uncle?' There was a too-casual note in his voice that made Iris glance at him, puzzled.

Well, she could hardly deny it. She had told the dinner table last night. 'Yes, I am.'

'Will he be in Colombo to meet you?'

'I'm hoping so,' she said carefully, looking away. 'I've written, of course, but when I didn't get a reply, I decided that the best course of action was to come out and find him.'

Guy glanced at her averted face. 'Brave of you.'

'Not brave,' she said in a voice too low for him to hear. 'Desperate.'

15

Roz

London, present day

Much to her surprise, Roz loved working at Ballantyne's. She and Hugo agreed that she should come in three days a week, but just for four hours, between eleven and three. It meant that she could work in the evenings at Cork & Candle and still have plenty of time to explore London.

Increasingly, though, she missed the shop when she didn't go in. Hugo was a restful person to be with. He never asked awkward questions or demanded that she tell him about herself. He accepted her as she was, stiff and guarded, and if he wondered what a young Australian was doing in an antiquarian bookshop, he never said.

Occasionally he went away to auctions, and Roz ran the shop by herself for a few hours. She kept herself busy sorting out the appalling mess on Hugo's desk and dealing with emails, but it wasn't the same when he wasn't there. He was always dressed in old cords, a faded shirt and a cardigan with leather patches at the elbows. In spite of his age and old-fashioned appearance, he had a warmth and kindness and gentle wit that reminded her of her father. He could be vague, constantly patting his pockets in search of his glasses, but his eyes were shrewd and she found herself able to talk to him in a way she hadn't talked to anyone for a while.

They spent a lot of time drinking tea and chatting, ensconced in two rather tatty leather chairs on either side of a fireplace over which Hugo had hung her painting. A *Not For Sale* tag dangled off it. Roz was always very aware of the picture. At times she stood and gazed at it, but at others she caught a glimpse of it out of the corner of her eye and then it was almost as if the sea was moving. A gust of salty air freshened the crowded room and voices echoed so faintly that she convinced herself she was imagining it.

She learnt to love the musty, dusty smell of old books and faded prints and cracked oil paintings. There was something magical about Hugo's shop, she thought. It was like stepping into another world, another time. She couldn't help feeling that the catalogue should, by rights, be written in a flowery copperplate hand instead of being entered onto a spreadsheet. Much of Hugo's business was done online, but when customers did come into the shop, she almost expected the men to be wearing top hats and the women crinolines.

Hugo laughed when she told him this. 'Lucy used to say that too. Lucy was my wife,' he added, when Roz looked enquiring. 'She died in 2020.'

'Oh, Hugo, I am so sorry. I didn't realise you'd been married.'

'We had forty-nine years together.' He took his glasses off, polished them fiercely, then settled them back on his nose as he cleared his throat. 'We weren't lucky enough to have children, but we used to joke that this shop was our baby,' he said, looking around the room with its walls covered in paintings, its eccentric collection of antiques and tottering piles of old books. 'It certainly took up as much money and attention as a child. Not that we minded,' he said hastily. 'We both loved it, and we were happy just the two of us . . .'

He trailed off, and Roz's heart cracked at the expression on his face. 'How did Lucy die?' she asked quietly.

'Covid,' said Hugo with a sigh. 'We were careful during the pandemic, especially as Lucy was always fussing over what she called my weak chest, but we had to go out and get food. In the end, it wasn't me that fell ill, it was Lucy.' His face twisted at the memory. 'I had to call an ambulance, and they took her to hospital. I never saw her again. A kind nurse rang and asked if I had an iPad or something so that Lucy could see me, but we never had anything like that. Old fool that I was, I thought technology wasn't for us, but if we could have just seen each other once more . . .'

He stopped and looked hard at a still life hanging on the wall.

'Oh, Hugo . . .' Roz remembered how grief could strangle you without warning, that sleeping dragon that reared up and fastened its claws around your throat so that you couldn't speak, couldn't breathe for the pain of it, and all you could do was wrestle it back into its box. 'You must miss her very much.'

'I do. I don't remember much about the couple of years that followed,' Hugo admitted. 'The shop was closed anyway because of the pandemic, and I just left it to gather dust. Then one day I decided to come back, and as soon as I opened the door, I remembered what we had both loved about it. I don't know what I would do without it now.'

Roz leant forward and put her hand on his age-spotted one. 'It's been a lifesaver for both of us then,' she said.

'Dear girl.' He smiled at her. 'What a blessing it was for me when you walked through the door that day. I was starting to feel overwhelmed by the mess, but now that you have done such a good job of sorting me out, you've made it a cheerful place again. I'm very glad that painting drew you in.'

'I am too.'

'You must have earned it many times over,' he said. 'Don't you want to take it home now?'

'Do you mind if I leave it here for now?' Roz said slowly. 'I haven't got anywhere to hang it in the flat, and . . . well, the truth is that it frightens me at little.'

Hugo's bushy brows rose. '*Frightens* is a strong word.' He looked up at the painting above the mantelpiece. 'I can see there's an eerie quality to it. Is that what you mean?'

'I'm not sure.' Roz followed his gaze. It was just a picture. Hills, sea, stones. Why, then, was she having to suppress a shiver? 'This is going to sound mad, but it's like the painting is *alive*.' She risked a quick glance at Hugo, but he wasn't laughing, just listening intently. 'And this ring,' she went on, holding up her hand with the opal ring so that he could see it. 'It sort of . . . warms up when I look at the scene. It's weird.'

'How extraordinary!' Hugo leant forward, intrigued. 'I've noticed that ring. It's very striking and unusual.' His gaze went back to the painting. 'I wonder if there's a connection?' he mused.

'Between the ring and the painting?'

'Well, you said that the ring seems to react to the painting in some way,' he pointed out mildly.

'Yes, but that can't be *real*,' Roz protested, startled by the idea. 'You're not suggesting that there's some kind of magic involved, surely?'

He lifted his shoulders. 'I'm just saying that I think there are some things in life that can't be explained, that's all.'

'True, but . . .' Roz trailed off. She couldn't believe she was even talking about magic. She was a twenty-first-century girl. Her father had been a scientist, and like him, she had never had any time for superstition or magic. She respected cultures that had other beliefs, of course, but her experience had always been that what you see was what you got.

And yet this ring, tingling on her finger. How could she explain that? Or her strange compulsion to possess a painting of a place she had never seen before?

She swallowed.

'Where did the ring come from?' Hugo asked.

'My grandmother, I think.' Roz told him how her father had been killed while picking up the ring from a jeweller, and how she had found it in his jacket before she left Australia.

'So if you hadn't been clearing your mother's house, you might never have found it?'

'No, I suppose not,' she said, trying to shake the uncomfortable idea that her mother had died just so that Roz could find the ring.

'And you've no idea how it might have come to your grandmother?'

Roz shook her head. 'I don't know anything about my mother's family. Mum never talked about them. But my grandmother was definitely an Aussie. As far as I know, there's no connection to Scotland.'

'Hmm.' Hugo stroked his chin, thinking. 'Did you manage to find out any more about Amelia Blackmore?'

'I did some research, but I didn't get very far.' Roz sat back in her chair and picked up her tea, feeling better now that they were back in the realm of facts. 'I did a bit of googling, but I haven't been able to find out that much about her. She was born Amelia Davidson in Edinburgh in 1889, and she married Charles Blackmore in 1910. I get the impression he was a self-made man. It seems he was very wealthy, but her family didn't approve.'

'He must have been the wrong class,' said Hugo. 'They wouldn't have objected otherwise.'

'Perhaps. Anyway, there's not much after that, just that she died in 1931. She painted landscapes, all in Scotland, and like you said, some have come on the market over the last few years, but she wasn't famous in her lifetime, and not really after her death until there was an exhibition of early-twentieth-century Scottish landscape painters in Edinburgh in 2002.'

'Ah, yes, I remember going to that with Lucy. I like her work. There's a quality to her painting that I can't quite put my finger on,' Hugo mused as he studied the painting. 'Uncanny is the best word, perhaps.'

Chewing her thumb, Roz stared at the painting too. At the standing stones, set against the restless sea and the distant blue hills.

'I wish I knew where the stones are,' she sighed. 'I've spent ages googling images of standing stones on the Scottish coast.

I've seen the ones at Calanais on the Isle of Lewis, and there are some in Orkney, but none of them look quite like these. I think I may be going a bit crazy,' she admitted, with an uncomfortable laugh. 'I'm getting obsessed about a bunch of old stones!'

Hugo frowned. 'Obsessions are dangerous things,' he commented after a moment.

Roz thought about Richard's obsession with neatness, about her mother's refusal to admit how tightly he was controlling her.

'I know,' she said.

His eyes were kind. 'Why don't you take some time off?' he suggested. 'Have a break. I can manage here for a week or two, and it'll do you good.'

'I *could* have a holiday,' Roz admitted. 'I had an email from my solicitor in Australia last night. The sale of my mother's house has gone through and he's transferring the funds to my account, so I could afford to go away.'

'There you are, then. The universe is telling you to take a break! Of course, I hope you'll come back. The painting is yours whenever you want it, but it sounds to me as if you need to think about something else for a while. Go away, have a good time, take your ring off and forget about the picture, forget about the stones. Just be a young traveller enjoying Europe.'

'You know what? That sounds like good advice.' Roz tugged at the ring. It seemed to resist, but she persisted and at last it slid resentfully off her finger.

She caught herself up on the thought. Rings didn't have feelings. How could it be resentful? That was ridiculous.

She was surprised at how much lighter she felt without it. Hugo was right, she needed a break from all this.

'Thank you, Hugo,' she said, and kissed him on the cheek. She tucked the ring into her pocket and didn't even give the painting a backward glance as she left.

There was no one else in the flat when she let herself in. Drawing the ring from her pocket, she studied it for a moment, and rubbed a thumb thoughtfully over the strangely shaped opal. It was a beautiful ring, but there was an uncanniness to it that both intrigued and repelled her. She was tempted to put it on her finger again – the impulse was almost physical – but she remembered the expression in Hugo's eyes. *Obsessions are dangerous things.*

Abruptly she dropped it into a small pottery bowl she kept on her bedside table, where it was lost in a tangle of cheap earrings, bangles and necklaces. She would take Hugo's advice and forget about the ring *and* the painting for a while.

16
Iris

Orphea, the Mediterranean, May 1931

'Come on, Iris! Make sure you've got a good grip!'

Bertie put his hands on the deck and thrust his legs back towards her. Iris averted her eyes from the hairy thighs she could glimpse as his baggy shorts gaped, and bent to take a tentative hold of his ankles. Fortunately, he had sturdy socks up to his knees so she didn't have to touch his skin, but still, it felt uncomfortably intimate. She had hugged her father, and kissed Ian, but Bertie was a virtual stranger.

She had tried to demur when he'd asked her to partner him in the wheelbarrow race, but he had looked so disappointed that in the end she had given in.

'One of these days, Iris, you're going to have to learn to say no,' Ariadne observed languidly from her position on the sunlounger that she occupied every morning, wearing a bathing costume, a large hat and huge sunglasses.

Rose always said the same thing, Iris remembered with a trace of resentment. 'Stand up for yourself, Iris,' she would command. 'You're too soft-hearted. Just say no!'

Which was all very well, Iris would think, but how was she supposed to do that? Bark out a negative and turn her back? It felt *rude*.

Bertie's legs were surprisingly heavy. Iris shifted her grip, hoping this would all be over soon.

'Three, two, one . . . Go!'

'Off we go!' Bertie shouted over his shoulder, setting off on his hands. Iris had to scramble to keep hold of his ankles. She trotted after him, feeling ridiculous. Beside her, a married couple were getting into a frightful muddle, the husband barking at his wife to keep up, while on her other side, a flinty-eyed woman was driving on her partner.

Bertie was jubilant as he crossed the finishing line. 'Well done, old girl!' he crowed, jumping to his feet when Iris dropped his legs with some relief. 'What a team! We're through to the semi-finals. It's all to play for, what?'

Iris managed a weak smile to disguise her sinking heart. Now they would have to do it all over again.

The misery of seasickness had been quickly forgotten as *Orphea* sailed into the Mediterranean. The afflicted ventured out of their cabins one by one and blossomed in the warmth and carefree atmosphere of the ship. For some, like Ariadne, it was enough to bask in the sun in the morning before changing for lunch and perhaps an afternoon of bridge, and then again for the evening. Others, like Geraldine, approached the day in a more disciplined manner, striding sternly around the promenade deck the requisite number of times before allowing themselves to occupy a lounger.

For Bertie, the voyage offered endless opportunities to indulge his competitive spirit. He badgered Iris into taking part in races of one kind or another, or games of deck quoits, when she would much rather sit and sketch. At least the activities gave her plenty of material to write home about. When she could escape from Bertie's attempts to win wheelbarrow races or demonstrate his prowess with the egg and spoon, she would find a quiet corner in the writing room and try to describe life on board to her sisters. She added to the letter every day and looked forward to being able to send it from Naples, their first port of call. Her account was liberally illustrated with little sketches of the people she had met: Ariadne looking languidly elegant with a cocktail; Bertie playing ping-pong, face screwed up with effort; Geraldine marching round and round the deck.

She drew the grand staircase with its glittering chandeliers, the dining room laid with white tablecloths and silver cutlery. She drew herself sitting in the writing room, scribbling industriously at a table, while moustachioed colonels shook their newspapers and harrumphed at old news in the solid leather chairs behind her. She drew the intent expressions on the faces of the bridge players who took over the lounge every afternoon. She drew the promenade deck with its rows of loungers and passengers at the rail exclaiming at the sight of a flying fish or turning their faces up to the sun.

And sometimes, when the homesickness threatened to overwhelm her, she drew from memory: Rose, Lily and Daisy, and Ian, on the beach or riding up in the hills on their rugged mountain ponies. Or the view she loved so much, from the stones where she had sat with her sisters after their mother's funeral.

Iris often thought about the legend of the stones, of those four sisters who had been snatched away from home. What had it been like for them, tied up and forced into boats? Had they lain terrified, wet and cold, or were they braver than Iris? Perhaps they had lifted their chins and refused to be cowed. She liked to think so; she hated to imagine them being separated and fearful for each other. Bad enough for them to face the sea as captives in an open boat. Sometimes she thought about the unimaginable comfort of her own voyage and felt ashamed at how easy her fate was in comparison to those ancient sisters.

This journey was nothing like theirs. It was such a strange, hedonistic life, Iris thought. For just these few weeks, there was nothing to do but enjoy oneself. At first, she had set herself a strict routine of walking a mile around the deck every morning the way Geraldine did, but as it grew hotter, she became less energetic. Instead, she tucked her hair into a rubber cap, pulling the strap tight under her chin, and ventured into the swimming pool. She was glad Rose had insisted that she bring a bathing costume with her. It was a very modest affair compared to some, but she was still self-conscious about how much flesh she had on display when she hauled herself up the steps to get out.

Once, she pulled off her cap to shake out her hair, and when she looked up, she found Guy Henderson watching her. The colour rushed to her face as his eyes travelled over her, and her stomach dipped. Jerking her eyes away, she snatched up a towel. She hated the way he made her feel, as if she were prickly all over.

Fortunately, Ariadne, who could be uncomfortably perceptive at times, hadn't noticed. Iris was dismayed to see that she was absorbed instead in the sketchbook that she had left on her lounger.

'Iris, how clever you are!' she said, flicking through the pages and ignoring Iris's attempts to retrieve it. 'You've caught everyone exactly! There's Bertie, and oh, there's me.' She looked pleased. 'Am I really that elegant? I had no idea that hat suited me so well,' she added unconvincingly.

She turned a few more pages. 'Oh, and there's that sour-faced Geraldine Woolstone. You've got *her* down to a T!'

'I didn't mean to make her look like that,' Iris protested. 'I was hoping we could be friends,' she added sadly, 'but I don't think she thinks much of me.'

'She's jealous of you.' Ariadne pulled her sunglasses down her nose so that she could roll her eyes at Iris over the top of the frames. 'Good Lord, Iris, don't look so surprised!'

Iris realised that her mouth was hanging open and shut it. 'Why would Geraldine be jealous of *me*? She thinks I'm too silly for words.'

'Maybe, but in spite of those appalling clothes you wear, you're also a very pretty girl, and Bertie has certainly noticed.'

'I remind him of his sisters,' Iris said, and Ariadne sighed.

'You are such an innocent, Iris!'

'It's true,' Iris protested. She and Bertie were quickly on first-name terms, and in spite of his ponderous manner, she found him kind-hearted and easy to get on with.

'What about Guy Henderson? Does he think of you as a sister too?' asked Ariadne with a sly smile. She pushed her sunglasses back into place with the tip of a finger. 'I notice you've drawn him very well. Anyone would think you'd been observing him.'

Iris flushed. 'He's got such strong features, he's easy to draw,' she explained, flustered.

'Ah, is that it?' Ariadne handed back the sketchbook, clearly disbelieving. 'I must say, you've really caught that fierce expression. It gives one quite a little frisson.' She wriggled her shoulders to illustrate. 'I quite fancied him myself, but it seems he's more interested in you!'

'Mr Henderson isn't interested in me – or not in *that* way,' Iris added, as Ariadne raised her brows. 'He never even asks me to dance.'

Then she wished that she hadn't admitted to noticing. It was true, though. Guy danced occasionally with Ariadne. It seemed to Iris that the two of them were coolly amused by each other.

But there was no amusement in those watchful eyes when they rested on Iris, which they did often, she had to admit.

She and Ian had ridden high up into the hills on Skara once. They had sat on their ponies and watched a golden eagle soaring and circling remorselessly above its prey before that final savage swoop. Guy Henderson made Iris feel like that small creature frozen below the eagle's ferocious gaze.

'He frightens me a bit,' she confessed, sitting on the edge of the lounger and looking at the sketch she had drawn of Guy. 'He watches me as if he's waiting for me to ... well, I don't know what he's expecting. It's ... unsettling.'

'Unsettling's good, darling. Much more fun than predictable.'

Iris couldn't agree. Unbidden, a memory of Ian slid into her mind, knife-sharp and bittersweet. He was standing sturdily on a hillside, the wind ruffling his sandy hair, his blue eyes smiling. She knew him so well. Ian never made her feel nervous. Who would want unsettling and unpredictable when you could have safe and loving? She couldn't understand it.

Ariadne was watching her face. 'Well, there's always Bertie,' she said lightly. 'I don't imagine he'd unsettle a girl, and he's clearly besotted with you.'

Blinking away the memory of Ian, Iris shook her head. 'I think he's just lonely and missing his family. He'd much rather be with one of his sisters.'

Ariadne lay back in the sunshine, her smile eloquent with disbelief.

Evenings on board ship followed the same pattern every night. Ariadne appeared in a succession of chic outfits while Iris's two evening gowns were soon looking tired. Bertie was always there, meticulously dressed in dinner jacket, and ready to order drinks with heavy gallantry. Ariadne had no compunction about accepting a cocktail and then flitting off to find more interesting company, which left Iris to be entertained by Bertie.

She soon knew all about his three sisters, all of whom clearly adored him. Sophia was the clever one. Bertie was inordinately proud of the fact that she had written an obscure book about the medieval practice of embalming organs and burying them in different places. It didn't sound like something Iris would read, but she was suitably impressed. Em, it seemed, shared Bertie's love of puns, while Cath was famously greedy. 'I must remember to describe this for Miss Cath,' Bertie would say whenever he was served a particularly delicious pudding.

She knew about Jimbo, too. Bertie's dog had had to be chained up to stop him following the pony and trap to the station. Bertie had looked close to tears when he told Iris how Jimbo had lifted his muzzle and howled and howled at being left behind again. Remembering her own painful farewells, Iris had put her hand over his in sympathy.

To distract him, she asked about Ceylon, and he soon cheered up. He told her about his pet mongoose and how it had not only killed a cobra but had also bitten his servant before escaping and killing eleven chickens.

'Are there a lot of snakes in Ceylon?' she asked.

Bertie was oblivious to her shudder. 'Yes, indeed. And many of them are extremely venomous.' Ignoring Iris's look of horror, he began to list the worst snakes she might encounter. 'There's the common krait, and several vipers – Russell's viper, for instance, or the hump-nosed pit viper – all of which can kill you, and not forgetting the *naja naja*, the famous cobra.'

The snakes were the worst, but Iris also heard about the vagaries of the weather in Nuwara Eliya, where he was posted, and the best way to deal with leeches and 'problems with the digestion'. He told her in exhaustive detail about a crocodile shoot he had been on, and kindly explained everything he had read about the Vedda, the forest people of Ceylon. Sometimes it seemed to Iris that the only thing Bertie didn't know was the whereabouts of her uncle.

Nobody knew. Iris had asked everyone she could think of, even Geraldine, but they all shook their heads. It was worrying, but there was little she could do about it until she reached Ceylon. She told herself not to fret, and resigned herself to smiling and nodding along to Bertie's stories.

17

Finn

Skara, present day

By the time Finn got back to the Anchor Inn, he was filthy. Morag clucked when she saw the state of his clothes. 'I told you you'd regret going there,' she said.

'On the contrary, it was a very productive day,' he said.

Her lips tightened. 'Last orders at seven thirty,' she said, turning to go. 'I trust you'll change before you sit down to eat.'

By the time Finn had showered and changed, the bar was empty except for a solid-looking man with a humorous face. A golden retriever at his feet got up to greet Finn with a gently waving tail.

Finn patted the dog's head and ordered a beer from Morag. 'I'm ready for this,' he said when it came, and he drank it in one go before setting the empty glass back on the bar with a sigh.

The dog's owner raised his brows. 'Difficult day?'

'You could say that.'

'So you didn't find what you were looking for at Rubha Clachan?'

Finn glanced at him. 'Morag, I suppose?'

'Of course, but I already knew. I saw you drive past,' the man explained. 'I live at Dundonan, across the bay from Rubha Clachan, and once you pass our gates there's nowhere else you can be going.' He lifted his empty glass to Morag, who had come through from the other side of the bar to check if they needed anything. 'I'll have another, please, Morag, and one for our friend here.'

'Thanks.' Finn offered his hand. 'Finn Drummond.'

'Drew Malcolm,' the man returned, shaking hands.

Finn frowned. 'Isn't Dundonan a hotel now? I'm afraid it's beyond my expense account.'

'Mine too,' said Drew frankly. 'I was advised that the only way to get punters to come out here to Skara was to go right to the top of the market and appeal to the people with silly money. So I got in a Michelin-starred chef, mortgaged myself to the eyebrows and redecorated. The bar at Dundonan is the place for the finest whisky money can buy, but this is where I come if I just want a quiet pint.'

'Industrial espionage, I call it,' said Morag, pretending to scowl as she pushed the beers across the bar.

Drew winked at her. 'I'm still new at this business. I'm picking up tips.' He turned back to Finn as Morag rolled her eyes and moved away. 'So, what are you doing at Rubha Clachan? Morag would only say that you were messing around with things you shouldn't.'

'Are you going to tell me that the house is cursed too?'

'I spent ten years in the army,' said Drew. 'They don't encourage us to believe in curses. On the other hand, nobody round here will go near Rubha Clachan. When we were kids, we'd dare each other to sneak in there at night, that kind of thing, and I don't mind admitting that I was shit scared. I did two tours in Afghanistan, and running away from Rubha Clachan was the most frightened I've ever been.'

Finn thought about the way he had glanced over his shoulder, and the uncanny sense of stillness and waiting in the house. Then he imagined himself going back to James Kingan and babbling about curses. That would be a sure way to get himself consigned to cold cases for ever. He might never see the inside of a courtroom again.

'It's odd, don't you think? Leaving a house like that standing empty? You'd think *someone* would want it.'

'Nobody round here wants anything to do with it,' said Drew. 'I can see that an upstanding Edinburgh solicitor wouldn't set much store by curses, but the fact is that no one will go near the place. Shame, really,' he added. 'It's a fine example of an art deco house. I'm surprised the heritage people haven't been on to it. Of course, it's possible nobody knows who owns it,' he said.

'It's still owned by the Blackmore Trust,' said Finn. 'I work for the trust's solicitors,' he said, as Drew's brows rose with interest. 'I've checked the title deeds in the Land Register, and the house and land are still part of the trust.'

'Is that right? And who owns the trust?'

'That's the problem. It was left to the four daughters of Charles Blackmore or their successors, but nobody seems to have been able to track any of them down. I was hoping someone round here might be able to tell me what happened.'

'I doubt anyone remembers. You're talking nearly a century ago.'

'They seem to remember the fact that the house was cursed,' Finn pointed out. 'What does this curse consist of, anyway?'

'Ah, well, that's where it gets confused.' Drew drank his beer. 'Some say its origins are lost in the mists of time, and that a god or magician cursed the headland because some sacred standing stones had been pulled down. There's another, more recent version that seems to hold Charles Blackmore responsible for taking down the stones in the 1920s.'

'Can't they just put them back up again, if that's the problem?' Finn asked. 'I saw the stones when I was there this morning. It shouldn't be beyond modern technology to set them upright.'

'You would think so, but apparently every time it's been tried, disaster strikes. The first attempt was soon after Charles Blackmore died in the thirties. All the younger men went up to Rubha Clachan with ropes and levers. If people thousands of years ago were able to move the stones, they reckoned they could do the same. But a sea mist rolled in and the men got disorientated. It's easily done.'

Finn nodded. 'It's the same in the hills when the clouds come down.'

'You'll understand, then. On this occasion, the mist was particularly thick. Three men ended up in the sea and drowned. Others came out babbling about devils and evil spirits and were never the same again. I believe they had another go in the fifties, with a tractor, but there was an accident and the driver was killed. There was a third attempt in the eighties, but whenever they tried to get up there, the mist would come in, and it was impossible to see what they were doing. Half the men ended up with chest infections, the other half with bad backs. In the end, it was decided just to leave the headland alone. If you got a frosty reception from Morag, that's why. She's afraid that anyone disturbing things at the house will reactivate the curse.'

'I've got no intention of activating any curses,' said Finn, irritated. 'I was only there to see if I could find information about the Blackmores and where they went.'

'Any hidden treasures or clues?'

'No,' he admitted. 'I did find some letters, though, so I've taken those and I'm hopeful they'll give me leads to track down Blackmore's descendants.'

'Well, good luck with that.' Draining his glass, Drew set it back on the counter, then pushed himself away from the bar and prepared to leave. 'If half the legends about Rubha Clachan are true, you're going to need it.'

18
Roz

Paris, present day

Paris was Sasha's idea. Roz's flatmate and fellow waitress was keen to see more of Europe, and when she heard that Roz had asked for a week's leave from Cork & Candle, she promptly asked for the same. 'Let's go and see Paris,' she said. 'It'll be fun.'

Roz hadn't really thought about what she would do with her week, but why *not* Paris? She didn't know Sasha well, but the other Australian had a breezy attitude to life that Roz wanted to try to emulate. She wanted to be normal for a change, to be someone who might go to Paris on an impulse, who could slip on a ring without it tingling or pulsing. Who could walk past a painting in the middle of London without thinking that she could hear gulls crying or waves breaking on a distant shore.

'Paris is always a good idea,' said Hugo, when she told him of her plans. 'It's a beautiful city. Go and enjoy yourself.'

They took the Eurostar from St Pancras and ended up in Paris two hours later. Sasha had found a cheap hotel with luridly patterned orange wallpaper and a minuscule lift that wheezed and rattled alarmingly on the way up to the fifth floor. 'I'm taking the stairs next time,' Roz said with feeling, when it clunked into place and they managed to pull back the door.

Apart from the lift, she loved Paris. They ticked off all the tourist hot spots: the Eiffel Tower, Notre-Dame and the Rive Gauche. They wandered down the Champs-Élysées and enjoyed an ice cream sitting by the Seine. They skipped the Louvre in favour of Montmartre and the famous square, where they peered nosily at the artists and caricaturists. Sasha wanted to see the shops along the Faubourg Saint-Honoré, but Roz preferred the flea markets, where she picked up a dark green velvet blazer from the seventies and an off-the-shoulder eighties sweatshirt. Sasha was so envious of the blazer that she sulked for an hour, but was coaxed back into good humour with an *apéro* in a rooftop bar with views of the iconic Paris skyline.

Roz's hand felt lighter now without the opal ring on her finger. When she was packing, she had caught sight of the ring glimmering through the cheap costume jewellery. It felt almost as if it was trying to catch her eye, but she resisted the impulse to put it back on. If a thief could be bothered to climb all the way up to the top floor, they would see little of interest in a pile of ordinary necklaces, bracelets and earrings. It was safe enough left where it was, she decided.

Still, it was odd not to be wearing it.

Sasha was good company, but to Roz's dismay, she took endless photos. Every drink, every meal, every tourist attraction had to be recorded on Instagram. Roz's avoidance of social media was a matter of wonderment to her companion. 'You don't do *anything?*'

Roz didn't want to tell Sasha about her mother's death, or Richard's harassment of her before he was imprisoned. She just wanted to be normal for once.

'I'm taking a screen break,' she said instead. 'I'm not even checking my emails this week.'

'But what if someone needs to get hold of you?'

Who would need her? There was no one, she realised. But that was how she liked it, she reminded herself quickly. It was easier to know that no one was depending on her, and that she didn't need anyone in return.

'Just while I'm on holiday,' she said.

Sasha had no intention of taking a break from social media. She bossed Roz into appearing in numerous selfies. 'Jeez, Roz, relax!' she ordered. 'You're on holiday in Paris. Smile!'

Be normal, Roz told herself. Sasha was right. She should relax. It wasn't as if the other girl was an influencer with millions of followers. Who would see her posts, or connect her brightly smiling friend with the tense, bitter young woman who had given evidence at Richard's trial in Ridgewell? So Roz posed gamely and hammed it up for the camera. Of all the millions of photos being posted in Paris, who would notice hers?

But on their fourth morning, they were sitting at a café in the Marais with a coffee and a pain au chocolat, debating whether to head to Versailles or hit the shops again, when Roz's phone pinged and her heart jerked at the unexpected sound.

'There you go,' said Sasha, vindicated. '*Someone* wants to be in touch!'

Roz read the text.

Enjoying Paris? Make the most of it.

A cold, sick feeling was gathering in her stomach.

'Who's it from?' asked Sasha.

'I don't know,' said Roz slowly. 'The number's withheld.'

But she did know. The text was from Richard. He knew where she was. And he would be coming for her.

'Are you sure it's from him?' asked Hugo. Roz had gone straight to Ballantyne's when she got back to London. Later, she would wonder that she had turned so instinctively to Hugo, who she barely knew, but at the time, he felt like a safe harbour. She hadn't told him much about her past before, but now she related the whole sorry story, and his face was very grave.

'I'm sure,' she said, moving restlessly around the shop. 'He's playing with me. This is what he used to do before he was arrested. The messages were innocuous enough, but they were designed to intimidate me. They were all anonymous, and there was never anything I could take to the police, even if I hadn't known the police were his colleagues and on his side. They were just reminders that he always knew where I was and what I was doing – and that he would always be able to find me.'

'But how could he have known that you were in Paris?'

She sighed. 'The police use software to track people all the time. I don't know exactly how it works, but I suspect those images that Sasha was posting must have triggered an alert with one of his mates in the police, who passed it on to him. I *knew* I should have kept out of her photos,' she said bitterly. This was what happened when she tried to be normal and have friends.

Hugo rubbed his chin. 'Could you go to the police here?'

'And say what? He sent me a message asking if I was enjoying Paris. It's not a threat, even if I could prove that it was from him. It's easy enough to send an anonymous message,' she added. 'You just need to google how to do it.'

He grimaced an acknowledgement of her point. 'It's worrying that he knows your number.'

'I know.' Roz dropped into the chair opposite him at last, unaware that she was twisting the ring on her finger. She had thought she had left the ring in a bowl, buried under a pile of cheap jewellery, but somehow while she had been in Paris, it had found its way to the top and, when she walked into her bedroom, it had been lying there, glinting, as if waiting for her. Preoccupied with worry about Richard, Roz had picked the ring up and put it on without thinking, and it felt reassuringly familiar on her hand once more.

'I don't know how he found my number, but there's some pretty sophisticated software out there that he might have access to through mates. We don't know the half of it. And there's worse. After I received the text, I checked my email. There was a message from my solicitor saying that Richard had been released. Apparently the defence had discovered that some evidence was contaminated. The forensic analysis was faulty, apparently. So he's free.' She shuddered abruptly.

'Roz, this sounds serious,' said Hugo. 'I don't want to sound melodramatic, but do you think he'll come after you?'

'He's a sociopath,' said Roz, after a moment, 'and a murderer, whatever the forensic analysis says. He blames me for his conviction. He's certainly not someone you'd want to cross, and

I've crossed him.' The box in her mind pulsed with dangerous memories. 'I found my mother's body. He blames me for that. I wasn't supposed to be in Ridgewell that day, and I saw him leave the house. I don't know whether he was going to do something with her body or put her death down to an accident or an intruder. Either way, in his head I'm sure he thinks she asked for it,' she added bitterly.

She made herself think it through logically. 'He's got access to technology thanks to his contacts in the police, but he doesn't have financial resources, especially now I've sold the house. My mother had the money. That was why he married her, but once he was convicted, he couldn't claim on her estate. So what can he do?'

Roz looked up at the painting, talking almost to herself. 'He knows I'm in Europe, but it's a big place, and I won't be appearing in any more posts. I've told Sasha and Keeley that I'm leaving the flat. Sasha thinks I'm overreacting, but what if he manages to track her down? I've got a new phone with a new number, so I've done what I can.'

She blew out a sigh. 'I know I sound paranoid, but I'm afraid, and I'm angry with myself for being afraid. I'm so sorry, Hugo, but I think I have to leave London. I won't be able to help you in the shop any more.'

'As if the shop matters!' said Hugo robustly. 'I will miss you terribly, but of course you must be safe. But ... where will you go?'

Roz's eyes went back to the painting. The sea seemed to shift invitingly, and a breath of gorse-scented breeze touched her cheek. 'I thought perhaps I'd try to find the Four Sisters in my painting,' she said.

'An excellent idea.' Hugo nodded approvingly. 'And the timing is so good that it must be meant! I was going to tell you before you put it out of my mind with your news, but I've had a notice about an auction in Edinburgh later this week. There are some maps I want to look at, but buried away in the back of the catalogue are some papers from the Blackmore estate, and a couple of unframed paintings by Amelia Blackmore. You might find some clues there. Why don't you come to the auction?' he suggested. 'I can safely promise I won't be posting anything on social media. I'll book everything in my name, so we won't leave a trail.'

'And I'll use cash as far as possible.' Roz sat up, energised. 'Thank you, Hugo, that sounds perfect. When shall we leave?'

A stiff breeze blew Roz's hair around her face when they got off the train in Edinburgh, and she shivered. Shouldn't July be warmer than this? Hugo didn't seem to notice, but she turned up the collar of the velvet blazer she had bought in Paris and wished that she had brought a proper jacket with her.

She had seen pictures of Edinburgh before, but nothing had prepared her for the drama of the scene as they emerged from Waverley station: the castle rearing out of the rock above them, the towering grey tenement buildings jostling together up the hill towards it, Princes Street Gardens ahead.

She sniffed at the air. It was fresh and invigorating and laced with something she didn't recognise.

'What's that smell?'

'Hops,' Hugo told her. 'The wind must be blowing from the brewery. That's the smell of Edinburgh to me.'

While Hugo rested, Roz spent the afternoon exploring the

city. Her first stop was an outdoor shop, where she bought a cherry-red jacket that was both warm and waterproof. Once properly equipped, she climbed endless steep steps between the tall grey-stone buildings, pausing every now and then to get her breath and enjoy the glimpses of hills or the Firth of Forth gleaming silver in the distance.

It was hard not to notice how many CCTV cameras she passed, and she found herself ducking her head whenever she noticed one. Her solicitor in Adelaide had assured her they would appeal Richard's release, but the process would be another tortuous one, and in the meantime, Richard was out there. Roz pictured him at a computer, scanning the world for a sight of her, his fists closing and unclosing in frustration, and she shivered again, but this time not because of the cold. She had hoped that leaving London would make her feel safer, but Edinburgh was a big city too. It was time she headed for the countryside, where there were fewer cameras swivelling and watching.

Hugo was like a small boy, fidgeting with excitement as they waited for the auction rooms to open the next morning. 'One of Fries' early maps of Ceylon is up for auction. I've been trying to get hold of one for ages.' He rubbed his hands together. 'It shows Ptolemy's misconceptions about the island, which was then called Taprobana, and—' He broke off, catching Roz's affectionate grin. 'Well, it'll be jolly exciting to see, anyway.'

Roz tucked her hand into his arm. 'Ceylon's Sri Lanka now, isn't it?'

'It is. Pearl of the Indian Ocean, they call it. It's supposed to be the most beautiful place.'

'I'd like to go,' said Roz. She shifted from foot to foot, glad of her coat. The wind was biting. If it was this chilly in July, what would it be like in the winter?

When the doors opened at last, she was glad to hustle into the warmth. She hadn't realised that the auction itself would take place the next day. Today was just a chance to assess what was on offer. It was a very specialised sale, and all was quiet and sedate.

She was glad that Hugo knew the ropes. He arranged for her to sit down and look through Lot 71, the Blackmore papers. 'What am I looking for?' she whispered.

'You won't know until you find it,' said Hugo. 'I'm not trying to be cryptic,' he added at Roz's sideways look. 'It's just the way it usually works out. Skim through everything and see if you can find any reference to the stones, or some hint about where Amelia might have been painting. Something will jump out at you.'

She started with one of the unframed watercolours signed by Amelia Blackmore. Roz was no expert, but she could recognise Amelia's style. She thought she recognised the hills, too, painted from a slightly different spot. There was no sign of the stones, but she was sure it was the same place. When she turned the watercolour over, she saw an inscription in a faded hand: *Rubha Clachan, 1929.*

She found herself glancing down at her ring, half expecting it to warm the way it did when she looked at her painting, but it sat innocently on her finger, glinting subtly in the light from the lamp beside her but otherwise doing nothing untoward.

Ridiculous to expect that it would.

The second watercolour showed a different angle again, this one looking across to a castle standing on a headland. It seemed to Roz like something out of a fairy tale, with its towers and turrets, but the back of the canvas was blank.

The second part of the lot consisted of a large envelope containing packets of letters tied together with thin ribbons. She pulled them out gingerly. The paper was very fine and the ink faded but still legible. They smelt faintly exotic.

It felt wrong to be reading private correspondence, but that was what she was here for, wasn't it? She pulled out a letter at random and looked at the top: *Colombo, May 1931*, she read. Her first reaction was disappointment. This letter wouldn't answer the mystery of the stones. Roz hadn't been to Sri Lanka, but she was fairly sure that the stones in her painting were set not in the tropics but against a backdrop of northern hills.

Carefully she unfolded the letter anyway and began to read.

19
Iris

Orphea, Indian Ocean, May 1931

Iris held onto her hat as she stood at the railing, chewing her lip, her eyes on the horizon. They would be arriving in Colombo the next day, and she had no idea what to do if Ralph wasn't there to meet her.

It was hard to believe that the voyage would end. She had lost all sense of time on board ship, with one indolent day following another. They had stopped at Pompeii and Port Said, where she had had some cool dresses made overnight, and had invested in a plain straw hat. The purchases had depleted her remaining funds, but the tailor was very cheap, and she had been afraid that she would simply expire if she didn't find anything cooler to wear.

Her new frocks were deliciously cool and loose, but without a girdle and stockings, or the zips and buttons she was used to, she felt oddly exposed.

When Guy Henderson came to lean on the railing beside

her, she was instantly conscious of the warm wind blowing her skirt around her legs.

'I've been meaning to say that I like your new look,' he said. 'You look less buttoned up.'

Iris was unusually exasperated. 'You have quite a talent, Mr Henderson, for offering a compliment with one hand and taking it away with the other.'

An unexpected smile lit the saturnine face. 'You look very nice. Is that better?'

'Thank you,' she said primly.

But she was uncomfortably aware of her bare legs, and the whisper of the silky material against them. Aware, too, of the flat dark hairs at Guy's wrist, where the sleeve of his white shirt was rolled up above his worn leather watch strap. Of the angles of his face and the hard set of his mouth.

The trouble was that she *felt* unbuttoned without her sensible tweeds and felt hat. She felt as if she were standing at the top of a slippery slope, desperate to keep her place, but it was hard to stay steady when the air was warm, the sun was glittering on the sea and the heat was making her feel fuzzy.

'What's the problem?' Guy asked, and Iris stiffened.

'I don't have a problem,' she said sharply.

'I thought you seemed worried. Aren't you looking forward to getting to Ceylon?'

She put on a bright smile. 'Of course I am.'

'And to meeting your uncle, I suppose?'

'Of course,' she said again, but her eyes slid away from his. 'Well, perhaps I am a little nervous about what it will be like,' she conceded. He was standing a little too close for comfort and she shifted sideways as subtly as she could. 'Life on board ship seemed strange at first, but now I'm used to it. I'm wondering how different life in Ceylon will be.'

'It's no place for a girl like you, I can tell you that now,' he said abruptly, and she stared at him.

'What on earth do you mean?'

'You're an innocent. I've never met anyone with such a transparent expression,' he told her. 'You won't fit in with the old hands who run social life in Ceylon.'

'I thought you'd never been there,' said Iris defensively. 'You can't know what it's like.'

'I know places like it. Hot, steamy, exotic places ruled by the British, who sit on their verandas and drink their gin and march around in their topees and have no idea about what life is really like for the people who live there. The British men are desperate for wives, and their wives are desperate for something to do. It's too hot to do more than gossip and drink. It's too hot to keep up morals. I think it'll be a louche world for someone as fresh and innocent as you are.'

'You sound very bitter,' said Iris, not sure how to react to his description of her.

'I do, don't I?' he said. Bitterly. 'I've learnt the hard way that everyone's your friend in these communities until you lose your money or your status, and then nobody wants to know.'

Iris shifted uncomfortably. She took off her hat and smoothed down her hair. 'Bertie isn't louche,' was all she could think of to say, and Guy's face was lit by a sudden, startling smile. He gave a bark of laughter.

'You've got me there,' he said. 'Perhaps I should have said

that most of the British you'll encounter are either louche or pompous prigs.'

'That's not fair,' said Iris, ruffled. 'Bertie isn't a prig. He's ...' *Boring.* 'Kind,' she finished firmly. 'Anyway, why are you going to Ceylon if you dislike that world so much?'

Guy hesitated. 'There's something there that I need.'

'What?'

'Restitution.'

'Restitution?' she echoed, puzzled.

'Do you believe in it, Iris Blackmore?'

Iris wanted to look away from those stern eyes, but it was as if she was skewered into place. 'Yes, of course,' she managed, moistening her lips. 'If it's fair.'

'Ah, fairness. That's the issue, isn't it?' Guy levered himself away from the rail. 'You've been out in the sun too long,' he said. 'You've got a bit of sunburn, just here ...' He brushed a finger at the nape of her neck. The touch of his hand sent a shivery shock through her and she stepped quickly away. 'Sorry,' he said, not sounding it.

She mustered a smile. 'No, it's fine. I'm ... er ... I'm going inside anyway.' Their eyes met in a jarring look and hers slid away first. 'You're right, I've been out in the sun too long.'

The captain hosted a cocktail party to mark the last night at sea. Iris wore the same blue gown she had chosen for the first night, remembering how her sisters' letters had comforted her. *Wear the blue*, Daisy had advised.

The party was in full swing when she arrived with Ariadne. Funny to remember how strange everything had seemed on the first night, she thought, accepting a cocktail with aplomb. Now almost everyone was familiar. Ariadne was looking dazzling in a floor-length satin gown with diamanté straps, and a diamanté belt, and as always, Iris knew that she was dowdy in comparison. But she was less shy now, and although the room was packed with her fellow passengers, many of them already tight and ready to let their hair down with the end of the voyage in sight, she was able to circulate by herself – at least until she glimpsed Guy Henderson by the door, lean and dark in his tuxedo and looking sardonic as always. She turned away before he saw her and bumped into Bertie.

His face lit up. 'I was hoping to see you,' he said. He tugged at his collar. 'Gosh, it's hot, isn't it? Shall we go on deck?'

Iris agreed with relief. 'Yes, let's get some air.'

Other people were on deck, but most were happily crammed into the party, and apart from the sound of it spilling out whenever a door was opened, it was blissfully quiet. The water swelled dark and mysterious around them, and the warm air was threaded by a welcome breeze from the motion of the ship.

Iris rested her elbows on the rail and gazed out at where moonlight laid a bright stripe across the surface of the sea. She hardly noticed the churn of the propellers now, or the constant throb of the engines. 'It's hard to believe that this is our last night,' she said.

Bertie cleared his throat. 'I say, I will miss you awfully, Iris.'

'I'll miss you too,' she said, because what else could she say?

'Will you really?' he asked eagerly, and then to Iris's consternation, he grabbed her hand and dropped to one knee. 'Miss Blackmore, Iris, will you do me the honour of being my wife?'

'Oh, Bertie...' Dismayed, Iris tugged her hand away from his desperate grip. 'I had no idea... I never dreamt...'

'I love you desperately!' he told her, his face pink and sweating with nerves.

Flustered, Iris looked up and down the deck. 'Bertie, do get up,' she begged. 'I can't marry you.'

'I'm in a position to support a wife now,' he assured her, though to her relief he scrambled to his feet. 'And you are everything I have ever dreamed of!'

'I'm so flattered, Bertie,' Iris was acutely uncomfortable, 'but I really can't marry anyone at the moment. I need to find my uncle and look after my sisters.'

'I can support you,' Bertie insisted.

'And my sisters?'

She saw him blench before he straightened his shoulders. 'If that is the only way I can marry you, then of course I would support you all.'

'Oh, Bertie, you are so kind,' said Iris, touched, 'but you have your own sisters to think of. And it wouldn't be fair of me to marry you. The truth is, I'm in love with someone else.'

He looked downcast. 'I should have realised. Why would you want a chump like me?'

'You're not a chump, Bertie. You're kind and sweet and one day you'll make some lucky girl a lovely husband. Until then, I hope we can be friends.'

'I hope so too.' Bertie summoned a smile. 'I'll have to go straight up to my post in Nuwara Eliya when we arrive, but may I write to you?'

'Yes, of course. If you send a letter care of Lady Carsington, I'm sure it will reach me – and I'll write back,' she promised.

Bertie was making a heroic effort to hide his disappointment. 'Let me take you back to the party,' he said, but Iris held out a hand.

'Actually, I'd like a little time alone, if you don't mind. I might stay out here a few minutes longer.'

'Oh. Yes, of course. I'll see you at dinner.' Disconsolate, Bertie took himself off, and Iris pressed the heels of her hands against her eyes, more shaken than she wanted to admit. She had not expected a proposal!

'So, who *are* you in love with?'

Guy Henderson's voice made her spin round in shock.

'You were eavesdropping!'

'I couldn't help it,' he said. 'I was having a cigarette behind that bulkhead. It would have been too awkward if I had appeared when Bertie was down on one knee.'

Iris glared at him. 'That was a private conversation. You had no business listening in! A gentleman would have made himself known as soon as we came out, or moved away to the other side of the deck,' she said, her voice shaking with a mixture of fury and embarrassment.

'Clearly I'm no gentleman,' said Guy, unperturbed. 'I'm quite intrigued to know about your lover. Isn't he suitable? Is that why you've been sent off to your uncle?'

'It's none of your business!' She turned back to the rail, blinking away tears of rage.

'You know, you're very mysterious.' Guy joined her at the rail and Iris jerked a shoulder away from him, not that he seemed to notice. 'You seem such a simple girl on the surface, but the more I get to know you, the more intriguing you are. I feel like there's more to you than I realised at first. A lot more.'

Unbidden, a memory of her mother giving her the ring came to Iris. *The opal has always reminded me of you, so clear and simple at first glance, but so much more colourful and interesting when you look closely.*

'You don't know me at all,' she said stiffly.

'I know that you have no idea how beautiful you are,' he said, to her astonishment. 'And that being cross suits you.'

'I have no idea what you're talking about,' said Iris, turning to him in exasperation.

'I know that too,' said Guy, with a twisted smile. 'Let me show you.'

Before Iris realised what he meant to do, he had taken her face between his hands and kissed her. Sucking in a startled breath, she felt the deck drop away beneath her feet, and her lips parted as she toppled into him, palms against his jacket to anchor herself.

Guy had always seemed so fierce, but his mouth was almost gentle on hers, his lips cool and disconcertingly persuasive, his kiss unhurried and thorough. A thrill Iris told herself was shock shivered through her, and she floundered, her senses scrambled by conflicting sensations. Her heart was pounding in what might have been fear but felt more like treacherous excitement at the hardness of his hands when they dropped from her face to the slippery silk of her gown to pull her closer. The scrape of male-rough skin against her cheek. The coolness of his mouth, the liquid heat coursing along her veins.

Iris could feel his jacket against her fingers. She could feel the deck beneath her feet once more, the throb of the engines reverberating up to her belly. She could feel the warm air caressing the nape of her neck.

She could feel his lips on the sensitive spot beneath her ear and she squirmed and arched her neck in instinctive response, fisting her hand in the cloth of his jacket. When his mouth found hers once more, it was as if her body was acting of its own accord, pressing closer, touching him, tasting him, kissing him back.

Wait, what was she *doing*? Iris struggled to steady her spinning senses. She wasn't supposed to be kissing him. She wasn't supposed to be *feeling* anything. She was supposed to be pushing him away.

Fumbling, she laid her palms flat against his chest and shoved as she wrenched her head away.

'Stop it!'

Guy stepped back, lifting his hands in laconic surrender. He wasn't even breathing heavily, unlike Iris, whose heart was racing. She was trembling all over.

'Why did you do that?' she asked unsteadily.

He pulled down the corners of his mouth – his *mouth* – as if considering. 'I wanted to,' he said.

Iris gave a cross between a squeak and splutter of sheer frustration at how impossible it was to ruffle him.

And how easy it was for her to be ruffled.

'Didn't you like it?' he asked.

'Of course I didn't!' she said, and he smiled, his teeth gleaming in the darkness.

'Liar,' he said.

20
Finn

Edinburgh, present day

'Use one of the meeting rooms,' James Kingan said, when Finn said that he had finally made contact with someone in connection with the Blackmore estate.

'I put the papers and paintings I brought back from Skara up for auction,' he explained. 'I hoped it might bring a member of the family out of the woodwork. The buyer was a Roz Chatton. She sounded Australian on the phone, and she wanted to meet me as the seller. I'm not sure what the connection is, so I invited her here,' he added, eyeing James nervously. It was always hard to know which way the senior partner would go. 'I thought it would be the easiest way to see if she might be a descendant of Charles Blackmore.'

Fortunately, James was in a jovial mood. 'Good, good,' he said. 'Face to face is often the best way to get information. Australia, eh? It wouldn't be the first time a family has ended up there.' He nodded approvingly. 'Good work. It's time we got this trust sorted out, so let's hope your Australian can shed some light on it all.'

To Finn's surprise, Faiza, the intimidating office manager, assigned him the meeting room that looked out over George Square. It was an impressive room, with high ceilings and walls lined with glass-fronted cupboards containing leather-bound legal tomes that could now be accessed online. A long, polished table filled the room, upright chairs with plush leather seats ranged around it.

Finn looked around, feeling the weight of Scottish law on his shoulders. Would his father be impressed that he was holding a meeting somewhere like this? Probably not, he acknowledged with an inner sigh. He would always be found wanting in comparison with Angus. His older brother was clever, charming, good-looking. He was even good at sport. Bypassing Scottish universities, he had gone straight to Oxford and then on to a top London law firm. Finn wasn't jealous of his success, but he couldn't stop himself jumping up and down in a futile attempt to get his father to notice him. *Here I am. Look at me. I'm your son too.*

At his interview with Kingan, Kingan & McVean, Finn had insisted that he had ambitions to be a criminal lawyer, but was that true, or was he just trying to impress his father? He liked the certainty of the law, the steadiness of it. Whatever he said about wanting to get into the courtroom, deep down, he knew that he was more suited to the day-to-day rigour of a solicitor's work.

He had been disappointed at being allocated cold cases, but was that not the strength of the law, that a property like Rubha Clachan couldn't just be handed over to anyone who fancied it because the fate of Charles Blackmore's daughters had been forgotten? There was a process to be gone through before matters at the house could be settled. Finn approved of that. Since his visit to Skara, he had been intrigued by the mystery of what had happened. He wouldn't go so far as to say that the atmosphere had been haunting, but there had been a strange sense of anticipation about the house. Almost as if the Blackmore girls were playing a game of hide-and-seek with him. As if they were lurking behind a door, laughing. *Find us*, they seemed to be saying.

And now perhaps he was on the verge of finding a descendant of one of them.

Finn organised his papers about the Blackmore Trust at one end of the table and tried to look as if he was used to meeting clients in such grand surroundings.

He had been imagining Roz Chatton as blonde and gregarious, but the woman who was ushered in was slight and dark, with wary grey eyes. In jeans and a faded green velvet jacket and with a striking opal ring on her hand, she was stylish in an offbeat way, or at least to Finn's eyes. He wondered what Aileen would make of her.

She smiled briefly as she shook his hand and introduced herself. 'I hope you don't mind, but I've brought my friend Hugo Ballantyne with me,' she said, drawing forward an older man with twinkling eyes and a horseshoe of tufty grey hair. 'He's as interested as I am in what you can tell us about Amelia Blackmore.'

They seemed an unlikely couple, Hugo elderly and genial, Roz young and guarded, but they were clearly fond of each other.

'I was rather hoping that *you* could tell *me* more about the family,' Finn admitted, only to see from their disappointed expressions that he had got the wrong end of the stick. 'Do sit down,' he said, gesturing to the chairs at the end of the table. 'Perhaps we can pool our information, if nothing else. Can I offer you something to drink?'

When the whole refreshments hoo-ha was over and they were settled with cups of coffee, Finn took a seat and pulled his notebook towards him.

'What exactly is your interest in the Blackmore estate?' he asked Roz.

'I don't know exactly.' She spread her hands in a helpless gesture. 'Hugo had a painting for sale in his shop. I saw it and ... well, this is hard to explain, but I felt a real connection to it. It's by Amelia Blackmore and is called *Four Sisters*, and it seems to be of somewhere in Scotland. I've been able to find out a little bit about Amelia, but I'd really like to know exactly what the painting is of. It's become a bit of an obsession,' she confessed. 'When we saw the papers for sale at auction, I hoped they might tell me more, but they're just letters from someone called Iris on board a ship going to Sri Lanka.'

'Iris Blackmore,' Finn agreed. 'Amelia's daughter. I read those letters too,' he told her. 'As I explained on the phone, Kingan, Kingan & McVean are trustees for the Blackmore Trust, which was created by Charles Blackmore before his death. It appears that Amelia, his wife, died in 1931, and their four daughters left Skara, although we don't know exactly where they went or what happened to them. If you've read the letters, you'll know that Iris set off for Ceylon in search of her maternal uncle, leaving the other three behind. I've had a look through ship manifests and passenger lists for the period, and she did indeed arrive in

Colombo, but I haven't been able to establish what happened to her after that. I was rather hoping that you might be the connection I've been looking for,' he admitted.

'I'm afraid not,' said Roz. 'Or at least not as far as I know. What happened to the other sisters?'

'That's just it. Nobody knows. Their father, Charles Blackmore, left the house to them or their female descendants equally when he died, but there's no trace of where the girls went. They seem to have disappeared.'

'How sad,' Hugo commented.

Finn nodded. 'It is. Their father died alone, and as none of the girls came back, the house is still owned by the trust. When I put the papers up for auction, I hoped that someone would recognise the Blackmore name and get in touch.'

'Instead you just got me,' said Roz ruefully. 'Sorry about that.'

'Is there any chance you could be a descendant of one of the Blackmore daughters?'

'The name doesn't mean anything to me, so I don't think so,' she said. 'Hugo asked that too, didn't you?' she added, with an affectionate glance at her friend.

'You said you didn't know where your grandmother came from, so it's possible,' Hugo pointed out. 'It's easy for families to lose track of each other. Iris could very well be your great-grandmother, or great-great-grandmother perhaps.'

Roz turned back to Finn. 'You think Iris might have gone to Australia? I haven't read all the letters yet, but she seemed to be going to Ceylon, not Australia.'

'Who knows?' said Finn. 'It would be helpful if there were more letters.'

'Where did you find the ones from Iris that you put up for auction?' Hugo asked.

'In the family home. The Blackmore house was named after the headland it stands on, Rubha Clachan.'

'Rubha Clachan?' Roz made a good stab at echoing his pronunciation.

'It means a headland with rocks or stones. Stone Point, I suppose.'

'Stones?' Roz exchanged an excited look with Hugo Ballantyne. She leant forward. 'Are there four standing stones at this place?'

'Not any more,' said Finn. 'At least, they're not standing—' he added, and then broke off as Roz gave an exclamation and looked oddly at the ring on her hand. 'Is everything all right?'

'Yes,' she said, but she sounded distracted. 'Yes, I'm fine.'

After a curious glance at her, Finn went on. 'My predecessors at Kingan, Kingan & McVean made various attempts to track down the Blackmore daughters – advertisements in newspapers, that kind of thing – but without any success. Charles Blackmore died a couple of years before war broke out, and I suppose there were other priorities at the time, so the issue of Rubha Clachan and the trust was rather forgotten. It's only now that storage space is such an issue that we're looking to close some files, and this particular one has been passed to me.'

He offered a self-deprecating smile. There was no point in trying to convince them that they were dealing with anything other than a junior solicitor. 'I hoped I might find something at the house to shed some light on what happened to the family. I found the packet of letters in what I assume was Charles Blackmore's desk, but as I said, Ceylon seems to be a dead end.'

Roz leant forward. 'Might there be more letters?'

'I'm hoping so,' said Finn. 'I'm planning to go back to Rubha Clachan next week, in fact. The house has been abandoned since Charles Blackmore's death. In the absence of any family members, I need to arrange a survey at least. I'll have a look and see if I can find any more letters when I'm there.'

'Could I come?' Roz asked impulsively. 'I mean, not *with* you,' she added, picking up on his instinctively doubtful look, 'but could I see the house?'

Finn hesitated. 'The house is in a very poor state,' he said. 'It's really not safe.'

'It's safe enough for you to go inside and look for the letters.'

'Well, yes, but—'

'*Please.*'

She clasped her hands together, her eyes shining. Finn couldn't help noticing that they were a beautiful silvery grey colour, the kind of eyes that made you think of moonlit nights or the still sea at dawn.

Moonlit nights? The still sea at dawn? He imagined Aileen hooting with laughter, and shifted in his chair. He was a steady, sensible solicitor, not a poet.

Roz kept those eyes fixed on his face. 'I don't want to make a nuisance of myself,' she said, 'but I really would like to see the house, if only from outside.' She turned to Hugo. 'I could hire a car, couldn't I?'

It was Hugo's turn to look doubtful. 'It would mean using a credit card,' he said, in what sounded to Finn like a warning tone, and Roz's face fell.

'Yes, I didn't think of that.'

She looked so disconsolate that his professionalism deserted him. 'Look, I can't stop you going to Skara, and there's no point in two cars driving there,' he said. Perhaps it wouldn't be appropriate, but she wasn't a client, she seemed like a nice woman, and judging by the guarded air, she clearly had a problem of some kind. What harm could it do to help her? 'I'm going anyway, so I could give you a lift if that would help.'

'Oh, it would!' The brightening of her expression was reward enough for him. Strange, she hadn't seemed that attractive when she first came in, but when she smiled, she lit up the room and he felt unaccountably flustered. '*Thank* you,' she said.

He cleared his throat. 'Well, it's a long journey,' he said. 'I'd be glad of the company.'

21
Iris

Orphea, Indian Ocean, May 1931

On the horizon, a hazy lump of emerald green was emerging. 'Well, there it is,' said Ariadne. 'Ceylon at last.' She glanced at Iris from under another spectacular hat, tilted at exactly the right angle. 'You're very quiet. I thought you were desperate to get there?'

'I was. I am,' Iris corrected herself. She didn't want to explain about Bertie's proposal and certainly not about Guy's kiss. It had taken all her efforts to avoid looking directly at either of them the night before, and now she was annoyingly conscious of Guy lounging further along the deck, elbows on the rail, hands clasped loosely in front of him. She remembered the feel of those hands through the thin material of her evening gown, and a slow shiver snaked its way down her spine. She looked determinedly away.

'I suppose I'm nervous,' she confessed. 'What if Uncle Ralph isn't waiting for me?'

'You can come and stay with us,' said Ariadne, waving a careless hand. 'It's not as if there isn't masses of room.'

'But your husband . . .?'

'Oh, Johnny won't mind,' Ariadne said with a faint undercurrent of bitterness. 'And I'd be glad of the company, to be honest. I always have to be on my best behaviour here, and I can't tell you how tedious it is sometimes.'

'Well, that would be awfully kind of you,' said Iris gratefully. 'I've been getting into a panic thinking about what to do if my uncle isn't waiting to meet me. I'm not even sure I'd recognise him if he is,' she confessed.

Why hadn't Ralph replied to any of her mother's letters? Iris remembered how casually she had dismissed Lily's questioning. And if her uncle *was* there to meet her, how soon would she be able to tell him that she needed money from him? It was all going to be so awkward. Lily had been right. She should have thought of all this before haring off to Ceylon. She wasn't sure if she wanted him to be there or not now.

But it was too late to do anything about it either way. The tug boats were bustling around *Orphea*, guiding her into the port. The air was soupy, almost stifling, and it was very hot. Iris took off her hat and fanned herself with it, glad to have a reason to ignore Guy Henderson.

Nobody had ever *handled* her like that. Certainly not Ian, who had always been so sweet and tender. He had never done more than kiss her, and the touch of his lips on hers had made her feel loved and safe and happy. Whereas Guy's mouth had been cool and sure and had sent shock and outrage and a treacherous excitement tumbling through her.

Why, why, *why* had she kissed him back? Iris had tried desperately to convince herself that she hadn't responded. She wanted to blame Guy, but she couldn't shake the memory of curling her fingers into his jacket, of leaning into him, of her lips seeking his, and she burnt with humiliation at the memory. 'You're too honest for your own good,' Rose had always said.

She would never need to see Guy again once the ship had docked, she reminded herself. All she had to do was ignore him and put the whole incident down to . . . to . . . shipboard madness, she decided at last. Madness, anyway.

Iris had thought Naples was chaotic, but the clamour on the dockside was beyond anything she had imagined. And the smell! Fish and salt, engine oil, sewage, all threaded through with something spicy and enticing.

What seemed like thousands of Sinhalese milled around, shouting and gesticulating. Porters and hawkers and officials, a mass of humanity into which *Orphea*'s passengers were swallowed. Bertie made a punctilious farewell and pressed Iris's hand meaningfully, but for most there was barely a chance to say goodbye. There were taxis waiting. A hat or a hand might be lifted in farewell, but then the people Iris had shared the last few weeks with were gone.

Ariadne, in a stylish crêpe silk two-piece suit and her usual sunglasses, had sent Baxter to supervise the moving of all her trunks and was not inclined to rush off. 'I've told her to check with the shipping office,' she added. 'They'll know if your uncle is waiting to meet you.'

Overwhelmed by the heat and the noise and the smell, Iris stood alone at the rail, her eyes searching the crowd below for anyone who might be her uncle. When she saw Baxter heading back up the gangplank, she leant forward anxiously, but Ariadne's maid shook her head and Iris stood back, her shoulders slumping.

'He's not here,' she said dully.

'You didn't really think he would be, did you?' Ariadne settled her sunglasses on her nose and adjusted the tilt of her hat. 'I'm not convinced this uncle of yours wants to be found. Come along,' she added briskly, 'the car's waiting.'

At least she wasn't completely on her own, Iris reflected as she scurried after Ariadne down the gangplank, afraid that she would lose her in the jostling crowd. Baxter was to follow with the trunks and Iris's suitcase, but a gleaming Rolls-Royce was waiting for Ariadne, grandly ignoring the envious stares of those around it. A bowing Sinhalese chauffeur, immaculately dressed, ushered Iris into the back next to Ariadne and closed the door.

Iris sank back into the plush leather, overwhelmed at first by heat and strangeness and disappointment, but as the car nosed its way through the busy Fort area, she sat up and took notice of her surroundings. This was the administrative heart of the city, Ariadne told her. The buildings were more solid and substantial then she had imagined, many of them painted white, with deep arcades to keep out the fierce sunlight, while the roads were crowded with trams and rickshaws and people on bicycles, and two-wheeled bullock carts with towering loads of pineapples or bananas, all weaving in and out of each other. Iris had to cover her eyes on several occasions, but the Rolls-Royce purred through it all with disdain for other road users.

'This is the commercial centre too,' Ariadne said. 'We'll come shopping here. Look, there's Cargills, and over there is

Whiteaway, Laidlaw & Co. Everyone calls it Right-away & Paid-for, as it's a strictly cash department store.'

Iris craned past Ariadne to see where she was pointing. London had been busy, Naples and Port Said chaotic, but Colombo was in a different league. She had never seen so many people crammed into the streets, had never had her senses assaulted by quite so much colour, by so much noise, by so many different smells: coconut, cinnamon, and something spicy frying.

She could see little shops selling everything from buckets to sewing machines to vibrantly coloured fabrics beneath signs covered in a strange squiggly lettering that she couldn't imagine ever being able to decipher. Rickety stalls were piled high with pineapples and bananas and other fruits that she didn't recognise. There were tea stalls and hawkers selling street food, and children playing, and snake charmers, and dogs scavenging. The air was raucous with the sound of traffic and workshops, of bicycle bells and blaring horns and street cries, and in every spare patch of land, lush greenery sprouted: stately palm trees swaying in the hot breeze, native trees, and glossy, exotic bushes with fruits and flowers that Iris had never seen before. Their names felt strange on her tongue when she tried to repeat them: bougainvillea and frangipani, rambutan and mangosteen, jacaranda and hibiscus.

How strange to think that while she was here having her senses buffeted, at Skara the breeze was still bending the seagrass, the storm petrels were fluttering over the water and the gulls were wheeling and calling above. That, on the other side of the world, life was carrying on as normal. Her head reeled at the thought.

After the chaos and energy of the Fort, the roads in Cinnamon

Gardens were quieter. Flat and a dark red, they shimmered with heat, and were lined by tall, dramatic trees. Amused by Iris's wide-eyed wonder, Ariadne listed the names of the trees indulgently: slender, graceful casuarinas, cinnamon, pomegranate and vanilla, and the flamboyant tree, which was covered in a mass of fine red flowers.

They passed a shimmering lake before the Rolls-Royce turned at last into a grand entrance and slid to a halt in front of the steps up to a sprawling single-storey building. Surrounded on all sides by a deep veranda supported by round white columns, it was set in a perfectly manicured garden.

Ariadne's expression was hard to read as she got out of the car and looked at the house. 'Well, I suppose this is home,' she said.

Servants in pristine white uniforms were waiting to welcome them in, but there was no sign of Ariadne's husband. It was cooler inside, and very quiet, all murmuring voices, marble floors and ceiling fans that slapped lazily at the hot, thick air. The rooms led into each other, linked by large open archways to keep the air circulating

'There's some crisis at the office,' Ariadne said with a brittle smile after a discussion in Sinhalese with the butler. 'Johnny will be back later.' She jerked off her gloves. 'Well, what would you like to do?' she asked Iris. 'Shall we have lunch? Or would you like to rest?'

'I think I'd like to rest,' said Iris honestly. 'I'm not used to this heat and it's all been so . . . overwhelming.'

Hands were clapped and a graceful servant showed Iris to her room. It had a high ceiling and louvred doors, and was furnished in dark, exotic wood. In the centre of the room a large bed swathed in mosquito netting stood beneath a ceiling fan that slapped in a desultory way at the hot air.

From the window she could see the garden beyond the veranda. The grass was cut neatly and the luxuriant foliage was splashed with brilliantly coloured flowers. It was beautiful, but it made her uneasy. The garden was so lush, so green, that she could almost see it growing. Given half a chance, she could imagine it sending wild tendrils into the house to smother everything inside in green too.

Iris shook herself out of her fearful mood. She must stop this. She was in Ceylon at last, and staying in luxury. Perhaps it was disappointing that Uncle Ralph had not been there to meet her, but she wasn't ready to give up yet. She was just tired.

Taking off her shoes, she fought her way through the mosquito netting and lay fully dressed on the bed. The sound of the fan sent her to sleep, and she dreamt of being adrift in an open boat not far from the shore at Skara. The waves got higher and higher, blocking off her view of home and spinning the boat around. She would get a glimpse of the familiar shoreline, but then another huge wave would rear up and it would be lost to view again, and the more she craned her neck to keep it in sight, the higher the waves swelled, until abruptly the sea quieted, but when she looked, the shore was gone.

She woke herself up with a cry of distress. She lay for a while looking up at the blur of the fan, swallowing the fear of her nightmare. She was not lost. She was where she was supposed to be, doing what she was supposed to do. Saving her sisters, keeping the family together. And when it was done, she could go home.

The ring on her finger throbbed.

She felt better after a bath and changed into an evening gown. She even powdered her face.

Ariadne was alone on the veranda when Iris found her. She was moodily drinking a cocktail and Iris suspected that it was not her first. 'Ah, there you are!' She waved her glass at Iris. 'Gimlet?'

'Just a lime juice, please.'

Ariadne rolled her eyes extravagantly, but clapped her hands for the bearer. She ordered drinks and then gestured vaguely to the chair beside her. 'My dear husband hasn't deigned to join us yet,' she said. 'I thought it might be nice for you to have a familiar face at dinner, so I rang up Guy Henderson and asked him to join us.' She raised her brows at Iris's expression. 'Ah, that was a mistake?'

'No, of course not.' It seemed too late to admit why she felt awkward. She could hardly refuse to see him now.

'You don't sound very pleased,' Ariadne commented.

Iris concentrated on smoothing her dress over her knees. 'It's just ... well, I suppose the truth is that he makes me a little uncomfortable.'

'Darling, it's called sexual tension,' Ariadne drawled, then smirked as Iris blushed fierily.

'It's not that ... that thing,' she stammered, unable to bring herself to use the words. 'I just don't think he likes me.'

'Do you like him?'

'No!'

'That's what I thought,' said Ariadne. 'Sex-u-al tension,' she repeated, drawing out the word and enjoying how Iris squirmed with embarrassment. 'It's perfectly natural.'

Iris was relieved when the bearer arrived with a tray. He offered her a glass filled with deliciously cold lime juice and had brought another gimlet for Ariadne.

Guy arrived as the sun was setting in a magnificent blaze of gold and orange. He stepped out of a rickshaw in full evening dress and looked up at the veranda from the bottom of the steps, his eyes mocking as he took in Iris's wooden expression.

Ariadne greeted him with far more warmth than Iris considered necessary, insisting that he sit next to Iris and ordering him a beer.

Iris was furiously aware of him as he sat easily beside her. How could he look so cool when there was a drip of sweat making its way slowly down her spine and her dress was sticking clammily to her? She looked determinedly at the sunset. The sky was red now, a deep, hot red that was intensifying and darkening into a fiery purple as she tried to force down unwanted memories of his hands on her, of his mouth against her skin, of the solidity of his body.

'It's an unexpected pleasure to see you again so soon, Miss Blackmore,' Guy said, when his beer had arrived. He lifted the glass to her – mockingly, she was sure – his expression as sardonic as ever. 'Do I gather that your uncle wasn't able to meet you after all?'

He must have been well aware of that, as he had left the ship after them and Iris was certain that he had been watching her.

'No,' she said.

'Have you been able to find out where he lives?'

'Not yet,' she said, tight-lipped.

'It must be an unsettling time for you, not being sure where he is. Can I do anything to help?'

'Thank you, but I'm sure I'll manage.' Iris bit out the words, hugely relieved when headlights swept over the veranda and a car pulled up at the bottom of the steps.

Ariadne's husband had arrived.

22
Iris

Colombo, May 1931

The main post office in Colombo was huge and echoed with the sound of what seemed like hundreds of people jabbering excitedly at each other. Electric fans overhead whirred ineffectively at the hot air, and Iris dabbed at her face with a handkerchief. She couldn't wait to get out of there, but she was desperate for word from home.

Long, sweltering minutes later, an official appeared with a packet of letters. She practically snatched them out of his hands. 'These are from my sisters,' she told Ariadne. She finished rifling through them. 'Nothing from Uncle Ralph.' She sighed. Finding a letter explaining why he couldn't meet her had been her last hope.

'Why don't I ask if anyone has collected the letters you sent him?' Ariadne suggested, languidly fanning herself with her hat.

'Are you allowed to do that?'

'Darling, I'm Lady Carsington. Lord Carsington's wife. I can do what I like.' To demonstrate, she unleashed a dazzling smile on the official, who blinked visibly and hurried to oblige as soon as he understood what was wanted. When he returned, he had a clutch of letters in his hand, and he offered them to Ariadne with a bow.

Iris looked through them in growing dismay. 'They're almost all from me! And a few bills, by the look of it.' Had coming out to Ceylon been a complete waste of time? 'He's not here.'

'But he's *been* here,' Ariadne pointed out. 'The bills tell you that. And you said your mother had written, didn't you? He collected those letters. Now you just need to find someone who knows him and knows where he might have gone. We'll ask around, but first let's go and have a curry lunch at Mount Lavinia.'

Iris glanced longingly at her sisters' letters, but she could hardly insist on going back to the residence alone. She would have to read them later.

The Mount Lavinia hotel was perched on a headland at the end of a golden beach. Palm trees leant over the sand and were planted around the hotel. They dipped and swayed in the welcome breeze from the ocean. Iris ate a proper curry for the first time, her eyes watering, while Ariadne pushed most of hers to the side of her plate and drank instead. It took several minutes for them to leave, as she stopped at almost every table, gathering invitations as she went.

Iris observed a mixture of admiration and disapproval in the way the British greeted her erstwhile employer – not unlike the way Lord Carsington treated her, in fact. Johnny Carsington was a distinguished-looking man with grey hair and an aloof air, clearly much respected by everyone except his wife. It made Iris uncomfortable to see how brittle Ariadne seemed in her husband's presence. To Iris, she had always seemed to be indolence and elegance personified, but with her husband she was taut and jagged. In the evenings, they sat on the veranda and listened to the shrilling and whirring of the tropical night. It should have been relaxing, but Iris was constantly on the qui vive in case Ariadne said something provocative.

She herself found Lord Carsington quietly charming and thought she saw yearning in his eyes when he looked at his beautiful wife. It was clear that all was not well in their marriage, but Iris was hardly in a position to judge, she reminded herself.

'They all hate me,' Ariadne said as they climbed back into the Rolls-Royce. 'I like to make sure they have to invite me to their parties.'

'I'm sure they don't *hate* you,' said Iris, much as she would have done to Daisy if she had said such a thing.

'They do. They adored Johnny's sainted first wife and I can never live up to her reputation.' Ariadne's expression verged on the resentful before she put a bright smile back into place. 'But who cares what they think? We've got lots of lovely parties to go to and there's bound to be someone amusing there.'

Iris excused herself as soon as they got back to the house. Carrying the letters to her room, she propped a couple of pillows behind her and settled herself on the bed. She read her youngest sister's first.

I miss you, Daisy wrote. *When are you coming home? I have been making a new frock from one of Mummy's dresses since Rose says we cannot afford to buy anything new now. I cut a piece off the bottom and* made a frilled collar and covered a belt and I think it looks very smart. Mrs Grierson thinks the hemline is scandalously high, and she tuts every time she sees me wearing it. I take that as reassurance that I look fashionable at last! I asked Rose what she thought of my new look and she said that it wasn't very practical and why didn't I put on a cardigan, which was so very Rose of her, don't you think?

Lily wrote about what she had been reading and how Rose was snappy sometimes. *But I know it's just because she's worried and she misses you and Mummy like we all do.* Iris pressed her lips together at that. Lily was the most observant of the sisters. She was clever and clear-eyed and could mimic accents beautifully. She had practically taught herself French and German and had dreamt of travelling on the Continent so that she could practise both. At one time, Charles had promised that she could go to university, but there was no chance of that now, of course.

Rose apologised for not having any good news to send. *Papa is very low. The other day he went rampaging around the house in search of a bottle and he pulled all the books from the shelves in his library. I put them back when he was asleep so that Mrs Grierson didn't have to do it. Iris, darling, I don't know if I should tell you this, but there has been an announcement at Dundonan. Ian is to marry an American heiress called Margaret Ricci. We bumped into her walking with him and Lady Malcolm on the headland and it was very awkward, but we were polite as I imagine you would wish us to be. Ian coloured up as he introduced us. His fiancée had nothing to say for herself. When I asked how she was finding Skara, she just said that it was colder than she had thought. Lily tried asking her about New York but didn't get anywhere either. Daisy said she was wearing too much lipstick and that it was the wrong shade of pink and that she would make a horrible Lady Malcolm.*

Iris smiled at that as she knew Rose intended her to. She was glad she'd heard about Margaret Ricci on board ship or it would have been a horrible shock.

Aunt Edith is threatening a visit next week, Rose finished. *I will try and sober Papa up before she gets here. We all send you so much love, darling Iris, and can't wait to hear that you have found Uncle Ralph and can be on your way home very soon.*

Tears blurred Iris's eyes as she folded the letters and put them away. Oh, if only she *could* go home! She *must* find Ralph somehow.

But before she could do anything useful, she was sucked into a whirl of social activity. Cocktail parties and picnics on the beach. Tennis and bridge parties, shopping trips and more curry lunches. Walks on the esplanade at the Galle Face and dancing in the hotel's ballroom after dinner in its restaurant, where the tables were covered in pristine white tablecloths and separated by elegant potted palms. The Galle Face menu featured staples like steak and kidney pie and roast wild duck with apple sauce that Iris couldn't even contemplate eating in the heat. There was a frenetic quality to Ariadne's insistence that they should always be out. Iris asked everyone she met if they had ever encountered a Ralph Davidson, but she met with blank looks or shaken heads every time.

'Tea planters aren't quite out of the top drawer, darling,' Ariadne told her at last. 'It's very unlikely that any of these people would have come across your uncle.'

They were sitting on the veranda, having returned from yet another drinks party followed by a dinner elsewhere in the

Cinnamon Gardens. For once, Johnny Carsington had accompanied them, but the moment they returned, he shut himself up in his study.

Ariadne watched him go and turned to Iris. 'Let's have another toot.'

Iris didn't really want anything else to drink, but she didn't like the shuttered expression on Ariadne's face.

Ariadne sighed as she tipped her head back against the cushions of her chair. 'There's nothing like a tropical night.'

Iris didn't answer. She hated the nights here. The thick darkness, the clammy heat. The silent servants, with their dark, fine features, always smiling and graceful, but what were they thinking? She couldn't read their expressions. The intense, rich scents. Those millions and millions of ghastly insects frantically shrilling and whirring and rasping, going on and on and on and never pausing. She would do anything to breathe in the tangy air of Skara, to feel the cold nip at her cheeks, to let the sea wind blow away all the festering doubts and uncertainties.

When the sky split with jagged light, and thunder cracked, Iris jumped.

'Oh, good,' Ariadne said. 'A storm will clear the air. Here comes the rain now.'

Iris was no stranger to rain, but she had never seen anything like this. It fell straight like a curtain, crashing onto the roof and bouncing off the earth. The sound was deafening. There was no way they could have had a conversation, so they just had to just sit and watch the display.

The storm rolled over and the rain stopped as suddenly as it had begun. The air steamed. Foliage dripped and the insects resumed their incessant noise, punctuated by the occasional howl of the pariah dogs that roamed the streets.

'Thank you for being here,' Ariadne said abruptly, swirling her drink in the glass. 'I've been glad of your company the last few days.'

'I don't know what I would have done without you,' Iris replied, touched.

'I wonder if you're ever going to find this uncle of yours?'

'I don't know.' She looked down into her lime juice. 'I'm not sure what I should do now.'

'You need a husband to help you,' said Ariadne. 'If you don't fancy Guy Henderson, which I think rather odd of you, what was wrong with Bertie Spencer? He's very industrious. Johnny thinks he'll go far, and it's time he had a wife. I saw him take you out onto the deck that last night on the ship,' she explained at Iris's look of surprise. 'He came back in looking disconsolate, so I guessed you'd said no, but you'd just need to lift your little finger...'

'Oh, no,' said Iris in instinctive denial.

'Well, perhaps he *is* a little ponderous, but there are any number of young men here who would be delighted to marry you. I've seen them clustering around you at parties. Why not consider one of them? At least let them take you out for the evening and spoil you,' Ariadne went on. 'Even if you don't marry them, a little affair would do you the world of good. You need someone to take your mind off your broken heart.'

'What...?' She had never mentioned Ian to Ariadne, she was sure. 'How did you know?'

'Oh, darling, it's obvious. Who was he?'

'We were neighbours,' Iris admitted at last. 'Childhood sweethearts, I suppose.'

'Well, then, it would never have worked,' Ariadne declared robustly. 'You don't want someone who remembers you as a child. You want someone to see you as a woman, mysterious, alluring.'

Iris couldn't help laughing. 'I don't think that would ever be me!' But even as she said it, she remembered that Guy Henderson had called her mysterious once.

'Oh, I don't know.' Ariadne eyed her critically. 'In better clothes and if you did something with your hair . . . You've got beautiful skin. All that Scottish rain, I suppose. What have I said?' she asked as Iris's eyes filled with tears.

'I'm sorry.' She brushed furiously at her cheeks. 'I'm just homesick. I can't marry anyone, Ariadne,' she said. 'I only want Ian.'

A shadow touched Ariadne's eyes. 'Oh, my dear, I know. I *do* know. I was married before, did I ever tell you that? I was only eighteen. We were madly in love, but then war broke out.' She let out a long sigh. 'When Freddie came back on leave, he wasn't the same. The war changed so many young men,' she added sadly. 'I loved him desperately, even when I couldn't reach him. When he was killed at the Somme, I truly thought I would die of grief.

'But as you see, I didn't die,' she said. 'I carried on, because what choice do we have? After a few years, I married Johnny, because he wanted a wife and he could keep me comfortably and I was tired of struggling by myself. And I thought perhaps there would be children to love to fill the hole that Freddie left inside me, but . . . well, it hasn't happened.'

'Ariadne, I am so sorry.' Iris spoke quietly, moved by her story. Who would have guessed from her languid, frivolous manner that she carried such sadness in her?

'I'm only telling you this, Iris, because you mustn't waste your life wanting a man you can't have. You will find someone else, and perhaps you won't love him the way you loved Ian, but you may love him enough. You don't believe me, I know,' Ariadne went on, 'but you are such a sweet girl. You deserve to be happy, and sometimes you have to *decide* to be happy and to enjoy yourself and eventually it becomes a habit.'

Iris looked at her thoughtfully. 'Are *you* happy?'

'Of course!' Ariadne laughed, but then she looked away. 'I think Johnny regrets marrying me,' she said in a low voice. 'He shuts himself away, and the only way I can think of to get him to notice me is to behave badly. Stupid, isn't it?'

Impulsively, Iris put out a hand to the arm of Ariadne's chair. 'I don't think Lord Carsington regrets marrying you at all,' she said. 'I've seen the way he watches you, when you're not looking at him. And I've seen his expression when you hold him at arm's length. I think he doesn't know how to reach you either.'

'Wise little thing, aren't you?' Ariadne's laugh was a little shaky. 'What a pair we are. Well, if you won't marry anyone, we'd better find your Uncle Ralph, hadn't we? I wonder if Guy Henderson is still around. He looks like the kind of man who would be useful in this sort of situation. Why don't you ask him to help?'

'I'm not asking Guy Henderson,' said Iris flatly. 'And it's not because of ... of what you think. I just don't trust him.'

23

Roz

Skara, present day

'I'm glad to see that you've brought some wet-weather gear,' Finn said, when he picked Roz up from her hotel that Monday morning. She was waiting for him outside, wearing a bright red walking jacket and trying to stop the brisk Edinburgh wind from blowing her hair about her face.

'I wasn't expecting it to be quite this cold in July,' she said, as she let him help her lift her case into the back of his car. 'I went to an outdoor shop and told them I was going to Skara, and they kitted me out.' She lifted her feet, one by one. 'New boots. I bought walking trousers and a fleece, and gloves too,' she added, indicating the gloves poking out of her jacket pocket.

'You'll need all of that and more,' he said, opening the passenger door for her.

It had felt extravagant to buy quite so much, but Roz had had the weekend to kill and her one day in Edinburgh had been enough to make her realise that her wardrobe was hopelessly inadequate for Scotland. Besides, she was excited about going to Skara and seeing where Iris Blackmore had lived. After waving Hugo off on the train, she had spent much of the weekend reading Iris's letters and trying not to think about Richard Heissen walking around Ridgewell a free man.

Or sitting at a computer screen trawling the internet to find pictures of her.

There had been no messages since Paris, but waiting for the ping of her phone, dreading it, was almost worse. Richard had found her once, and he would keep looking. She was certain of that. She had done her best to dodge CCTV cameras around Edinburgh, but surely they would be few and far between somewhere like Skara?

Surely Richard would never find her there.

Finn's car was as neat and tidy as his appearance. Stocky and sandy-haired, he had abandoned his suit for jeans and a green jumper, which made him seem younger and more approachable. Over the weekend, Roz had had a few qualms about putting herself into a stranger's hands, but Finn seemed so steady and dependable, and there was something reassuring about his soft Scottish accent. Even Hugo had thought she would be safe with him.

And the alternative, putting her credit card into some car hire company's system, had seemed too risky.

'This is really kind of you,' she told him as they set off, tyres juddering over the Edinburgh cobbles. 'I know I made it difficult for you to refuse to give me a lift. I hope I haven't put you in a difficult position.'

'Not at all,' he said politely.

Roz felt that she owed him an explanation. 'I can drive, and

I could afford to hire a car,' she began, 'but, well, it's a complicated situation.'

'So I gathered,' said Finn. He hesitated. 'You don't need to tell me anything, but if there's anything I can do . . .'

'You are doing something. You're driving me to Skara.'

'It's my pleasure,' he said, tacitly accepting that she didn't want to say more. 'As I said, I'll be glad of the company, as we've a way to go. We'll stop for a bit of lunch about halfway, but in the meantime,' he added with an unexpectedly charming smile, 'there's a bag of toffees in the glovebox.'

'Is that a hint?'

'It is,' he said gravely.

Smiling, Roz leant forward to find the toffees. She unwrapped one and handed it to Finn, then settled back into her seat, letting another dissolve on her tongue as she watched the countryside unfold. It was a raw, grey day – 'dreich', Finn called it – and at first Roz could see little beyond the heavy clouds that were slumped over the tops of the hills. It was oddly restful to be driven by someone as comfortable with silence as Finn seemed to be, with just the gentle swish of the wipers sweeping the mizzle from the windscreen as a counterpoint to the radio, which was playing quiet classical music.

They stopped for lunch in Bridge of Orchy, and as the afternoon drew on and they headed further west, the clouds lifted, slowly at first, until the odd patch of blue sky squirmed between them and pushed the rest away. Roz was left gaping at the majestic mountains that dwarfed the car. Until then, everything she had seen in the UK had been on a tiny scale compared to everything in Australia, but this was more like it.

'Wow,' she said inadequately. 'This is so cool. I had no idea.'

Finn permitted himself a modest smile. 'Not bad, is it? I grew up in the hills,' he told her. 'In fine weather, there's no more beautiful place in the world.'

'Really?' Roz swivelled in her seat to look at him. 'I'd imagined you as a city guy.'

'I live in Edinburgh now, but no, when I was growing up, I lived in a place a friend of mine calls "a bus stop on the way to nowhere".'

There was something in his voice. 'A female friend?' she asked, and he glanced at her in surprise.

'How did you know?'

'Call it feminine intuition.'

He returned his eyes to the road. 'Aileen and a few other friends from university came to do some walking once. They were impressed by the hills, but Glenussie itself, not so much. And she's right. There's very little there.'

'It must be strange growing up somewhere that remote. You're not tempted to go back?'

'And do what? There's not much call for a solicitor in Glenussie. No, I won't go back,' he said. 'At least, not to live. My parents are still there, so I go and see them when I can, and this area will always be home to me.' He nodded at a signpost. 'There's the turning to Glenussie now.'

Roz sat up straighter. 'Do you want to go and see your parents now?'

'No,' he said quickly. 'Thanks, but I'll go another time. My father's not very well and he gets flustered by unexpected visits.'

Finn seemed embarrassed, and Roz offered an understanding smile. 'My mother was the same,' she said.

Remembering Millie's contorted efforts to explain why Roz couldn't stay in her own home just reminded her of Richard, though, and her smile faded into a shiver.

'Cold?' Finn asked, and she shook her head and fixed on a smile.

'No, I'm fine.'

She *was* fine. The hills soared around her, empty of any sign of human activity apart from the road winding along the valley. There were no CCTV cameras, no drones following the car, no tourists to inadvertently catch her in their videos. When she had checked out of the hotel, she had told them that she was heading to Norway next. Nobody would be able to make a connection with Finn. She was as safe as she could be.

Finn told her that in the west, the weather often cleared in the evenings, but Roz was still unprepared for her first glimpse of Skara. A silvery-blue sea gleamed between hills that faded purple into the distance beneath a sky streaked orange and gold, and her blood thrilled at the sight of it. She forgot Richard as she gaped at the view, aware that the ring on her finger was almost glowing, and when Finn pulled into the uninspiring car park beside the hotel, her throat was so tight she could barely speak.

He pulled out the ignition key and wriggled his stiff shoulders before glancing at Roz and noticing her face. 'Okay?' he asked cautiously.

She put a hand to her mouth, unable to explain the churn of emotion inside her. 'Sorry, I . . . No, it's okay,' she said, when Finn looked terrified at the prospect of tears.

Almost as terrified as she was. She never cried. Why should she start now? It was just sea, just a sunset. Beautiful, but just a view.

'I'm fine. It's just... I'm fine.'

Blinking away the stupid tears, she got out of the car. It was very cold, and she dragged on her jacket and gloves to keep her warm as she carried her suitcase across the car park. It seemed a lot for one night, but she had to take everything with her now.

A stocky woman with beady eyes came out from an office when Finn rang a bell on the worn wooden reception desk.

'You're back,' she said, with a dour look.

'I am,' said Finn, apparently unbothered by the frosty welcome. 'Hello again, Morag.' He nodded at Roz. 'And this is Roz Chatton. I've booked a room for her too.'

'Aye, I heard.' Morag pushed a form across the desk for Finn to complete. 'Don't forget your registration number.' She turned to Roz, who was gazing around her, still grappling with her weirdly emotional response to the place. 'What brings you to Acheravie?'

Finn trod on Roz's foot and she looked at him in surprise. It didn't seem like him to be clumsy. 'I'm interested in the house where the Blackmore family once lived,' she replied.

Morag's sharp gaze snapped to Finn. 'Didn't you tell her?'

'Tell me what?' asked Roz, puzzled.

Finn sighed. 'Morag believes the house at Rubha Clachan is haunted.'

'Not haunted,' snapped Morag. 'Cursed. Some folks will no take a telling.' Her lips were pressed firmly together as she pushed two old-fashioned keys on wooden tags across the desk. 'You be careful,' she said to Roz. 'Room three, on the left at the top of the stairs. I've put you back in room five,' she said to Finn. 'Last orders at seven thirty, as usual.'

'Sorry about that,' Finn muttered as they made their way up the stairs. 'I meant to warn you about local sensitivities.'

'What did she mean about a curse?'

He checked his phone. 'It's quarter past six. Why don't you have a rest and I'll meet you in the bar at seven. I'll tell you then.'

Roz dropped her suitcase inside her room and looked around. The decor was faded – a lot of tartan – but a large window looked out over the sea to the hills of the mainland. It was almost the same view as in her painting, but not quite.

She was tired, but there was a fluttery feeling beneath her skin, as if she was excited or nervous – she couldn't decide which. Either way, she was glad to be on her own. Still close to unfamiliar tears, she wanted to think about the deep hum of recognition inside her, the sense of coming home after a very long journey. As if she had been carrying a great burden of grief and loneliness and had stepped through a door where she could lower it to the floor at last.

Frowning at the thought, she blinked it away and turned to inspect the room more closely. The furniture was as dated as the decor, but the four-poster bed looked comfortable and there was large, echoing bathroom. She took a shower to wash off the strange feeling along with the tiredness from the journey, and by the time she had done that and dressed in jeans, T-shirt and a warm checked shirt, she was feeling more herself.

The packet of letters she had bought at the auction seemed to beckon from her suitcase. Roz checked the time. She had a few minutes to spare, and the itch to discover more of Iris's story was overwhelming. She hadn't yet had a chance to read through all the letters properly. Sitting cross-legged on the sagging bed, she pulled one out at random. Iris had written from Colombo, she saw, and she smoothed out the sheets of paper carefully and started to read.

Iris described the strangeness of the Colombo garden and the birds she couldn't see but could hear, their whistles and guttural squawks and liquid bubbling notes so different from the call of the kittiwake or the familiar screech of the gulls wheeling in the Skara sky. Roz could see the effort she had made to make it sound amusing for her sisters, including some vivid sketches of an elegant colonial house set in a lush garden, but it was obvious how desperately homesick she had been, poor girl. How she had longed to be where Roz was right now.

The buzz of a text jolted Roz back to the present. *I'm in the bar*, Finn had typed, too polite to send *Where are you?* or *You're late* as he probably wanted to.

Reluctantly scrambling off the bed, Roz folded the letter and put it carefully back in its envelope before heading downstairs, half her mind still in Colombo.

She found Finn in the bar, talking to a tough-looking man with an easy, humorous face. A golden retriever was flopped at his feet but got up to welcome Roz with a gently waving plumed tail.

Finn interrupted his conversation to greet her with a smile. 'Feeling better?'

'Much better, thank you,' she said, embarrassed at how strangely she had reacted to reaching Skara at last. She glanced at the stranger, hoping to change the subject, and Finn took the hint.

'Roz, this is Drew Malcolm. Roz Chatton,' he introduced her.

'Hello.'

They shook hands. Drew's palm was warm, his grip firm, and Roz was conscious of an unsettling jolt of her pulse.

'Welcome to Skara,' he said. His gaze was a clear blue and held a smile that warmed his whole face, creasing his cheeks and deepening the laughter lines at the edges of his eyes. To Roz, used to guarding her feelings, the easy warmth was almost shocking, and her gaze slid away as she withdrew her hand, feeling oddly ruffled and annoyed with herself for wishing she had taken a little more trouble over her appearance.

'Is this your dog?' Glad of the distraction, she bent to stroke the silky head.

'It is.'

'She's beautiful.'

'And knows it,' said Drew. 'Stop flirting, Bonnie, and lie down.'

Finn's eyes were flicking between them, and Roz felt ridiculously self-conscious. 'I've ordered you a glass of wine,' he said. 'Is Sauvignon Blanc okay?'

'Perfect.' She took the glass he handed her and cleared her throat. 'Thanks, Finn.'

Drew leant casually against the bar, watching her with glinting eyes. 'Finn was just telling me that you're Australian. You're a long way from home.'

It was odd that he should say that, Roz thought, when her overwhelming feeling was that she had just found her way home.

'Yes, I am,' she said, trying to ignore the embarrassing flutter of her pulse. This wasn't like her. She had always been cool and in control. She wanted to wriggle her shoulders, shake off this awkward awareness. It wasn't even as if this Drew Malcolm was doing anything. He was just *there*, with his warm blue eyes, making the air tingle.

'What about you?' she asked stiffly. 'Are you a local?'

The corner of his mouth quirked. 'You could say that.'

'According to Morag, the Malcolms have been at Dundonan since the fourteenth century,' said Finn, in a dry voice.

Roz flushed, feeling foolish. She recognised the name now from Iris's letters. Drew must be a descendant of Ian Malcolm.

'Seven hundred years? Wow.'

'Barely enough to not be considered outsiders round here, to be honest,' said Drew, the crease in his cheek deepening in a way that set a strange fizzy feeling uncoiling inside Roz, and in spite of herself, she found herself laughing. 'Skara people have memories that go back thousands of years.'

'To the Four Sisters?'

'Ah.' He glanced at Finn. 'Finn's told you about them?'

'That's why I'm here,' Roz said, when Finn nodded. She forced her gaze away from Drew's smile. It wasn't really a proper smile, anyway, just a dent in his cheek, a curl of his mouth, a glimmer in his eyes. No reason for her insides to snarl up.

She cleared her throat. 'I bought a painting of the Four Sisters and it got me interested. That led to me buying some old letters, and then to Finn, and now ... here I am.' Deliberately, she turned to Finn. 'So,' she said, taking a sip of her wine, 'tell me about this curse.'

24

Roz

Finn brightened, but then gave a self-deprecating shrug. 'Drew's your man for that,' he said, which meant Roz had to look back at Drew.

Drew took a pull of his beer. 'You don't want to take Morag too seriously,' he told Roz. 'She does a grand job of frightening guests away from Rubha Clachan in the interests of health and safety, if nothing else.'

'I'm not frightened,' Roz said, irritated by the undercurrent of amusement in his voice. More irritated by the way her gaze kept snagging on his mouth. 'I'd just like to know what Morag meant.'

'It's a local legend,' Drew said, half apologetically. 'I told you people on Skara have long memories. This one goes back thousands of years, to when a man lived on Skara with his four beautiful daughters. They had wandered for years and found a home here at last. He may have been a wizard of some kind.'

'A wizard?' Roz must have looked sceptical, and he spread his hands.

'I'm just telling you the story.'

Out of the corner of her eye, she could see Finn looking peeved, but he was the one who had passed the story-telling on to Drew.

'Go on,' she said.

'Well, whatever he was, this man was proud of his daughters. Then one day when he was out fishing, they were taken by raiders who stole in under cover of a sea fret, and were never seen again. He raised four stones to guide them home and laid a curse on anyone who cast the stones down. They would be doomed to misfortune and their family would be scattered, fated to be homeless for ever. The village was entrusted to make sure the stones would always stand on the point.'

Drew paused to drink some more beer. 'Fast-forward to the 1920s, when a thrusting Englishman called Charles Blackmore bought the land. Dismissing the legend, he built a modern house and knocked down the stones that were blocking his view, thus triggering the curse.'

The hairs were rising at the back of Roz's neck. Her ring was warming up. Turning it uneasily on her finger, she gave a tentative laugh. 'You don't believe in curses, do you?'

'I don't,' he said, 'but after Charles Blackmore knocked down the stones, his family certainly suffered a series of misfortunes. Blackmore himself lost his fortune, his wife died and his daughters left one by one.' He turned to Finn. 'Didn't you say that he died alone and never saw any of his daughters again?'

'That seems to have been the case,' Finn agreed cautiously. 'He had four daughters too, which may have given rise to the legend in the first place.'

'And one of those daughters was Iris,' said Roz, thinking of the letters she had read. Poor homesick Iris had never made it home. 'I wonder what happened to her,' she added, almost to herself.

'Still keen to explore the house?' Drew asked, and her gaze met his in spite of herself. His eyes were warm and blue and glimmering with . . . *something*, something that tightened the air and made it suddenly hard to breathe.

Somehow she wrenched her own away and swallowed. 'Even more so now I know more about the history,' she said, horribly aware of how thin and breathless her voice sounded. She lifted her chin to make up for it, although she didn't dare risk another look directly at him. 'I don't think the curse will apply to me.'

'Well, just be careful,' he said. 'Cursed or not, that house has been abandoned for nearly a century. It won't be safe.'

'I've already explained the safety situation to her,' said Finn a little stiffly.

Drew's gaze flickered between the two of them. 'I'm sure you have.' He nodded at their empty glasses. 'Another?'

'Thank you, but it's last orders for food soon. Roz, we'd better go.'

'Sure.' Roz drained her glass and set it on the bar. Finn didn't make her feel like this, jarred and . . . *fizzy*. The sooner they went in to eat, the better, she told herself.

Still, she could hardly scuttle away without saying goodbye. She wasn't a silly shy schoolgirl, she reminded herself, even if Drew made her feel like one. She made herself smile at him. 'Nice to meet you,' she said, carefully neutral.

'You too.' He looked back at her, and all at once the air was thrumming with awareness. 'We'll meet again,' he said.

Roz had to jerk her eyes away from his. 'Um ... er, well ...' So much for not being silly and shy!

It was a relief when Morag appeared behind the bar and eyed them sourly. 'Are you eating or no?'

'Morag, you can't glare at your guests like that,' said Drew, pulling a face of such exaggerated dismay that Roz had to smother a laugh. 'You'll never get a decent Tripadvisor review that way.'

'I'm not glaring. I'm just telling them their tea's ready.'

'You could try a smile. Go on,' he teased, and Roz bit her lip and looked away. 'Just a little one.'

Morag was clearly used to him. 'I'll smile when they tell me they're not planning to mess around any more at Rubha Clachan.'

'Drew here has just been telling us about the curse,' Finn put in.

'And I suppose he made it into a funny story, did he? The curse is real enough. That Blackmore man should never have come here with his fancy ideas. He brought ruin on this place and on his family.'

'We heard about the stones he took down,' Roz said, thinking with a pang of her painting, where the stones had stood tall on the headland. 'The Four Sisters.'

'He was a fool,' spat Morag. 'Taking down the stones wasn't enough for him. No, he went further. He commissioned a beautiful necklace for his wife. It had four exquisite stones, all different, but all a similar shape to the standing stones, linked by diamonds and pearls. He boasted to everyone that the stones represented *his* four beautiful daughters, so everyone should forget about ancient curses. It was a deliberate taunt.' Her voice shook with anger. 'Charles Blackmore had no understanding of the past or care for the community. He thought he could build his modern house and install his modern gadgets and ignore the ancient forces at work in the landscape here, and that didn't sit well with my great-great-great-grandmother, Nessa. She was a wise woman.'

'What, like a witch?' asked Roz, caught up in the story in spite of herself.

'No, not like a witch,' said Morag, annoyed. 'Like a woman who knows a lot of things. A woman who is in tune with nature and understands the power of the past. Nessa warned the Malcolms about selling the land in the first place,' she added with an accusing scowl at Drew, who held up his hands.

'Hey, don't look at me. I didn't do anything.'

He winked at Roz, who was betrayed into a smile that she had to quickly convert to a cough. How did he do that, make her jitter one moment and laugh the next?

'No, but James Malcolm did,' said Morag. 'He sold Rubha Clachan to Charles Blackmore to pay off his gambling debts. He should have known better.'

'Why weren't the Malcolms cursed in that case?' Finn put in.

'Who says they weren't?' said Morag, with a glance at Drew. 'And the village was cursed along with them. We were supposed to protect the land and ensure that the stones remained standing. Ever since then, there's been bad luck here. Inexplicable accidents, children dying, lives broken. People have left. This is nothing like the village it was in the 1920s.'

Roz's ring was pulsing. 'And the necklace? What happened to that?'

'Nessa cursed it,' said Morag, matter-of-fact. 'Why should Charles Blackmore's stones not be cursed just as the Four Sisters were? Whoever wore that necklace wore bad luck around their neck – and they still will. The stones in it carry the curse with them.'

'Where is it now?'

'No one knows,' she admitted. 'Presumably Amelia gave it to one of her daughters, who took the curse with her. Good riddance,' she added. 'We've had enough trouble here without that necklace as well. Now, are you coming to eat or not?'

Roz fiddled with her cutlery as she and Finn waited for their venison burgers to arrive.

'What did you make of all that?' she asked him.

'It was interesting what she said about the necklace.' His voice was carefully neutral. 'I'll see if I can find anything about it in the Blackmore papers. If the necklace is still out there somewhere and we can trace provenance, it might be a way of tracking down one of the daughters. You'd think Amelia would have given it to Iris, though, wouldn't you? She was the eldest.'

'I haven't come across anything about a necklace in the letters I've read,' said Roz. 'But she wouldn't necessarily have mentioned it to her sisters. They would have known she had it.'

'Perhaps we'll find something tomorrow.' There was a pause. 'What did you think of Drew Malcolm?' asked Finn, almost reluctantly.

Roz didn't answer immediately. She could still feel Drew's smile burning behind her eyelids, still feel that crackle in the air. She remembered how he had winked at her, tugged a smile out of her.

'He's . . . not what I expected,' she said at last.

'What do you mean?'

'Isn't he a lord, with his own castle? I thought he'd be more . . . serious.'

'Oh, I imagine he can be serious enough when he chooses,' said Finn, a touch glumly. 'He's turned Dundonan into one of Scotland's top hotels, and you don't do that by playing the fool.'

'Well,' said Roz after a moment, 'I liked his dog, anyway.'

That night, Roz dreamt of being at sea in an open boat. The waves reared up around her, the wind screamed, the rain pelted, and when she woke in her comfortable bed at the Anchor Inn, her cheeks were wet with tears.

Shaking off the lingering terror of the dream, she went over to the window, and was instantly soothed by the sight of a still, silvery sea and the mountains across the water. She would have to find a map to see whether she was looking at the mainland or an island.

With Finn's advice about the state of the house at Rubha Clachan in mind, she dressed warmly in walking trousers and the fleece she had bought in Edinburgh before heading down to the dining room, where she found him eating porridge.

He looked up with a smile. 'Ready to tackle the haunted house?'

'I can't wait!'

After breakfast, they drove cautiously up the track to the entrance to Rubha Clachan, and then got out to walk. Roz was glad of her jacket, although it wasn't really raining. A fine mizzle settled on her face and spangled her hair as she strode ahead, impatient to reach Rubha Clachan after so long.

They rounded a bend, and there it was, sitting square on the headland. *Home.*

Except how could that be right? She shook her head slightly. Surely home was in Australia, with its brilliantly bright light and tones of dusty greens and reds, not this misty grey headland.

But this was the place. She could see the view she had gazed at so often in the painting, though it was missing the four standing stones.

The Four Sisters.

Finn offered to show her inside, but Roz walked round to the front. It was as if she knew exactly where she was going. And there, laid low, in a sort of hollow in the overgrown grass, were the four great stones.

Careless of the damp, she sat on one of them and set her palms against the rough granite. In spite of the chill morning, it felt warm and welcoming, and the opal ring on her hand was humming.

Home, whispered the wind that was soft against her cheek. *Home at last.*

25

Finn

Skara, present day

Finn watched Roz's face. There was something other-worldly about her expression as she sat on the fallen stone and tipped her face up to the breeze.

He hoped that she wasn't letting all the talk of curses get to her. She seemed a refreshingly sensible woman. He liked her reticence and the fact that she was comfortable with silence. She had been good company on the drive up from Edinburgh, though, without chattering. Roz had none of Aileen's golden beauty. She wasn't conventionally pretty, but still, he had been very aware of the dark sweep of her lashes against her cheek, the graceful turn of her head, the way her mouth curved in her rare smile.

He was not the only one who had noticed. Drew Malcolm had too. There had been a spark between him and Roz as soon as they had met. Even Finn could see it, and Aileen was always telling him that he didn't have a clue about reading signals.

Which was rich coming from her, Finn always thought. Throughout university and afterwards, she would tell him that one girl or another liked him. 'Honestly, Finn, you're so *dense* about women,' she would say while apparently oblivious to the fact that she was the only girl he wanted.

Roz Chatton was the first woman he hadn't immediately compared to Aileen and found wanting. He found her guardedness, a complete contrast to Aileen's flamboyance, oddly appealing. He sensed that she was dealing with a major problem and wished he could help her, but she clearly wasn't yet ready to confide in him.

He hoped she wouldn't turn to Drew Malcolm.

At least he and Roz had a shared interest in finding more letters, Finn reassured himself. He was glad to know that she was as intrigued as he now was to find out what had happened to Iris Blackmore.

He was eager to get going and see what else they could find in the house. 'Shall we go in?' he suggested again, and Roz turned as if startled out of her thoughts.

'Oh, yes, of course.' She smiled as she got up, and Finn actually felt his stolid heart miss a beat.

He wanted to sweep her up and into the house, to insist that she join him on an adventure and solve the mystery of Iris Blackmore with him, but of course he didn't.

'Please do be careful, though,' he said instead. 'I'm not at all sure how safe the house is.'

Why not give her a lecture on health and safety while he was at it? he thought bitterly. Aileen was right. He didn't have what it took to sweep a woman off her feet.

The front door opened with a satisfying creak, and they stepped into the entrance hall together. Through the open door behind them, Finn could hear the sea, but inside there was only the quivering silence he remembered from before.

Roz stepped up beside him, and to his delight, she reached for his hand. 'There's nothing to be scared of,' he said, hoping to sound protective.

'I'm not scared,' she said. 'It's just ... it's like they're waiting for us.'

'They?'

'The sisters.'

He had felt the same thing, he remembered. That uncanny sense of someone waiting, just out of sight. The light in the hall was dim, but enough to see the cobwebs festooned along the staircase and around the windows and hanging from the ceiling. The dust was thick on the floor, and Finn could still see his footprints from his earlier visit. The contrast with the stark art deco lines of the room was somehow eerier than if it had been some Gothic castle.

Roz had noticed the old telephone. 'Look at the—' she began just as a door slammed somewhere, and they both jumped before exchanging a shamefaced smile.

'What was that about not being scared?' she said.

Finn's heart was banging uncomfortably against his ribs. 'I think it's just the wind,' he said, uncomfortably aware of the croak in his voice as he went to close the front door.

'I'm sure you're right,' said Roz, 'but I'm glad you're here!'

'Me too,' he confessed.

'Can we have a look around?' she asked.

'We should stay downstairs for now,' he warned, back in health-and-safety mode.

'All right. I'll be careful.'

Finn led the way to the drawing room, and saw Roz gasp at the view when she went in. She turned slowly in the middle of the room, taking in the piano, the abandoned books and the gramophone with the untidy pile of records beside it, just as he had done.

'Take away the dust and it's like they could walk in at any minute,' she said.

'There's no sign of Charles Blackmore in here,' Finn realised, looking around. 'It sounds as if he was drinking heavily. I'm guessing he retreated to his study. I saw a few empty bottles in there.'

'Or perhaps he couldn't bear it in here without his daughters?' said Roz. 'If we can sense what it must have been like when they were here, how much worse must it have been for him?'

'Perhaps,' Finn agreed. 'We don't yet know what happened but my sense is that Blackmore somehow drove his daughters away. He set up the trust when he was dying alone, and he must have known then that he'd never see any of them again.'

'I wonder why none of them ever came back?' said Roz.

'Let's see if we can find some clues in the study.' Finn led the way across the hall and opened the study door.

'I see what you mean,' she said, pulling down the corners of her mouth at the state of the room. 'This feels very different.'

'This room is where I found those letters from Iris,' said Finn. 'I'm hoping there might be more, but Charles Blackmore doesn't seem to have had an efficient filing system.' He eyed the piles of papers, bulging cupboards and abandoned bottles and glasses with disapproval.

'Where shall we start?' Roz looked at him expectantly, and Finn straightened his shoulders.

'I only looked through the desk drawers,' he said. He had been glad to find something to show for his trip and then go, he remembered, but he didn't think he would tell Roz that. 'There are some cupboards at the front that we could try.'

Roz bent to inspect them. 'They're locked.'

'I saw some keys in here.' Finn pulled open one of the drawers and tossed Roz a ring bristling with keys of different sizes. 'Try these,' he said. The fact that the cupboard was locked was surely promising, and he wanted Roz to have the thrill of finding some letters for herself. 'I'll start with the cupboard in the corner and work round.'

She grimaced at the sight of the papers spilling out of the stuffed cupboard. 'Good luck!'

Careless of the dust, she sat cross-legged on the floor and began trying the keys while Finn took a breath, tugged a sheaf of papers from the cupboard and began to look through them.

'Ah!' Roz exclaimed in satisfaction as she turned a key with a click. 'Let's see what's in here . . .'

For a while they worked in companionable silence, broken only by the rustle of papers or the occasional grunt of disappointment from Finn as he discovered yet another set of bills. Roz moved on to the second desk cupboard.

The quiet thickened around them until Finn could feel it pressing against his eardrums. He glanced at Roz, who lifted her head at the same moment.

'What was that?' she asked.

'What was what?'

'I thought I heard something. A giggle?'

An icy finger seemed to press at the very top of Finn's spine. 'I didn't hear anything,' he said, mortified to hear the squeak in his voice. He was prepared to bet Drew Malcolm had never squeaked in his life.

Roz shivered and stretched out her legs. 'Probably just my imagination. I can't shake the feeling that the girls are hiding behind the door, waiting to surprise us.'

'Have you found anything useful?' Finn asked.

'No,' she said glumly. 'It's hard to see when the light is so bad too. I miss electricity! I've been using the torch on my phone.' She demonstrated as she reached into the cupboard for a thick envelope and shook out the contents.

'We should have a break,' said Finn. 'I wish I'd thought to ask Morag for a flask of coffee—' He broke off as Roz cried out.

'Letters!' she said, shaking out the envelopes and showing one to him.

'They're from Iris,' he said. 'I recognise her handwriting now.'

'And her little sketches! Oh my God,' said Roz, unfolding some pages and passing them on to him. 'They're wonderful! Look at the market! And the veranda! I'm sure I recognise Lady Carsington from the letters Iris sent from the ship.'

They exchanged smiles. In her excitement, Roz glowed, the guardedness dropping from her expression, and Finn's heart warmed. It was good to know that she was as thrilled as he was. Hard to believe now that he had been disappointed to have been given the task of sorting out the Blackmore Trust.

'It looks like she made it to Ceylon, anyway,' he said. 'These are all written from Colombo.'

They put the packet aside after a while and continued their search until Finn noticed that Roz had stilled. He glanced over curiously.

'What is it?'

'Come and look at this!' Her voice sounded strange.

He hurried over to crouch beside her as she smoothed out a paper and shone the torch at it.

'It's a receipt,' he realised.

'From a jeweller,' said Roz. 'Listen: "To remove four fine gemstones from twenty-four-carat gold and diamond necklace and set into four rings."' She glanced up at him. 'This must be the necklace Morag talked about.'

'It certainly sounds like it.'

Her eyes dropped back to the receipt. 'Then it describes the rings one by one. First, a central rectangular blue opal, six claw-mounted, tapered shoulders on a plain shank...'

'What is it?' asked Finn as she trailed off.

When she looked up, her eyes were huge in her pale face. She lifted her hand to show him the ring she always wore. 'This is a rectangular blue opal,' she told him. 'It has six claws and a plain setting.'

Finn gaped at her. 'You mean... you think your ring is part of Amelia Blackmore's necklace?'

'It would explain...' She stopped, rubbing the ring, and then gave an embarrassed laugh. 'I don't want to sound too woo-woo, but it might explain what drew me here.'

'If this is true, you might be one of the Blackmore descendants,' he said slowly.

'Or my grandmother might have bought the ring, or been given it.'

'True. We'd need to establish provenance, but it's a start, surely.' What were the odds? 'Do you have any family papers? Birth certificates, that kind of thing?'

'In Australia.'

'Are you planning to go home any time soon?'

A shadow crossed her face. 'No.'

Something about her expression made Finn decide not to ask any more. 'Well, this is a great find anyway,' he said. 'I'll take the receipt and see if I can find out more about it.' His knees creaked embarrassingly as he straightened. 'It's too dark and dusty to read these here. Let's call it a day and look through them properly back at the hotel.'

'Okay.' Roz seemed to have recovered her composure as she stood up, a lot more elegantly than Finn had, and stretched. 'I won't be sorry to get out of this dust,' she said, looking round. 'It's such a sad house now—'

She was interrupted by Finn's phone beeping. His heart jerked, and he had the oddest sensation that the house around him had flinched, as if equally startled by the jarring noise.

Roz was patting her throat. 'Oh, that gave me a fright.'

'It's very unusual to get a signal here,' he said, pushing the idea of a frightened house away – what a ridiculous idea! – and frowning at the phone. 'Hmm, a voicemail. I'll take it outside,' he said. 'There might be a better chance of catching enough signal to listen to it.'

26

Iris

Colombo, June 1931

Iris was having breakfast alone in the dining room when Kasun, the butler, brought her two letters on a tray.

'Thank you.' She put down her toast and took the letters eagerly. One was from Rose, while the second, she saw with a sinking heart, was from Bertie Spencer. He had written to her from Nuwara Eliya several times, inviting her to visit. *I feel sure you would enjoy the climate here*, he always wrote. *It is so much more pleasant than in Colombo.*

Reluctant to give him any encouragement, Iris had prevaricated. She was still anxious to have news of her uncle, she had replied, and would be uneasy leaving Colombo until she did.

'Very tactful,' Ariadne had observed. 'But it won't put Bertie off. He's the doggedly devoted type, and he won't give up.

Iris put Bertie's letter aside with a guilty sigh and slit open the envelope with Rose's letter.

Darling Iris, I must be quick, her sister had scrawled. *Aunt Edith has been, and she has told Papa that his daughters must be properly cared for as he cannot. I tried to explain that we were managing very well, but she just looked at me in that withering way she has. It seems that Aunt Bessy – remember, she married the American with the strange name, Hiram Beckerdorf, that used to make us laugh? – is over from America and Aunt Edith has talked to her about taking Lily and Daisy back to New York with her. Aunt Edith says Bessy would give them a comfortable and loving home.*

Needless to say, when I told the girls of the plan, both dug in their heels and refused to leave. As for me, Aunt Edith has reluctantly offered me a home with her in Edinburgh, which I shall not be taking up. Iris, I have a plan! If you are unable to find Uncle Ralph, I will introduce myself to Papa's brother instead. Uncle Percy sent a letter the other day telling Papa that he was on his way to Egypt, where they have hopes of finding a new tomb in the Valley of the Kings. He might be able to help us. But the flaw in my plan is that I can't leave Lily and Daisy here on their own. I'm afraid of what Aunt Edith will arrange if we cannot come up with a better solution ourselves. I don't trust Papa not to hand them over to her. Please, Iris darling, can you come home, and I will go and find our other uncle in Egypt?

Iris dropped the letter and put her head in her hands. What was Rose thinking? She was nineteen! The idea of her sister setting off for Egypt – Egypt! – on her own made Iris's blood run cold. Rose had never given two hoots for respectability, but surely she must realise that it was too dangerous to even consider such a trip? And what would happen to Lily and Daisy if she went dashing off to Egypt before Iris could get home?

But what was the alternative if Iris herself couldn't find Ralph?

Distracted, she pulled out Bertie's letter and opened it. She skimmed over his apologies for not writing earlier, and was about to put it aside to answer later when her eye snagged on the word *uncle*.

I know how anxious you are to have word of your uncle, he had written. There followed a complicated story about one of Bertie's cases that had involved a tea planter, but the upshot, Iris read with rising excitement, was that at last someone had recognised Ralph Davidson's name. *I cannot say he spoke of your uncle in flattering terms*, Bertie wrote, *but I thought you would be glad to know that he has been here in Ceylon. Unfortunately, it seems that this Davidson – if he is indeed your uncle – has left the country, which will be disappointing news for you.*

Iris, who had been sitting bolt upright, dropped the letter and slumped back in her chair. She had made it all the way to Ceylon only to discover that Ralph wasn't there any longer! What a fool she had been to set off without being sure, but what else could she have done? And what should she do now?

Disconsolate, she picked up the letter once more. Bertie ended by telling her that a tea planter named Roy Markham had purchased the plantation from Ralph and therefore might be able to tell her more. *I would be delighted to escort you to Mr Markham's plantation so that you can speak to him yourself*, he finished. *It is a four- or five-hour drive from Nuwara Eliya, and I can arrange for you to stay at the Hill Club here if you are able to make the journey from Colombo.*

Iris reread the letter more carefully. It was disappointing to realise that her uncle was no longer in Ceylon, but if she could find out where he had gone, it might be possible to follow him. It was worth a try, anyway.

She dashed off a reply telling Rose to stand firm against Aunt

Edith and promising to come home as soon as possible. *At last, I have a lead*, she scribbled. *I will tell you more when I have found out where Ralph is now. But please, Rose, do not go to Egypt, and certainly not on your own! It is far too dangerous.*

She gave the letter to Kasun to post and went to find Ariadne, who was lounging on her bed flicking through fashion magazines.

'You can't go haring off to Nuwara Eliya on your own,' Ariadne said when told of Iris's plan. 'Ring Bertie up and tell him we'll both come.' Energised, she tossed aside the magazine she had been reading. 'It's so hot here at the moment. A trip to Nuwara Eliya is just what I feel like. It's so much cooler up there.'

Bertie was delighted to hear from her. 'Oh, I say, that would be very jolly,' he said. 'I'll book you in at the club and get on to Markham for you.'

It was a long and winding drive up to Nuwara Eliya. Hill upon hill upon hill, every shade of green pressing into the car from every side. The saris of the women plucking tea made bright splashes of colour against vivid green of the tea estates sweeping over the hillsides, with the darker green of the rainforest behind. They shared narrow roads with working elephants and bicycles and bullock carts laden with coconut palm fronds, and passed stalls where coconuts, pineapples and other exotic fruits were piled high, until at long last they arrived in a cool, misty grey town that felt completely surreal.

Iris had thought that Ariadne was joking when she told her to pack her Scottish clothes, but high up in the hills, Nuwara Eliya had a completely different climate to Colombo. A low mist hung over the lake and wide avenues were lined with half-timbered buildings that looked as if they might have been designed as

English houses by someone who had never been to England.

The Hill Club was a huge barrack-like building with a sweeping gravel drive. Bertie was waiting to greet them when they arrived, weary after the long drive. Beaming, he ushered them inside, shouting conflicting instructions over his shoulder to the servants who came out to take their cases. Iris was pleasantly surprised by her room, which had a fireplace and a dressing table and pictures of fox hunting on the walls.

She would have liked to have had a rest in the blissful cool, but Bertie was hovering to take them to dinner, so she contented herself with a trip to the cavernous bathroom at the end of the very long corridor. She took her toilet bag with her to wash her face before she changed into a fresh frock for the evening, but she was so tired that somehow she managed to catch her hand in the door, which slammed against it so hard that she had to suck in a scream. Her head rang and for a ghastly moment she was afraid that she might actually pass out on the black-and-white tiled floor, but it seemed that her ring had borne the brunt of the impact. Terrified that the opal might have been cracked, she pulled it off her throbbing hand to inspect it, but although the setting was dented, the stone itself still glowed a deep, pure blue.

It was cold in the bathroom. Iris hurried through her ablutions and back along the corridor to her room. She was glad now that she had taken Ariadne's advice and brought a cardigan, though the weight around her shoulders felt strange after being hot for so long.

Bertie was waiting for her in the hall and was concerned when he saw her cradling her injured hand. 'Have you hurt yourself?'

She explained about the accident with the door. 'I'll have to get the ring checked when I get back to Colombo,' she said. 'I'm worried that the stone might be loose.'

'There are plenty of jewellers in Nuwara Eliya,' Bertie hastened to assure her. 'I can go with you if you like.'

'That's kind, Bertie, but I'd like to see Mr Markham first. Will we be able to go to his tea estate tomorrow?'

'I'm afraid not,' he said. 'I sent him a message, but his butler says he's travelling and won't be back until the day after tomorrow at the earliest.' He must have noticed Iris's dismayed expression, because he hastened to reassure her. 'I'm very happy to take you there on Thursday. I gather Markham isn't the most sociable of chaps, but I'm sure he'll be prepared to see you.'

Iris sighed to herself. 'I suppose I'll just have to wait.' After all this time, would two days really make so much difference?

Bertie began guiding her towards the bar. 'I say, it's jolly good to see you again,' he said. 'I'm so glad you were able to come up. I've planned a few things to amuse you until Markham gets back. I've got a few people together for a picnic tomorrow, when the mist is supposed to clear. There's a beautiful waterfall not too far away. I hope you'll like it.'

'I'm sure I will,' Iris murmured politely. 'Is Lady Carsington down yet?'

'She's waiting in the bar. I thought we'd have a drink before dinner, just like old times on *Orphea*.'

The bar was furnished with leather chairs and comfortable sofas that would not have looked out of place at Dundonan. There were more hunting prints on the walls and a lot of dark, heavy furniture, with old magazines and newspapers laid out. A fire burnt at the end of the room where Ariadne was sitting, elegant as ever, talking to someone who was seated in a deep winged armchair turned away from the door.

'Here we are,' Bertie cried, leading Iris towards the fire, and a man rose from the armchair and turned to greet her.

She stopped dead in dismay.

It was Guy Henderson.

Ariadne's smile held a touch of devilry. She had known quite well that Iris would be aghast, but was clearly enjoying watching from the sidelines. 'Quite the shipboard reunion, isn't it?'

'We meet again,' Guy said, and Iris was too fed up with everything to be polite.

'What are you doing in Nuwara Eliya?' she asked.

He raised his brows at her tone. 'I'm waiting to meet somebody. And you?'

'Miss Blackmore has managed to find news of her uncle at last,' Bertie put in importantly, though Iris would rather he had kept the news to himself. She didn't know why Guy Henderson riled her so much, but she didn't want him knowing her business.

'I wondered if you had,' Guy murmured, with one of those sardonic looks that made her feel prickly with resentment.

Then, of course, he had to be invited to join them for dinner, which they ate in the dining room. There were a few other diners there, but Iris found it rather gloomy. The lighting was dim and the ceiling decorated with mock beams in imitation of a Tudor house, adding to the strange, surreal air of the place.

Dinner was the usual fare: oxtail soup, devilled eggs, a rabbit and vegetable curry or venison stew, followed by spotted dick and custard or blancmange. At least it was cold enough to eat what was on the menu for once, but Iris had lost her appetite. Why did Guy Henderson keep popping up?

He seemed content to sit and listen to Bertie, who held forth about the delights of Nuwara Eliya and the picnic he had planned for the next day. Iris did her best to listen too, and ignore the hard line of Guy's cheek and the occasional gleam of his smile.

Afterwards, someone put a record on the gramophone and there was desultory dancing at the end of the dining room. A few couples took to the floor, but when Bertie asked Iris to dance, she excused herself, saying that her hand was still sore. Instead, Ariadne danced with Guy, which Iris found even more annoying although she didn't care to understand why.

She was very glad when the evening was over and she could go to bed. Just a couple of days, she told herself. Then she could find out where Ralph had gone. He might even have returned to Scotland or England, she thought. What a relief that would be. She could get a passage back to Southampton, find her elusive uncle and then, at last, she could go home.

And she would never have to see Guy Henderson again.

27

Roz

Skara, present day

Giving Finn some privacy to listen to his voicemail message, Roz wandered down to the stones once more. She didn't want to admit how relieved she was to get outside. It wasn't just the dust or the gloomy light. It was the eerie sense of being watched, of the air tightening remorselessly around her. It reminded her too much of how she had felt in Ridgewell before Richard was imprisoned.

But at the same time, the pull to be there and discover more of Iris's letters was too strong to be resisted.

She looked up as Finn approached. 'Everything okay?'

'No, not really. That was my mother. It seems my father is in hospital.'

'Oh no! I'm sorry, Finn. What's happened?'

He pulled a face. 'She wasn't very coherent. It sounds like a heart attack, but last time this happened, it turned out to be a panic attack. Anyway, I'm afraid I'll need to go.'

'Of course.' Roz jumped up. 'Is it just you?' she asked, as they walked back down the overgrown drive to the car after gathering up the letters they had found and carefully closing the front door once more. 'Or do you have brothers and sisters?'

'I've got an older brother, Angus.' There was a trace of reserve in Finn's voice. 'He's a barrister in London. I gathered from my mother's message that he's got a high-profile court case on at the moment and can't spare the time to come up. Or, more likely, they don't want to bother him because he's so busy and successful.'

'Ah. But you can be bothered?' said Roz, with a sympathetic look, and he smiled a little crookedly.

'I may not be a high-flyer like Angus, but I'm reliable.' He sighed. 'I'd better go and see what's going on, anyway.'

'Where is the hospital?'

'In Fort William. Would you mind very much if we drove up there this afternoon?'

'You won't want to be bothered with me in the middle of a family crisis,' said Roz. 'Besides, I'd really like to stay here for a while.'

Finn frowned. 'How will you manage without a car?'

'I've got legs,' she pointed out. She didn't want to go back to a town with cameras and ways to track her. 'And I can come back to Rubha Clachan and see if I can find some more letters. I'll be very, very careful,' she added, seeing him open his mouth to object. 'I can't explain it, but I feel that I need to be here. It was such a thrill to find those letters, wasn't it? There *must* be more if I keep looking.'

'Well ...'

'Oh, *please*, Finn,' she said. 'You've got enough to think about with your father.' She held the letters on her lap as he turned the car around. 'Why don't I keep these here and read them until you get back? You *will* come back, won't you?'

'Yes, of course. I'll need to order them all and—'

'I can do that for you,' said Roz eagerly.

'It's not very professional,' he said, clearly torn.

'Who's going to know?' she countered, guiltily aware that she was taking advantage of his distraction.

He glanced at her and she smiled at him. 'Please,' she said, and his face relaxed.

'All right,' he said, with a rueful answering smile. 'You keep the letters safely here and I'll be back as soon as I can.'

Morag was not at all happy when she learnt that Finn would not be taking Roz with him when he left, a day early. She was even less pleased that Roz wanted to stay on for at least another week.

'We're fully booked,' she said flatly, and when Roz arched a disbelieving eyebrow, she announced that she would be arranging for decorators in any unoccupied rooms. There would be nowhere for Roz to stay.

Finn fretted, but Roz insisted that she would fine. 'Don't give me a thought,' she told him. 'You just worry about your parents.'

'But how will you manage?' He paused as he opened the boot of the car to sling in his overnight case. 'You weren't thinking of camping at Rubha Clachan, were you?'

'Well . . .'

'Roz, it's too dangerous. I won't leave unless you promise me that you won't even consider it. There's Dundonan Castle, of course. It's a five-star hotel with prices to match, I gather, but perhaps if you asked Drew Malcolm directly, he could offer you a better rate?'

'I don't need to ask him,' said Roz, uncomfortable at the idea of asking Drew, with his glinting blue eyes, for help. 'I can afford to book a room there, for a while anyway. And if the worst comes to the worst, I'll ring for a taxi or get a bus or something.' She relented at the sight of Finn's worried face and on an impulse gave him a hug. 'You go. I hope your dad will be okay, and don't worry about me. I'll be absolutely fine.'

She felt less sure of that after Morag had grudgingly given her breakfast the next morning and informed her that there were no local taxis available.

'In that case, I'll walk,' said Roz, refusing to beg the other woman for advice.

She set off up the long hill that led to Dundonan and Rubha Clachan, trundling her case behind her. The fine morning had clouded over and a steady drizzle was seeping into every tiny crack and crevice. She was glad that she had sealed the letters and packed them carefully away in the middle of her case to keep them dry. When the wind picked up, driving the rain into her face and blowing her hood from her hair, however, she began to regret her decision. She could have been sitting in Fort William, warm and dry, she remembered.

She set her teeth and plodded on. It hadn't seemed so far when Finn had driven past the castle on the way back from Rubha Clachan the day before. She wondered how he was getting on. It had been sweet of him to let her keep the letters they had found. She sensed that he was not a natural rule-breaker, and it was probably making him uncomfortable to know that he had behaved in what he considered an unprofessional way. She didn't want him to feel bad, as he had been so kind to her, but she felt such a strong connection to Iris already. She hadn't been able to bear the thought of waiting to read the letters.

She had broken her own rule on using her phone and had messaged Finn earlier that morning. He had replied to say that his father was being kept in for observation for a couple of days, but that it seemed time to set up some care at home for his parents. He wouldn't be able to get back to Skara for a few days, he told her. Would she be all right?

I'll be fine, she had replied.

The drumming sound of the rain on the hood of her jacket was so loud that Roz didn't hear the car coming at first, and it was almost upon her before she dragged her case to the edge of the narrow road and did her best to get out of the way. A battered Land Rover pulled up beside her, and when the window came down, she saw with a sense of inevitability that it was Drew Malcolm. She had hoped to slip into Dundonan without him noticing her among the other guests. She really didn't want him to think that she was trying to manoeuvre another encounter.

'Hello,' he said, and the amusement in his eyes made her skin prickle all over. 'It's Roz, isn't it?'

'It is.' She was tempted to pretend that she had forgotten who he was, but that would be childish. 'Hi, Drew.'

'Where are you off to?'

'Actually, I was hoping to get a room at your hotel,' she said with as much dignity as she could muster with rain dripping from her nose.

'At Dundonan?' His brows shot up. 'Can't you stay at the Anchor?'

'Morag says she's full.'

He shook his head. 'That's nonsense. She's never full.'

'Perhaps, but she doesn't want me there any longer, so I'm looking for somewhere else to stay.'

Drew opened his door. 'Hop in, I'll give you a lift.'

Well, what could she do? 'Thank you,' she said.

He slung her case easily into the back while she climbed gratefully into the passenger seat and turned to pet a happily panting Bonnie, who was sprawled in the back, glad of the distraction from her ridiculous awareness of Drew.

'How long do you need a room for?' Drew asked, as he put the car into gear.

Roz narrowed her eyes at him. 'Worried that I might not be able to afford your prices?'

'Touchy, aren't you?' Drew countered, amused, and she shifted uncomfortably in her seat

'Sorry, it has been said before,' she admitted. 'To answer your question, I'm not sure.' She told Drew about Finn needing to go and see his father in hospital. 'I really want to stay in Skara for a while,' she said.

'I was asking because, unlike the Anchor, we really are booked up at this time of year. But we might be able to squeeze you in for tonight, and maybe tomorrow.'

'Oh, well, thank you,' said Roz, wrong-footed. 'That would be great.'

She had seen the castle from Rubha Clachan, but it was even more impressive at close quarters. From the outside, it was like something out of a fairy tale, with massive walls, high windows and higgledy-piggledy turrets, towers and stone steps. An immaculate gravel drive swept around the courtyard to a great carved doorway, where Drew parked.

'Welcome to Dundonan,' he said.

Roz was relieved to be out of the Land Rover, where she had felt much, much too close to Drew and far, far too aware of his hands on the steering wheel, of the firm line of his jaw and the shivery warmth of his smile. 'Um, would you like me to go in the back way? I'm so wet.'

'Don't worry about that,' he said. 'Our guests often go out walking and return sodden.'

Ignoring her objections, he carried her case to the reception desk, which stood at one end of a huge baronial hall. At the other end, a fire burnt in the biggest fireplace Roz had ever seen, but there the fairy-tale setting had been brought bang up to date. There were the usual comfortable chairs and sofas, but in place of leather or chintz or – the Anchor's choice – tartan, the colours were bold and stylish. She took it all in with a designer's eye and was reluctantly impressed.

'Wow,' she said, craning her neck to look up at the panelled ceiling. 'This is amazing.'

'I'm glad you like it,' said Drew. 'Let's ask Douglas if he can find you a room.'

In spite of its size, the hall felt warm and welcoming. Guests were reading by the fire or having tea and scones. Roz could smell the magnificent floral displays mingling with the indefinable scent of luxury as she stood dripping by the desk, feeling awkward as Drew conferred with Douglas.

After much peering at the computer screen, he turned to her. 'We've got a room for tonight,' he told her, 'but someone has booked it from tomorrow, I'm afraid.'

'I'll take it for one night in that case.' She would worry about tomorrow later. 'How much is it?'

She just about managed not to wince at the price, but her smile was rather fixed. 'That's fine,' she said, very aware of Drew Malcolm watching her with those blue eyes of his.

Douglas smiled charmingly. 'Could I take your credit card, Ms Chatton?'

'It's Roz, please, and I'd prefer to pay cash.' She felt Drew look at her curiously, but Douglas didn't even blink. 'Certainly,' he said, as she dug into her bag and counted out an eye-watering amount of money.

'I'll leave you in Douglas's capable hands,' said Drew, whistling for Bonnie, who had wandered over to greet some of the other guests. 'I'll see you later, Roz.'

'Oh, er, yes . . . great.'

What was it about Drew Malcolm that turned her into a dithering idiot? He was just being polite. He probably said 'see you later' to everyone he met. It didn't mean anything.

He smiled at her then, amusement dancing in his blue gaze. He knew what effect he had on her, Roz was sure, and she was mortified.

'Um, thank you for the lift,' she said stiffly.

'My pleasure,' he said, and turned away, leaving her relieved but still obscurely disappointed that he had gone.

28

Iris

Nuwara Eliya, June 1931

'Sandwich?' Bertie held out a plate to Iris. 'I wasn't sure what you'd like, so I got my cook to make up a selection. Tongue, egg mayonnaise, fish paste, and cucumber!'

Iris wasn't at all hungry, but Bertie had gone to so much effort and seemed so desperate to please her that she didn't want to disappoint him again. 'Lovely,' she said, eyeing the sandwiches dubiously and eventually selecting a fish paste one.

Afterwards, she would associate the smell of fish paste with horror, but then it was just a bit of bread and butter with a filling.

'My sister Cath is very fond of a picnic,' Bertie confided. 'Fish paste is her favourite too. She likes it with lashings of ginger beer.'

Poor Cath. Iris was sure his sister had plenty of other interests, but according to Bertie, all she ever did was eat.

Bertie had chosen a spot near a waterfall for his picnic. Impatient as she was to find Mr Markham and learn more about where Ralph had gone, even Iris had gasped at the sight of the water tumbling down over the rocks to a clear green pool. The party numbered seven, not including the servants, who had trekked ahead of them through the rainforest to set up a table spread with a white cloth. By the time Bertie, Iris and the others arrived, the table was laden with sandwiches and sausage rolls, cakes and little curry puffs, pineapple and mango. For the men, there was bottled beer, and for Iris and Susan, the only other woman there, a thirst-quenching lime juice. Ariadne had claimed to loathe picnics – 'too many crumbs, darling' – and opted to stay at the club.

The tumbling water sent deliciously cool silvery drops into the air, and the sound of it mingled with the exotic squawks and squeals of the birds that flapped from tree to tree and the constant thrum of hidden insects. Iris hadn't really enjoyed the walk to the waterfall. It was hard to concentrate on the beauty of the brightly dangling flowers that Bertie told her were called angel's trumpets when there was all that rustling and slithering in the undergrowth, and she kept hearing the alarming shriek of monkeys. The dark, rich smell of the vegetation gave her a headache. The rainforest was too lush, too close for her taste, and she was glad when they stumbled out from the narrow path into a clearing.

Bertie was being very solicitous, finding somewhere for Iris to sit and pressing food on her. To her dismay, Guy Henderson had joined the party. He made no effort to interrupt her conversation with Bertie, but she had a feeling that he was listening to everything she said, which was disconcerting.

'How long will it take us to get to Mr Markham's plantation tomorrow?' she asked Bertie, who was chomping on an egg mayonnaise sandwich with relish.

'It's quite a way.' Bertie picked up a piece of egg that had fallen and popped it in his mouth. It seemed Cath was not the only one who enjoyed their food. 'Four or five hours at least, I'd say. What do you think, Carstairs?' he asked Susan's husband.

'Five hours easily,' said Ronald Carstairs. 'Why do you want to see that curmudgeonly old . . .' he caught his wife's eye, 'so-and-so?' he finished lamely. 'He's suddenly very popular.' He turned to Guy. 'Weren't you asking about him the other day, Henderson?'

'Yes, I was,' said Guy coolly. 'I'm hoping to see him tomorrow, as a matter of fact.'

Iris stiffened. Why was *Guy* going to see Mr Markham?

'Tomorrow?' Bertie put in before she could stop him. 'But I'm taking Iris to see him tomorrow too! What a coincidence. We should travel together.'

Guy met Iris's glare with a hint of malice in his smile. 'What an excellent idea.' He drained his beer. 'Thank you, Spencer. That would be very convenient.'

'That's settled, then.' Bertie was never happier than when he was organising everybody, Iris realised. No wonder he was such a good administrator.

As the conversation grew general, Guy got up and wandered down to the edge of the waterfall. Iris, who had been watching him suspiciously, got up to follow him.

'Why are you so interested in Mr Markham?' she demanded when he acknowledged her with a nod.

'For the same reason you are,' he said. 'I'm hoping he can tell me where Ralph Davidson went when he left Ceylon.'

'You're looking for Uncle Ralph?' Iris gaped at him. 'Why? Wait...' She frowned, remembering a conversation on the ship. 'Restitution?'

'Restitution,' he agreed.

'But...' Iris had so many questions she didn't know where to begin. 'How long have you known that you were looking for my uncle?'

'I've been searching for Ralph Davidson for a very long time. I only discovered that he was your uncle on board ship, when I heard you asking Spencer if he knew of him.'

'Why didn't you say anything?' she demanded. 'And why are you looking for him anyway?'

'It's a long story.'

'I have time,' she said tightly.

Guy sighed, lit a cigarette and blew out a cloud of smoke before realising he had forgotten to ask if Iris would like one. She shook her head impatiently.

'I don't want a cigarette. I want to know why you've been lying to me.'

'I haven't lied,' he said. 'I just haven't told you the whole truth.'

'Why don't you start now?'

'You know, you should be angry more often,' he said. 'It improves your looks.'

Iris narrowed her eyes at him and he held up a hand in apology. 'All right, all right. I'll tell you, though I'm not sure you're going to like it.'

He gestured towards a fallen log, and after a moment, Iris sat next to him, her lips pressed together tightly.

'How much do you know about your uncle?'

'Not much,' she had to admit. 'He was my mother's favourite brother and he came out to Ceylon to take over a tea plantation.'

'And before that?'

'I don't know. I think he travelled around a bit.'

'That's true. I met him in Malaya,' Guy said, and Iris stared at him.

'You *know* him?'

'I was just a boy, fourteen years old and home for the school holidays. My parents moved out to Malaya from Dundee before I was born, but like all good children of the Empire, I was sent to boarding school. I only got to go home once a year, for the summer, and that year my parents had a new friend. He called himself Ralph Jamieson.'

Iris frowned. Jamieson had been her grandmother's maiden name.

'Ralph was great fun,' Guy went on. 'Everybody liked him. He was good company and sympathetic. He even had time for an awkward boy like me. He treated me as if I were a man, and if you'd ever been a teenage boy, you'd know what a difference that makes. He'd sit and chat as if we were equals. I felt as if he was really interested in my opinion.'

He gave a mirthless laugh. 'Of course, everybody felt that, especially my father. He was very impressed by Ralph, who was a successful financier – or so he said. Ralph had been to school at Fettes and knew all sorts of Edinburgh people that my father had only ever heard of. He'd drop their names into the conversation, and my father would nod along as if he knew them too. My father was a successful businessman, but he came from a humble background and there were some things he had a blind spot about. He'd agree to anything Ralph said, just because Ralph was upper class.

'Anyway, Ralph had been around for a while before I got there. He made that summer special. He'd take us to lunch at the Eastern & Oriental Hotel, where they had the best curries, and he was completely self-assured and generous. I always hated going back to school, but it was worse than ever that year.'

There was a sinking feeling in Iris's stomach. She didn't like the way this story was going.

'I'd only been back at school for a couple of weeks when the headmaster called me into his study to tell me that my father had killed himself.'

Iris drew in a shocked breath while Guy swallowed, his jaw set hard.

'He asked me if I wanted to sit down, so I knew straight away that it was bad news. I can still remember the feel of the upright chair. It had a leather seat. Everything smelt of leather. It was a windy day, and the ivy outside the study windows was tapping on the glass. Tap, tap. Tap, tap. I remember wishing someone would cut it back. I remember looking at old Taffer, as we called him, and wondering what he was talking about. My father wasn't dead. How could he be dead? I'd just seen him.'

'I'm sorry,' said Iris. 'It must have been a terrible shock.'

'I think I said something stupid like "thank you, sir" and walked out.' Guy dropped his cigarette on the ground and used the heel of his shoe to grind it out. 'It wasn't until my mother came back to England that I learnt the whole story. Ralph Jamieson had persuaded my father to invest in a supposedly sure-fire business scheme that was nothing more than an old-fashioned swindle. It left him bankrupt and unable to honour his debts. His reputation was in tatters and Ralph had disappeared. Not content with destroying my father's business, Ralph had also seduced my mother. My father must have felt that putting a gun to his head was his only option.'

'Oh Guy, how awful.' Iris could only imagine how a young boy must have felt learning of his father's humiliation and death. Her own father had also lost everything, but he hadn't done *that* to them. 'I'm so sorry,' she said again.

Could this be true? Was the uncle she had sought so eagerly no better than a common swindler? She turned the ring on her finger in agitation. What would her mother have said if she had known what her beloved brother had done?

Scapegrace, Aunt Edith had called Ralph. If Guy was right, he was far worse than that.

Guy was leaning forward, resting his arms on his knees, his eyes on the silvery torrent of water. 'We'd lost everything, so my mother was dependent on her brother for support. He paid my school fees and gave her an allowance, so I suppose we were fortunate, but my mother was never the same. She'd been so gay and pretty. I remember the perfume she used to wear, and the sound of her heels on the polished wood floors. She loved to dance. When I was a little boy, she would let me stand on her feet and twirl me round and round.'

His mouth twisted at the memory.

'But after Ralph ... she was so bitter, and riddled with guilt.

She hated being poor. All she ever talked about was finding Ralph and taking revenge on him. I promised her that I wouldn't rest until I'd tracked him down, but we could never find any trace of a Ralph Jamieson. It was only when my mother died that I made any progress. A friend of my father's who'd been to Fettes came to her funeral, and I told him about how my father had been embezzled. He said, "Sounds an awful lot like Ralph Davidson, chap at school who could charm the birds out of the trees but you wouldn't trust to see you across a road."

'When I started looking for Ralph Davidson, I got on better. I went to Edinburgh, and eventually managed to track down his older sister.'

'Aunt Edith?' Iris was struggling to take all this in.

'She didn't seem to have much time for her brother. All she would tell me was that Ralph had last been heard of on a tea plantation in Ceylon, financially supported by his doting sister Amelia.'

'My mother,' said Iris numbly.

'I took the first ship I could to Ceylon, which by coincidence turned out to be the one you were travelling out on.'

'But... I don't understand,' she said. 'Why didn't you tell me who you were straight away?'

'I had no reason to make a connection between Blackmore and Davidson until I overheard you asking Spencer if he knew of Ralph.'

'So that's why you...' Iris stopped. She didn't want to explain how puzzled she had been by the way Guy had seemed interested in her but not in the way she had expected.

'I wanted to get close to you, but I didn't want to give myself away. For all I knew, you were like your uncle and out for all you could get.'

'What?' Iris was outraged, and a smile softened his mouth briefly.

'As I got to know you, I realised that wasn't the case, but I couldn't understand why you were looking for him. I hoped that if I hung around, you would lead me to him. Not that hanging around you was a chore,' he added with a faint smile. 'You may not be a fashionable beauty like Ariadne Carsington, but there's something about you all the same.' His gaze rested thoughtfully on her face, considering. 'Yes, you're not fashionable, but in your own quiet way you are beautiful, you know. Ah, no, you *don't* know, do you?' he went on when Iris stared at him, at a loss to know how to react. 'You have no idea at all. That's what makes you beautiful, Iris Blackmore.'

29

Iris

Iris wrenched her eyes away from his and found her voice. 'We were talking about my uncle,' she reminded him, sounding constricted.

'So we were.' To her relief, Guy dropped the subject. 'Yes, I was hoping that you might introduce me to Ralph, but you didn't seem to be having any better luck finding him. Although we both appear to have found out about Markham buying the plantation from him. How did you hear about that?'

'Bertie wrote to me,' she said stiffly.

'Ah.' He nodded. 'Since we're both going to talk to Markham tomorrow, it makes sense to pool our efforts, don't you think?'

Iris didn't reply immediately. She was twisting her ring mechanically around her finger, distressed by what she had learnt.

'You said you wanted restitution. What did you mean by that?' she asked at last.

'Ralph Davidson owes me my inheritance. He needs to repay the money that he stole from my father.'

Somewhere in the forest behind Iris, monkeys shrieked, and there was a flurry in the branches of a tree that made her flinch.

'I hate this place,' she said.

Guy simply shrugged.

Iris turned on the log to look at him directly.

'You're not going to . . . hurt him?'

'I'd like to,' said Guy. 'I'd like to knock him down the way my father should have knocked him down for what he did to my mother, but I'll settle for an apology and the money.'

'So, in fact, you're just after money?' said Iris with a bitter look.

'Restitution, like I said. What do *you* want from him?'

She bit her lip. 'My mother lent him the money to buy the plantation,' she said defensively. 'He promised to repay her, and now we . . . my sisters . . . I was hoping he would help us.'

'So, in fact, *you're* just after money?' Guy echoed, and she flushed.

'I suppose it sounds like that. But it's not just money. I hoped he might offer us a home.'

'Why can't you stay in Scotland?'

Iris watched the waterfall spilling through the lush greenery, and thought about the burns bubbling down the hillsides on Skara. No lushness there, just the smell of heather and the cheep of pipits. Longing for its cool quietness clenched inside her.

'We'd rather do that, of course,' she said with difficulty, 'but my father . . . is not well. He drinks,' she made herself add.

'Ah.' Guy gave an understanding nod. 'Look,' he said, 'we both want to find Ralph, don't we? It makes sense to pool our resources. I don't mind admitting that my funds are running low.'

'Mine too.'

'So what do you think? Let's go and see Markham tomorrow and see what we can find out. Doubtless Ralph has moved on to swindle someone else by now.'

Iris could feel his energy vibrating through the log they sat on. If she wasn't careful, she would be dragged along in Guy Henderson's wake, and who knew where that would end?

'I need to think,' she said.

Guy got to his feet. 'I'll leave you to decide. It's up to you, of course, but one way or another I'm going to track down your crooked uncle and make him pay for what he did to my family.'

Iris got up too, pressing the tips of her fingers to her temples as Guy walked off. She didn't want to believe him, but the fact that Ralph had never replied to her mother should have set warning bells ringing long ago. Reluctant to rejoin the picnic party but unable to sit still, she paced up and down, pretending to admire the waterfall but really fretting. What if Ralph *was* as dishonourable as Guy claimed? She had assumed that his sister's family would be important to him, but what if he just didn't care?

Had she been a fool to dash off to Ceylon in search of someone who clearly didn't want to be found? But what choice had she had? She twisted the ring on her finger, blind to the beauty of the scene. There had been nowhere else to turn.

Now everything felt up in the air. She thought of the letter Rose had sent, and shuddered. She *must* find some money from somewhere, and her uncle was still her best bet. Perhaps she could shame him into helping Amelia's daughters, and if that failed, she would beg him, she decided. She would do whatever it took to keep her sisters together.

And if that meant pooling her meagre resources with Guy, that was what she would do.

Iris was glad when it was decided to pack up the picnic and go back to Nuwara Eliya. Solicitous as ever, Bertie walked beside her, rhapsodising about his glimpse of a black-capped kingfisher. 'Such a brilliant blue colour . . . and that bright red beak!'

Worried about what she would do if it turned out that Mr Markham had nothing to tell them about Ralph's whereabouts, Iris fiddled distractedly with her ring, then frowned. Something felt wrong.

Glancing down at her hand, she stopped dead. 'Oh, my ring!' she exclaimed.

'What is it?' asked Bertie in concern. 'Have you lost it?'

'I've got the ring, but the opal has gone,' said Iris, distressed. 'How could I have been so careless? I need to go back!'

The others had realised something was wrong and had gathered round.

'When did you last see it?' asked Susan.

'When I was by the lake, talking to Guy.' Iris remembered looking down at the ring then and twisting it as she thought. It was a bad habit. 'The bathroom door banged shut on my hand the other day. The opal may have come loose then. I meant to get it fixed . . .' She wrung her hands together.

Bertie hollered something in Sinhalese. 'I'll send the servants back to look.'

'No, I need to go back myself. That's my mother's opal. I can't lose it. I can't!' Hearing the hysterical note in her voice,

Iris caught her breath and made herself speak more calmly. 'The rest of you, please do carry on. I'll catch you up.'

She was already turning and hurrying back up the path. 'Iris, wait!' Bertie called, but she was in a panic to find the missing opal.

Guy caught her up easily on his long legs. 'I'll help you look,' he said.

Bertie followed her too, with a couple of the servants, and together they went down to the log where Iris had sat talking to Guy. Why, oh why, had she been pacing around so much afterwards? She had been too distracted to notice the ring.

If she had lost the stone, she would never forgive herself. Never. Iris had a terrible sense of foreboding. Yes, it was just an opal, but losing it would feel like losing her mother all over again, losing all hope of getting back to her family. She *had* to find it!

Desperately she paced the area, her eyes fixed on the ground, but her vision was so blurred with panicky tears that she couldn't see anything.

'We should be methodical.' Guy put out a hand to stop her. 'There's no point in trampling everywhere. You take this section here and go over it inch by inch. We'll divide up the rest of the area. We'll find it.'

It was sensible, Iris realised. She took a deep breath and made herself calm down. She was being hysterical. What would Rose and Lily think to see their steady sister in such a state? Daisy, of course, would have revelled in the drama, she thought with a twist of longing for home.

They searched in silence, and Iris was just beginning to despair when Bertie gave a shout. 'I see it!'

Iris ran over as he bent down to reach into the undergrowth at the very edge of where she thought she had been.

'Oh, Bertie, tha—'

Her grateful cry was cut off as he jerked back with a yelp of pain, and to Iris's horror, she saw a snake wriggle away through the grass.

She hurried to his side. 'Bertie, are you all right?'

'Something bit me.' His voice taut with pain, he handed Iris the opal. She shoved it into her pocket, more worried about Bertie now.

'I saw a snake,' she said worriedly, as Guy and the others came up.

'What did it look like?' Guy asked. 'Quick, it's important!'

'Um, it was black, I think, and it had white lines on it as if it was divided into sections.

Bertie blenched, and the servants muttered anxiously.

'Sounds like a krait,' he said, his face contorted with agony.

'Is it poisonous?'

'It can be.' He swallowed and looked at his hand, where Iris could see an ugly puncture wound.

'Quick, give me a knife,' ordered Guy, holding out his hand, and one of the servants hastily passed one to him.

'Apologies, Spencer,' he said, and made a slash over the bite. 'We need to try and get the poison out.'

'Thank you.' It was obvious that Bertie was in a lot of pain.

Iris watched helplessly as Guy held Bertie's hand downwards to let the blood flow onto the ground.

'Think it's worth sloshing some brandy onto it?' Bertie asked, very stiff upper lip.

'Can't do any harm,' said Guy. 'You'd better drink some as well.'

'Don't mind if I do.'

'We need to get him to a doctor,' Iris said anxiously, when Guy had done what he could with the wound and bandaged it up. 'Can you walk, Bertie?'

'I'll be fine,' he said, mustering a smile. 'Don't worry about me.'

They set off slowly, but it soon became clear that Guy's quick thinking with the knife hadn't been enough to stop the poison spreading through Bertie's system. His steps began to become unsteady, and he doubled over in pain, vomiting into the undergrowth.

'Sorry,' he managed, wiping his mouth with a shaking hand. 'Very bad form.'

'Don't think about that, Bertie,' said Iris. She looked at Guy. 'We need to carry him.'

He nodded. 'I agree. It'll take too long to fix up a stretcher. Come on, old chap,' he said to Bertie. 'Put your arm around my shoulder.'

'Can't see very well,' said Bertie.

One of the other men took the other side, and between them they half carried, half dragged Bertie back to Nuwara Eliya. One of the servants had been sent ahead to warn a doctor, and they went straight to the hospital. By then, it was clear that Bertie was having difficulty swallowing, and his breathing was alarmingly short.

The doctor looked grave when Iris described the snake that she had seen. 'It does sound like a krait. I'm afraid that's bad news.'

'There must be something you can do!'

'The venom is attacking his nervous system. It's making it difficult for him to breathe. All we can do is make him as comfortable as possible and hope for the best.'

Bertie lay on his bed, sweating profusely. Iris wiped his face with a flannel and murmured comfortingly, but she felt so helpless.

Her fingers closed over the opal in her pocket at one point, and guilt swamped her. If she hadn't lost it, if she hadn't insisted on going back for it, Bertie wouldn't be lying there suffering.

He was struggling to breathe. His eyes rolled wildly as he tried to swallow, and his jaw worked convulsively.

'Ma . . . Ma . . . Mama . . .'

Iris took his good hand, realising that he was calling for his mother. 'She's coming,' she told him, hoping it would calm him. 'Cath and Em and Sophia too,' she added, remembering his adoring sisters. She hadn't valued Bertie as she should have done. When she had sent sketches of him home or talked about him in her letters, it had always been as a figure of fun, a little ponderous, a little too eager. She hadn't thought about his intelligence or his sense of duty. The way he supported his family. How much he loved animals. She thought of Jimbo, the dog that had howled when he left home, and she wanted to cover her face and weep.

He thrashed around on the bed, mumbling incoherently.

'Please, Bertie, lie still if you can,' she begged him, her voice breaking.

If only, *if only* she could go back. She would listen, fascinated, to what he had to tell her about the woodpecker or the kingfisher or whatever bird he had been describing, instead of fretting about her own concerns. She would realise the opal had gone when they reached Nuwara Eliya, and perhaps they would still have gone back, but the snake would have slithered away from the stone by then. Bertie wouldn't be lying in bed, fighting for every breath, his face contorted with pain.

Guy Henderson had stayed at the hospital with her. He was unobtrusive in the background, but his presence was obscurely reassuring. Bertie's servant, Dinesh, was there too, red-eyed and shaking. He brought Iris tea that she didn't want, but she drank it as she knew it kept him occupied.

When the doctor came round again, he shook his head. 'There is nothing you can do here, Miss Blackmore.'

'I'm staying with him.' She wouldn't leave Bertie all alone so far from home.

He must have thought that she and Bertie were engaged, for he patted her shoulder before he left. 'I'm very sorry, my dear.'

Ariadne came and held Iris's hand. Others came and went, whispering, and Guy dealt with them all. Iris sat bowed forward, crushed by distress. Bertie, who could be so pompous, who could be a bit of a clot, but who was kind and decent and adored by his mother and sisters and his dog. She hadn't loved him, but she was fond of him, and to watch his agonising struggles was almost more than she could bear.

But she sat on, eyes burning with unshed tears, until night fell. A nurse took his pulse, her face grave. Bertie grew weaker and weaker and his breathing more and more laboured. It was agony just to listen to it, so when it stopped at last, there was a moment of exquisite relief before Iris realised what it meant.

Only a few hours before, Bertie had been plying her with fish paste sandwiches, and now he was dead.

30

Roz

Skara, present day

As the rain appeared to have settled in for the day, Roz abandoned her idea of returning to Rubha Clachan. She wouldn't even be able to see the headland, let alone decipher any letters she might find groping around without electricity.

There were worse places to be stuck on a wet day, she thought, looking around her luxurious hotel room. It was beautifully decorated, warm and comfortable, so she opted to make the most of her short stay at Dundonan and go through the further letters she and Finn had found. Some she had already read, but she had kept getting distracted by the little sketches Iris had included. She would begin by sorting them into date order.

It was very peaceful sitting cross-legged on the carpet while outside the wind howled and tossed rattling gobbets of rain at the window, and Iris's sketches transported her to another world altogether. There was one of a ship steaming into Naples, others of a visit to Pompeii. One of the later sketches was labelled

Colombo, and showed an elegant woman reclining on a veranda, cigarette holder in one hand, a glass in another. And there were more portraits: the same woman, this time captioned *Ariadne*; a portly young man; the captain of the ship, with magnificent whiskers. And a man with lean features and a bitter twist to his mouth. Roz peered more closely at the name Iris had written carefully on the edge. *Guy Henderson.*

Something tingled at the back of her mind. Something about that name. She shook her head in frustration. It was no good. She couldn't think why it might mean anything to her.

There were some charming drawings of Dundonan itself, too. It was obvious that Iris knew it well. Other sketches, lovingly executed, showed a young man in a kilt. There was an unreachable quality to those, though, and Roz couldn't help feeling that they were drawn from memory, unlike the vivid pictures of the other passengers on the ship, which were clearly sketched from real life.

Setting the drawings aside, she unfolded one of the later letters, dated June 1931. 'Nuwara Eliya,' she read out loud. Her knowledge of Sri Lanka was hazy, but she had a feeling the town was in the hill country. What had taken Iris there?

It has been a long day, Iris had written, *but we are in Nuwara Eliya at last and I have hopes of more news of Uncle Ralph soon. What a strange place this is! They say the houses here are mock Tudor, but really they are not like any houses I have ever seen at home. Not that there are many houses in Skara, of course. We are staying in the Hill Club and I am actually cold, for the first time I can remember since I left home. For once I may be cooler than you! I am imagining a long June evening on Skara, and the three of you sitting on the stones without me. It's too early for midges, at least in my imagination, and the sky is suffused with gold . . . Oh, I had better stop or I will get in what Mrs Grierson calls 'a state'.*

Poor Iris, Roz thought. How homesick she had been! Then her gaze sharpened as she caught sight of the word *ring*.

I had a fright this evening when I caught my hand in the bathroom door. I thought for one awful moment that I had broken the ring Mummy gave me, but although my hand is jolly sore, the ring itself seems undamaged. I was so *relieved. I don't think I could have borne it if I had not been able to wear it. It is such a comfort to me, as if I have a bit of Mummy with me wherever I go.*

A knock on the door startled her. Absorbed in the letters and sketches of another life, she had barely noticed the time. Wincing at the stiffness in her legs, she hoisted herself up and opened the door to find Drew Malcolm holding a tray with a pot of tea and some exquisite sandwiches.

'Room service,' he said.

Roz blinked at him, thrown by his sudden appearance. 'I didn't order anything.'

'Douglas said you hadn't been down for anything to eat, so I wondered if you'd like some tea. On the house,' he added with a smile.

'Do you provide free tea and sandwiches for all your guests?'

'We do, in fact, but I can take it away if you'd rather not have it.'

Roz hesitated. She had forgotten about lunch, and now she came to think of it, she was hungry.

'No, that's all right,' she said, opening the door wider and aware that she had been less than gracious. 'Thank you. Something to eat would be welcome.'

Drew carried the tray into the room, raising his brows at the sight of letters and sketches scattered all over the floor and the coffee table that stood between a little sofa and the fireplace. He looked around for somewhere to put the tray and settled on the dressing table, while Roz stood tensely by the door, hoping that he would leave. It wasn't that she didn't like him, but he seemed to take up too much of the room, too much of the oxygen, so that she was left feeling short of breath and edgy and out of control.

And she *hated* feeling like that.

When he showed no sign of leaving, she went over to the tray and poured some tea to give herself something to do.

'What are you doing here?' he asked with interest, squatting down by the coffee table to study some of the sketches. 'Hey, that's here,' he exclaimed, picking up a drawing of Dundonan Castle.

'I know.' Roz took a bite of a sandwich. 'Iris drew lots of pictures of Dundonan as well as Rubha Clachan. I think she must have loved it here.'

'She was a good artist, wasn't she?' Drew looked thoughtfully at a drawing of a garden.

In spite of herself, Roz was drawn to join him by the sketches, still eating her sandwich. 'Her portraits are excellent,' she agreed. 'I'm not sure, but I think she had some kind of relationship with someone at Dundonan. She doesn't talk much about it in her letters, but I've found a few drawings of the same man.'

She finished the sandwich, brushed the crumbs from her hands, and searched through the sketches on the table, pulling out a couple of the man in a kilt. 'Any idea who that might be?'

'What date are we talking?' Drew straightened to consider the picture.

'Around 1930, 1931.'

His mouth pulled down at the corners as he thought. 'It could be my great-grandfather, Ian. There's a portrait of him on the stairs. I'll show you later, if you like.'

'Thank you,' she said. 'I'd love to see it.'

Drew handed back the sketch. 'I'll leave you to your tea. Would you like to have dinner later?'

Roz hesitated. 'Do you invite all your guests for dinner?'

'Only the ones I find interesting,' he said, 'but if you'd rather be alone, that's fine.'

'No,' she said, feeling obscurely wrong-footed once more. 'No, I'd be glad of the company.'

'Good.' He turned for the door. 'We'll have a drink first, shall we? Is six o'clock okay?'

Roz spent more time than she wanted dithering about what to wear that evening. She remembered reading the letter Daisy had sent to Iris, full of advice on what to wear for her first night on board the ship. She wished that *she* had a little sister to tell her how to make it clear that she understood it was only the most casual invitation to dinner, that if she put on a dress instead of jeans, it didn't mean that she cared what Drew thought. Her mother would have been good at that too, she thought with a pang. Millie had always been immaculately groomed, and was disappointed that her daughter had never shown an interest in clothes.

She could have tried harder, Roz thought. Maybe she and Millie could have bonded over shopping trips and long discussions about colour palettes and hemlines. It had been easy to blame Richard for keeping them apart, but if Roz had suggested a shopping trip, her mother might have come. They might have talked. Roz might have known exactly what was happening in her mother's marriage before it was too late.

She sighed. She had no mother and no sister, so she would have to make a decision on her own.

She was furious with herself for changing no fewer than three times before she settled on black trousers and a silvery-grey top. Her dress was gorgeous – but no! She stopped herself sternly. The dress was too much.

In the end, she was glad when Drew knocked and it was too late to change her mind again.

'You look nice,' he said, and when he smiled, her heart did an alarming somersault. 'That top is exactly the colour of your eyes.'

That was the thing about Drew, Roz realised. He might seem carelessly amused, but he noticed. He *saw* her. 'Thank you,' she said, quite easily after all.

'Come and meet my great-grandpapa.' He led her to the ornately carved staircase that descended to the great hall. About halfway down, he stopped and pointed to a traditional oil painting. 'There he is. Ian Malcolm, ninth Laird of Dundonan.'

'He looks sad,' said Roz, studying the portrait. Ian Malcolm had been painted up in the hills, with his hand on a stick and a dog at his feet. 'I know it wasn't the fashion to paint people smiling, but still, look at his eyes.'

'Hmm, I never thought of it like that before. Always thought he looked a miserable old sod.'

'Iris must have known him,' said Roz. 'I think she must have loved him to have drawn him so carefully from memory.' She caught Drew's side-eye and thumped a fist against his arm. 'Don't look at me like that! Why else would she draw him?'

'Don't ask me,' he said, making a big show of rubbing his arm. 'I'm just a bloke. Blokes don't *draw*.'

'I thought you were going to say blokes don't love,' said Roz tartly, and he smiled at her, a slow smile that set her blood fizzing alarmingly.

'No, we know how to love,' he said, holding her eyes, but then he grinned and she rolled her eyes, and all at once the tension broke and she could let out a breath she hadn't known she was holding.

From the dining room, Roz could hear the subdued murmur of voices and the chink and clink of cutlery on china, but the bar was quiet and comfortably furnished with the same bold take on traditional designs that she had noticed in the hall. They sat on stools at the bar, behind which was a whole wall of whisky bottles.

'What would you recommend?' she said, when Drew asked her what she would like to drink.

He smiled and nodded at the wall. 'What about a whisky? When in Rome and all that.'

'All right, I'll try a small one.'

He turned away to consult with the barman, and she took the opportunity to study him under her lashes without those blue eyes on her. He wasn't particularly handsome, but he had such an easy air about him, as if he was comfortable in his own skin the way she never could be. There was just something about the way he leant on the bar, the humorous lift in his voice, the way his mouth curved in a smile . . .

She jerked her eyes away. 'Where's Bonnie?' she asked him a little breathlessly, and she was glad to distract herself by taking a small sip of the whisky he handed her. It burnt and then warmed her throat.

'She's resting after another day of being told that she's beautiful by everyone who meets her,' said Drew, unsuccessfully trying to disguise the affection in his voice.

'Well, she *is* beautiful,' said Roz.

'She's my wife's dog really.'

Roz's heart dipped dismayingly. 'Oh?'

'Ex-wife, I should say,' Drew corrected himself, and Roz was almost equally dismayed at the lift of her spirits. 'Ella was big on looks,' he added. 'She's an interior designer.' He nodded around the bar. "She chose all the fabrics and did all the decorative stuff when we decided to upgrade.'

'She did a good job,' said Roz, following his gaze. 'It's nice that there's nothing twee here. Everything is bold and stylish. I like that.' She took another sip of her whisky. 'Have you always wanted to run a hotel?'

For once, Drew's laugh held little humour. 'Far from it! This was the last thing I ever saw myself doing. I grew up here, but I was sent away to school when I was eight, and then this was just somewhere I came in the holidays. My parents divorced when I was eleven, so a lot of my memories were of arguments and tension. I joined the army straight from university, and for a few years I was happy not to come here at all.'

Army? That explained his straight shoulders and the tough, self-sufficient air, Roz thought.

'It was my grandmother's idea to turn Dundonan into a hotel,'

Drew went on. 'It was that or sell up. She persuaded my father to go along with it, and he did his best, but his heart wasn't really in it and they were struggling to get guests. When he died, my grandmother insisted on carrying on alone, but it was obvious that she couldn't manage by herself, so I resigned my commission and came back to help her.'

He looked down into his glass. 'So no, it wasn't my dream to do this, but Dundonan is my home. I can't just let it go. And the longer I stay, the more I realise that this is where I want to be. So I took some advice and went upmarket. It was a huge investment, but it seems to be paying off at last.'

'I'd say so,' said Roz. 'It's a beautiful place.' She hesitated. 'What happened with you and Ella?' she asked.

'Oh, nothing dramatic. When I first broached the idea of coming here to help Granny, Ella was all for it. She threw herself into the redesign, but once it was done, there was nothing else for her here. She was bored, and I can't blame her. She's a city girl at heart. She didn't grow up here like I did.'

'Do you have kids?'

'Luckily, no. We divorced a couple of years ago now and it was as amicable as these things can be.'

'Sounds like you had a very civilised break-up,' she said.

He lifted his shoulders. 'We did our share of shouting early on, but then it was just dreary. I guess it helped that we didn't have children, but I don't know . . .' He stared broodingly at the whisky bottles. 'You feel such a bloody failure when you can't make it work, don't you?'

Roz didn't say anything. The truth was that she had never really tried to make a relationship work. Seeing her mother with

Richard had taught her a hard lesson. She had no intention of tying herself down with anyone. She wanted to be able to run if she needed to.

'How about you?' Drew asked after a moment, and she took another sip of her whisky before answering.

'Never committed,' she said lightly.

'Why does that not surprise me?'

She sat back, wondering whether to be offended. 'What does that mean?'

'I guess you don't strike me as someone who lets anyone close.'

She was really getting a taste for this whisky, Roz reflected, taking a bigger mouthful this time. 'No, well, I've found it easier that way,' she said.

Drew leant forward. 'You know what they taught us in the army? The easy way is for cowards. And you don't strike me as a coward, Roz Chatton.'

She swallowed, her eyes sliding away from his. 'Maybe I am,' she said, but he shook his head slowly.

'Nope,' he said. 'You're tough, but you're not a coward. You just need to be sure that it's worth letting go.'

'How can you ever be sure of that?' Roz asked her whisky. She couldn't look at Drew, but she felt his smile warming her skin.

'I guess you won't know until you try,' he said.

31
Finn

Glenussie, present day

'Why don't you go and lie down, Mum?' Finn chivvied his mother towards the bedroom.

'Oh, but your father... I don't want to leave him.' Her hands fluttered indecisively.

'He's sleeping. I'll keep an eye on him.'

Once he had persuaded his exhausted mother to rest, Finn put his head round the door of his father's room. Donald Drummond was asleep, or pretending to be. With the sheet drawn up under his chin, he looked old and vulnerable, and Finn felt a surge of pity. His father had always been a big man in every way, dominating the family until a series of health scares had made him shrink steadily. Being diagnosed with a panic attack once had humiliated him, and he refused to believe the doctors now.

When Finn had seen his father in hospital, Donald had been querulous and snappy. He was frightened, Finn understood that. This time he'd been told that he'd had a small stroke. 'All very manageable,' the doctor had said breezily. 'You've been lucky, Mr Drummond.'

'Lucky?' Donald spat. 'What's lucky about having a stroke? I'll have your mother fussing over me all the time. I won't be able to drive. I won't be able to do anything.'

'It'll take you a while to get back on your feet,' Finn started to say, but his father overrode him.

'What would you know about it? What are you doing here anyway?'

'I'm trying to help.'

'You can't help.' Donald turned his face away. 'No one can.'

'Should I ask Angus to come up?' Finn had tried, but his father fired up immediately.

'Don't you go bothering Angus. He's got more important things to think about.'

Now, closing the door quietly, Finn went along to the kitchen, unchanged since he was a boy. He sat at the table with the faded cherry oilcloth and called his brother.

'They're going to need more help around the house,' he said.

'Yup.' Angus was clearly busy. Finn imagined him scribbling notes on some document, beckoning to an underling with his other hand, gesturing for more coffee, all while talking on the phone. 'Yup, yup.'

Finn set his teeth. When he moved to London, Angus had adopted all the mannerisms of a traditional Englishman. He bought his shirts at Turnbull & Asser, his suits in Savile Row. His shoes were hand-crafted, and his wines came from Berry Bros. & Rudd. Finn had nothing against the English, but he couldn't understand why his brother had buffed away his Highland accent to cut glass, keeping only a soft remnant, which he used whenever it suited him but not otherwise.

'Can't you sort something out?' Angus said. 'Get on to social services or whatever you think. You're on the spot, after all.'

'Hardly,' said Finn in a dry voice. 'Edinburgh's a good four-hour drive from Glenussie.'

'Yes, well, you're there now, aren't you?'

Only because he had taken time off work, much to James Kingan's displeasure. But Finn's job was not important, not compared to Angus's.

There was a fourteen-year gap between Finn and his older brother. Angus was the golden only child until Finn came along, and Finn had always understood that his own existence was considered a mistake. His parents had thrown everything into caring for their firstborn and had no energy left for another child. Angus was sent away to school in Edinburgh. Clever and ambitious, he had studied law at Oxford before being head-hunted by a top law firm.

Finn was an also-ran. He worked hard for his parents' approval, but he could never measure up to Angus.

Sighing, he ended the call. He would call social services in the morning. Of course he could stand his ground and insist his brother did his share, as Aileen was always urging him, but if Finn didn't do it, it wouldn't get done. As Angus well knew.

Glum, he sent Roz a message.

Sorry. Still here. Won't be able to get back to Skara for a while.

A few minutes later, Roz rang him back. When the phone buzzed, Finn jumped. It reminded him of being with her at Rubha Clachan, and how his mother's call had startled them both. He remembered the smile in Roz's eyes, the scent of her shampoo when she had hugged him goodbye.

'Is everything okay?' he asked, concerned by her call.

'Yes, I'm fine.' The Australian accent was more obvious over the phone. 'I just wanted to tell you not to worry. I've got a job, and somewhere to stay!'

'A *job?*'

'It turns out that Dundonan is short of a couple of servers. Drew says the hotel is so remote they struggle to keep staff, even though they get decent quarters and their own bar and facilities. I was a waitress in London, so I'm working in the restaurant now. Drew says I can have one of the staff rooms in the old stables, and I can stay as long as I want.'

Drew says. Finn made a face at the phone. Drew, who would get to see Roz every day.

With an effort, he summoned some enthusiasm. 'That's great.'

'Isn't it?' said Roz happily. 'I haven't forgotten the Blackmore Trust, though. I've sorted the letters out and read through them all. Iris is still in Ceylon and can't find her uncle, but I'm going back to Rubha Clachan after my lunch shift tomorrow and I'll keep looking through the study. I'm sure there must be more letters to find. It won't be as much fun without you,' she added, and the smile in her voice warmed him. 'I wish you could be here.'

'I wish I could be there too,' said Finn wistfully. 'Are you sure you'll be okay on your own?' *Please tell me Drew isn't going with you,* was what he meant.

'I'll be fine,' said Roz, and he had to be content with that.

32

Roz

Skara, present day

Roz pushed open the door to Rubha Clachan and stepped into the silent house. She stood for a moment in the hall, head cocked, certain that she could catch ghostly echoes of girlish laughter, the sound of light footsteps on the broken stairs, the slam of a door in sudden temper.

In spite of her bravado, she missed Finn's undemanding company. It wasn't that she was *scared*, of course, but the compulsion to get to the house was disquieting. Roz didn't like being out of control. She had guarded herself for so long that feeling as if something outside her was pushing her to Rubha Clachan made her uneasy.

And yet it had been her choice, surely, to come to Skara. Her decision to look for Iris's letters. Nobody was *making* her do anything.

It wasn't frightening, she decided. If anything, the echoes of the lost Blackmore girls were keeping her company, but she was conscious of a sense of anticipation, as if the house was waiting for her to do something, realise something.

'But what?' she said aloud, frustrated rather than alarmed, as she stood at the drawing room window, turning the ring on her finger. It was a bright, blowy day. Great billowing clouds sailed majestically across the sky, sending scudding shadows over the mountains as they blotted out the sun.

She was trying to imagine what the view would be like if the stones were still standing. What had Charles Blackmore been thinking? He could so easily have built the house a few yards over and avoided the curse, and then maybe his daughters would have been able to stay safe at home.

If you believed in such things. Which Roz didn't.

She didn't think so, anyway.

The ring on her finger hummed.

In the study, the light was much better than when she had been there with Finn. It poured in through the big windows, highlighting a century of dirt and neglect with cruel clarity. Roz paused in the doorway, momentarily daunted by the task ahead of her, which seemed greater on her own, but then she squared her shoulders and stepped into the room. She would carry on with the cupboard Finn had started to empty. There were so many papers and books in there, all jumbled up. She needed to be methodical about it if she was going to find anything.

She dug out piles of papers and blew the dust off them as best she could, then sat on the floor to look through them. Most she set aside for Finn to see in case they were relevant to the estate, but she was rewarded at last by finding another envelope of letters from Iris.

Unable to resist having a quick look, she was soon absorbed in the letters.

My dearest sisters, Iris had written. *I write with the heaviest of hearts. A good man is dead, and I cannot shake the feeling that it is all my fault. If I had not damaged Mummy's ring, if I had been more careful with it when I knew the stone was loose, if I had not been so shocked by what Guy Henderson had told me about Uncle Ralph . . . if, if, if! There is no end to the 'if onlys' and I am numb with grief and guilt. I cannot stop imagining poor Bertie's beloved sisters hearing of his death, and how I would feel in those circumstances. Guy tells me there is no use blaming myself, but how can I not?*

Roz's opal ring caught her eye as folded the letter and put it back in the envelope. Was this the same opal that Bertie had found for Iris? The same opal that had killed him? Finn might warn about definitive proof, but she was sure in her heart that it was the same ring and her throat ached for the young man who had tried so hard to please Iris and who had saved the opal that Roz now wore.

She was pulling out another envelope when Bonnie bustled in to stick a cold nose in her face, and she yelped in shock.

Drew followed the dog in, and the air instantly tightened.

It had been a nice evening. Drew was good company, and there was no denying the zing in the air between them. He hadn't pushed it, sensing perhaps that Roz would back off if he did. When he said goodnight, he just lifted a casual hand in farewell and said that he would see her tomorrow. Roz told herself that she was relieved he hadn't tried to kiss her.

No, she *was* relieved. Definitely.

He was wrong about her not being a coward. She *was* a coward, she knew. She was afraid of letting herself go. Afraid to get in too deep. Afraid of caring too much in case she got hurt, and that dragon sleeping inside her woke and flexed its claws.

Drew was an attractive guy, there was no doubt about it. He seemed funny and warm and kind. The trouble for Roz was that he was too attractive. Too funny. Too warm and kind. She could feel herself teetering on the edge of a chasm. It would be so easy to fall for him, and perhaps it would be thrilling, but she couldn't afford to take that risk, to tumble over and hope that all would be well. Safer by far to step back and think of him as just a friend.

So when he appeared, she ignored the way her heart stuttered and kept her voice casual. 'What are you doing here?' she asked. 'I thought you were terrified of Rubha Clachan?'

Over dinner, he had made her laugh with the story of how he had been dared to go into the house after dark, only to bolt home in fear. 'But I was only eleven,' he had excused himself.

'I am,' he said now. 'But I've got Bonnie and you to protect me.' He held up a thermos. 'I brought you some coffee and a sandwich. I thought you might have forgotten about lunch.'

'I did.' Oh yes, it would be so easy to fall for him. Friends, Roz told herself firmly. Keep it casual. 'And I was just thinking that I'd kill for a coffee.'

'Well, there's no need to go that far.' He held out a hand to help Roz to her feet. His palm was warm against hers.

'You're very good to your staff,' she said lightly, pulling her hand away, trying to ignore the tingling where her skin had touched his.

'Aren't I?' he said, equally light. 'But I do have a favour to ask.'
'What?'

'Let's have coffee outside and I'll tell you.'

Roz quirked an eyebrow at him. 'I thought you weren't scared?'

'Rule one in Scotland: never waste the sunshine,' he said with a virtuous air.

They sat on the fallen stones, and the ring settled to a silent hum of satisfaction. Drew poured her coffee and offered a sandwich. 'Smoked salmon, poached chicken and tarragon mayonnaise, or avocado, hummus and broad bean?'

'Wow,' said Roz. 'I was expecting cheese and pickle!'

'The advantage of having a Michelin-starred chef on the premises.'

'It's delicious,' she said, taking a bite of the avocado sandwich. 'I hadn't realised how hungry I was,' she added with her mouth full.

It might have been delicious, but it was a messy sandwich to eat. Broad beans and bits of avocado kept falling out. Roz touched the side of her mouth with her finger. She was very aware of Drew beside her, eating his own sandwich with his usual economy of movement, and annoyed with herself for noticing his hand around the thermos, the firm line of his jaw as he chewed.

When he had mentioned over dinner that he needed staff, she had leapt at the idea. There had been an awkward moment when he had started to talk about wages, and she had insisted on not being paid at all. 'I'll work for the room,' she said. 'I don't want any more than that.'

Drew had been puzzled but had eventually agreed. Roz knew that she should have told him why she didn't want to appear on any system, but she was reluctant to talk about Richard just when everything else seemed to be falling into place. The knowledge that he was free simmered always at the back of her mind, a low-level throb of fear. Her solicitor had warned her that the appeal would take some time.

Roz would feel better if Richard was back in prison, but for now she felt safe in Skara. 'How can he find me here?' she had asked Hugo when she rang him to tell him that she had a comfortable room in the stable block and could stay in Skara as long as she liked.

'So what's the favour?' she asked Drew.

'My grandmother is very keen to meet you.'

'Me?' Roz looked at him in astonishment. 'Why?'

'Come on, Acheravie's a small community. Mysterious Australian turns up, determined to poke around a haunted house... *of course* she wants to meet you.'

Roz laughed uncomfortably. 'I'm not mysterious.'

'Aren't you?' Drew's eyes rested on her face. 'You seem like someone with secrets.'

'Not secrets exactly,' she admitted after a moment. 'Just things I'd rather forget.'

'Ah, well, we've all got those.' He got to his feet. 'I'll leave you to get on,' he said, as he packed away the remains of the sandwiches and tucked the flask under his arm. Bonnie danced around him, eager for the next adventure. 'Unless you'd like a lift back?'

'I might see if can find any more letters, but thanks,' said Roz, remembering how aware she had been of him in the Land Rover. 'Can I walk back along the beach? It looks a lot shorter than using the road.'

'Be careful,' he said. 'The tide comes in quicker than you

think, and it can bring a sea fret with it. All that land between here and Dundonan is bog, so even if the mist holds off, if the sea's in, you'll struggle to get across it.'

Re-energised by her lunch, Roz set about emptying another cupboard, and crowed with pleasure when she unearthed some old photograph albums bound in musty brown leather. She couldn't wait to tell Finn about them!

Opening one very carefully, she peered at the photographs. They were fixed into the pages with special corners and were so small that it was difficult to see much detail. She eased out a family group so that she could look at it more closely. It showed the Blackmores standing in front of Rubha Clachan, and when she turned it over she saw the date: 1928.

Before the Great Depression. Before everything went wrong.

Charles Blackmore was easily identifiable, his chest thrust proudly forward. Beside him stood his wife, Amelia, her face half hidden by a cloche hat, and on his other side, her hands behind her back but leaning affectionately towards him, was a girl with a bright smile.

Iris? Roz wondered, studying the four girls. But no, that was Rose, she thought. Iris was obviously the eldest. She had a sweet expression and stood by her mother, one hand on the shoulder of a younger girl with a sharp, clever face. That must be Lily, Roz decided, and the youngest was Daisy, right at the front, smiling directly to the camera as if she already knew how much it was going to love her.

Roz put the photo back between its corners, feeling sad. They looked like a close family. You could tell by the way they leant towards each other, as if bound by an invisible thread.

A thread that had snapped.

Slowly Roz turned the pages, poring over the photos of the sisters, preserved for ever young in celluloid. The longer she looked, the less she noticed that the photos were all in black and white, and she imagined the girls instead in full colour, not frozen for one moment in time but relaxing after the camera had clicked, shading their eyes from the sun or calling out to the photographer or sticking out a tongue behind their mother's back, turning away from the camera to dance away out of the shot.

She spent so long over the photos that she forgot the time, and when she did glance at her phone, she saw with an exclamation that it was getting late. How could she not have realised? The clouds had clustered together, blotting out the light and lowering threateningly over the hills.

She would go back to Dundonan the short way, Roz decided, packing up the albums and the letters and putting them carefully into her backpack. She eyed the beach, remembering Drew's warning about the tide, but it seemed safe enough. There was still plenty of sand.

At the top of the path to the beach, she hesitated, reluctant in a way she couldn't explain to go further. It was almost as if the house didn't want her to leave.

She had to almost force herself down onto the sand. This was the beach that Iris had walked on so often. Roz had read so many of her letters that she almost felt as if she knew Iris now. She felt her homesickness, and her distress at Bertie's death, and her desperation to keep her sisters together. It made for sad reading when she knew that none of them had ever come home.

Lost in thought, it took her a while to realise that the tide was rushing inexorably in, bringing with it a mist and a fine mizzle. As the sand disappeared under water, she found herself edging further and further towards the rocks.

She looked at the tufty grass behind the rocks. Surely it would be safer to walk up there? The last thing she wanted was to get the albums and letters wet. She clambered carefully over the rocks and up onto the grass, but soon discovered why Drew had warned her about it. There were boggy pools of water between the clumps, and she had to jump from one to the next. Inevitably she stumbled into water, and in her struggle to stay upright, she didn't notice at first that the mist had thickened around her.

Her ring was throbbing. She stopped to catch her breath, disorientated. Where was she? She couldn't have got lost so close to the shore, surely? She strained to hear the sea, but the mist muffled all sound.

Wait, were those *screams* she could hear? She stood very still, her pulse thudding in her ears. There was sobbing too, and scuffling. A murmur of reassurance. A slap. A cry. The noises were so faint that Roz couldn't be sure she wasn't imagining them, and yet so real.

The four sisters for whom the stones had been raised, being dragged from their home.

She could *feel* them in the mist, feel their despair and their defiance as they were dragged, stumbling, down to the beach, the deer sinew cords rubbing painfully against their wrists.

Roz's mouth was dry. She couldn't move, could only stand there, her heart banging against her ribs, but when Bonnie bounded out of the mist without warning, she screamed in fright.

'Bonnie! Oh, thank God!' She was so grateful to see the dog that she bent and hugged her. 'Where's Drew, Bonnie?'

The next moment, she heard his voice calling. 'She's here!' she yelled back. 'I'm here!'

'Follow Bonnie,' he shouted.

The dog bounded easily from clump to clump, but kept coming back to check that Roz was following.

'Good girl,' said Roz, almost sobbing with tiredness. 'Good dog.'

Quite suddenly the mist cleared and she staggered out of it to see Drew standing by his car, Bonnie barking and bouncing proudly around him. Bedraggled, filthy and exhausted, Roz didn't even think. She stumbled towards him and clutched at his old waxed jacket, too relieved to be out of the mist to remember that she barely knew him, knowing only that he was real and solid and that when his arms went around her, she felt safe at last.

She clung to him for a moment before she made herself let go. 'Sorry,' she said awkwardly.

For once the blue eyes were serious as Drew looked at her. 'You okay?'

'Yes.' She was beginning to shiver with reaction. 'Just wet and ... I was frightened.' She couldn't tell him about her conviction that the four sisters of the legend had stumbled past her on the beach. 'The mist came down so quickly.'

'I know.' Drew frowned. 'I've never seen it do it quite like that before.'

Already it was dispersing into insubstantial rags. Roz could see the beach again in the distance.

'How did I get *here*?'

'It's disorientating when the mist drops like that. I was worried when you didn't come back, so I went to Rubha Clachan to see if you wanted a lift. You'd gone by then, though, and I saw the mist come down, so I stopped here and Bonnie just took off. She must have sensed you.'

'You're the cleverest dog in the world,' Roz told Bonnie, patting her affectionately. 'I was *so* glad to see you.' She looked up at Drew. 'I'll use the track next time.'

'Is there going to be a next time?' he asked, opening the passenger door for her.

'Yes.' Roz climbed wearily into the car. 'There has to be. I need to know what happened to Iris,' she said, and the ring on her hand warmed approvingly.

33

Iris

Nuwara Eliya, June 1931

Bertie's funeral was held two days later. 'In this climate …' Ariadne explained with a grimace.

Lord Carsington came up from Colombo to read the eulogy. He talked about Bertie's career, but it meant little to Iris. The Bertie she had known was clumsy and generous and eager, dogged rather than brilliant perhaps. She preferred to remember how he had flung himself into the games on board ship. He had been a terrible dancer, but he had loved his sisters. He liked dogs, and birds, and picnics.

She sat in the church next to Ariadne, numb still. Listening to the English people around her, singing English hymns, their voices floating out over Lake Gregory, the strangeness of it hit her. Outside lay the rainforest, the lush hills, the peeping, whistling, screeching birds, the thrumming insects, but inside they might have been in any parish church at home. Bertie's father had been a clergyman, she knew. This would all have been so familiar to him.

Iris watched as Bertie was lowered into a grave thousands of miles from his home and she thought she would shatter with sadness.

'We should go back to Colombo with Johnny,' Ariadne said as they walked into the Hill Club after the service. Iris agreed, because she couldn't think what else to do.

'What about you, Guy?' Ariadne said. 'Do you want a lift?'

'Thank you, but I'm going to go and see Markham tomorrow.'

Iris looked at him angrily. 'How can you think about your vendetta now?'

'It's not a vendetta.' Guy set his jaw, clearly keeping his temper with an effort. 'I just want what I'm owed. That hasn't changed. What are *you* going to do?' he sneered. 'Sit around and blame yourself for Bertie's death? How will *that* help your sisters?'

'That's enough, Guy,' said Ariadne sharply, seeing how Iris flinched at every question.

Guy blew out a breath and dragged a hand through his hair. 'Sorry, we're all on edge. Look, I'll talk to Markham and I'll let you know what he says. How about that?'

Iris sighed. 'I'm sorry too,' she said, adding as he turned to go, 'Thank you.'

It was a sober drive back to Colombo. Iris stared out of the car window at the mist drifting between the hills, at the brilliantly coloured saris among the tea bushes, at the elephants lumbering along the road, but she could find no beauty in any of it. A downpour left the glossy vegetation laden with huge drops of rainwater that dripped slowly from the leaves and the ground faintly steaming in the heat. The road wound its way down through an impenetrable wall of green. Iris imagined the forest teeming with wild animals, with monkeys and shrilling insects and slithering snakes, full of sudden shrieks and unexplained rustlings, and she shuddered at the idea of the eyes that might be watching them, alien intruders in their motor car.

How she longed for the open hills of Skara! For clean, fresh air that wasn't clogged with heat and spice and the heavy fragrance of jasmine and wild orchids.

Her hand kept going to the finger where she always wore her mother's ring, only to fall back into her lap. She had taken it off until she could get the blue opal reset, and it was strange not to have it to worry at. Part of her missed it, part of her hated it now. It had cost Bertie his life. She wanted to throw it out of the window.

She could almost hear Guy Henderson's reaction if she told him that. *It's not the ring's fault*, she imagined him saying in his harsh way. *Don't be hysterical. You can't throw away a perfectly good ring because of an accident.*

Besides, she loved the ring, Iris reminded herself. It had been her mother's, and she had promised Amelia that she would wear it always.

A letter from Rose was waiting for her when they got back to the residence at last. She snatched it up from the tray and took it to her bedroom to read.

Darling Iris, I must be quick as everything is happening very fast. Aunt Edith came back yesterday. Things are very difficult here and I am afraid to say that Papa has become violent. Yesterday he smashed up the sitting room because he could not find anything to drink. Iris, I am afraid. I don't want to think he would hurt Lily or Daisy, but it is as if he is possessed by some demon. He is not himself and they are not safe right now.

The three of us have talked about it, and for now we cannot see an alternative to the refuges Aunt Edith has found for us. So Lily and Daisy will go to Aunt Edith's until Aunt Bessy arrives and takes them to America. I hate the thought of them being so far away, but Lily will keep an eye on Daisy, and you know what Daisy is like: she will be on the silver screen before we can get her home!

As for me, Aunt Edith has (rather grudgingly) offered me a home in Edinburgh. I have not yet told her that I have made my own plans. She doesn't approve of Papa's family, but I am going to try and find Uncle Percy in Egypt. I am sure that he will help us if Uncle Ralph cannot, for Mummy's sake if not for Papa's. We have not given up on you and we talk about you and miss you so much. We will all keep in touch, and as soon as you have found Uncle Ralph and he has repaid the money Mummy gave him, the four of us can be together again.

Aghast, Iris dropped the letter in her lap and covered her face with her hands. This was the news she had been dreading. She couldn't blame Rose, but oh! to think of Lily and Daisy being sent to live so far away, with an aunt they barely knew! They were brave girls, her sisters, and they would be putting a brave face on it for each other, but they must be scared. And as for Rose, setting out for Egypt on her own ... How would she get there? It was too dangerous! She must send a telegram telling her not to think about it.

She jumped up in agitation, but when she looked again at the date on Rose's letter, she realised that she was too late. They had probably already left Skara. If only they could have stayed together! This was all her fault! She should never have left her sisters alone, she berated herself.

As she paced the room, Guy Henderson's unwelcome voice snuck into her mind.

What are you going to do? Sit around and blame yourself for Bertie's death? How will that help your sisters?'

He was beastly to be so abrupt with her. But at least the thought of him had the effect of making her drop into a chair and think more calmly.

Her sisters were making the best of it, and so would she. She needed to find her uncle more urgently than ever. She should have gone with Guy to see Mr Markham instead of heading numbly back to Colombo. Now she would have to wait for him to bring her any news, but once he did, she would go with him to find Ralph. She would demand her uncle repay his debt, and then she would gather her sisters from around the world and they could all go home.

But what was home like now? She reread the letter and her face twisted with distress at the news that her once-adored father was reduced to violence. She remembered him as he had looked when she left, slumped dishevelled in his chair, peering up at her bleary-eyed, the reek of whisky and despair hanging around him. Her wonderful, boisterous, loving Papa. Where had it all gone wrong? Had it been the stock-market crash? The court case over a patent? Her mother falling ill? Or did it go further back, to Charles's decision to take down the stones that had stood on the headland at Rubha Clachan since time immemorial.

He threw down the stones. He'll pay for that.

Iris shivered, remembering the legend of the four sisters snatched from their home on Skara, dragged across the beach and shoved into boats by men with wild hair and cruel eyes and bitter mouths. Swallowed up by the mist. No one knew where they had gone or what had befallen them.

And now it seemed that she and her sisters were to be scattered just as the curse had foretold.

But in their case, it would not be for ever, she vowed. Yes, they would be in different countries for now, but they were not *lost*. Rose knew where they were. Iris would find Ralph, and then she would find her sisters, and she would take them home.

At least she could do that, unlike poor Bertie, who could never go home.

She had written to Bertie's mother and sisters, telling them what had happened. She told them how much Bertie had loved them all, and that his last thoughts had been of them. Would they be glad that she had been with him at the end, or would they blame her as she blamed herself, whatever Guy Henderson said?

For once she was eager to see Guy again, but he didn't come.

In Colombo, the heat was suffocating. Social life closed seamlessly over the news of Bertie's death. There were dances at the club, cocktails on the veranda, excursions to the beach.

'Darling, one can't sit around and mope,' said Ariadne, when Iris expressed reluctance. 'It's terribly sad, but life goes on. I learnt that when Freddie died.'

So Iris put on her tennis dress and played doubles matches at the club. She put on her afternoon tea dress for curry lunches and her old evening gown to accompany Ariadne to drinks parties. She put on her bathing costume for a picnic at Mount Lavinia. She swam in the sea and sat in the fringed shade of the coconut palms, digging her toes into the white sand while she wondered what was keeping Guy. What if he had found Markham and had gone in search of Uncle Ralph by himself?

'He won't do that,' said Ariadne.

'Then why hasn't he come back?' Iris fretted. 'Should I go and find Mr Markham myself after all?' She hated the thought of going back to Nuwara Eliya, where the flowers would already be wilting on Bertie's grave, but she would do it if she had to.

'There's no point in you haring off on your own,' said Ariadne firmly. 'What you need is a distraction. Let's go shopping.'

Shopping was the last thing Iris wanted to do, but she agreed to take her mother's ring to be repaired.

The first jeweller they visited took the ring and the opal to inspect, but then his face closed and he pushed them abruptly back over the counter.

'No, I cannot do this.'

'Why? It's a simple job, surely?'

But he turned away. 'No good,' he said.

Iris met with a similar response at the other jewellers she tried. Their welcoming smiles vanished when they held the stone in their hands. They shook their heads or made a sign to ward off evil.

'Bad ring,' said one simply.

'Oh, this is ridiculous!' said Ariadne. 'We'll try one more, and if he won't do it, I'll glue that wretched opal back into the ring myself.'

Iris watched as the next jeweller examined the ring and the opal in disquieting detail. Eventually he lifted dark, avaricious eyes to her face. 'I can fix this, but . . .' he tilted his head from side to side, 'it will be very expensive.'

'I'll pay for it,' Ariadne said, overriding Iris's attempts to protest. 'I'm bored of this.' She turned to the jeweller. 'Do whatever is needed and send word to Lord Carsington's residence when it's ready.'

'Strange, isn't it?' Iris said uneasily as they left him bowing. 'It's as if they're all frightened of the ring.'

'The Sinhalese are a superstitious lot.' Ariadne waved a dismissive hand. 'Don't think of it. Now, let's go to Chatham Street and buy some lovely fabric. We could both do with a new frock.'

34

Iris

Guy Henderson was waiting on the veranda when they got back from the city. He had been lounging on one of the planter's chairs, but he got to his feet when he saw them.

'Oh, you're back!' Iris hurried up the wooden steps towards him, but when he raised a brow, clearly surprised at the welcome on her face, she stopped, flustered. 'Where have you been?'

'Iris! Darling! Give the man a chance to sit down. Let's go inside, it's too hot to be out here.' Ariadne swept them into the cool interior and clapped her hands for her butler, who appeared noiselessly. She ordered a beer for Guy, lime juice for Iris and a gimlet for herself. 'I imagine this is going to be a long story,' she said, 'and I, for one, am gasping for a drink.'

Iris perched on the edge of her seat, desperate to hear news of Ralph, but to her irritation, Guy took his time, chatting to Ariadne about the train journey. How did he always look so cool in this heat? Her frock was sticking to her spine, and her skin felt clammy in spite of the ceiling fan whirring overhead. Surreptitiously she wiped the perspiration from her upper lip.

'So where *have* you been?' Ariadne asked at last, when the drinks had arrived and Guy had taken his beer with a nod of thanks to the bearer.

'Markham wasn't there when I arrived,' he explained. 'I had to hang around for another week before he came back, and in the meantime I asked around at the local club to see if anyone else there remembered Ralph Davidson.' He took a drink of his beer while Iris held her icy glass to her forehead to try to cool herself down.

'And?'

'I talked eventually to a man called Fothergill.'

'Did he remember Uncle Ralph?'

Guy permitted himself a sardonic smile. 'He certainly did. His wife apparently made a fool of herself with Davidson. Your uncle bought a tea plantation, above Trincomalee, but he fell out with the manager and decided to run it himself. Unfortunately, in Fothergill's words, he didn't know a damn thing about tea. Although he may have expressed himself more colourfully than that,' he added, with a wry look.

'Then one day, about three years ago, he just upped and disappeared, leaving countless debts behind him. Including his bar bill, which Fothergill was particularly aggrieved about as he was club secretary at the time. It turned out that he had sold his tea plantation for a vastly inflated price to Markham, who Fothergill describes as "a credulous Welshman" who knew even less about tea than Ralph did – which according to Fothergill was saying something.'

'He didn't know where Ralph went?' Iris asked.

Guy shook his head. 'No, I'm afraid not. So then I had to wait to get hold of Markham, who is nearly as elusive as your uncle and not the most sociable of chaps. He was very bitter about the state Ralph left the plantation in, but after listening to him rant for a while, I asked if he knew anything about where Ralph had gone. According to Markham, Ralph told him that he was bored with tea and had a new plan in mind, so he was leaving Ceylon.'

'Did he say where he was going?'

'He did.'

'Where?'

'You're not going to like this,' Guy warned

Iris pressed a hand to her throat. 'He's not dead?'

'Worse than that. He's in Australia.'

There was a moment of silence.

'Australia,' Iris repeated expressionlessly.

'He talked about a cattle station in Queensland, but he took a ship to Adelaide in the first instance.'

It was so unlike Iris to feel real anger that it took her a moment to recognise it for what it was. 'Could he not have found somewhere further away?' she demanded bitterly. How could her mother have loved and supported her feckless brother for so long? What use was Ralph to her in Australia? 'We'll never find him now.' She felt close to tears.

'I'm certainly not giving up,' said Guy. 'There's a ship leaving for Melbourne via Adelaide next week. I plan to be on it.' He looked straight at Iris. 'Do you want to come with me?'

Iris didn't want to go to Australia. She wanted to go home. But she couldn't go back empty-handed. Her sisters were depending on her. She would have to do *something*.

'How long will it take, do you think?'

Guy lifted his shoulders. 'A couple of weeks on the ship. Then we'd have to find him – but there can't be that many crooked Scots masquerading as upper-class Englishmen in the outback. He shouldn't be hard to track down if we pool our resources.'

She turned the glass between her hands, chewing the inside of her cheek while she thought.

'I've very little money left,' she confessed at last.

'I can pay for your passage. You've got other resources. You're Ralph's niece, which means people will be more likely to give you information.'

Iris lifted her eyes to his. 'So we go to Australia?'

'That's where he is. He owes us both, don't you think?'

'Now just a minute,' Ariadne put in. 'I know I'm not the most conventional woman, but Iris, you're only twenty! You can't just go off to Australia with Guy! You'd ruin your reputation.'

'Oh, what does that matter?' Iris said impatiently. 'I need to find my uncle and then get back to my sisters, and if that means going to Australia, that's what I'm going to have to do.'

'What do you think your mother would say about it?' Ariadne challenged her.

Iris sighed. 'Very well, I'll see if I can find another position as a companion on the journey,' she said.

'That's going to take too long,' said Guy. 'And what happens when you get to Australia? Where are you going to find a chaperone in the outback?'

'Have you got a better idea?' she snapped.

'I do,' he said. 'Let's get married.'

Iris laughed sarcastically. 'Yes, let's. What a super idea!'

'I think so.'

'I'm not being serious!'

'I am.'

There was a pause. 'Don't be ridiculous, Guy,' said Ariadne after a moment. 'You can't just get married like that.'

'We've got a week. We could get a special licence if necessary. Lord Carsington would help us with that, surely?'

Ariadne put down her glass. 'You *are* serious!'

'Why wouldn't I be?' Guy sounded exasperated. 'Look, I can see there are problems about Iris and me travelling together, but we both need to get to Australia and this seems to be the most straightforward way around the problem. Nobody can object to her travelling with me as my wife.'

Iris found her voice again. 'But you don't want to get married,' she said.

'When did I say that?'

She stared at him, puzzled, unable to read his expression.

'Look, I know you don't love me,' he said more gently. 'I know you don't want to marry anyone, unless it's whoever broke your heart back in Scotland.'

'I never told you about . . . about that!'

'You told Bertie,' he reminded her.

'You were eavesdropping!'

'I was,' he agreed equably.

He had listened to her conversation, and then he had kissed her.

Iris hated the fact that she could still remember how that had felt. The delicious, dangerous jolt of response. The warmth of his mouth. The strength of his hands.

She looked away.

'Ian's married now,' she said in a stifled voice. 'That's over.'

There was a pause. She could feel Guy's eyes on her face, but she couldn't look at him.

'I'm not asking you to love me, Iris,' he said at last. 'I know you can't do that. I'm asking you to marry me so that we can find Ralph Davidson. It could be a purely practical arrangement. We wouldn't be the first people to marry for convenience. And if you really can't bear to be married to me, we can always divorce once we've got our money back.'

Instinctively Iris reached for her ring, but she had to be content with fingering her knuckle. 'We're strangers,' was all she could think of to say.

'Are we? I know you.'

She bridled. 'I doubt that very much.'

'I know you're an artist. I know that you're kind. I know you hate saying no to people. You feel responsible for things that are not your fault. I know you're desperately homesick for Scotland. And that you have no idea how lovely you are.' He smiled crookedly. 'I know that when you're worried, you twist your mother's ring around your finger,' he went on, 'and that when you smile, which isn't as often as you should, a little dimple appears right there ...'

His finger barely grazed her cheek and Iris stepped back as if burnt.

'I know enough about you to marry you,' he said softly.

'Perhaps I should have said: I don't know anything about *you*.' Her voice sounded thin and breathless.

But was that true? Iris thought about Guy as a boy, hearing the news of his father's death. About his grim determination to track down the man who had destroyed his family. About the unexpected thoughtfulness in Nuwara Eliya. He was sardonic and impatient and he made her feel edgy. She wasn't sure that she liked him, but the fact was that she trusted him.

And she could have drawn his features in her sleep.

He reached for her hands. He turned them over and studied them before lifting his eyes to her face. 'You know the important things about me, Iris,' he said. 'I think you know enough about me to marry me.'

There was another long silence. Iris could hear her heart thud, thud, thudding in her ears. She could smell the frangipani blossoms that Kasun had laid in a bowl of water to scent the room. Guy's fingers tightened around hers, warm and strong, and his eyes held an expression she couldn't identify but that made the air leak out of her lungs.

'Can I think about it?' she asked with difficulty.

He dropped her hands, and she had the oddest feeling that he was disappointed.

'Yes, you can think about it,' he said, 'but don't think too long. The ship sails next Thursday, and I mean to be on it, with or without you.'

When he had gone, Iris looked at Ariadne. 'I don't know what to do,' she said helplessly.

'If you can't marry the man you love, you might as well marry Guy,' said Ariadne practically. 'At least you'll know what you're getting. You know more about each other than some people do when they get married. And Guy wants you, that's obvious.'

'To get to my uncle.'

'No, he wants *you*. You can tell by the way he looks at you. I can't believe you haven't noticed.'

Iris swallowed. 'He doesn't love me.'

'Oh, love...' said Ariadne dismissively. 'How many marriages do you think are love matches?'

'Ian and I loved each other.' In spite of herself, Iris's voice cracked. 'We would have been happy together.'

'My dear, I do understand,' Ariadne said in a gentler tone. 'I loved Freddie that way and it was wonderful, but would it have been so wonderful ten, twenty years down the line? He died before we had a chance to find out. But you don't have to be passionately in love to have a successful marriage. Before you say anything, I know I'm in no position to lecture about successful marriages, but Johnny and I have been trying harder...' She spread her hands. 'If you want my opinion, you could do a lot worse than Guy Henderson. I know he can be a bit forbidding, and I imagine he won't be *easy*, but he certainly won't be dull, which is fatal, and he desires you. If Johnny looked at me the way Guy looks at you, I would be a very happy woman,' she added with a twisted smile.

Iris looked out at Johnny Carsington's garden. The cloying scent of jasmine and hibiscus drifted in from the veranda, and in the dense tropical night the insects rasped frantically.

'Sleep on it,' Ariadne advised. 'Decide in the morning.'

But Iris couldn't sleep. She lay under the mosquito net and opened herself up to memories of Ian. Of how happy they had been. Of the plans they had had. Of how certain they had been that they belonged together, that they would walk along the shore at Skara hand in hand for ever. Never had he seemed so far away from her. Instead of pushing the memories away, instead of pretending, she let the old grief and pain press on her raw heart as she lay in suffering silence, but by the time the dawn brought its chorus of shrill, squawking tropical birds, she had made up her mind.

She sent Guy a note.

I'll marry you. Book me a passage to Australia as Mrs Henderson.

35

Roz

Skara, present day

Roz dropped the letter and grabbed her phone. 'Finn!' she said when he answered. 'Iris went to *Australia*!'

She read out the letter Iris had sent to her sisters telling them how she had discovered where their uncle had gone and about her marriage. She had described her new husband in cagey terms that had Roz intrigued.

'She's included a lovely sketch of her on her wedding day,' she added. 'It's funny how little she had mentioned Guy Henderson to her sisters before, isn't it? But the main thing is that we know where she went and that she was travelling under a different name,' she finished excitedly.

'Iris Henderson . . .' She could hear Finn scribbling it down. 'That's excellent news,' he said. 'Now we've got a name, I can check the passenger lists on ships from Colombo to Australia. Iris doesn't say anything about where exactly Ralph had gone?'

Roz skimmed the letter again. 'No, she just says Australia . . .

but her husband had booked a passage to Adelaide. They might have gone anywhere from there, though, and Australia is a big place.'

'Still, this information is a good place to start,' said Finn.

'Oh, I almost forgot! I found some photo albums too.' Roz had been so spooked by her experience in the mist that she hadn't unpacked her bag straight away when Drew dropped her at the entrance to the staff quarters. She'd been cold and wet and thoroughly unnerved, and it was only after a hot shower and a cup of tea that she remembered the letters. Finding out that Iris had gone to Australia had put everything else out of her mind.

'I don't think they tell us anything we didn't already know, but they're interesting,' she said. 'I can't wait to show them to you.'

She wished Finn was there to share her excitement. On impulse, she picked up the phone and called Hugo to tell him what she had discovered. She had been keeping in touch with him by email, using a new address that he had set up for her, but she knew he would love to hear about Iris's marriage and the photos.

She hadn't thought twice about calling him, she realised after a long chat. Until recently, she had been wary of using the phone in case Richard was somehow able to track her, but she had a new mobile and a new SIM card since Paris, and there had been no more messages. She had called Finn without thinking to find out about his father, and again just now when she had been desperate to share her discovery with him. She felt safe here.

Skara was good for her. It was hard to stay tense with the sea and the quiet hills as a constant backdrop. She was learning to love the way the light moved over the water and the blue hush at twilight. The smell of the gorse and the constant rustle of the wind.

But the mist... She shuddered at the memory of it. She hadn't felt safe then. She had been frightened by the uncanniness of it, by the fear and the violence and the aching grief that had swirled around her. She thought of Morag's warnings, and the sense that she was messing with things she didn't understand.

Her ring tingled and she turned it absently on her finger. Yes, she loved Skara, but she wouldn't forget that there was a dark side to its history.

Roz was glad to be working the next day and to have something else to think about. It hadn't taken her long to get back into the groove of working shifts, although she had soon learnt that Dundonan Castle operated to more exacting standards than Cork & Candle. The kitchen was led by an intense Yorkshireman who kept his chefs terrified by saying almost nothing at all, but the food was so exquisitely prepared and presented that he was worth whatever Drew was paying him. In the restaurant itself, Gordon, the maître d', held sway, insisting that the tables were precisely laid, the crisp white cloths were immaculate, each piece of cutlery was polished and every glass sparkled. It was a far cry from the casual jeans and T-shirt approach of Cork & Candle, but Roz picked it up quickly.

It was a few days before Drew was able to arrange tea with his grandmother. Henrietta Malcolm lived on the ground floor of the private wing at Dundonan. She sat fiercely erect in her chair and sent Drew to make tea in the little kitchenette. Bonnie settled herself at Henrietta's feet and Roz was made to sit down and give an account of herself.

She explained about coming to London and finding the painting of the Four Sisters, which had led her to Iris's letters and to Skara. At ninety, Henrietta Malcolm was clearly still a forceful character. She had limited mobility, but her mind was still active, and she listened to Roz with interest.

'I've got a theory,' Roz told her as Drew came in with the tea. 'Drew thinks I'm being over-romantic, but I think Ian Malcolm and Iris Blackmore were in love, and then she left him – or, more likely, Ian dumped her because he needed to marry money. We know Charles Blackmore had lost his fortune, so presumably Iris wouldn't have been a good match any more.'

'It might have been like that.' Henrietta considered the idea. 'It would certainly explain why Ian was so unhappy always. The Blackmores were obviously long gone before I married James and came to Dundonan, so I only ever heard stories about them. They were supposed to be lovely girls, who just left one day and were never seen again.'

'So you *knew* Ian Malcolm?' Roz was thrilled at the idea.

'He was my father-in-law,' said Henrietta. 'He died not long after James and I were married, but I remember feeling very sorry for him. He seemed such a disappointed man, and really, for someone who'd inherited an estate like Dundonan and lived a long and healthy life, that's so sad, don't you think?'

'I do,' Roz agreed, thinking of her own mother and how she too had been permanently disappointed, as if life had failed to give her something she was somehow owed.

'He married an American called Margaret,' Drew's grandmother went on. 'There's a portrait of her somewhere. Get Drew to show you. Rather a hard face, but perhaps I'm prejudiced. She wasn't a good mother.'

'I wonder why he married her?' said Roz, sipping her tea.

'No wonder about it,' said Henrietta firmly. 'Ian's father, James, was a gambler and a fool, though perhaps they're the same thing. He brought the estate to its knees, and then he sold the opposite headland to Charles Blackmore and that was that.'

'So you've heard about the curse?'

She pursed her lips. 'I've heard all the stories, of course. I don't believe in curses, but there's no doubt nothing has quite gone right for Dundonan since that land was sold. Ian did his best to turn things around by marrying an heiress, but apart from the money, it wasn't a success. From the little he told me, Margaret was carried away by the romance of living in a Highland castle but not so impressed by the reality of it. I believe the plumbing and the lack of central heating did for her. Although if she had all that money, I'd have thought she could have installed a few bathrooms,' she added, dropping another piece of ginger nut to a grateful Bonnie and ignoring Drew's tut of disapproval.

'No wonder he looks so sad in his portrait,' said Roz.

'He was wretched, I think,' said Henrietta. 'Once James was born, Margaret seemed to spend the rest of her life in the London house. Poor James hardly ever saw his mother, and she died while he was at school, so that was the end of that. It affects men badly, you know, when they don't have a strong feminine influence in their lives. I had a difficult time with James – no use pretending otherwise – and he soon ran through what was left of Margaret's money, but I made sure that I stuck around for my son. Hamish turned out all right, though he married a minx. Ginny led him a pretty dance before she found someone who could keep her in more comfort. She's now on her . . . what, fifth husband?'

'Fourth,' said Drew.

'At least she's spending someone else's money now,' said Henrietta. 'And then there's Drew here. Ella was a nice enough girl, but she wasn't tough enough for Skara.'

'As you can tell,' Drew said to Roz in a dry voice, 'the Malcolm men don't have a good track record when it comes to marriage.'

'I guess we all make bad choices at times,' she said, thinking of her mother again.

'Bad choices or a curse?' said Henrietta. 'It depends what you believe, I suppose.'

'Morag believes in the curse,' Roz remembered. 'She was there when I tried to buy a dustpan and brush in the village shop the other day and the shopkeeper refused to serve me.'

Drew frowned. 'What on earth did you want a dustpan and brush for?'

'I wanted to see if I could clean up Rubha Clachan a bit,' she said.

He stared at her. 'You're a crazy woman! Remove a hundred years of dirt with a dustpan and brush! The only way to clean that house would be to demolish it and start again.'

'Oh, don't say that!' Roz protested. 'It would be so lovely to see the house restored. Although obviously Morag wouldn't agree,' she went on glumly. 'She practically pushed me out of the shop.'

'I'm sorry about that, but you'll have to make allowances for Morag,' said Drew. 'She's not quite rational on the subject of Rubha Clachan.'

'She's had her share of tragedy,' Henrietta put in. 'Her father broke his back after he had been up on the headland, and then she had a son, wee Jamie, who drowned.'

'How terrible for her,' said Roz, sobered.

'You can see why, for Morag, the curse is easier to blame than the unfairness of life.'

'Yes, I do see. I must be a horrible reminder to her of everything she's lost. But . . .' She hesitated. 'I don't want to make trouble, but I feel that I need to stay here and find out what happened to the Blackmore girls.'

'Do you think you're connected to the family?' Henrietta asked.

Roz lifted her hands. 'We can't be sure. We know that Iris took a ship to Australia. Finn's looking into ship's manifests and immigration records to see if he can find out any more.' She turned to Drew. 'He's hoping to come up in a week or two. Is there any room for him to stay here rather than at the Anchor? I meant in the stables, rather than the hotel itself. I don't think his firm's budget will stretch to Dundonan Castle.'

'I'm sure we can squeeze him in somewhere,' said Drew. 'Find out when he's coming and let Douglas know. He'll sort something out.'

'That would be great. A friend of mine from London is going to come and stay too. I've been telling him about the hotel and how good the food is, so he said he'd book a room. I can't wait to see him again,' she added, thinking about how much she had missed Hugo.

'We'll do our best to make him comfortable,' said Drew,

sounding rather pinched, and his grandmother threw him an amused glance before turning back to Roz.

'How nice for you to have your friends make the effort to come all the way to see you,' she said innocently.

'I know,' said Roz, thinking fondly that in Hugo and Finn she had found two real friends. 'They're both great. Hugo in particular is so special. You'll love him,' she told Drew, who smiled thinly.

'I'm sure I will,' he said.

36

Iris

Australia, September 1931

'Julia Creek?' Iris repeated. 'Where on earth is that?'

'North-west Queensland.' Guy unfolded a map of Australia and spread it on the table. He pointed. 'There. According to my sources, a Ralph Davidson bought a property near there in 1929.'

Iris looked at the map, which showed towns and cities clinging to the shore and a huge space in the middle, empty apart from a few isolated settlements. Guy's finger sat on a tiny dot along a straight road leading in from Townsville on the Queensland coast. Her gaze travelled down the map to find Adelaide.

'That's miles away!'

'Miles and miles and miles,' Guy agreed. 'And more miles. More than a thousand, in fact. With very few sealed roads.'

'It's going to take for ever to get there,' Iris said in dismay. Just when she thought they were at the end of their journey, it appeared they still had a long way to go.

'It would if we tried to drive. I suggest we fly instead.'

'Fly?' she echoed dubiously. 'Is that safe?'

'It's fast, which is what matters. We can take a train to Broken Hill, just over the border into New South Wales, and fly to Julia Creek from there. It should only take three days.'

'I've never been on an aeroplane before. It sounds dangerous.'

'It will be fine,' he said, with a touch of impatience. 'People fly all the time here. Come on, Iris, we're almost there! All we need to do now is get to Julia Creek and then find a way to get to Strathann – that's the name of the property. Then we'll be able to pin down your elusive uncle at last.'

And what then? Iris couldn't help wondering. Guy was driven by the need to find Ralph, but what would happen when they came face to face with him after all this time? She doubted her husband would get the humble apology and full restitution he craved

Her husband.

It was over a month since they had been married in Colombo, and Iris was still getting used to the idea. Johnny Carsington had given her away and Ariadne had thrown a party the evening before they sailed.

It had been harder than Iris had thought to say goodbye to Ariadne. When everyone else had gone and Johnny was in his study, the two of them had sat in comfortable silence on the veranda, listening to the raucous tropical night.

'How are you feeling?' Ariadne asked at last. 'Nervous?'

'Incredibly,' Iris admitted with a shaky smile.

'You're a brave girl, Iris. I hope this marriage will be the making of both of you. I know it's not what you wanted, but perhaps Guy will turn out to be a better husband.' Ariadne hesitated. 'He can be brusque at times, but I don't see him letting his parents tell him who he should and shouldn't marry the way your Ian did.'

'It's not that. I think we both understand why we're getting married.'

'Are you thinking about the wedding night?' Ariadne asked delicately. 'Your mother did tell you what to expect, didn't she?'

Iris was glad the darkness hid the embarrassed colour that flooded her cheeks. 'Oh, yes, yes . . . she did.'

'I hope she told you that sex is one of life's great pleasures?'

'She didn't put it *quite* like that.'

The truth was that Amelia had been vague and Iris's understanding of the whole business was sketchy in the extreme, but she didn't want to talk about it. She had already had an excruciatingly awkward conversation on the subject with Guy. Well, she had felt awkward; Guy didn't seem at all bothered by it. Iris had steeled herself to ask him exactly what he expected from the marriage.

'You said it would be a purely practical arrangement,' she reminded him.

'Yes?'

'So you wouldn't expect . . . that you . . . that *we* . . . you know . . .'

'I do know,' he said with a crooked smile. 'I know exactly what you mean.' He got up and went to lean on the veranda rail, staring out into the darkness before turning back to her. 'If we're going to get married, let's have a proper marriage. I want you to be my wife, with all that entails, but not if you lie there wishing that I was someone else.' His mouth twisted. 'No, I couldn't bear that.' He paused, considering. 'I can promise you that I won't force you to do anything you don't want,' he said at last. 'It will be your choice, Iris. If you decide that you want to be a real wife, all you have to do is ask, but until you do, I won't lay a finger on you.'

It should have made her feel better, but somehow it hadn't.

Guy had kept his word. They had shared a poky third-class cabin on the voyage to Port Adelaide, which was all he could afford by then. It was nowhere near as comfortable as the first-class cabins on *Orphea*, but thankfully it at least had separate bunks. At night, he waited until Iris had been down to the bathroom so that she was always undressed and in bed before he appeared, but it was hard not to be preternaturally aware of him. The sound of him settling into bed, the sound of him breathing. Sometimes she would wake in the night and see him lying on top of his bunk, the end of a cigarette glowing in the dark, his eyes on the ceiling. She would touch her mother's ring – now repaired and retrieved from the Colombo jeweller, who had practically thrown it in his eagerness to get rid of it – and remember what Guy had said.

All you have to do is ask.

The *Ormonde* had docked in Port Adelaide on a still morning. The sea was milky and the light was dazzling. 'I'm in Australia,' Iris kept repeating to herself. 'I'm on the other side of the world.'

She hadn't expected Australia to feel quite so foreign. Of course, there was much that was familiar. Everyone spoke English, and they ate the same food, albeit in much larger quantities, but the light was startlingly clear, and the air smelt different too, a dry, tangy, citrusy smell.

'Right,' said Guy briskly as they made their way down the gangway. 'Let's go and find your uncle.'

They'd stayed in Largs Bay, at the Pier Hotel, which was clearly the first port of call for many of the migrants who had been on board the *Ormonde*. It was an imposing building from the outside, with a curved corner and an elaborately colonnaded facade, looking out over the Moreton Bay pines that lined the roads, but inside, the rooms were basic. Iris reflected that she must have been spoilt by the luxurious surroundings in Ceylon, as life felt much harder here in Australia. The people she had met were bluntly spoken and brown-skinned, their eyes creased at the corners from squinting in the harsh sunlight. The food was plain and plentiful, usually great slabs of meat grilled until leathery. Guy had taken to the beer, but Iris was given great glasses of sherry, and she couldn't help feeling nostalgic for the fresh lime juice she had enjoyed on Ariadne's veranda.

Every day, Guy had gone out in search of any trace of Ralph. He spoke to officials at the port, at the railway station and anywhere else he could think Ralph might have been, and now that he had a definite location, nothing was going to stop him

Flying rather than driving across the interior had seemed a sensible idea to Iris, but that was before she was strapped into her seat on the aeroplane. The noise of the engine was tremendous, and the sides of the plane seemed all too fragile. There was a single line of seats on either side of the aisle. She sat opposite Guy and clutched at the armrest, her knuckles white, as the propellers whirled faster and faster until they were no more than a blur on the wings, and the pilot turned at the end of the runway. And then they were speeding, faster than Iris had ever gone, and she squeezed her eyes shut in terror. They would never get off the ground. They would crash. They would die here in this dry, distant land. She would never see her family again ...

A hard hand covered hers. 'Think of how you'll draw this scene for your sisters,' Guy said.

Oddly, it helped. Iris imagined the sketch she would send of herself, jaw clenched, rigid with terror, gasping as the plane lifted off the ground and her stomach dropped. She would draw Guy and the other passengers sitting smiling and relaxed, as if they hadn't realised that they were stuck in a metal can up in the air.

She would send it with her next letter, by which time she would be able to let her sisters know exactly where she was. For now, all letters had to be sent to Rubha Clachan, from where she hoped Mrs Grierson would forward them. Telling her sisters about her marriage had been tricky, especially as she had barely mentioned Guy before, but she had glossed over it as best she could. She had included a quick sketch of their wedding day, Guy dark and saturnine in his tropical suit, she in a cream silk suit that Ariadne had lent her, carrying a bouquet of scented flowers from Lord Carsington's garden.

'See, we're off the ground.'

When Iris risked opening her eyes to glance at him, she saw that his expression was amused. He wasn't exactly smiling, but the creases in his cheeks and at the edges of his eyes had deepened. It gave her a strange buzzing feeling inside, and without thinking, she turned her hand over so that their palms met and their fingers interlocked.

The plane landed at a place called Charleville, where they

spent the night before boarding another plane, which hopped its way up through the outback, stopping at two-bit towns with a single dusty street, and what seemed like every sheep or cattle station in between, when everyone would get off the plane and troop into the homestead for a cup of tea and an exchange of gossip. Guy and Iris were objects of intense interest, and when they explained that Iris was Ralph Davidson's niece, it seemed that everyone knew about his purchase of Strathann.

'He picked the wrong time to invest in cattle,' was the common opinion. The beef export trade had collapsed in 1921, they heard. Ralph was variously considered unlucky or a 'daft beggar' for thinking he could buck the trend, and now they came to think of it, nobody had heard much of him for a while.

Iris exchanged a dismayed glance with Guy. Surely, *surely*, he wouldn't have moved on yet again? But it was too late to turn back now. They would have to get to Strathann and find out for themselves.

By the time they landed at last in Julia Creek, Iris was exhausted and practically fell off the plane. If she ever got back to Skara, she was never, ever leaving home again, she vowed to Guy, who just picked up her case and nodded at a scattering of buildings shimmering in the heat haze amidst a vast expanse of grey-green scrub the locals called blue mallee.

'Chin up, we're nearly there. Now we just need to get ourselves to Strathann.'

The Club Hotel was the only two-storey building in the town. Like the other houses, it was built of wood and had a corrugated-iron roof. Wearily Iris climbed the wooden steps to the deep veranda and Guy held open the door for her.

Inside, it was dark and dusty and the smell of beer was overpowering. Fighting the urge to grimace, Iris hesitated while her eyes adjusted to the gloom. A cluster of men in singlets and cattleman hats leant against the long wooden bar. They stopped talking when they saw Iris, and stared at her. She felt very self-conscious in the summer dress she had bought in Port Said, and with her pale skin. 'Hello,' she said nervously, waving a cloud of flies from her face.

'Ladies in the back parlour,' said the barman, jerking his head.

Guy let the door swing shut behind him with a clatter and dropped the cases on the floor, which gave off a puff of dust.

'We're not staying. We're looking for a place called Strathann,' he said to the room at large. 'Do you know it?'

There was some suspicious muttering, but the man behind the bar finally admitted that he knew it.

'Is it near here?'

'Yeah, pretty near.'

Oh, thank goodness, Iris thought.

'A hundred miles or so, I'd say.' He looked around at his mates for confirmation, and when they nodded, added reassuringly, 'Not far.'

'Do you know where I can get hold of a vehicle?' Guy asked.

'Now?'

'Yes.'

'No!' said Iris. 'I'm not going another hundred miles today! We're going to stay here tonight and think about it in the morning.'

The barman smiled slyly. 'What's it to be, mate? You or your missus going to have the final say?'

Guy glanced at Iris's face. 'We'll take a room,' he said through gritted teeth. 'I presume you have one free?'

'Oh yeah, I reckon we might be able to fit you in.'

It turned out they were the only guests. Which wasn't a surprise to Iris when she saw the room. There was a rough-and-ready table, a rickety wardrobe and a dusty mirror. The door opened onto the covered walkway above the veranda, shaded by the inevitable corrugated-iron roof, and there was a bathroom down the hall. A plain iron bed stood on a bare wooden floor.

One bed.

She eyed it. 'Don't they have a room with two beds?'

'You go and ask if you want a different room.' Guy was in a bad mood. 'You're the one who wanted to stay. Sort it out yourself.' He dumped the case and headed for the door. 'I'm going to have a beer.'

37
Iris

Guy had acquired a dusty old truck by the next morning. Iris eyed it with misgiving as he tossed their cases into the open back.

'They'll get filthy,' she protested

'Where else do you want me to put them?' he said shortly. 'I'm sorry I couldn't find a Rolls-Royce for you, but this is the best I could do.' He stood back, brushing the dust from his hands. 'They call it a ute out here.'

Iris suppressed a sigh and waved a cluster of flies away from her face. Why did Australians have to shorten every word?

The outback was an awful place. Why on earth had her uncle chosen to come here? While Guy was drinking beer the previous afternoon, she hadn't had the heart to write to her sisters, and had taken herself for a walk around the town instead. It hadn't taken long. The main street was wide and sparsely lined with a store, a post office, a bank, a motor works and a few houses, all with corrugated-iron roofs painted red for some reason. The creek itself was a dry riverbed overhung by gum trees, and the air was raucous with the incessant cawing of crows.

It was very hot, but when at breakfast she had said as much to Mrs Foster, the hotel owner had hooted with laughter. 'This is lovely cool weather for us,' she had said. 'Wait until it gets hot.'

Iris could only smile weakly and hope that she would be long gone before then.

Now she and Guy were both in a bad mood. Neither of them had slept well; Iris because she was so self-conscious about being trapped under the mosquito net in the same bed as her husband, and Guy because she had kept him awake with her fidgeting. Dinner had been a huge plate of roast meat with tinned vegetables, and tea with the milk also out of a tin.

For breakfast, Mrs Foster had deposited plates of steak with fried eggs on top in front of them. Iris had stared at her plate, appalled. 'Could I just have some toast?' she asked.

'Just eat it, Iris,' snapped Guy. 'You don't know when your next meal will be.'

She climbed into the ute with some difficulty and settled her skirts around her as best she could. Inside, the vehicle was as rudimentary as the rest of it. A single tattered seat stretched across the cab and a tangle of wires dangled below the bare metal dashboard. Guy swung himself into the driver's seat and put the ute into gear.

'Do you know where you're going?' Iris asked.

'No, I'm just going to drive off and hope for the best.'

'There's no need to be sarcastic.'

She subsided into offended silence as they set off. The road stretched straight to the horizon. It was unsealed, which meant the ute juddered over the corrugations and Iris had to cling to the strap to stop herself being jolted and jarred. As it was, the uncomfortable ride was soon making her stomach react uneasily. The Bay of Biscay had been a breeze compared to this, she thought bitterly. At least then she hadn't had to contend with steak and greasy fried eggs. To make matters worse, they were travelling in a billowing cloud of dust. She tried winding up the window, but then it was unbearably hot. The dust still seeped in through every crack, and she was soon coated in a fine layer of grit.

They hadn't passed a single other vehicle. Iris's eyes were aching from the glaring light. There seemed to be nothing here, just mile upon mile upon mile of spindly mulga trees and sparse dry scrub.

'There's the turning.' The relief in Guy's voice made Iris think that he hadn't been as certain as he pretended about the directions.

He swung the ute off the road onto an even rougher track, and her heart sank as her stomach squirmed in protest. They had only been driving for ten minutes along the track, lurching in and out of ruts, when she shouted over the sound of the engine, 'Stop!'

'What? Why?'

'I'm going to be sick.'

She clapped a hand over her mouth as Guy slammed on the brakes, and he had scarcely stopped before she almost fell out of the cab and ran for a patch of scrub, where she lost her breakfast in humiliating fashion. Not that there was anyone to witness it, she thought as she straightened at last and wiped her mouth shakily with her handkerchief.

The thin trees offered some meagre shade, and when a hot

wind lifted her hair, she arched her neck, rubbing the aching muscles there and savouring the blessed relief of standing still. Above her, the sky was a glaring blue bowl, and the heat beat down on her. It was terribly quiet, apart from the sound of the inevitable flies that had somehow located her in the middle of nowhere and were buzzing infuriatingly around her head.

'Iris!'

She ignored Guy's call and kept her back to the truck. Surely she could have a few more moments out of that wretched ute?

'*Iris!* Hurry!'

The urgency in his voice got through at last, and she turned to see him running towards her. Puzzled, she stared at him until she realised that he was gesturing behind him, and her eyes lifted and widened in horror at the sight of a huge, churning brown cloud that was gobbling up the blue sky and bearing down on the truck at terrifying speed.

For a moment she could only look, paralysed with shock at the suddenness of it, and then she began to run. She met Guy halfway and he seized her wrist and dragged her back with him. The dust storm was on them like a roaring, ravaging beast just as they reached the ute. He shoved her inside.

'Wind the window up!' he shouted above the noise, making a hand gesture in case she hadn't heard, and she fumbled frantically with the handle. The dust was swirling and screaming around them, and she could barely make out Guy struggling around to the driver's side. The wind was so powerful that he couldn't get the door open, and Iris had to lean over and push it, but at last he was inside, coughing and spluttering, and had slammed the door closed behind him.

The ute was being buffeted by the wind, and dust scrabbled at the windows, looking for a way in.

'Cover your nose and mouth,' Guy yelled, demonstrating with his handkerchief, and Iris followed suit, but hers was so small and her hands were shaking so much that it barely made any difference. The dust was stinging, and the more she coughed, the more she inhaled. The vicious, screaming storm seemed to have come out of nowhere. One moment she was looking at blue sky, the next she had been plunged into a nightmare of noise and darkness and fury.

The air in the cab was already cloudy, and it was getting hard to breathe. Iris started to panic, flapping frantically at the dust and coughing wildly, until Guy's hand closed around her wrist.

'I can't breathe!' she shouted, wild-eyed.

'You can. Come here.' He pulled her towards him, dragging her onto his lap and drawing her face against his shoulder to protect it from the worst of the storm. He kept his handkerchief over his own face and turned his head into Iris's hair, holding her close.

'You can breathe,' he said into her ear, his voice reverberating through her. 'Just take it slowly.'

Terrified, Iris huddled into him, pressing her face into his throat, but she made herself take a breath and then another.

'Good girl,' he said.

She was so close, she could feel his heart beating, slow and steady, while her own was racing. It was too noisy to speak, so she just clung to him, taking comfort in his solidity and calm.

Afterwards, she was never sure how long they stayed like that. It could not have been as long as it felt given the ferocity of the wind, and in the end the storm passed as abruptly as it had arrived. It took a few moments for Iris to realise that the horrible noise had stopped, leaving an eerie silence behind it. Only then did she become aware that her face was still pressed into Guy's neck and his arms were holding her tightly against him. For one treacherous moment, she wanted to stay safely there, but then she felt him stir, and his grip loosened.

She sat up shakily. She was still on his lap, their faces as close as lovers'. Guy's skin was coated with dust. It was the first time Iris had looked properly into his eyes. They were a cool grey, almost silver, in startling contrast to his dirty face. As she stared into them, a disquieting warmth uncoiled in the pit of her stomach. Tearing her eyes away from his, she cleared her throat.

'Thank you,' she said huskily. 'I panicked.'

'It was a frightening situation.' Guy's voice sounded as croaky as hers. He coughed. 'I think we could both do with some water.'

Disentangling themselves was awkward, but they managed it in the end, and climbed out of the ute to brush themselves down as best they could. They could see the dust storm sweeping malevolently onwards towards the horizon, and Iris shivered at the memory of its power.

'Are you all right?'

'Yes, thanks to you.' She pushed her hands through her hair, grimacing at the feel of the dust. 'I'm sorry about yesterday. If we'd set off when you wanted, we would have missed that.'

'I'm sorry too,' said Guy. He splashed water from a jerrycan into a cup and handed it to her. 'I should have realised how tired you were.'

They exchanged rueful smiles. 'Well, I suppose a dust storm

is one way to clear the air,' she said. 'But next time, let's just talk about it.'

It was a feeble attempt at a joke, but when Guy laughed, the warm feeling in her belly uncurled further.

The water was tepid and tasted metallic, but it was the best drink Iris had ever had. The last thing she wanted to do was to get back into the ute, but they couldn't stay where they were, and when Guy suggested they get going, she climbed back in without protest and took a good hold of the door handle so that she stayed firmly on her side and there was no chance of sliding over against Guy, which would give him quite the wrong impression.

On and on they jolted through the pitiless scrub. Iris kept an anxious eye on the sky in case of another dust storm, but it stayed clear and blue and immense. The horizon stretched horrifically in every direction, its flatness punctuated only by what looked like towering red pillars that Guy said were termite mounds.

And then, just when she had resigned herself to the fact that they would be driving for ever, there was a flash in the distance.

She sat up in her seat. 'What was that?'

'Sunlight on an iron roof is my guess,' said Guy. 'We must be nearly there.'

'Nearly' was an exaggeration. They had to cross several dry riverbeds, bumping slowly over the rutted earth. At least there were some trees along the riverbeds, great leaning gums with ghostly white bark, though Iris could not imagine how they ever got enough water to live.

As they drew nearer, they could make out a sprawling homestead with ramshackle sheds around it and a windmill next to a corrugated-iron water tank. The fences were broken and the whole place had a neglected air to it. A few horses penned in a paddock raised their heads and watched curiously.

'Is this it?' Iris said, dismayed.

'Looks like it.' Guy's expression was grim as he brought the truck to a halt in front of the homestead and put on the handbrake.

Iris sat numbly, hardly able to believe that she had reached the end of her journey at last, a journey that had taken her from her beloved Skara to Ceylon, and now to a place that was as different from both of them as it could be. It seemed deserted.

'He'd better be here,' said Guy, obviously thinking the same thing.

Stiffly Iris climbed down from the ute and touched her hair. She hadn't planned on meeting her uncle covered in dust, but there was no help for it. She shook out her dress and squared her shoulders before climbing the wooden steps to a veranda.

'Hello?' she called, her voice swallowed up in the dense silence. 'Hello, is there anyone there? Uncle Ralph?'

She pushed open the screen door and found herself in a long corridor with a dusty wooden floor and two other corridors leading off it. 'Uncle Ralph?' she called again as the door clattered into place behind her. Where was everyone? Surely her uncle couldn't live here on his own?

When an indigenous woman appeared noiselessly at the end of the corridor, Iris nearly screamed.

'Oh! You startled me!'

The woman was barefoot, dark-skinned with dark eyes that regarded Iris in expressionless silence.

'Ralph?' Iris tried. 'Ralph Davidson? I am his niece. Family,' she tried to clarify, having no idea whether the woman spoke English. How was she supposed to communicate?

There was a pause, and then the woman nodded, beckoning. Iris followed uneasily, her footsteps echoing on the wooden boards. The woman stopped and opened a door. 'Sick,' she said to Iris.

Inside, blinds had been drawn to shut out the light, but in the dimness Iris could make out a figure lying in a bed, coughing feebly.

'Uncle Ralph?' she said tentatively, and with an effort he turned his head on the pillow to stare at her.

'Amelia?'

38

Roz

Skara, present day

In defiance of Drew's ridicule, Roz had borrowed a broom and a dustpan and brush from the hotel store and attempted to sweep up at least some of the thick layer of dust in the study at Rubha Clachan. He had been right, of course, she thought, as she went outside to tip out the contents of the pan, blinking dust out of her eyes: she was a crazy woman. It would take for ever to make a difference to the house, but she hadn't managed to find any more letters and she was sick of sitting on the filthy floor and blowing dust off papers.

She rested for a moment, enthralled as always by the view, the majestic mountains rolling away, the shifting sea gleaming between the hills. It had called to her on that Kensington street, beckoning from the painting, and it was part of her now.

Her gaze drifted to the beach. She had avoided it since she had been lost in the mist. Even on a clear day, she always came by the track.

Perhaps she was being foolish. The beach was so beautiful, particularly on a day like this, when the sea glittered turquoise in the shallows and the sand was a bright, brilliant white. It was hard to believe the horror that had happened here: the treacherous mist concealing savage marauders, the four girls snatched from their home, dragged across the sand and flung into open boats.

Roz rolled her shoulders, trying to shrug away the memory of the terror she had sensed in the mist. She must be careful not to get too entangled in this place, where it was all too easy to succumb to the pull of the past. At least she had Dundonan, and a job that anchored her to the real world. She liked working again. She liked the other staff.

And she liked Drew. No use pretending that she didn't. She liked the smile that creased his cheeks and snarled her insides. She liked his hands, square and capable. She liked the easy way he walked, as if he was sure of where he was going and what he was going to do.

She wanted him, she could admit that, but she didn't *need* him.

As if her thoughts had conjured him up, the sound of an engine made her turn, and she saw his Land Rover bumping over the track. It could get much further than Finn's city car.

When Drew got out, Roz raised a hand in greeting, ruthlessly quashing the skip of her pulse.

'I hope you've brought coffee?' she said, keeping it casual as she bent to pat Bonnie.

'I'm empty-handed, I'm afraid.' Drew nodded at the dustpan in her hand. 'How's the cleaning going?'

'Slowly,' she acknowledged.

'Well, if you can tear yourself away, I might have a more rewarding job for you.'

'Really?'

'It's just a one-off,' he said. 'Did you hear that a film production company is coming up next week? They're doing a reality show, behind the scenes at a luxury hotel sort of thing.'

Roz nodded. 'Yes, we were talking about it in the kitchen earlier. They're going to do a piece on sourcing the produce and how the menus are put together?'

'That's right, and they want to do another segment on our picnics.'

'Picnics?'

'It's one of our most popular activities,' said Drew. 'Guests can book a special boat trip to one of the uninhabited islands. They see a lot of marine life on the way, and then disembark at a beach, where we give them a picnic. And not just any picnic. We set up a table and chairs and serve the food. The guests love it.'

'And the TV crew are going to film a picnic?'

'Exactly. It should be good publicity. Anyway, I was talking to Gordon and we wondered if you'd like to be the server on the picnic.'

'Me?'

'Gordon says you're "all right", which means he thinks you're fabulous.'

Roz bit her lip. 'Isn't there anyone else who could do it?'

'Sure,' said Drew in surprise, 'but the others have done it before and it's quite an experience.

'I'm sorry, Drew, I can't.'

He regarded her, puzzled. 'Because?'

'I might be on television.'

'A glimpse or two, maybe, but it wouldn't be about you.'

She shook her head. 'I can't,' she said again.

There was a pause. 'Let's walk on the beach,' Drew said, after a moment. 'I think we need to talk.'

Roz hesitated, then nodded. She set down the dustpan and brush and shrugged on her jacket instead. She wasn't sure about walking on the beach, and she was definitely not sure about talking, but Drew was already heading towards the path through the shifting dunes, Bonnie prancing around him.

She followed him onto the firm sand, where she paused and eyed the sea, so tranquil today, remembering how remorselessly it had swept in, bringing with it the mist that had gobbled her up, driven her into the bog.

'Tide's on its way out,' said Drew, as if he could read her thoughts. 'It's quite safe.'

Roz stuffed her hands into her pockets, excruciatingly aware of Drew walking beside her with easy strides, the wind lifting his hair. She concentrated on the crunch of shells beneath her boots, on the froth and bubble of the waves breaking on the beach. A salty breeze stung her cheeks. Above her head, a gull wheeled on the wind. Little brown birds were skittering up to the waves and then away, lifting in small flurries if Bonnie bounded too close, only to settle back on the sand when she ran on.

Drew followed her gaze. 'Dunlins,' he told her.

'They're cute.'

He seemed content to walk in silence for a bit. Roz watched Bonnie run in joyous circles and gradually felt her muscles loosen, her shoulders lower. She breathed in the air and tasted the damp, brackeny smell of the hillside, the cool, clean breeze.

'What did you want to talk about?' she asked at last.

'You,' he said. 'How I can help you.'

'I don't need help,' she said instantly. 'I don't need anyone.'

Drew ignored that. 'You're scared,' he said.

'I don't know what you mean.'

'Come on, Roz. You're afraid of appearing on television. You only use cash. You don't even want to be paid if it means going onto some system. You're like a drawn bow, ready to run the moment anyone gets too close to you. You're running away from something.'

'It didn't feel like running away,' said Roz. 'It feels like I've been running *to* here.'

'But you don't want to be found?'

'No, I don't want to be found.' She let out a sigh. She might as well tell him. It didn't mean she was going to rely on him for anything. It didn't mean she needed his help.

'Who's looking for you? A boyfriend? A husband?'

'No, nothing like that. My mother was killed,' she said, quite easily after all. 'By her husband. I found her body.'

Drew bent to pick up a stick. He sent it spinning out into the waves so that Bonnie could splash after it, but he was listening.

'I saw him leave just as I arrived.'

Roz stopped walking, transported from the cold Scottish beach to Ridgewell, getting out of the car into the bouncing heat and glare, into the smell of wattle and gum.

She told Drew how she had walked through the house that day, how she had been distracted by the dripping tap. 'I told myself that Mum was in the garden and that I would turn the tap off first. We don't waste water in South Australia,' she said in a feeble attempt to lighten the mood. 'But I think I knew, even then. I went into her bedroom and opened the door into the en suite, and then I . . . then I . . .'

Her throat closed up. In her mind, the box of memories was bulging and shaking with images of horror.

'You don't need to talk about it if you're not ready,' Drew said quietly.

'No, I can do it.' She took a breath, and then another. Her eyes rested on Bonnie's sleek head in the water, but she saw again her mother's bathroom. The basin with the dripping tap, set into a marble vanity unit. The mirror Millie was so proud of, with its special lights all around. The expensive moisturisers lined up on the shelf with military precision, the way Richard insisted they were left. The gleaming shower with the huge waterfall head.

But then the soft towels, which should have been hanging neatly on the towel rail, were slithering to one side, slumping on the floor.

It was difficult to remember now. Had she seen the towels first and realised that something was wrong? Or had she taken in the scene in one horrifying glance?

'My mother was on the floor. I could tell straight away that she was dead.' Her heart was racing but she made herself go on. 'Her eyes were open and she looked . . . she looked terrified.'

She swallowed. 'There was a gash on her cheek, and one arm was twisted underneath her. The other was sticking out at an angle.' Roz had been reminded of a plastic doll whose limbs had been twisted this way and that for a cruel child's amusement. Quickly she shoved all the memories back in the box and slammed the lid shut.

'I've never told anyone all that before,' she said. She took a deep breath to calm her pulse rate and started to walk again. She felt strange, light-headed and shaky, half ashamed at having let the memories escape, but oddly purged too.

Drew kept pace with her. 'I'm sorry,' he said simply. 'You've had a hard time, Roz.'

'There was an investigation, of course, and a trial, and Richard was convicted. He is – was – a police officer, so it was difficult for local people to accept that he was guilty. I was the main witness, and lots of his friends blamed me. *He* certainly blamed me. Once he was safely in prison, I could get on with my life. I came over here, got a job in London, met Hugo.' She smiled fondly. 'I felt as if I could relax after two long years. I let myself make friends. I thought I could be normal,' she said bitterly. 'Then my solicitor told me that Richard had been released on a technicality.'

'Oh, Roz.'

Her throat tightened and she scowled. She didn't want to be pitied. 'My solicitor is appealing,' she said briskly, 'but it all takes time.'

'I've never heard of anything to do with the law that doesn't,' said Drew. 'In the meantime, Richard is free and you're scared that he'll come after you. How would he find you?'

'I don't know how he does it,' said Roz. 'I know I sound paranoid, but he was able to send me anonymous messages in Australia even when I changed my phone. I thought I'd be safe over here, but he tracked me down in Paris. I think he has friends in the security services, and they seem to be able to find you anywhere. He sent me another message. Nothing threatening, just enough to let me know that he knew how to find me. I panicked. I left London. I was afraid he'd pick me up on CCTV cameras, or through my credit card. That's why I only use cash now. Hugo set up a new email address for me and bought me yet another new phone – I don't know what I'd have done without him – but I couldn't think clearly. I was too afraid that having tracked me down once, Richard would do it again.

'So I suppose I did run away,' she went on. 'I didn't know what else to do. I told you about the painting of the Four Sisters, and all I could think of was to come here and find them. And I've felt safe here. I can pretend that what happened to my mother wasn't real, that Richard's not real. That he's not in Ridgewell right now, hating me. Blaming me for sending him to prison. Looking for me.'

The fear that she had been suppressing for so long erupted, and she began to shake. She put a hand to her mouth. 'Sorry, I—'

'You don't need to be sorry.' Drew wrapped his arms around her and pulled her close. He was solid and steady, and Roz let herself cling to him, breathing in the leathery smell of his jacket, lulled by the soothing rubbing of his hand on her back, until the trembling stopped. 'It's okay,' he said quietly at last. 'Hold on to me. I won't let you go.'

39

Iris

Strathann, September 1931

'Amelia?' Ralph whispered again, incredulous.

Iris moved forward so that he could see her properly. 'No, not Amelia. I'm her daughter, Iris.'

He moved his head restlessly on the pillow. 'I can't see a damn thing.'

Iris wasn't surprised. She could barely see anything herself. The room smelt fetid and was full of flies. Wrinkling her nose, she went over to raise the blind and open the window, and turned to see her uncle properly for the first time.

He had once been a handsome man, that was obvious, but now he was diminished by illness. His face was grey and drawn, his skin clammy, and he plucked fretfully at the single sheet that covered him. 'Thirsty,' he muttered.

There was a glass by the bed, but it was empty, and flies had settled on the rim. Iris picked it up with a grimace. Her uncle was too sick to talk at the moment, that was clear. 'I'll get you some more,' she said as Guy loomed in the doorway.

'Is he here?' he asked menacingly, and stepped forward, fists clenched.

'Guy, he's ill,' said Iris, moving towards him and laying a hand on his arm. His muscles were rigid, his mouth twisted with bitterness. 'He doesn't even know we're here.'

'Who's that?' Ralph's voice was no more than a thread in the stifling room.

'My name's Henderson,' said Guy, shaking off Iris's hand, and for one awful moment she thought he would lift her uncle up from the bed and shake him. 'I'm Duncan Henderson's son.'

'Thirsty . . .'

'Leave him, Guy,' said Iris. 'There's no point in trying to talk to him now.'

Thwarted, Guy turned with an exclamation of disgust and stalked out of the room.

Iris sighed. There was little point in trying to talk to Guy either right then.

Still carrying the filthy glass, she found her way to the kitchen at the back of the homestead, where she looked around, aghast. The screens on the door and window were torn, and flies swarmed over dirty plates. Iris thought of the immaculate kitchen at Rubha Clachan, with its gleaming refrigerator and the electric cooker that was Mrs Grierson's pride and joy, and her throat tightened. This place was awful.

Awful.

The Aboriginal woman was squatting on the back porch. With some miming, Iris established that her name was Polly.

'Where can I find water, Polly?' she asked. 'And a cloth?'

Leaving Guy to stew for the time being, she carried a fresh glass of water, a bowl and a cloth back to her uncle's room. The stench of it hit her again. Somehow she would have to wash those sheets.

She helped Ralph lift his head enough to drink some water, but even that tiny effort was clearly exhausting, and when he slumped back against the pillow, he looked at her hazily. 'Amelia?' he asked again.

'Iris,' she said. 'I'm Amelia's daughter.' But it was obvious that he was too ill to understand what she was saying. Biting her lip, she used the damp cloth to clean his face and hands, and straightened his dirty sheets as best she could. Then, having exhausted her medical knowledge, she left him tossing and muttering feverishly and went to find Guy.

He was on the front porch, glaring out at the dusty yard. A muscle jumped and jerked in his jaw, and his fists opened and closed in frustration.

'All these years,' he said bitterly. 'All these years looking for Ralph, waiting to tell him what he did to my family, waiting for the moment I could plant my fist in his face, and he's just a sick old man in a bed.' He almost spat out the words.

'I'm sorry—' Iris began, and he turned to her angrily.

'Stop apologising for things that aren't your fault! It's as bad for you. I know you were counting on Ralph to help you.'

Iris dropped onto one of the upright wooden chairs and rubbed her forehead. 'What do we do now?'

'There's not much we can do until he gets better – or at least well enough to have a conversation about money.'

'And in the meantime?'

Guy shrugged. 'I'll take a look around the property, see what state it's in – though nothing we've seen so far is very encouraging.'

Iris looked down at her dress, barely recognisable now that it was ingrained with dust from the storm. Her skin felt as if it was covered in a layer of grit. 'I'm going to clean up a bit before I do anything else.'

With Polly's help, she filled a metal bath of cold water and scrubbed herself clean. It was a far cry from the modern bathrooms at Rubha Clachan, but once she had changed into a fresh dress, she felt a bit better. She checked on her uncle. He was sleeping, so she left him and set about cleaning the kitchen instead.

By the time Guy came back, she had explored the house. It was bigger than it had seemed from the outside. Clearly it had once been a substantial homestead, but its glory was now faded and the rooms were grubby and largely empty. There were several bedrooms with iron bedsteads and thin, lumpy mattresses under torn mosquito nets, much like the one Iris had shared with Guy in Julia Creek.

Had it only been the night before?

She thought about how Guy had held her in the dust storm, how it had felt to press her face against his throat.

Would he expect to share a bed again?

All you have to do is ask.

Not now, she told herself. Not when you're both tired and bitter with disappointment. She put her heavy leather suitcase in one room and left Guy's in the corridor. She would let him choose where he slept.

Guy didn't come back alone. 'Look who I found.' He gestured down to a cattle dog with a brindled coat and alert brown eyes. 'He was tied up on a chain,' he added with heat. 'That's no way to treat a dog! As if I didn't despise your uncle enough. This is my dog now,' he said. 'I'm calling him Toby.'

When Toby sat, Guy grinned. 'See, he's clever! He knows his name already.' The smile made him look suddenly younger and more carefree.

'I hadn't thought of you as someone who liked dogs,' said Iris a little breathlessly.

'I like them better than people.' He glanced at her. 'Most people, anyway.'

The air seemed to tighten before Iris made herself look away. 'There's not much in the larder,' she said, her voice too high. 'But I found some eggs and a bit of cheese. I could make an omelette.' It was the limit of her repertoire.

'What happened to the woman who was here?'

'Polly? She seems to have disappeared. She must have her own place to stay. She doesn't seem to be a maid,' Iris added doubtfully, 'or not like any maid I've ever known, so if we want to eat, you'll have to put up with my cooking.'

'An omelette will be fine,' said Guy.

He straddled a chair and leant on the back while he watched Iris beating the eggs and told her about the property. 'I didn't see a single decent fence,' he said. 'The windmill works, but that's about it. The creek's almost dry. I drove out as far as I could, but I didn't see any cattle. The whole place is dying,' he said grimly. 'Unless Ralph has it hidden under his mattress, there's no money here.'

'It's the same with the homestead,' said Iris, swirling butter into a pan. 'Once it must have been quite grand. There's even a proper dining room, although it's hard to imagine eating a formal dinner out here. Now it's just sad.'

Guy nodded. 'What about your uncle?'

'He's much the same. Sleeping mostly. I sat with him for a while, but he doesn't know who I am.' She had tried to get him to drink and had dabbed at his sweaty face with the cloth, but she'd felt useless. 'There's so little I can do.'

'You're doing what you can,' said Guy.

After they had eaten, Iris stood up to take the plates. 'I'll look in on Uncle Ralph, then I'll bring tea to the veranda. It's cooler now.'

She had looked in vain for a teapot earlier. Polly had taught her how to make tea by boiling some coarse tea leaves in a can set over a flame instead. Iris poured it into two battered enamel mugs and carried them out to the veranda.

The sun had sunk behind the creek and now the sky was burning, blazing red, purple, orange. The heat was evaporating, leaving a welcome cool behind, and as the birds squabbled and settled at last in the gum trees, a great hush descended over the outback. Even the windmill had stopped creaking.

Never had Iris felt so far from home. So far from all the rules, from knowing the right thing to do.

Guy sat on a hard upright chair, hunched forward, turning the mug morosely between his hands.

Iris was very tired, but at the same time her senses were on high alert. She was excruciatingly conscious of Guy beside her. She kept remembering how it had felt to press her face into his throat. Her lips had been so close to touching his skin. She could feel the soft cotton of her dress slipping over her thighs and her toes curling in her shoes. Her eyes kept skittering to his profile, to the line of his jaw and the hard angles of his face and the edge of his mouth.

All you have to do is ask.

Stop it, she told herself fiercely.

Guy pulled himself out of his thoughts and sat up. 'There's no restitution to be had here,' he said, as if coming to a decision. 'Finding Ralph Jamieson – Davidson, or whatever his name really is – has been my purpose, and now I've found him and he's a sad, pathetic old man. A sad, pathetic, *bankrupt* old man.'

Draining his tea, he glanced at Iris's averted face. 'You're not going to find an answer to your problems here either.'

'No.' She let out a long sigh. 'I suppose I hadn't thought beyond finding him. What did I think would happen? That he would give me a cheque and send me home? That it would be that easy? I thought this would be the end, but it's not. It's just the beginning of a new problem. He's really ill, Guy.' Her voice cracked. 'What if he dies just when we've found him? What happens then?'

'You're tired,' he said. 'We both are. Let's worry about it tomorrow. For now, let's just sit and look at the sunset.'

The unexpected gentleness in his voice brought a sting of tears to her eyes, and she blinked them quickly away. Guy was right. They couldn't do anything else right then, so they might as well just sit.

The blazing sky faded to a deep red and then a brilliant purple before it darkened. Guy and Iris sat on in a kind of stunned quiet as above them the stars came out one by one, and then in their millions, until the whole sky was a blur of starlight and the only sound was Toby scratching under Guy's chair.

'I've never seen so many stars,' Iris said at last. A yawn slipped out before she could stop it.

'Time for bed,' said Guy. He got up, held out a hand and helped Iris to her feet. His fingers were warm around hers.

The breath clogged in her throat, but she couldn't bring herself to ask. 'Yes, I am tired,' she said, embarrassed by the squeaky note in her voice.

He still held her hand. 'What did you do with my suitcase?'

'It's in the corridor. There are several bedrooms,' she said, her eyes sliding away from his. 'I thought you might like to decide where you wanted to sleep?'

She had made it a question. It was like asking, she told herself, and for a moment she thought that Guy had understood. His hand tightened around hers, but then, abruptly, he dropped it. 'I'll choose my own room, then,' he said. 'Goodnight, Iris.'

40

Iris

'We need to decide what we're going to do,' said Guy the next morning. He had taken Iris to show her the creek and they were sitting on a smooth sun-bleached log.

Iris had been glad to get out of the gloomy house with its stench of sickness. Toby trotted with them as they walked down the creek, past the derelict sheds, past some chickens scratching in the dust, past a paddock with a patched-together railing penning in a few skittish horses. Past what Guy said had clearly once been a cookhouse and stockmen's quarters. Past the windmill, and the water tank, and the empty yards populated only by the ghosts of great mobs of bellowing cattle.

The creek was dry, but the gum trees provided a fractured shade. It was very quiet, apart from the crunch of dried leaves under their feet, and the air had a sharp, dry tang to it.

Tormented by mosquitoes and worry, Iris hadn't slept well. She looked wearily down at her hands. 'I can't leave Uncle Ralph now. He's dying.'

'You don't owe him anything, Iris.'

'He's my mother's brother.'

'Who took her money and never bothered to write,' Guy pointed out.

She sighed. 'I know you're right, but ... he's family and he's ill. Even if he wasn't my uncle, I don't think I could leave him there, not like this. But I understand if you want to go,' she added bravely.

'Go?' he echoed bitterly. 'I can't go anywhere until Ralph either recovers or dies.'

'Then we'd better manage as best we can in the meantime,' said Iris, struggling to be practical. 'We need food. I've had a look around and found a few tins, and there are still eggs, but they won't last us long.' She hesitated. 'Have we got any money to pay for food?'

'Don't tell your swindling uncle, but we've got some left.' Guy stretched out his legs as if glad to have a plan. 'All right, I'll drive back to Julia Creek tomorrow and pick up some supplies. Will you be all right on your own?'

'Of course I will,' said Iris, although the thought of being left alone in this terrible place made her quake inside.

She was up early the next morning to see him off. She gave him a letter to post to her sisters, and another for Ariadne in Colombo, telling her how the search for her uncle had ended. If Rose had written to her in Colombo, Ariadne would forward the letter, Iris was sure.

Arms folded to conceal her trepidation, she stood at the top of the steps as Guy came out and the dog scrambled up to greet him. He had found an old hat of Ralph's and settled it on top of his head as if he had been a cattleman his whole life.

'You will come back?' she said, only half joking, and he touched a finger to her cheek, a brief, burning contact.

'I will,' he said. 'Of course I will.'

Their eyes met, and his words seemed to echo around the outback like a marriage vow. *I will ... I will ... I will.* As if to mark it, a flurry of birds exploded from the gums in a burst of pink, and swooped chattering and squabbling over the creek.

Iris watched the ute until its cloud of dust faded from sight, and then she turned and went inside.

For more than a week, Ralph sweated and thrashed in his bed, growing thinner and greyer by the day. Iris struggled to nurse him. She wrung out endless cloths to wipe the sweat from his body and bring his temperature down, but there seemed almost nothing else she could do. One day he seemed ready to eat something, and she fed him a broth that he promptly brought up all over the sheets she had just changed.

Guy carried him to a chair while Iris stripped the soiled sheets and put on clean ones. At her signal, he lifted her uncle back into bed, but he was scowling as he watched her gather up the dirty sheets.

'You shouldn't be doing this,' he said. 'You're exhausted!'

'He's my uncle, Guy.' Wearily Iris pushed her hair from her face with her forearm. 'I can't just let him die.'

They were scratchy with each other a lot of the time, trapped in a strange place with a man Iris feared was dying. Guy prowled around the abandoned cattle yards, Toby at his heels, and poked around in sheds to see if there was anything of value. He fiddled with the radio as they had seen people do in the stations they'd visited on their flight north, and managed to work it, which was a relief to Iris, who could at last talk to a doctor in Cloncurry.

'Sounds like typhoid,' the doctor said laconically. 'We've had an epidemic in Queensland lately. You're doing what you can,' he told her. 'If he's lucky, he'll start to get better in three or four weeks – though don't be surprised if he relapses. If not . . .'

'Four weeks!' Guy exclaimed when he heard. 'How much longer are we going to have to kick our heels here while we wait for your uncle to decide whether he's going to live or die?'

'As long as it takes,' said Iris, an unfamiliar crispness to her voice. 'If you want to make yourself useful, you could mend those screens. I can't bear the flies!'

Polly turned up at unpredictable times and helped with Ralph, moving noiselessly around the homestead in her bare feet, part of the vast, daunting landscape in a way that Iris knew she could never be. How would the Aboriginal woman feel if she were transported to Skara? she wondered. What would she make of the damp sand and the choppy waves, the smell of the gorse and the curling fronds of bracken?

At least Polly's presence gave Iris a chance to get to grips with the kitchen. There was a wood-burning hearth to cook on, and a kerosene fridge stood in one corner next to a meat safe covered in wire gauze. Other than that, the kitchen contained a cupboard and a rickety table, some chipped crockery and a set of battered saucepans.

When Iris had scrubbed every inch of it, she moved on to the other rooms in the homestead, until it was as clean as she could make it. She tied up her hair in a scarf and wrapped herself in an old apron she had found, presumably belonging to some long-vanished mistress of Strathann. She smiled sometimes to think of her sisters' reaction when they saw her sketches. Rose wouldn't mind the primitive facilities – she would love the adventure of it all, Iris thought – and Lily would just get on with it, but she doubted whether Daisy would be impressed. There were no modern bathrooms at Strathann; just a large tin bucket and a 'long drop' in the back yard, which Iris inspected nervously for spiders and snakes whenever she had to use it.

The outback was an eerie place, so vast, so silent, so strange. Every morning Iris woke early to the sound of birds squawking and squabbling down in the creek. It wasn't all bad. She liked sitting with Guy on the veranda in the hushed light of evening, watching the sky blaze and darken and then blur with starlight. She was getting used to the beautiful parrot-like birds Polly told her were called galahs. They would erupt squawking from the gum trees without warning, wheeling up into the sky and tipping their wings, flashing pink and white, white and pink in the bright, bright sun.

Just as Iris was beginning to despair, there came the day when Ralph's fever broke. She went into his room one morning to find that her uncle's eyes were clear at last.

'Oh, you're awake! I'm so glad.'

'Amelia?' he croaked. 'I thought I was hallucinating!'

'Not Amelia. I'm her daughter, Iris.'

'Good God!' Ralph struggled up onto his pillows and lifted a weak hand to beckon her closer. 'No, you're not Amelia,' he agreed. 'I can see that now. You've a tougher look about you. What are you doing here?'

'It's a long story,' said Iris. 'Why don't I get you some tea and we can talk?'

But by the time she had made the tea, washed his face and hands and straightened the sheets, Ralph was exhausted and collapsed back onto his newly plumped pillows.

'What did you say your name was again?'

'Iris.' She paused. 'You've been very ill, Uncle Ralph. Typhoid, we think, so I'll leave you to sleep. We can talk later.'

Guy was furious when he heard. 'Why didn't you tell me he was awake?' he demanded.

'Because he's not strong enough to talk yet,' said Iris. 'And if you go barging in and start haranguing him, he'll have a relapse.'

'Iris!' Guy clutched at his hair. 'We're been waiting all this time!'

'So a day or so won't make any difference, will it?'

In fact, it was three days before Iris judged that Ralph was able to have a discussion.

'About time,' said Guy, stalking into the room.

Propped up on his pillows, Ralph looked at him with interest. 'Who's this?'

'My husband, Guy.' It still felt odd to say it: *my husband*.

'Guy *Henderson*,' Guy said with meaning, as he pulled up a chair for Iris by the bed, and then another for himself. 'Perhaps you remember my father, Duncan Henderson?'

Ralph moved his head restlessly. 'Dear chap, I can barely remember yesterday.'

'Guy, wait.' Iris put out a hand as he made a gesture of frustration. She turned to face her uncle. 'You're probably wondering what we're doing here?'

'I imagine you want some money,' said Ralph with a cynical look. 'I can't think why else you'd want to find me.'

'You're right about that,' said Guy, his jaw set pugnaciously. 'It's taken me a long time to find you. Not made easier by you changing your name along the way. When I knew you, you called yourself Ralph Jamieson.'

Something flickered in Ralph's eyes. 'Did I? How original of me.'

'You were in Malaya at the time. Do you remember that? Surely you do,' Guy said. 'It must have been one of your more successful swindles.'

'Ah . . . Penang. That was a lovely place.'

'Memory coming back?'

'Vaguely. Did I know you?'

'I was a boy. Duncan Henderson was my father.'

'Oh, yes, rather a fierce boy, if I recall.'

Guy's mouth tightened. 'Perhaps you could recall the fortune you embezzled out of my father while you're at it?'

'Embezzling is a hard word. Is it my fault if a successful businessman allowed himself to be impressed by a bit of flair and a good idea, and failed to check that everything he'd been told was correct?'

'So you do remember my father?'

'There were plenty of businessmen like him,' said Ralph, and Iris's hand crept to her mouth. She was shocked by how casually her uncle admitted what he'd done.

'He shot himself after you left,' said Guy brutally. 'My mother never recovered from the guilt of letting herself be seduced by you.'

'Ah . . . it's coming back to me. Judy? Jane?'

'Janet.' Guy barely opened his lips.

'Janet, yes. So fresh and unspoilt!'

Iris put a hand on Guy's arm as his fists clenched, but he shook her off. 'I'm not going to hit a man lying in bed, much as he might deserve it,' he snarled. He turned back to Ralph. 'We lost everything thanks to you.'

'Well, if you're here to exact your revenge, you're too late,' said Ralph frankly. 'I'm dying and there's no money left. I thought there'd be mining potential here, but it seems not, and the grazier I bought the land from misinformed me.'

Guy gave a crack of laughter. 'Don't tell me you got stung in the end?'

'It happens to the best of us, dear boy. I've always been a gambler. Sometimes you win, sometimes you lose, and this time I lost.'

'It sounds as if you've been a better gambler than businessman,' said Guy. 'That tea plantation went bust, and now this cattle station is going to rack and ruin.'

'And now I'm too sick to move on,' Ralph agreed equably. 'Not where I would have chosen to end my days, but there we are.'

Iris leant forward. 'What about the money my mother lent you? To buy the plantation?'

Ralph gestured. 'Nothing left. All invested in this place, and good luck trying to realise any cash. Why do you want it anyway?' he asked. 'I thought your father was rich as Croesus.'

'Not any longer. The recession . . .'

'Hah! That damned recession has done for the lot of us. Do you mean to tell me that you've come all this way to ask me to repay Amelia?'

'She's dead,' said Iris baldly, and Ralph sobered.

'I'm sorry to hear it. She was the best of my sisters.'

'Or the most willing to overlook your flaws.'

'That too.'

'Before she died, she told me you had promised to repay the loan,' Iris said with a touch of desperation. 'She said you had called it a debt of honour.'

'Ah, well, I'm all out of honour, I'm afraid,' said Ralph. 'If it helps, I would give it to you, but as you can see, all I've got is this godforsaken homestead and a few thousand acres of desert. You're welcome to them if you can do anything with them.'

41

Iris

Guy rubbed a hand over his face. 'So there it is. I'm not inclined to believe anything your uncle says, but in this case, I don't think he's lying about there not being any money. The best we're going to get is a tumbledown homestead and a thousand acres of scrub – and that's if he keeps his word about including us both in his will.'

Leaving Ralph to sleep, they had walked down to the creek and sat on the same smooth log.

Iris turned her mother's ring on her finger. 'What shall we do now?'

'Well, we can give up and leave Ralph to his squalor. Or we can wait for him to die and then try to sell this place. We can divide the money straight down the middle and you can go back to Scotland. If you want to,' he added, the faintest of questions in his voice.

'That might not be for years.'

'True, and knowing your uncle, he'll live for ever to spite us,' said Guy sourly.

Iris crumbled a dried gum leaf between her fingers and looked around her. The colours were so alien here: red earth and dusty green and brittle brown leaves, and the serene white of the ghost gums leaning over the creek bed. The soft blues and greys of Skara, the violet light, the hills purple with heather, belonged to a different world.

She would go back if she could. Of course she would.

She glanced at Guy sitting on the log beside her, his face shadowed by his hat.

'And you?'

He shrugged. 'Who knows? I might stay in Australia. I like the light here. I like the people. They're straightforward.'

'So what are we saying?' said Iris at last. 'We're both going to stay until Ralph dies?'

'Unless you want to go home now,' he said evenly. 'I've got a little money left. I could probably scrape together enough for a passage back to Scotland for you. It wouldn't be first class, mind, but if that's what you really want...'

'No, Guy. I couldn't let you do that,' she said, disconcerted by her instinctive jolt of protest. 'It's not fair. We're in this together. I'll stay, and we'll decide what to do with Strathann when the time comes.'

A tension she hadn't been aware of before evaporated.

'Good,' said Guy, the rigidity in his shoulders relaxing. 'And if we *are* going to stay, we might as well try and get Strathann back on its feet. At least then there might be something worth selling. There's a lot of work to be done, if you're up for it.'

Iris brushed the fragments of leaf from her fingers. She was glad the decision had been made. 'Where do we begin?' she said.

'Let's start by talking to your uncle again.'

Ralph laughed himself into a coughing fit when they told him they were going to try and make a success of Strathann. 'What do you know about running a cattle station?'

'Probably as much as you did,' said Guy tightly.

'You won't be able to do anything without help. I employed some stockmen at first, but I couldn't afford to keep them.'

'What did they think you should be doing?'

Ralph coughed again, and Iris handed him a glass of water. 'There are a lot of wild horses out there, eating the grass the cattle need. If you can herd them back here and break them in, then you can use them to muster in any cattle you can find. See what you've got. But of course, to do that, you need to be able to ride.' He cast Guy an amused glance, well aware of his dislike. 'Ever been on a horse before?'

'No,' said Guy. 'But there's a first time for everything.'

'I can ride,' said Iris clearly. Was it only a year or so ago that she and Ian had ridden almost every day, high into the hills, the damp Scottish air spangling their hair?

'These aren't tame little ponies,' said Ralph, but she set her mouth stubbornly.

'I know horses,' she said. 'I can ride.'

'You can teach me,' said Guy. 'How hard can it be?'

That night they sat at the kitchen table and worked out a list of jobs they needed to tackle just to start. 'We can't do this alone,' Guy said when they looked at the length of the list. 'I'm going back to Julia Creek tomorrow to hire some stockmen.'

'Can we afford it?' Iris worried.

'That money I would have used for your passage home should be enough to get us started.'

Iris pulled her mother's ring from her finger. It was harder than she had thought to wiggle it off. 'I've been thinking: I could sell this.'

She held it out to Guy, but he put it back in her palm, closing her fingers over it. 'No, Iris. That's your mother's ring. I know what it means to you. We'll manage, I promise you.'

Guy brought three lanky stockmen back from Julia Creek. They looked at their dusty boots and mumbled inarticulate greetings. To Iris, Jed, Bob and Danny were strange creatures, who squatted rather than stood as they rolled their cigarettes, their hats tipped over their eyes.

They said little, at least not to her, but she didn't mind. She was just glad that they seemed to know what they were doing

Guy set them to repairing the cattle yards and building new fences. It was a tough job, as they had to cut posts to length, take them out to the distant paddocks in the back of the ute, dig holes in the hard red soil and then tighten the wire. He went with them, and came back with his hands torn and cut.

'We need to get the cattle in to see how many we have, and there's no point in doing that until we've got some fences to keep them here,' he said, when Iris exclaimed at another painful-looking tear on the side of his hand. She was getting used to the stubborn way he set his jaw when he refused to give in.

Once there was a decent paddock, Bob, Jed and Danny rode out to the north, where the land was rocky and they hoped to find some of the horses that had run wild over the last few years.

While they were away, Iris tried to teach Guy how to ride. Ralph was right, these were no gentle ponies, but the horses already in the paddock had been broken at least.

She showed him how to put on the saddle and bridle, but getting onto a horse proved a challenge for him, and staying on even harder. He had barely got his foot in the stirrup before the horse was dancing around, and he had no sooner settled into the saddle before it was bucking and rearing and he was sprawling back in the dust.

Iris winced at his bruises but admired his persistence. The same determination that had driven him across the world to find Ralph kept him getting back up, and while the muscle in his cheek jerked in frustration, he wouldn't rest until he succeeded.

It was a red-letter day when he was able to manage a short ride outside the paddock. The horses were hot, or bored, or had simply decided to behave for once, and Iris let herself relax as they ambled along. She had borrowed some trousers from Ralph and tightened them with a belt, and wore a long-sleeved shirt to protect herself from the sun. In the afternoon quiet, she could hear the creak of the saddles and the chink of the harness as the horses shook the flies off their manes. Their hooves scuffed through the dried leaves, sending the distinctive citrusy scent drifting up to mingle with the smell of leather.

Toby quartered the bush around them, putting up a family of wallabies, who bounded unhurriedly away, while above the cockatoos and galahs squabbled among themselves.

The stately ghost gums leant over the empty creek. Iris wished she had some paints: sketches gave no idea of how different the colour palette was out here, the silvery grey and pale pastel greens and reds and browns so different from the soft blues and greys she would paint with in Scotland.

Out of the corner of her eye, she watched Guy, who was concentrating harder than he needed to on keeping his horse under control. His hat cast a shadow over his face and all she could see was the firm line of his mouth. Something inside her clenched alarmingly, and she wrenched her gaze away, remembering his words a lifetime ago in Colombo.

All you have to do is ask.

He turned his head as if she had spoken out loud. Oh Lord, what if she *had*?

'All right?' he asked, obviously noticing her flustered expression.

'Yes, of course. You seem to be getting the hang of it,' she said, willing her heart to stop booming.

'I must have a good teacher.'

'Or a good horse.'

They lapsed back into silence. The opal in Iris's ring glimmered blue in the sunlight, and she remembered, as if in a dream, riding along the hillside above Dundonan and seeing her whole world laid out before her: the ancient castle with its turrets and towers, the starkly modern house her father had built, and stretching between the two, the bay. It had been a beautiful winter's day. The sea had been a glittering blue, the beach a curve of brilliant white.

It had been a moment of piercing happiness, with Ian by her side and everyone she loved contained in her view. Her mother was still alive then, her father still boisterously optimistic. When she rode home, her sisters were there: Rose, Lily and Daisy.

At least she had known then that she was happy, she thought. She hadn't taken any of it for granted. She just hadn't realised how quickly it would end.

'You're thinking about Scotland.'

Guy's voice broke into her thoughts, and she looked at him, startled. 'How did you know?'

'You look sad.'

Iris leant forward to pat her horse's neck. 'It does make me sad,' she confessed. 'I was wondering what they would all say if they could see me now.'

She was as far from Skara as it was possible to be, in every way, she thought. No hills, no sea. No green, no cool air. No one she loved.

'They?'

'My sisters. And Ian.' She said his name deliberately.

'Ian is the man you're in love with.' Guy's voice was flat, and it wasn't a question.

'We were childhood sweethearts.' Iris kept her gaze fixed between her horse's ears. 'We were going to get married.'

'What happened?'

She couldn't tell Guy about the curse her father might have unleashed by taking down the stones. 'The stock-market crash in America. The Depression,' she said. It sounded more plausible, and it was true. 'My father lost his fortune and Ian had to marry money,' she added, carefully expressionless.

'Why?' Guy asked harshly. 'He could have chosen you instead of money, couldn't he? He could have gone with you and helped you look for your uncle if that was what you needed.'

'It wasn't like that,' said Iris, instantly defensive. 'Ian's family have lived at Dundonan since the fourteenth century. It's part of them in a way I can't explain. Not just the castle itself, but the land. The hills, the sea. It's his birthright. He did offer to leave it and come with me, as it happens, but I couldn't let him do that. I knew how miserable he would be away from Skara.'

'So you have to be miserable on your own instead?'

'Why are you so angry about it?' Iris was feeling scratchy.

'Because it doesn't seem fair on you.'

She sighed. 'Lots of things aren't fair, Guy. It wasn't fair that Ralph cheated your father. It wasn't fair that Bertie died. It's not fair that Ralph sank everything he owed us into this godforsaken cattle station and now we're stuck here.'

Stuck here.

That was the problem with the outback. It was so vast that there was nothing to absorb your words. They kept on reverberating towards the far horizon, and once they were out, it was too late to call them back.

Iris bit her lip. She hadn't meant to sound so negative.

In silence they let the horses pick their way along the edge of the creek, in and out of the tattered shade.

'What about you?' she asked in an attempt to make amends. 'Have you ever come close to being married?'

'You mean before now?' Guy still sounded bad-tempered, as if he shouldn't need to remind her that they were in fact married.

'Yes, before now.'

'No,' he said after a while. 'I suppose seeing what happened to my parents' marriage put me off taking that risk myself. My mother . . . she spent so many years blaming herself for having an affair with Ralph that I never had the chance to blame her too. Maybe it wouldn't have made a difference. My father would still have fallen for Ralph's cock-and-bull scheme, and he would still have lost all his money, but it was my mother's betrayal that tipped him over the edge and made him decide that life wasn't worth living. That's what my mother thought too, of course. That was the guilt she lived with. She tried to turn it into a search for revenge. She was obsessed with finding Ralph and making him pay for what he'd done. I think she thought that would make it right for me, and I wanted to do it to make it right for *her*, but when I look back, what was the point? Nothing was going to change the fact that my father was dead.'

Nothing was going to change the fact that Guy hadn't been enough for his father to want to go on living, thought Iris. That he hadn't been enough for his mother either.

'Were you afraid that your marriage would turn out to be like your parents'?'

He shrugged. 'Perhaps. In any case, I couldn't afford to marry. I never met anyone I wanted to marry either.'

Until now. The unspoken words hung in the air.

'And yet here we are, married,' said Iris, and he turned to look at her.

'Yes, here we are,' he said.

42
Iris

Strathann, January 1932

Gradually Iris grew used to life in the outback. Guy was out all day with the stockmen, so for most of the time she was alone with her uncle, and sometimes Polly.

'Polly's been good to me,' Ralph said. 'She turns up if she feels like it, and I give her money when I've got any.' Other than that, he was vague about the arrangement, and Iris accepted that Polly would do as she liked.

Although he had recovered, Ralph remained weak, and he seemed content to leave the running of the station to Guy. 'Why not let him do all the work?' he said with a glint of mischief. 'I've got you to cook for me and keep the place clean, and Guy running everything. It suits me fine.'

Iris wanted to be cross with him, but she could never quite manage it. Her uncle was selfish and lazy, but he could be excellent company when he wanted, and it was all too easy to see how he had charmed his way through life.

The stockmen slept in swags in their own quarters, but Guy said they couldn't afford a cook for the men, so they came to the homestead for their meals and ate in the once grand dining room. Iris soon learnt to cook on the wood-burning hearth, and was glad that the men's needs were simple. Her day began at 4.30 a.m., when Guy and the stockmen had steak and eggs for breakfast. The evening meal was always beef, usually boiled brisket, and lunch was cold meat and bread.

She had found a tattered old book of housekeeping advice left by some long-departed mistress of Strathann, and she pored over it for recipes to make for the tea breaks the men called smoko, using the limited ingredients in her larder: rock cakes and flapjacks and tea loaf.

The book was useful, too, when the men came in with minor injuries. She treated them as best she could with permanganate of potash or kerosene, which worked well enough as a disinfectant.

Sometimes Iris remembered growing up at Rubha Clachan, with Mrs Grierson presiding over the kitchen. Sumptuous meals served from silver dishes appeared three times a day, and if you wanted tea and freshly made scones, all you had to do was ring the bell. Now that felt like another world, another life. She could hardly believe that it was one she had lived.

On one occasion, after a long, wearying day, she stood on the back porch with a bucket of scraps for the chooks, as Polly called the chickens. She was thirsty and dreaming of a fresh lime juice like the ones she had drunk in Colombo. If she had still been staying with Ariadne, all she would have had to do was clap her hands and a servant would appear like a genie from a bottle and bring her whatever she desired. Had she really lived that life, she wondered, or had it just been a dream?

She laughed to herself. Putting down the bucket, she clapped. 'A lime juice, please,' she said to the dusty yard. 'With plenty of ice.'

Ice... ice... ice... echoed back at her until the words were swallowed up by the silent outback.

Shaking her head at herself, smiling wryly, she picked up her bucket once more and headed down to the chooks. Perhaps that had been her life once, but this was life now.

She enjoyed feeding the chooks, who came tumbling to meet her whenever she went to their run, and if she had a few minutes to herself, she liked to go down to the creek and sit in the shade of the ghost gums – at least until Polly told her how the branches could break without warning. Iris was more careful where she sat after that.

She was getting used to Australia, she realised, but it wasn't home. She yearned to hear from Rose and Lily and Daisy, but as the weeks passed, she remembered her aunt in Edinburgh. She should have thought to write to her before, she realised. Aunt Edith would surely know where her sisters were.

When Guy came back from Julia Creek one day, flourishing a letter, Iris seized on it.

My dear Iris, Edith wrote, *I was very glad to hear from you, although your situation sounds a difficult one. I dread to think what your mother would think about you married to a virtual stranger and living in such conditions. I am not at all surprised to hear that Ralph's circumstances are reduced. He was fickle as a boy and unreliable as a young man and unlikely to have changed much.*

As for your sisters, I am sorry to say that I have very sad news. As you may know, your Aunt Bessy and her husband were to give your two younger sisters a home, but Bessy felt that Lily would not fit in well with their life in America, and in the event they took only Daisy. Tragically, the ship went down off the coast of Newfoundland. It appears that it may have hit an iceberg just as Titanic *did. Dear Iris, they recovered the bodies of my sister and Hiram, but Daisy was listed as missing and we must presume that she is lost.*

'No!' The words blurred in front of Iris's eyes and she dropped the letter in horror. 'No!' She must have read that wrong. Daisy could not be dead, not her darling, sparkling little sister.

Guy heard her cry and looked up sharply from his own letters. 'What is it?' he demanded, but Iris could only shake her head. 'No, no, no, that can't be true,' she said, numb with disbelief.

He took the letter from her lap and read the first page. 'Oh, Iris,' he said with pity.

'All I wanted was news of them, but not this, not this!'

'What of Rose and Lily?' he asked gently.

'I don't know. I didn't get that far.'

'Do you want me to read the rest of the letter?'

Iris managed a nod. She couldn't get past the idea that Daisy's brilliant light was extinguished. Surely she would have felt it, have known somewhere deep in her bones that her youngest sister was no more? What had she been doing when the ship foundered? Had she been sleeping, oblivious? Had she been dancing or smiling while Daisy thrashed in the cold, black water? While she died alone and in terror?

Iris covered her face with her hands. She couldn't bear it.

Guy was reading Aunt Edith's letter quickly to check that there was no more desperate news. 'Lily and Rose are all right,' he said. 'At least, there is no bad news of them. Lily went to live on the Riviera – with someone called Florence?'

'Another aunt,' said Iris through stiff lips.

'When Lily heard the news about Daisy, it seems that she wrote to your Aunt Edith – what Edith calls "a most intemperate letter" – blaming her for splitting the sisters up. Aunt Edith has heard nothing from her since. She presumes that Lily is with Florence, but Florence, apparently, has never been a good correspondent. As for Rose, Edith has washed her hands of her. Rose announced that she was going to Egypt. "It was most unwise, and I advised her against it",' Guy read out. '"I will not repeat her reply."'

He turned the page. 'It sounds like she has taken umbrage. She talks about your father,' he went on. 'Says that she went all the way to Skara to see him after learning that Daisy was missing but that he refused to open the door and shouted at her to go away. "I am sorry to say that he has lost his reason entirely."' Guy laid the letter down. 'I'm sorry, Iris.'

Iris stared at him, her eyes stark. She felt as if she was slowly buckling under a great weight. 'That's the end,' she whispered. 'Lily and Rose are lost and I don't know how to find them, and Daisy . . .' Her voice cracked at last. 'I'll never see any of them again.'

She wept then, for her sisters, for her home. She wept for her father, alone and raving in his modern house. She wept for Ian, for her love. They were all gone.

Guy held her while she cried, smoothing his hand up and

down her back as though she was a trembling horse in need of soothing.

'They may not be lost,' he said quietly at last, when her sobs had subsided to juddering breaths. 'They may know exactly where they are, just like you know where you are.'

'Not Daisy.'

'She's missing, that's all you know,' he told her. 'Pretend that she's alive somehow, wondering where *you* are.'

Iris was sad for a long time after receiving Aunt Edith's letter. She wrote back asking her aunt for Florence's address, but had a letter in return from Edith's officious daughter-in-law, Veronica, who had spent many years jockeying with her mother-in-law for influence over Edith's hapless son, Robert.

Edith had died quite suddenly, Veronica wrote, and she and Robert had been clearing out the house. *Doubtless you remember what a hoarder of papers she was. We were able to burn it all.* They regretted that they were unable to help.

Iris heard from Ariadne too. Johnny Carsington had decided to retire, and they would be returning to England. It felt like a farewell letter. The last link connecting her to her past had gone, and she was left aching and untethered.

Except for Guy. The thought of him anchored her. She knew him now, knew the sound of his boots on the steps up to the kitchen door. She knew how he paused to brush the dust from his hat before letting the screen door clatter back into place behind him. At mealtimes she would find her eyes lingering on his hands, his jaw, on the pulse beating in his throat, and her mouth would dry. Then she would encounter her uncle's amused expression and have to make herself look away.

And still she couldn't find the words to ask him to love her. She was too shy, and Guy was preoccupied, worried about keeping the station going, exhausted by the gruelling work of making a living out of the harsh land.

Tomorrow, she would say to herself. I'll ask him tomorrow.

43

Roz

Skara, present day

'Hugo!' Roz felt a rush of affection as she saw his familiar figure climbing out of Finn's car. She had suggested that Finn pick Hugo up from the station in Fort William.

'I would have taken you to meet him off the train if you'd asked,' Drew had said.

But Roz didn't want to ask him for anything.

She was mortified at how tightly she had clung to Drew on the beach. She was *never* needy like that. Whenever she remembered the solid feel of him, how safe she had felt with his arms around her, she cringed.

Hold on to me, he had said. But she wouldn't. She couldn't.

Drew had behaved perfectly normally after that, as if nothing whatsoever had happened, but Roz couldn't bear the thought that he had seen her afraid. If only she could rewind time! She would still tell him about Richard, of course, but her teeth wouldn't chatter, her body wouldn't shake. *It's disturbing,* she would have said, *but nothing I can't deal with*. She would have kept her armour in place. She would smile and reassure him that she was fine.

What she wouldn't do was start trembling. She would step back before he could put his arms round her. She wouldn't burrow into him, clutching at him as if he were her only anchor in a terrifying world.

She hadn't let herself hold on to anyone since her father had died and left her to manage alone, and she wouldn't start now.

Roz had avoided Drew ever since. She knew that he was puzzled, but she couldn't help prickling with humiliation whenever she saw him. She perfected a smile that didn't reach her eyes when she encountered him and kept herself to herself. It was easier that way. She didn't want him to tell her that it didn't matter or that everyone was entitled to fall apart at times. She knew that. She just didn't have the luxury of believing it.

And she hated Richard even more because he could make her feel vulnerable and expose herself to pity.

Brittle with embarrassment, she had been wishing that she hadn't encouraged Hugo to come up, but the moment she set eyes on him, her doubts dissolved and she hugged him tightly, breathing in his comfortingly familiar smell of old books and beeswax.

'It's so good to see you again,' she said, pulling back to look him in the face. 'How was your trip? Did you manage to sleep?'

'Like a baby,' he said. 'Thanks to a large glass of Laphroaig.'

'A man after my own heart.' Drew had been watching tight-lipped, but at the sight of Hugo, his expression had lightened and he'd held out a hand.

With some reserve, Roz introduced the two men.

'So you're Hugo?' Drew said, and glanced at Roz. 'Roz has talked a lot about her special friend in London.'

Hugo followed Drew's look and smiled. 'Ah. Did she not mention that I'm in my eighties?'

'No,' said Drew, 'she didn't.'

'I really didn't think it was relevant,' said Roz, and turned to Finn. 'Thank you for coming,' she said, as she hugged him. 'What's the news of your dad?'

'He's getting better slowly,' said Finn. 'It's more my mother who needs help now. They both seem to have suddenly got older. I've arranged for carers to go in once a day to clean and help Dad have a shower, but he doesn't like it.'

'You're doing what you can.' Roz could feel Drew's eyes on her as she smiled at Finn.

Hugo had booked himself a room, which Roz knew Drew had quietly upgraded. He had arranged for Finn to have a room in the hotel as well. Roz knew she should feel grateful, but instead it made her more prickly than ever. She didn't want to feel grateful. She didn't want to feel *anything* for him.

Everything was spinning out of her control. It was good to see Hugo and Finn, of course, but Henrietta wanted to meet them both later, and that meant that Drew would be there too and Roz couldn't relax. She felt as if she were on a plane, taxiing down a runway, gathering pace, wanting to beat her fists against the door but realising that it was too late to get off.

They all met up for afternoon tea in Henrietta's rooms. Roz had brought along the letters and the photo albums she had found while Finn had been away. He and Hugo and Henrietta exclaimed over them while Drew sat, arms folded, as if supervising excited children.

'Since you discovered that Iris changed her name to Henderson on her marriage, I've been able to find out quite a bit more,' said Finn, when it was his turn to contribute. 'I checked the ship manifests and they did indeed sail from Colombo to Australia, on the *Ormonde*. The immigration records show that a Guy and Iris Henderson landed at Port Adelaide in September 1931. It's unclear exactly where they went next, but they pop up in the Queensland records in 1935 as owners of a cattle station called Strathann. Does that name mean anything to you?'

Roz shook her head. 'No. I've never even been to Queensland.'

'So there's still no direct connection between you and Iris apart from your ring?' he said, looking disappointed.

'There's no proof that the ring *was* Iris's,' said Roz, studying it. 'I'm sure that it is, but I presume Kingan, Kingan & McVean will need more than my gut feeling.'

'Very true,' said Finn with a sigh.

'I wonder if it's worth having the ring examined?' Henrietta suggested. 'You might learn something about its history.'

'That's an excellent idea,' said Hugo approvingly. 'I have a friend who is an antique jewellery appraiser. It's amazing what she can tell about a piece. She looks at any jewellers' marks and the style. She could at least tell us where the ring was made, and when. It's possible there'll be a record somewhere of the original necklace Morag mentioned,' he added. 'If it was a special commission, there might be designs and invoices, *something* to connect the stone in your ring to the necklace and therefore you to Iris. The invoice you found only mentions how the rings were made from an existing necklace. We can't be sure that was *the* original necklace.'

'It's an idea,' Finn said. 'Could you take it to Hugo's friend, Roz, and ask her to have a look at it?' He turned to Hugo. 'Is she based in London?'

'She is.'

London, with its swivelling cameras and myriad ways to track her. Roz chewed the inside of her cheek. Hugo saw her hesitation. 'I could take the ring to her if you like. You wouldn't need to come all the way to London.'

Finn was still thinking. 'Are you sure you don't have any papers?' he asked Roz. 'Anything about your family history?'

'There were some,' she admitted. 'I didn't look at them closely when I was clearing my mother's house. I just shoved them in a box along with some other stuff I felt I should keep – pictures, that kind of thing – and left them with a friend.'

'You don't remember what was in them?'

'Not really. My birth certificate, my parents' marriage certificate, that kind of thing.'

'That's all useful stuff,' said Finn. 'The further back you can go with your family history, the better it will be. Now we know more about Iris and where she ended up, it would be good if we could connect her to you somehow.' He looked at Roz hopefully. 'I don't suppose you were thinking of going back to Australia any time soon?'

'I wasn't, no.' Then she saw his expression. 'Do you think it would make a difference?'

'I think it would. Until now, it's all been supposition, but if I'm to make the case that you are indeed an heir to the Blackmore Trust, I'll need documentary proof.'

'What about this place Iris ended up?' said Hugo. 'What was it called again?'

'Strathann. It's a cattle station in north-west Queensland and still a working property. I googled it and found a website.' Finn pulled out his laptop, tapped a few keys and turned the screen to show them an aerial view of a homestead encircled by green, surrounded in its turn by a vast expanse of red earth covered in scrub. A carousel of images blended one into the next: some remarkably healthy-looking cattle; stockmen sitting on high rails around pens; a creek full of dark green mysterious water and bird life; helicopters swooping over great herds of beasts.

'Just the million acres,' he said in a dry voice.

'It looks like a prosperous place,' Hugo commented.

'I gather most grazing properties are owned by companies now, but Strathann is still family-run.' Finn looked up, clearly pleased with his research. 'Guess what the name of the family is?'

'Henderson?' said Henrietta, and Finn nodded.

'Henderson,' he agreed.

'If they're the same family, surely they would be Iris's descendants too,' said Hugo. 'Does that mean they would inherit the trust as well?'

'Only if they're female,' said Finn. 'Charles Blackmore was quite specific. It's an odd condition, but very clear. It's almost as if he wanted to summon his four daughters back. The fact that the Henderson name is still going strong suggests they've had boys, but Iris may have had a daughter too, and *she* may have had a daughter, and if they passed the ring on in each generation, there could be a direct link to Iris.'

'You think I should go,' Roz realised.

'Well, the firm certainly wouldn't authorise a flight to Australia for me, much as I would like it,' said Finn. 'And really, only you can look through your family papers. You could even go and see the Hendersons at Strathann. The answers are in Australia, I'm sure. I don't think we're going to find any more here.'

'Hang on.' Drew spoke for the first time, in a clear voice. 'There's no question of Roz going to Australia.'

Roz stiffened. 'That's up to me.'

'What about this Richard?' There was no trace of the warm humour in Drew's face now, no dancing amusement in his eyes. His expression was deadly serious. 'You told me that he's threatened you in the past, and now he's out of prison he'll be looking for you. And you're proposing to walk right back into his territory! He's a violent man, Roz. He killed your *mother*.'

'Drew, I *know*,' said Roz through gritted teeth.

'How can you even consider this?' he demanded angrily. 'It's a crazy idea!'

'I'm not afraid of Richard Heissen.'

'You should be.' He looked directly at her, and she knew that he was thinking about how she had trembled with fear on the beach. The memory stiffened her spine. She would not be that vulnerable again.

'I'll be careful.'

Drew clutched at his head in frustration. 'Then at least let me come with you.'

'I don't need to be looked after or protected, Drew. I'm perfectly capable of looking after myself,' Roz said fiercely. 'I've managed to get through my life so far without you, and I don't need you or anybody else to tell me what I can and can't do. If I decide to go back to Australia, I will.'

Deliberately she turned to Finn. 'I'll do it. I'll book a flight this afternoon.'

'Oh yes, book a flight in your own name using your own passport when you already know Richard has the resources to track you down digitally!' Drew exploded. 'Brilliant idea!'

Finn was looking from one to the other, concerned. 'Who is this Richard?'

Roz had forgotten she hadn't told him. 'You don't want to know,' she said, and looked defiantly back at Drew. 'If I stay with other people the whole time, what can he do to me?'

'Oh, I don't know . . . shoot you?'

'Drew!' said Henrietta, shocked.

'What?' Drew demanded, as angry as Roz now. 'Let's pretend guns don't exist? Richard sounds like a textbook psychopath. He's not going to play by any rules, and Roz is proposing to stand there effectively waving her arms to get his attention, and what for? To see if she might inherit a house that's too dangerous to live in and that may or may not be cursed!'

'Perhaps Drew is right,' Hugo worried.

'Drew *isn't* right.' Roz took a breath, infuriated by the way Drew had assumed command. Hugo, Henrietta and Finn were all looking at him for guidance now! 'I know Richard is dangerous – nobody knows it better than I do – but the more I think about it, the more I believe my story is tied to Iris's somehow. Until I find out where I fit into it, I can't move on, and I can't move on by being scared of Richard either. I can't keep running from him.'

'Or from commitment,' Drew said clearly. 'That's what this is about, isn't it? You have to manage everything by yourself. Nobody else is allowed to help you.'

'I don't *need* help,' said Roz furiously.

'I don't know about that,' Henrietta put in, 'but Roz is right about needing to get to the bottom of her connection to Acheravie. She's not the only one who can't move on until she does. Acheravie can't move on either. There's something wrong with Rubhan Clachan,' she said. 'It's ruined lives, and Dundonan has suffered ever since James Malcolm sold that land to Charles Blackmore.'

'There's a perfectly rational explanation for all of that,' said Drew, his jaw set.

'Like what?' Roz demanded

'Like economic factors driving young people away. Like trespassers fooling around on a derelict property. Like the Malcolm men having bad judgement when it comes to women. Like bad luck all round. It's ridiculous to keep going on about a curse. Dundonan isn't cursed. We're doing fine.'

'Thanks to you, yes,' his grandmother said, 'but at what cost? Your career, your marriage ... and all the unhappy marriages there have been here. That's a terrible legacy, and if there's a way to break that pattern, we should try. Or rather, we should help Roz try. She's the key to this, I'm sure.'

'Well I don't like it,' said Drew grimly.

'You don't have to like it,' said Roz. 'I'm going to do this. I'm going to Australia, and I'm going to do it on my own.'

44
Iris

Strathann, April 1932

Iris never forgot her first muster.

They set out before dawn and rode north to the stark beauty of rocky red gorges, crossing dry creeks and interminable scrubland of spinifex grass, mallee and spindly mulga to chase the cattle out of their retreats and herd them into a great bellowing mob. Iris wore a scarf tied over her nose and mouth so that she didn't have to breathe in the dust that hung thick in the air. The outback, usually so silent, reverberated with the cracking of whips and the stockmen's cries of *chah, chah, chah* to move the lumbering beasts along.

Twice during the day they stopped for smoko, tethering their horses and letting the mob amble to a halt. Bob, Danny and Jed squatted and rolled themselves cigarettes while Guy made tea in a billycan and Iris handed out some chewy biscuits she had made.

At night, she sat next to Guy by the fire and watched a huge yellow moon rise over the curve of the earth. She caught herself looking at him and marvelling that he was the same man she had first seen on the ship at Southampton. Then, he had been bitter and sardonic, self-contained as he was still, but now he seemed at ease. The night was vast and mysterious, and Iris had no idea where she was, but she didn't feel lost with Guy beside her. She found herself remembering how close he had held her in the dust storm, and she had an overwhelming urge to crawl into his lap again, not because she was terrified but because she wanted to press her lips against his neck and feel his arms close around her as she had then.

All you have to do is ask.

We're stuck here.

I didn't mean it like that, she wanted to say. We're not stuck. We're doing something. We're bringing this property back to life. We're doing it together.

Back at the homestead, the mob of cattle brought a great cloud of red dust with it. It settled over everything in a thick layer. Iris let Guy and the stockmen deal with the counting and the sorting of cows from bullocks, with the dipping and castrating. For a week the yards were full of noise, bellowing and stamping hooves and shouting and swearing, and then Jed, Bob and Danny drove the cattle to the great fenced paddocks. It would take them a day to reach the furthest one, so they would camp overnight and ride back the next day.

Iris stood and listened to the sound of the mob receding into the distance, until silence fell and she and Polly set about cleaning the homestead all over again.

She was very tired when she went out onto the veranda that night. Every evening, Guy came back to wash the dust of the day off while she got the meal ready. Then they would sit and watch the sunset together, talking about their day, before the stockmen arrived for supper. It was Iris's favourite part of the day.

Ralph was often there too, drinking a beer as Guy did, although Iris secretly preferred it when she and Guy were alone. She knew that Guy held in his resentment of Ralph for her sake, but he still felt bitter about her uncle. Ralph sensed it too and seemed to take a perverse pleasure in needling him. It wasn't so bad when the stockmen were there, but when it was just the three of them, Iris was tense, waiting for one or other of them to lose their temper.

That night, it was Guy.

'I'm hungry,' Ralph said, as Iris sat down and smoothed her dress over her knees. 'What's for supper?'

'For God's sake, man,' Guy snapped. 'She's only just sat down!' He was tired too. It had been a long week.

'Just asking, old boy.'

'Don't "old boy" me,' Guy said, with such savagery that Iris jumped in to defuse the tension.

'Canned meat tonight,' she said brightly. 'It's just the three of us, so I thought I would keep it simple.'

'It's always simple here,' sighed Ralph, who was obviously in a provocative mood. 'Couldn't you try something different for once? God, when I think of the meals I've had!' he reminisced.

'Like the curries at the Eastern & Oriental in Penang?' Guy suggested dangerously.

'Exactly. Now *that* was a civilised place, and the women there were always so beautifully dressed. You should have seen them, Iris,' said Ralph, eyeing her worn dress with distaste. 'You could have taken a lesson from them in how to dress for a hot climate. Your mother would have been horrified to see you looking like this. It can't be that hard to look like a lady instead of a dusty drab.'

'That's *it*!' Guy was out of his chair and had grabbed Ralph by the collar, ignoring his yelp of protest. 'I'm *sick* of you,' he said, lifting him up until his feet were dangling helplessly and shaking him. 'I'm sick of you sitting around all day, complaining and doing nothing to help.'

'Guy, please . . .' Iris began, but Guy had had enough.

'No! He's had this coming.' He shook Ralph again, provoking a choke of protest. 'You let Iris wait on you hand and foot, and now, *now*, you have the nerve to criticise her! Iris is a lady, and she's beautiful whatever she wears. Apologise to her!'

'It doesn't matter,' Iris said, biting her lip as Ralph could only gurgle. What if Guy strangled him?

'It *does* matter!' Guy was beyond reason. 'Do you have any idea what she has been through?' he demanded of Ralph. 'What she's had to do because of *you*? Because you swanned off with money that could have saved her and her sisters. You promised her mother you would repay it. It was a debt of *honour*, but you don't understand the meaning of the word. You let Iris struggle and struggle—'

'Didn't . . . know . . .' Ralph gasped, scrabbling at Guy's hands at his throat.

'Because you didn't ask! You didn't keep in touch, after everything your sister had done for you. If you had, you would have known that she was dead, and it might have crossed your mind to find out how your nieces were and to ask if they needed help, but oh no! You were too busy swindling your way through life, leaving a trail of ruin behind you.

'You're the most selfish, thoughtless, crooked person I've ever encountered,' he told Ralph, shaking him on every adjective. 'It's sheer luck that Iris found you, and since then she has nursed you, she's cleaned you and fed you and washed your clothes, while working her fingers to the bone to try to keep things going, things that *you* have let go, when if she'd had any sense she would have left you lying on your stinking sheets and gone home. And now you *dare* criticise how she looks!'

With an exclamation of disgust, he threw Ralph down the steps.

'Guy!' Iris was on her feet.

'Leave him,' Guy ordered. 'He's not hurt, but I hope he's had a fright.' He watched, face set, as Ralph struggled onto all fours, coughing and spluttering and pawing at his throat. 'Let him grovel around in the dust where he belongs. He's not coming back up here until he apologises to you.'

With an effort, Ralph hauled himself to his feet and brushed himself down, clearly shaken.

'I apologise for my thoughtless comment, Iris,' he said hoarsely.

'And for not repaying her mother's debt,' Guy said, remorseless.

Ralph swallowed. 'And for not keeping in touch with Amelia and asking if she or you needed anything,' he said obediently. He glanced nervously at Guy. 'I have indeed been a bad brother and a bad uncle.'

'While you're at it, you can apologise to me.' Guy stood at the top of the steps, glaring down at Ralph. 'You sneer at what we're trying to do here, but it's my money that's keeping you alive. Where do you think the canned meat you turn your nose up at comes from? We're not making anything from Strathann yet, but at least we're trying. You never did a day's work in your life. Easier for you to lie and cheat than to work for what you want, but you've failed at everything you've ever done – except for ruining other people's lives, or betraying and disappointing the people who love and care for you.'

'You're right,' said Ralph, 'and I'm sorry. Genuinely sorry.'

'If it was up to me, I'd turn you out and let the dingoes have at you, but Iris wouldn't let me do it.'

'She has a kind and forgiving heart,' said Ralph, who was rapidly recovering his old nonchalance. 'And you're right, Guy. She *is* beautiful.' He looked up at Iris. 'Iris, my dear, Guy is right about everything. I *am* thoughtless, but I *have* appreciated everything you have done for me since you got here, and I promise to never again cast a word of aspersion against your clothing or your cooking.'

'You'd better not,' growled Guy. 'I'm going to get another beer.' He stomped inside and let the screen door slam behind him, but he brought another beer out for Ralph when he came back, and oddly, the incident seemed to clear the air. They ate the simple meal amicably together and Ralph helped to clear up before taking himself off to bed.

'Thank you for defending me,' Iris said later, when she and Guy were back on the veranda. The crickets whirred in the darkness and she could hear the creaking frogs and the occasional howl of a dingo in the distance that made Toby prick up his ears.

Guy hunched a shoulder. 'He had it coming.'

'I'm not saying he didn't deserve everything you said. I just didn't expect my tired old dress to be the cause of the row.' She gestured ruefully down at it, but she shivered inside remembering how Guy had raged at Ralph: *she's beautiful.* 'And he's done much worse to you than to me.'

'I know.' Guy flexed his hands as if he could still feel Ralph's weight. 'I just saw red when he spoke about you like that. It's like he doesn't even *see* you. He doesn't see how you *shine*. But he's right in a way,' he went on. 'You *should* be wearing fine clothes and living like the lady you are. I can't give you anything at the moment,' he said, frustrated. 'Not even a decent dress.'

'You don't need to give me anything,' said Iris, touched. 'We're in this together, remember? Oh, look!' she added, pointing as a shooting star streaked across the sky.

'Make a wish,' said Guy.

Iris was surprised to find herself hesitating. Until that moment, her instinctive wish would always have been to go home to Skara and Ian, but now, she wasn't sure.

'Did you wish?' he asked.

'Did you?' she countered.

He nodded, and their eyes met. 'You should never tell a wish,' he said softly. 'It might not come true.'

Iris's heart was knocking painfully against her ribs, making it hard to breathe.

All you have to do is ask.

'Do you remember when we got married?' she said, and it was easier than she had expected. 'You said you wouldn't lay a finger on me unless I asked you to.'

In the dim light, an alertness crept into his eyes. 'I remember,' he said.

She swallowed. 'What would you say if I asked you now?'

'To lay a finger on you?'

She couldn't see his smile start, but she could hear it in his voice as he reached across and laid one finger on her wrist, where her pulse was pounding.

'Yes,' she whispered. 'Or more than a finger, if ... if you wanted.'

His hand curled round her wrist to tug her up to stand with him. 'I'd say: who said wishes don't come true? I'd say: what took you so long?'

'I didn't think you wanted me,' said Iris humbly, and she felt his jolt of surprise.

'What on earth made you think that?'

'You never asked me to dance once on the ship.'

He shook his head. 'I've wanted you since I first saw you on deck the day we left Southampton. You stood there with your clear blue eyes, always so straight and so true. You shone then, Iris, and you're shining still. Not want you?' He laughed softly in disbelief. 'It's true that I never asked you to dance, but that's because there were always other men there waiting to dance with you. I've never cared for standing in line. I didn't want to be just another man lucky enough to have his arms around you, just someone else who could pull you closer and breathe in the scent of your hair.' His voice was very low and reverberated over Iris's skin. 'I didn't want to share you, Iris. I wanted you all to myself, and if I couldn't have that, I told myself it would be easier if I didn't dance with you at all.'

His hand was warm around hers as he drew her down the

steps to the yard and pulled her closer. 'Dance with me now,' he said against her ear, and she shivered at the desire in his voice.

'There's no music,' she said unsteadily, but they were already swaying together, turning in slow circles in the dusty cattle yard. Guy held her tight against him. He took his time, his hand sliding, warm and persuasive, down her spine and his mouth drifting from her hair to nuzzle the lobe of her ear.

'Isn't there?' he asked as Iris gasped and arched her neck in response, and she felt him smile against her skin. 'I think we can make our own music, don't you?'

Iris melted into him, her hand creeping to his shoulder. 'I think we can,' she said, and their heads drew close as they held each other and danced together at last in the starlight.

45

Finn

Edinburgh, present day

'Yes, what is it?' James Kingan looked up irritably as Finn knocked on the door.

'I thought you would like to know that I've made some progress on the Blackmore Trust at last.'

The annoyance at the interruption faded from James's face as he put down his pen and sat back in his plush leather chair. 'Have you now?' He beckoned Finn in and pointed at the rather less comfortable chair on the other side of his desk.

'You'll remember I told you about Roz Chatton, the Australian who bought the Blackmore letters?'

'I do indeed.'

'Roz – Ms Chatton – has been at Skara for the last couple of months and has found a number of letters and photos that have been very useful in establishing what happened to the Blackmore daughters.' Finn skirted quickly over how Roz had discovered the letters. He didn't want James Kingan enquiring too closely into how she had been able to access the house. 'It seems that all four girls went overseas. We've established that Iris went to Ceylon and then on Australia. One sister seems to have gone to the Riviera, one to America and one to Egypt.'

'Egypt? Good grief, what was wrong with running away to Glasgow?'

'It certainly might have made their descendants easier to track down,' Finn agreed with a wry look. 'The letters we've found are from Iris Blackmore, and they've made it possible for me to check shipping and immigration records. She married in Ceylon and ended up on a cattle station in Queensland, which is still run by her descendants.'

'Ah. So Australia is the connection with this Roz Chatton?'

'It's looking likely,' said Finn cautiously. 'Roz has a ring that might well have belonged to Iris.'

James grunted and pulled at his ear lobe while he thought. 'We'd need more than a ring, though.'

'I've discussed that with her, and she's on her way back to Australia to see if she can find some family papers that will prove her descent from Iris Blackmore.'

Finn wasn't at all sure that Roz should have been going to Australia. Drew Malcolm had filled him in on the situation with her stepfather, and Finn, appalled, had tried suggesting that she rethink her trip, but she was adamant that she would go.

Clearly she and Drew had had a huge row of some kind. Finn was not a fool. He knew that the warm hug she had given him on arrival had been largely for Drew's benefit. Certainly Drew hadn't liked her decision to go back to Edinburgh with Finn and fly to London and then on to Adelaide.

'If I'm going to go, I may as well go as soon as I can,' she'd said briskly.

Having only just arrived, Hugo was to stay on at Dundonan for a few days and then take Roz's ring back to London to be examined by the expert he knew.

Roz had been quiet on the drive back to Edinburgh. 'You know Drew's just worried about you,' Finn had tried, but she turned her face away.

'I don't want him to worry about me. I can look after myself.'

'Is there anything I can do to help?' he asked after a moment.

'You're already doing more than enough by taking me to the airport,' she had said, mustering a smile. 'I'll be fine, really.'

Finn suspected she said that a lot.

Roz had hugged him at the airport, and this time Drew had not been watching. 'You're a good friend,' she told him. 'I'll be in touch as soon as I've looked at the papers.'

'That sounds more promising.' James cocked a tufty grey eyebrow in Finn's direction at the news that Roz was on her way back to Australia, and Finn wrenched his mind back to the office. 'What about the other sisters?'

'I've put out more feelers now that we know, or think we know, where the other three were headed. Tragically, the youngest sister seems to have died on her way to America, but I can start looking at manifests for ships to Alexandria. It might be harder to track down information for the daughter who went to the Riviera, though. Presumably she would have travelled there by train.'

'Well, keep at it,' said James. 'You've got one possible female descendant in Miss Chatton, so that's a start. Carry on, Findlay.'

He picked up his pen again in a clear dismissal.

Finn met Aileen for a drink that night and found himself telling her all about Roz and the argument with Drew.

'Sounds like she's absolutely terrified of relying on anyone, poor girl,' said Aileen. 'And I don't blame her with a mother like that. She's hiding behind a prickly hedge because that's where she feels safe. Let's hope this Drew can hack his way through to her and give her a happy ending.'

'I had hoped I might be able to do that,' Finn admitted, 'but I know that if I burst through the thorns instead of Drew, she'd be disappointed.' He summoned a smile to make light of it. 'It looks like I just get to be a good friend again.'

Aileen put her hand over his. 'You *are* a good friend, Finn. You don't know how special that is. You're a good son and a good brother, too, even if your family don't appreciate you. And one of these days you're going to meet someone who'll want you as more than a friend. I'm not sure what she'll be like, but I don't think it's Roz.' There was a tiny pause. 'And it's not me either.'

Finn sighed a little and turned his hand over to squeeze Aileen's. 'I know,' he said.

46
Iris

Strathann, February 1933

Iris sent no more letters back to Skara. She would never see her sisters again, she knew that now. She would never be able to go home.

Her heart cracked when she thought of the hills and the sea, of the cool, damp air. Sometimes she would squeeze her eyes shut and picture the beach below Rubha Clachan. She would tell herself that she could hear the sea shushing onto the sand, could smell the gorse. That she could look up to Dundonan and see Ian coming down to meet her. His features were blurry now, but she remembered the sweetness of loving him, the certainty of being loved in return and knowing that they belonged together.

And then she would open her eyes and see the heat shimmering on the horizon, and her chest would feel as if there was an iron band around it, tightening, tightening, until she forced herself to take a breath and remember that this sunburnt country was home now.

Though she never posted the letters, she wrote to her sisters still, to Rose and to Lily, and to Daisy, who she could not, would not, believe was dead. It helped her to feel that she was still in touch with them; that they were still out there somewhere. She told them about her life in the outback, about the flies and the thunderbox in the yard with its lurking spiders, and the snakes that coiled and slithered between sacks of flour. About the brutal heat. About the bellowing cattle and the incessant cawing of the crows and the red dust that got everywhere.

But she told them too about the light that etched every leaf in startling detail. The smell of the creek, hot and dry, and the blur of pink and white in the sky as the cockatoos and galahs wheeled above the trees. About the stars that blotted out the dark night with their brilliance. About the quiet and the stillness and the vast horizon.

When she wrote, she could imagine exactly how each of her sisters would react to her news. Rose would lean forward, her face vivid and eager to hear about sleeping in a swag under the stars. Daisy would clap her hand over her mouth and shudder dramatically at the mere mention of a snake, while Lily would listen, head cocked to one side, and quirk an eyebrow if she thought Iris was exaggerating for effect.

She didn't tell them everything, of course. Some things were private. She said nothing about the nights with Guy. His hands, hard and insistent. His mouth, warm and coaxing. The way his muscles flexed in response when she touched him. The way his pulse raced. The way he smiled against her skin. The breathless, gasping pleasure. That was not for her sisters to know, and even if it had been, how could Iris have explained it?

She and Guy never talked of love. Guy could be difficult. He was often touchy and short-tempered. But when he turned to her at night, and set the liquid desire burning through her, she knew a hunger and a need she could never have imagined before.

When she discovered that she was expecting a baby, it seemed yet another sign that her life was at Strathann now.

The news has brought Guy and Ralph into an unexpected alliance, she wrote to her sisters. *They are both insisting on treating me as if I were made of glass, until I had to snap at them to stop it. That shocked them more than the news of the baby! But I'm not ill. I will manage. But oh, how I wish you were here to be with me!*

They were all short-tempered in the enervating heat. The sky was a colourless glare. The rains had not come as expected in November, and as Christmas passed, and January, the last traces of grass had withered and browned. The cattle grew thinner, and Iris watched the worry lines deepen in Guy's face as he scanned the horizon for clouds.

'It's a cruel land,' Ralph kept saying unhelpfully.

'Then why the hell did you invest all your money – all *our* money! – in it?' snarled Guy.

Day after day, Iris would stand on the back veranda and pray for rain, for some relief from the crushing heat. The nights were hot and airless and she couldn't get comfortable in bed. Her back ached, her feet ached and she wished – how she wished! – that she could talk to her mother, or to one of her sisters. How could she have a baby out here in this dying brown land? It was impossible to imagine a time when the creeks would be full and the grass would grow.

Sometimes a breeze would set the windmill creaking and they would look up at the sky hopefully, but it did no more than lift the dust and send it swirling across the plain, making Iris shudder with memories of the time she and Guy had been trapped in the ute on their way out to Strathann. The well provided water for them to drink, but there was not enough to make the grass grow. They would survive, but their precious cattle would not. Unless it rained.

Iris dreamt about home as if it were a mythical place. She yearned for the sea, for the damp, cool air of Skara, where the burns tumbled down the hillsides and never ran dry.

The temperature soared and the drought tightened its grip on the land. They sent away what cattle they could on agistment further south, where there was grass still, but so many more died, their corpses bloating over the land, and only the crows and the flies prospered. Every day Iris prayed for rain, and every day the sky burnt pitilessly down and the heat pounded until the ground was cracked. Even Guy started to lose heart. They had to let the men go. They all lost weight.

For Iris, the drought was biblical in its horror. This surely was the end. How could they possibly survive here? Ralph was right. It was a cruel land, and the worry was making them all tense. Guy and Ralph argued, a new edge to their sniping that worried Iris almost as much as the lack of rain. Something would have to break.

And then one day she stepped out onto the back veranda with a mug of tea, as she did every morning, and a breeze, barely more than a breath, stole up the steps and lifted the hair at the nape of her neck. There was something different about the light. She stood with one hand pressed into her back and stretched, her eyes on the horizon. 'Was that . . .? Could it be . . .?'

'Guy!' she called excitedly as she saw him crossing the yard, with Toby ever faithful at his heels. She pointed at the horizon, where a dark line could just be made out. 'Clouds?'

He joined her on the veranda, and together they stared at the line, straining their ears. 'Thunder,' he said, his voice lifting with hope as they heard a long, low mutter. 'It's a storm.'

'Is it coming our way?'

The screen door clattered as Ralph joined them. 'I've just been talking to Jim Cressy at the store on the radio,' he said. 'He reckons there's a cyclone moving down from the north.'

They wouldn't let themselves believe it at first. They had had false alarms before, when the promised rainclouds skirted them or spun back to the ocean. But this time there was a heaviness to the air, a queer tension that made it impossible to settle to anything. All day they found themselves going back to the veranda to stare at the dark clouds massing on the horizon and will them to move their way.

By the afternoon, Iris had given up. She went inside to slice some beef for the evening meal. It was too hot to cook. The storm wasn't going to come their way, she thought in despair. They were going to miss the rain.

'Iris! Iris! Come here!'

Guy's call had her running out to join him and Ralph on the veranda, still wiping her hands on a tea towel. 'The wind's changed,' Guy said, his face blazing. 'Look!'

Sure enough, the breeze was picking up. It rattled the slatted wooden blinds that kept the sun off the veranda and swirled up dry leaves from the creek, sending them skittering along the ground. Toby whined.

'Come on, come on,' Guy muttered, just as a loud grumble of thunder rolled over the outback. The clouds roiled and rumbled as they moved nearer, boiling blackly up until they blotted out the sky, while thunder crashed and lightning cracked.

Closer and closer it came, seeming to devour everything in its path: the creek, the yards, the sheds, and then it was on the homestead with a great clap of thunder, terrifying and magnificent. They held their breath.

A single rain drop splattered into the dust.

'Here it comes!' shouted Guy over the noise of the thunder, and down the rain came, crashing onto the ground and drumming deafeningly on the corrugated-iron roofs, and they were all laughing wildly and hugging each other, and Toby, caught up in the excitement, was barking in a frenzy.

Guy pulled Iris against his side as they stood together, careless of the rain that was leaking through the veranda roof and splashing around them. 'It's raining,' he said, smiling in a way she hadn't seen him smile for months.

'It is,' she agreed as she leant into him.

His arm tightened around her. 'It's going to be all right,' he said, and she nodded.

'It is,' she said again.

47

Strathann, present day

Roz looked down from the helicopter at the roof of the homestead, where the name of the station was painted in huge letters: *STRATHANN*.

Around the building, she could see bright patches of grass, flowering jacarandas and the unmistakable turquoise of a swimming pool. Spread out around the homestead were other, smaller houses with the same low iron roofs and startlingly vivid green lawns set against the vast expanse of red earth and mallee scrub.

It was a far cry from the tumbledown property Iris had known. There was an airstrip where three helicopters sat with a couple of two-seater planes. There were great sheds, and a maze of cattle yards and paddocks, where horses stood flicking their tails in the shade, apparently used to the choppy mechanical whirr of the helicopter.

And there, the creek with its leaning ghost gums. Iris would have recognised that, Roz thought, but little else. How different her arrival had been, gritty with dust after a long and uncomfortable drive from Julia Creek.

Roz, in contrast, had merely had to climb into a helicopter to be transported easily over miles and miles of red earth. The immensity and power of the ancient land below her made her feel small. Ridgewell had space and scrub and gums, of course, but nothing like this, and she found herself longing, as Iris had done, for the softer blue-grey light of Skara, for the gleaming sea and the purple sweep of the hills.

It was a relief to leave Ridgewell. Bronwen had met her at the airport in Adelaide, but in spite of her pleasure at seeing her friend again, Roz was twitchy until they were in the car and on the road. She had had plenty of time to think on the flight from London, plenty of time to realise that she had overreacted. What if Drew was right and returning to Ridgewell was a crazy thing to do? As her passport was checked, she imagined alerts popping up on Richard's phone. Was the immigration officer texting him under the desk even now? She stood at the carousel feeling exposed and vulnerable; and she paused and took a deep breath just before leaving the baggage area, suddenly convinced that Richard would be waiting for her outside.

She wished she had listened to Drew.

She would be fine, she told herself. She just needed to find the family papers and go.

When they got to Ridgewell, Bronwen showed her into the garage, where she had stacked Roz's boxes. 'Okay if I leave you to poke around for the papers?' she asked. 'Mum's been looking after the twins, and I need to go and relieve her. I won't be long, so make the most of the quiet.'

'Sure,' said Roz, with a bright smile, but she was nervous when Bronwen had gone. She'd told Drew that she'd stick with other people, and yet here she was alone already.

It was very quiet in the garage. There was a small window at the side, half covered with a creeping plant that bobbed in the breeze and produced flickering shadows that made Roz start and glance up. Her stomach was tight as she searched quickly through the boxes. In one, she found a stash of small landscapes that had hung on her mother's wall for years. Roz's own taste was for a more modern style, and she had never looked at the pictures properly before, but now she pulled them out of the box. They were almost all outback scenes: a homestead with a rickety windmill, a creek. She peered at the artist's signature and wasn't even surprised when she made it out. *Iris Henderson.*

There was a gathering sensation in the back of her mind, a conviction that everything was falling into place. She glanced at her finger, half expecting the ring to warm in agreement, but it was back in London, where Hugo was having it assessed. It felt strange without the feel of it on her hand.

A scrabbling sound made her heart jerk, and she almost dropped the painting. For long moments she crouched, unmoving, on the garage floor, clutching the picture and listening desperately for another sign of an intruder, until she realised how she must look to an observer. The thought was enough to make her straighten and put the painting back in the box with hands that weren't quite steady.

Just possums in the roof, she told herself. She wasn't scared.

Except that, she realised slowly, she *was* scared.

Roz paused in the act of shoving the box with the paintings

back into the pile. How had it taken her so long to admit it to herself? She insisted that she was brave and strong, but the truth was that she had been scared since her father had died and left her alone with the dragon of grief. She had kept everyone at arm's length ever since, not because she was tough, but because she was afraid of being abandoned again. She was terrified that the dragon that had lurked inside her since her father's death would raise its monstrous head once more, that it would open its maw and breathe fire and shrivel her up completely.

That was why she had pushed Drew away. She knew that she had hurt him by withdrawing so abruptly and refusing to let him help her. It wasn't as if anything had happened between them, but she hadn't been able to deny that there was *something* there, a connection so powerful that she had been spooked. Roz could admit it to herself now. She had been too afraid of how Drew might hurt her to think about how happy he might make her. The fear of being left alone had made her insist on being alone. How stupid and stubborn she had been!

Was she really going to let something that had happened when she was eleven dictate the rest of her life?

Perhaps it was time to stop being scared.

Pondering her new realisation, she barely jumped when her phone beeped and a message flashed up: *Welcome home.*

Richard, telling her that he knew she was back.

She bit her lip. Well, she had insisted on coming here alone, she remembered. She would just have to get on with it. And be very careful.

Still, she was glad to be going to Queensland the next day.

She had found the family papers at last. Bringing the box

inside, she smoothed the certificates out on Bronwen's dining room table. There was her own birth certificate: Rose Chatton. It wasn't that she had forgotten her real name, but it was only now that the possible significance struck her. She had been named after her grandmother, another Rose, whose death certificate Roz's mother had evidently stuffed into an envelope. Roz unfolded it, and then shook out the envelope. There was another paper in there.

A birth certificate for Rose Bell, daughter of Jim Bell and Amelia Bell, née Henderson. Born at Strathann Station, Queensland, 6 May 1956.

Roz sat back, suddenly breathless. Here it was, proof at last, a connection to Strathann and to Iris.

Taking photos of everything she could find, she emailed it all to Finn.

She had already contacted the Hendersons through the website, mentioning a possible family connection to Iris, and Evelyn Henderson had responded immediately. *Come and stay*, she wrote. *Michael, my husband, is interested in the family history. He's Guy and Iris Henderson's grandson, but we've no idea where they came from. Maybe you can fill in some blanks for us. Get yourself to Julia Creek and we'll pick you up.*

Now she shook off the sense of being watched. Surely Richard's connections didn't extend to outback Queensland?

Evelyn Henderson came to meet her as Roz climbed out of the helicopter. She was a lean, grey-haired, capable-looking woman, but even in jeans and a shirt with *Strathann* embroidered on it, there was a certain dash about her. She wore a bright lipstick and her handshake was firm.

'Welcome to Strathann, Roz.'

She drove Roz back to the homestead, past men and women moving purposefully in and out of the sheds. There was a cluster of stockmen perched on high railings, evidently discussing the qualities of a penned bull. Others were shouting across the yard as they got onto quad bikes or unpacked a truck.

'It's busier than I imagined,' Roz said.

'Cattle stations are big business,' Evelyn told her. 'Most of them have been taken over by corporations now, but we're proud of the fact that Strathann is still a family business. That's why we're keen to know more about our history here.'

Roz recognised the homestead from one of Iris's sketches. The wide, low roof, the deep turned veranda, the old door. She climbed the same steps that Iris must have climbed so many times, but inside she could only gape. Ralph's ramshackle house that had so horrified Iris had been transformed. They had kept the elegance of the colonial house at the front, but the whole of the rear had been extended with a striking modern design. From the kitchen, equipped with the latest technology, she could look out past a beautifully shaded garden to the swimming pool.

'This is incredible,' she said to Evelyn. 'Iris would be amazed. I think she had to look out at the chooks.'

Evelyn laughed. 'We've still got chooks. I guess it was a bit different in her day. It was Duncan, Michael's father, who really turned Strathann around. He was a wily one, all right. He bought up a lot of neighbouring stations and made Strathann profitable before the corporations got their hands on it.'

Later, Roz met Michael Henderson. In his seventies, he was as lanky and grey-haired as his wife, his long legs bandy after years in the saddle. She was also introduced to three of their sons, all married and living in their own houses on the station.

She was thoughtful when she went to change before supper that night. The Blackmore curse, if curse it was, did not seem to have affected the Hendersons. No one looking at the homestead and surroundings could doubt that Strathann was a prosperous and well-run station, and she had heard no talk of any tragedies.

Over supper in the dining room at the homestead, she told the Hendersons about Iris's letters, and how Guy and Iris had come to Strathann in search of Ralph Davidson.

'I know they found him and that he was very ill, but after a while Iris stopped writing. I think she must have given up hope of a reply, but it's frustrating not knowing what happened after that,' she said.

'There's a Ralph Davidson buried with the family,' Evelyn said. 'We've often wondered who he was. I'll show you the graves tomorrow if you like,' she offered.

'I think there's a load of old letters in the box my dad kept in his office, too,' Michael added. 'I'll look them out for you, Roz, and you can have a read of them. There might be something in there.'

After the meal, Michael dug out a dog-eared photo album and turned it back to the beginning. 'There they are,' he said, pointing to a family group on the veranda, looking self-consciously at the camera. Roz recognised Iris at once from the photos she had found at Rubha Clachan, but she studied Guy with interest. He was unsmiling, but holding a small boy in his arms, and he looked completely at home in the outback. Beside them stood an older man with an amused expression and aristocratic features. They had found Ralph at last.

'That's Dad,' Michael said, pointing at the child in Guy's arms.

'Duncan?'

'That's right. He loved this place. We all do. Strathann's in our bones now.'

Fascinated, Roz turned the pages of the album until she came across a photo of Duncan with another baby.

'Who's this?'

Michael peered closer. 'Oh, that's his sister, Amelia. My aunt.'

That name again.

'That's a sad story,' he went on. 'I don't remember her – she died when I was just a baby – but by all accounts she was a pistol. She hurt her back falling off a horse when she was just a kid, but that didn't stop her. She learnt to fly instead, and helped with the mustering, just as we use the choppers today. Dad told me that she married some guy who came out to work at Strathann, but he was gored by a bull and died barely weeks after the wedding.

'Then it turned out she was pregnant, but she didn't show much interest in the baby. She wouldn't even name her daughter. She just wanted to get back in a plane. One day she took off for Townsville and never came back. They found the plane a couple of weeks later. Impossible to know whether it was an accident or she crashed it deliberately.'

'Postnatal depression, we'd call it now,' Evelyn put in.

'What happened to the baby? Did she ever get a name?'

'It was Iris who named her—'

'Rose?' said Roz before she could finish.

'That's right.' They looked at her in surprise.

'My grandmother,' she said. 'Her birth certificate says she was born at Strathann Station. I never really knew her, but I think she was quite eccentric.'

'That would be right. Rose grew up here with me, but she never fitted in,' Michael remembered. 'She didn't ride. She was difficult about everything. Looking back, I guess she was very unhappy, poor kid, but at the time I just thought she was a pain. She went right off the rails, and after Iris died, nobody ever saw her here again.'

Poor Rose, her grandmother, who had drifted in and out of communes and never found a place of her own; Roz's own mother, Millie, who had lost one husband and been killed by another; and Amelia, lost to her grief in the aching blue sky. It was a cruel curse that affected only the women, Roz thought bitterly. The sons had prospered and the daughters had all the bad luck.

But the connection was made. She was Iris's great-great-granddaughter. She couldn't wait to tell Finn and Hugo.

And Drew.

There was no mobile signal at Strathann, so it would have to be an email.

Before she went to bed, Michael handed her a battered box. 'These are the letters I was telling you about. You're welcome to have a read of them.'

Roz took the box as if it were a holy relic and carried it to her bedroom. She recognised Iris's handwriting on the first letter and unfolded it, puzzled. Why would Iris have been writing to herself?

My dearest sisters, Duncan is growing fast. He is the sweetest baby, with fat, dimpled wrists and a gurgling laugh. I wish you could see him. You would adore him too. Sometimes I watch him sleeping and everything about him seems miraculous: his tiny toes, his starfish hands, the bloom of his skin. When he squints sometimes, I think he has a look of Uncle Ralph about him (I haven't said this to Guy, who likes to think his boy is a Henderson through and through!). Ralph professes to have no time for babies, but if he thinks I'm not looking he will take Duncan on his knee and make funny faces until Duncan is helpless with giggles. Between you and me, our uncle is besotted! As for Guy, I watch him with his son, and the expression on his face makes me want to cry for some stupid reason. I miss you all, I miss Skara, but at the same time, my heart is so full here.

Roz put down the sheet of paper, absurdly touched to realise Iris had continued to write to her sisters even when she had lost hope of a letter ever reaching them.

She sat up long into the night reading the letters Iris had written but never posted. The next day Evelyn took her to a shady area near the creek with a cluster of simple headstones. Roz knelt and traced Iris's name carved into the stone with her fingertip. Iris, who had loved Skara so much and who had died so far from home. Guy was buried there too, next to Iris, and Ralph. There were gravestones for Michael's parents, and for tragic Amelia. How sad, Roz thought, that her own grandmother had not been able to find a place here too.

She spent two restful days reading Iris's letters and exploring the creek. She counted cattle with Evelyn and collected eggs from the chooks, and in the evening ate with the Hendersons. Afterwards, they sat on the screened-in veranda and chatted comfortably.

'I think Iris came to love it here,' Roz said. 'And I can see why. It's so peaceful.' With ironic timing, a scream of terror made her heart jerk, and she spilt her beer. 'What was that?' she said, horrified.

Michael laughed. 'Sounds like someone being tortured, doesn't it? Don't you have bush stone-curlews in the city? They're hard to see – they blend right into the leaf litter, but you can hear them all right.'

'That was a *bird*?' Roz's heart was still racing.

'Oh, yeah. They're noisy buggers but harmless. There's an Aboriginal legend that if you hear a bush stone-curlew crying in the dark, it means someone's going to die.'

Roz shuddered.

'Don't listen to him,' said Evelyn. 'It's just a silly story.'

Inside, a phone started ringing. Michael heaved himself out of his chair. 'I'll get it.' When he came back, his face was grave. 'It's for you, Roz. I'm sorry, it sounds like bad news.'

48

Roz

London, present day

Roz was appalled when she saw Hugo. He was heavily bandaged and seemed to have shrunk, dwarfed by the hospital bed. There was a tube coming out of his nose, and he was attached by wires to machines that beeped and whirred.

How could this be Hugo? He didn't belong here in the artificial light with the colourless floor and the smell of antiseptic and those ominously flashing lights. He belonged in his shop, in his saggy armchair, with books and pictures piled up around him and photos of his beloved Lucy on the wall.

Her heart was cracking, splintering. She thought of his gentle humour, his bright curiosity, the kindness and warmth he had shown her ever since she stepped inside his shop. She couldn't bear the thought of Ballantyne's desecrated, the beautiful books and paintings, his treasured maps, all burnt and black, sodden with water from the fire hoses.

Roz had lost count of the hours since she had stood in Michael

Henderson's office at Strathann and heard Drew's voice from the other side of the world.

'Hugo's in hospital. There's been a fire at the shop and he's been badly burnt. He's asking for you. Can you come back?'

The long journey to London was a blur. Roz sat numbly, uncaring of the discomfort, just desperate to get back to see Hugo.

Drew met her at Heathrow and took her straight to the hospital in a taxi, the situation too grim to remember the awkwardness between them when she had left for Australia.

'He's in a bad way,' he told her. 'The burns are bad, but the smoke inhalation is worse. It seems he got out, but went back into the shop to find your painting and then collapsed. When the fire officers found him, he was shielding the picture with his body.'

Roz's dry eyes burnt. 'Oh, why didn't he just *leave* it?' she cried. 'It's only a painting!'

'Hugo obviously felt it was more than that. He had your ring in his pocket, too.' Drew dug into the inner pocket of his jacket and pulled out the blue opal ring, but Roz threw out her hands in a gesture of repugnance.

'That bloody ring! Chuck it out of the window!' she said wildly. 'Morag's right, the whole business is cursed. I wish I'd never seen that painting or walked into Ballantyne's.'

'Then you would have missed getting to know a good man who cares for you very much.' Drew started to put the ring back in his jacket, but Roz snatched at it.

'Give me that! I don't want anything happening to *you* now!' She pushed it onto her finger, hating it, not trusting it to keep anyone she loved safe. 'Why have you got it anyway?'

'We got on very well after you left.' There was a slight reserve in Drew's voice. 'Hugo rang me when he returned to London to say that he'd been straight to see his friend the jewellery expert. She was apparently very excited and took lots of pictures. She promised to see what she could find and let him and Finn know as soon as possible.

'The police found his phone, and as I was the last number he'd called, they contacted me and told me what had happened. I came down straight away, and the hospital gave me his valuables, just his watch and the ring. I told him I'd keep them both for you. He's been unconscious most of the time, but he did ask for you.'

'Hugo?' Her voice cracked as she sat by his bed and took his hand.

His eyes flickered and opened. 'Lucy?' he murmured.

Roz swallowed. 'It's Roz.'

'Dear girl.' Hugo managed a squeeze of her hand. 'The painting . . . is it safe?'

'It is, but you shouldn't have gone back for it,' she said, her voice thick with tears. 'You're more important than any painting.'

'It was more than a painting. It brought you to me,' he said, his voice barely more than a whisper, but even now, being Hugo, he could manage a smile. 'My only regret is that Lucy never met you. She would have loved you too.'

'Oh, Hugo!' Roz dropped her head to the bed and wept.

She felt him lift his hand to her hair. 'Don't cry, dear girl,' he said. 'I'm ready to go. I want to see Lucy again.'

'Please don't go, Hugo,' she begged, lifting her head, careless of the tears running down her face. 'I can't manage without you.'

'You've got Drew now,' said Hugo faintly. 'He's a good man.

Let yourself be happy, Roz. Be as happy as I was with Lucy. Promise me you'll try.'

'I'll try,' she said, kissing his hand. 'Of course I'll try.'

Hugo died less than an hour later. 'I think he was waiting for you,' the nurse said to Roz. 'He wanted to see you one more time, but you could tell he was ready to go.'

Numb, Roz let Drew take her to a hotel. She let him take off her shoes and her jacket. She let him put his arms around her. 'You can cry now,' he said.

She hadn't cried since her father's death, but she was too weak to withstand the dragon of grief this time. It reared up, tail lashing, roaring fire, and she let it consume her. She clung to Drew while she wept for Hugo, wept for her father too, and her mother, and for her fear, and for all the time she had wasted throwing up barriers and refusing to let anyone close.

She cried until her eyes were swollen and her throat was raw and her head was pounding, until she was too tired to do more than draw a juddering breath. She let Drew put her to bed and stroke her hair until she fell asleep, and when she woke, the sadness was still there but the dragon had slunk away, its terror tamed at last.

Drew had dealt with everything while she slept, blurred by exhaustion and grief. Two days later, they flew back to Edinburgh airport, where he had left his Land Rover and where Finn met them, his expression sober.

'I'm very sorry to hear about Hugo,' he said, and Roz's mouth trembled as she hugged him.

That was the trouble with crying, she was learning. Once you started, it was difficult to stop.

'I realise it's the last thing you want to think about now,' Finn said, 'but I've brought the expert's report on your ring. I thought you might want to see it.'

They sat in a coffee shop in the airport terminal while Finn told them what Hugo's friend had managed to find out. 'The hallmarks show that the ring was made in Edinburgh by Duncombe & Lister, then one of the top Edinburgh jewellers. One of her students who has a particular interest in 1920s jewellery design did some research and was able to find a design for the original necklace in the National Museum.'

'Really?' Roz cupped her hands around her coffee cup, conscious of the first spark of interest since hearing the news about Hugo.

'It was an unusual commission, which is why the design was kept. Charles Blackmore wanted a necklace with four different but equally beautiful blue stones: an opal, a moonstone, a sandstone and a sapphire. And this is what they came up with.'

With a flourish, Finn pulled out a colour drawing of the finished necklace and showed it to Roz, who gasped, the ring on her finger pulsing. The necklace had been exquisite, the four glowing blue stones, each unique and yet complementing the others beautifully, set in a cobweb of fine diamonds and pearls.

Drew whistled. 'Amelia Blackmore must have felt desperate to break up a necklace like that.'

'Indeed,' said Finn. 'But the expert has been able to confirm that the blue opal in Roz's ring is the same as that in the necklace, so between that and her grandmother's birth certificate showing that she was Iris's granddaughter and born at Strathann, I think we can say that Roz is entitled to a share of the Blackmore Trust.'

If only she could tell Hugo, Roz couldn't help thinking. He would have been so pleased for her.

'So what happens now?' she asked.

'Well, as Drew pointed out before, it's not much of an inheritance as it stands at the moment. The house is certainly too dangerous to live in. We still need to establish whether there are any female descendants of Iris's three sisters. The provenance of the rings may give us a starting point. The rings are all distinctive, so I'm hoping that if I put out a query on various sites online, someone may recognise them.'

When they got up to go, Roz exclaimed at the sight of a wallet on the floor by Drew's chair. 'Is that yours, Drew?'

'That's odd,' he said, bending to pick it up. 'It must have fallen out of my pocket when I was carrying the coffees.'

'I hope you haven't been pickpocketed?' said Finn.

There was a faint frown between Drew's brows as he checked the contents. 'No, all my cards are still there, and a ten-quid note, which was all the cash I had. If it was a pickpocket, they got away empty-handed.'

Two weeks later, Roz went back to London and buried Hugo next to his Lucy. Drew went with her, and comforted her while she wept some more, and then he took her back to Dundonan.

'You look tired,' he said when they arrived. 'Why don't you rest?'

'I need some air,' said Roz. She *was* tired, but there was something she needed to do before she could sleep. 'Let's go down to the beach.'

It was a still September evening. The water gleamed gold in

the sunset. The hills rolled blue into the distance. An otter dived with a plop, leaving ripples in the tranquil water.

'I'm sorry I pushed you away before,' Roz said abruptly.

'Why did you?' asked Drew. 'I thought I was getting through your defences at last.'

'That's why,' she said, with a crooked smile.

She told him then about her father dying. She told him how scared she had been as a child that she would not survive the pain of his loss, and that ever since she had been terrified by the thought of loving someone again and losing them. 'I didn't realise that I was terrified, though,' she said. 'I thought I was independent and brave. I thought it was easier not to love at all. Easier not to get involved with messy emotions. Easier not to *need* someone.

'When I fell apart here that day, I was humiliated. I couldn't pretend that I was brave any longer. I was scared by Richard, but I was more scared by needing someone to lean on in a way I never had before. No, not someone,' she corrected herself. 'You. I wanted to lean on *you*.'

They had stopped walking, and Drew's eyes were fixed on her face. Roz's gaze slid away. She had wanted to apologise, to explain, but she was making a mess of it and she could feel her cheeks prickling with embarrassment.

'I know it's stupid,' she stumbled on, 'because it's not as if we ever had a ... thing.'

'A *thing*?' The undercurrent of amusement in Drew's voice deepened the humiliating flush.

'You know what I mean,' she said crossly. 'I shouldn't need you when we'd never even kissed, let alone ... you know.'

A smile was twitching the corner of his mouth. 'We can soon put that right,' he said, and reached for her, but Roz stepped back.

'I wasn't asking you to kiss me.'

'I wish you would,' said Drew. 'I've thought about kissing you ever since you walked into the bar at the Anchor that evening, with your silver eyes. I was determined to beat down those prickles, but it seemed obvious that you were wary about men, so I told myself to give you space to learn to trust me. When you let me hold you, I thought my patience had paid off at last, but then all your prickles went up again and you ignored me, although you rushed to give Finn a big hug, I noticed.'

Roz could feel a smile quivering. 'You weren't jealous, were you?'

'Yes, I was, and you knew it,' he said with mock severity.

She let the smile spread. 'I'm sorry,' she said. 'How can I make it up to you?'

'You can ask me to kiss you now,' said Drew.

Roz stepped forward deliberately and rested her palms against his chest. She smiled up at him.

'Kiss me,' she said obediently. 'Kiss me now, *please*,' she corrected herself at his look, and he pulled her closer.

'I thought you'd never ask,' he said.

September slid into October without Roz noticing. In spite of her sadness about Hugo, she was more content than she had ever been. Dundonan would soon close for the winter, leaving only a skeleton staff for maintenance, and Drew had asked her to design a new website. It felt good to be using her skills again, even if she suspected the job was a favour, and she was glad to be in the warm office when the autumn winds blustered around the castle and swirled the dead leaves in great flurries along the drive.

And then there was Drew. He didn't spend much time in the office, preferring to be out and about in the hotel and grounds, but whenever he came in, bringing the tang of sea air with him, their eyes would meet, and they would smile.

'Och, get a room!' Douglas would cry in mock disgust, but Drew only grinned.

'I can't help it,' he said, spreading his hands. 'I love her.'

'Stop it!' Roz always shook her head at him, embarrassed but laughing, but the truth was that she loved him too.

Loving had never been so easy before. She loved the way Drew would rest his hand at the nape of her neck when he leant down to study something she was showing him onscreen. She loved the way his eyes creased in a smile, how his voice deepened with desire. She loved the way he teased her and made her laugh, and how he made her gasp at the merest brush of his fingers.

She had pretty much moved into Drew's flat in the west tower, with its thick stone walls and windows that looked across the bay to Rubha Clachan. Drew hung the painting Hugo had saved from the fire above the fireplace in the cosy sitting room. Roz stood in front of it every day.

'I'm letting myself be happy, Hugo,' she murmured. 'I promised I would, and I am.'

Whenever the weather permitted, she walked over to Rubha Clachan with a new sense of belonging. Sometimes Drew went with her and helped knock down cobwebs and sweep up some of the dust, but she was happy to go on her own too. She was tied to this place, she knew now. She had promised Finn that she wouldn't take any risks in the house, so as much as she longed to explore upstairs, she had restricted herself to poking around in Charles Blackmore's study in the hope of finding more letters, or some clue to where Iris's sisters had gone.

One windy afternoon, she opened the front door and stopped, instantly aware of the change of atmosphere.

Someone had been there, she knew it. Someone who did not belong. She stepped into the hall. Were those new scuff marks in the dust? Her attempts at cleaning had made little impact on the century of neglect, and although the floors were clearer now, they were still dusty. Cautiously she opened the door to the study. Some books had been picked up and put down carelessly.

Her heart thudded. She strained to listen, but the house was creaking and rattling in the stiff breeze. Whoever it was had gone.

'A trespasser?' Drew suggested when she told him about it. He poured tea into a mug and handed it to her.

Curled up on the sofa with Bonnie's comforting warmth, Roz bit her lip. She hated the idea of anyone being in the house. 'I've felt that someone's watching me lately,' she confessed. A flash of binoculars in the sunlight. A boat passing a little too slowly. A solitary walker on the hillside, looking down at Rubha Clachan. Of course, he might have been looking at the view. He probably *had* been admiring the view, but it was making her uneasy. 'Nothing I can put my finger on, and I know I'm being paranoid, but I keep wondering if it's Richard.'

Drew put down the kettle in concern. 'You haven't had any more texts or messages, have you?'

'Nothing since that one welcoming me to Australia. But there's no signal here.'

'How would he find you?' Drew frowned. 'You've been so careful not to be in any photos that might go online, and you haven't given anyone this as your address.'

'No, you're right,' Roz said, wanting to be reassured. 'He can't find me here.'

But when all the talk locally was of an Australian who had hired a house on the other side of the peninsula for six whole weeks, unheard of at that time of year, Roz's nerves twitched.

'In the shop they think he said he was a New Zealander, not an Australian,' Drew reported. 'Morag says he's a writer and wants peace and quiet to finish a book.'

'What did he look like? Did you ask her?'

'I did, but she was a bit vague. She thought he was "nice".'

'My mother thought Richard was nice too,' said Roz bitterly.

'To be honest, they were all more interested in the news that Kenny Patterson had had his gun stolen from his vehicle. He swears he only left it untended for a few minutes while he went to check on a ewe, and there were no other cars around, so it's a mystery.'

Drew watched Roz, who was twisting her ring anxiously. 'Look, let's go and see this man,' he said. 'There's no point in wondering. If he's who he says he is, then you'll know and can stop thinking about him.'

'And if he's Richard?'

'I'll be with you,' Drew said. 'And like Kenny Patterson, I've got a licence for a gun.'

The house was a holiday let, set alone at the end of a rough track. Roz was very jittery as Drew's Land Rover bumped towards it. His gun lay across the back seat. She had a bad feeling about this.

What if it was Richard who had stolen Kenny's gun? What if he shot Drew? What if Drew shot *him*?

'Stop worrying,' said Drew, although she hadn't said a word. 'We're just going to walk up to the door and see who answers. Hopefully it'll just be a mad writer, cranky at being interrupted.'

But there was no answer when Drew knocked. He walked round the house, Roz scuttling nervously behind him, and cupped his hands to peer in the windows. 'Car's here, but there's no one home,' he said. 'Maybe he's gone for a walk.'

'Maybe.' Roz looked around. It was a bleak place. This side of the promontory was more exposed, and the landscape felt harsher, the hills dropping down to cliffs rather than the gentle sweep of beach that she was used to.

There were no trees at all, but she couldn't shake the feeling that someone was watching them. Crouched behind that clump of gorse bushes? Or inside, concealed behind a curtain?'

'Let's go,' she said to Drew. 'I don't like it here.'

She looked at the house reflected in the wing mirror as Drew drove away, and caught her breath as she thought she saw a curtain twitch, but the track was so bumpy that it could just have been a trick of the light.

49
Iris

Strathann, 1935

By the time Iris's son was born, there was green water in the creeks, and the trees were brimming with birds all twittering and piping and cheeping in a deafening chorus. Guy had been with the stockmen to bring the cattle back from agistment, and they fed on the long, lush grass and grew fat and glossy.

Iris planted some trees by the house and began to create a little garden with a patch of harsh grass where Duncan could sit and play. Guy had wanted to name his son after his father, in spite of Ralph, who, outrageously, had suggested that the child should be named after him as he had brought Guy and Iris together.

There wasn't usually time in the day to be homesick, but every now and then, Iris would be down by the creek, listening to the birds, and she would close her eyes and touch the ring on her finger. She would imagine that she was sitting on the stones at Skara, with the cool breeze in her face, feeling the pulse of the earth there and the pull of the past, and her heart would ache for home.

But she had a home in Australia too, she would remind herself. She had a husband and a son and another baby on the way. It had been impossible not to grow fond of Ralph, too. Her uncle was inextricably part of her life now.

One hot night, Iris sat with him and Guy on the veranda. She was at the lumbering stage of pregnancy and she couldn't get comfortable. When she heard the bush stone-curlews screaming in the darkness, she shuddered.

'I hate that noise!'

'You know what it means,' said Ralph lightly, and Guy frowned.

'Don't tell Iris things like that in her state! Besides, we've heard those bloody birds plenty of times in the past without anyone dropping dead.'

The heat soared again the next day. Guy was busy in the cattle yards, and Iris was edgy. 'Let's go to the creek,' she said to Ralph, attempting to puff strands of damp hair from her forehead. 'Can you keep an eye on Duncan?' she asked him. 'He moves faster than me at the moment and I want Polly to finish scrubbing the stockmen's quarters.'

With Ralph beside her, Iris waddled down to the creek while Duncan ran excitedly ahead. The shade was a blessed relief, and she took off her shoes, sighing with pleasure as the cool water closed over her swollen feet.

She stood for a while, hands pressed into the small of her back, watching an egret dipping and diving over the dark green water, until an ominous crack made her turn.

After that, everything seemed to be happening in slow

motion. She saw a huge branch tearing slowly from the ghost gum directly above where Duncan was bending to examine a leaf with the intense curiosity of a toddler. Her own mouth was opening, but it took for ever for a scream of warning to come out. Her limbs were reacting too slowly. She was too slow to turn, too slow to struggle out of the water and get her legs to run towards her child.

She was going to be too late... too late... too late... and then Ralph was there, pushing Duncan out of the way just before the branch fell onto her uncle with a crash that sent the cockatoos bursting out of the treetops with squawks of protest.

'Uncle Ralph!'

Duncan was yelling in outrage, more in surprise than hurt. Iris snatched him up and screamed for Polly. 'I need help! Fetch Guy! Fetch the boss!'

She dropped to her knees beside Ralph, who was pinned under the great branch, white-faced with pain.

'Can you move at all?'

'Can't... can't do... anything.'

The branch was solid, crushing him into the ground, and much too heavy for Iris to lift.

'I'll have to get Guy,' she said, making to scramble to her feet, but he groped for her hand.

'Don't go,' he croaked. 'Stay with me, please, Iris. I think I'm a goner this time, and I don't think it'll be long.' A faint smile touched his mouth. 'That bloody curlew had it right this time.'

'Oh, Uncle Ralph, no!'

'I'm sorry for everything I've done to you.' His eyes closed in pain and she kissed his hand.

'You don't need to apologise,' she said.

'Should have done. Hard for both of you,' he said with difficulty. 'But I can't regret all of it because some of those bad things brought you and Guy to me.'

Tears were standing in Iris's eyes as she held Duncan close with one arm and kept the fingers of her other hand twined tightly around her uncle's.

'Who would have thought I'd end up here, eh? I spent my life chasing wealth and adventure, but since you came, I've been happier than ever before. You're a brave girl, Iris,' he said, his voice fading. 'You and that man of yours have done a good job here. I hope you'll stay.'

By the time Guy and Polly came running, Ralph was dead.

They buried Ralph in the shade by the creek, and Iris and Polly both wept. It was very hot and it had to be done quickly. Sweating, the stockmen dug a hole and Guy read a prayer.

Afterwards, Iris left Duncan with Polly and went to find Guy. He was leaning on a rail and watching the horses in the paddock. It was her first chance to tell him what her uncle had said about the difference they had made to Strathann, and his mouth twisted.

'All those years, he was the big villainous figure in my life, and now ... goddammit, I'll miss him.'

'I will too.'

'Strathann is ours now, Iris,' he said.

She nodded.

'What do you want to do?'

'Do?'

'We can sell the property.' He kept his eyes on the horses, flicking their tails against the flies. 'Probably get a decent price for it now. And you could go home to Scotland. I know that's what you want.'

Iris leant beside him, not quite touching. She knew that she mustn't answer him too quickly. She watched the horses too while she turned her mother's ring on her finger.

How she loved Skara! She *did* long for the hills and the sea and the gentle light. But it wasn't home any more. What would it be without her sisters, without Ian? In her mind, Ian's features had grown blurry, and she could no longer remember the exact timbre of his voice. His memory was clouded in a golden haze of sweetness that now felt unreal.

When she looked at Guy, she saw not a dream, but someone solid, someone real. She knew him now. She knew how his nostrils flared when he was irritated, knew how he narrowed his eyes against the sun and tipped his hat back on his head. She could tell the sound of his boots and the slam of the screen door when he came into the kitchen. She knew the smell of his skin and the exact angle of his jaw.

'That's not what I want now,' she said carefully. 'We've worked too hard here. Duncan belongs here.' She touched her stomach. 'This little one will belong here. *You* belong here, Guy. And that means I belong here too.'

'It means you're stuck here,' said Guy. His jaw worked. 'That's what you said before. You were *stuck here*,' he repeated, as if the words were bitter in his mouth. 'And that was before Duncan and the new baby. I don't want you to be here because you have to be.'

'Guy.' Iris turned to face him. 'If I'm stuck, it's because I want to be. Yes, part of me will always be homesick for Scotland, but Strathann is home now. I want to be here, with you.'

'What about Ian?' He sounded as if the words were forced out of him.

'I loved Ian,' she said, quite simply after all. 'But I'm not that girl any more. I don't love him now. I don't know him now. But I know *you*. I love *you*.'

Guy stilled, then shifted to look down at her, and the dawning hope in his eyes made Iris feel foolish for not having understood. 'I thought you knew,' she said.

He shook his head. 'You never said.'

'You never said you loved me either,' she pointed out.

'I thought you knew,' he echoed, and the creases in his cheeks deepened with a smile.

'Well, I didn't,' said Iris almost crossly, but she was smiling too as she slipped her arms around his waist and leant into the familiar hard contours of his body.

Guy took his hat off and pulled her closer so that he could rest his cheek against her hair. 'I do,' he said softly, and Iris turned her face up to kiss him.

'I do too.'

Strathann, 1936

Iris and Guy had decided to call the new baby Ralph if it was a boy, but in the event, it was a girl, and Iris named her for her own mother, Amelia.

Amelia's birth made her miss her sisters anew, and for a while afterwards she felt desperately lonely. She so wanted to be able to tell her sisters that they had a niece named after their beloved mother. Just because she wasn't sending letters didn't mean she didn't think of them all the time. Where were they? she wondered constantly. What were they doing? Were they safe? Were they happy?

She was resigned now to never knowing.

Now, Iris carried Amelia on her hip down to the paddock, where Guy had lifted Duncan onto the saddle in front of him and was showing him how to hold on to the pommel. Watching his patience and his small son's delight, Iris could only marvel that this was the same dark and dangerous man she had first seen on the ship as they left Southampton. She would not have recognised him if she hadn't known that it was him.

But perhaps she wouldn't recognise herself either, she thought, remembering how wretchedly homesick she had been. There would always be a part of her that longed for her sisters and for Skara, but she had a new home now.

'Wave at Duncan,' she encouraged Amelia, and lifted her hand to show her how it was done. The sunlight caught the opal in the ring she still wore every day, and the baby gurgled and reached for it with chubby fingers. Seeing that her daughter was mesmerised by the sparkle of the stone, Iris twisted her hand back and forth to make it glint.

'This will be yours one day,' she told her. 'It's from a special place on the other side of the world, a place where the hills roll into the sea and the light is soft and the air is cool and clear.'

She smiled, remembering, and kissed the top of her daughter's head. 'I wish you could meet your aunts, Amelia. I hope you'll be like them, brave like Rose, clever like Lily, sweet and sparkling like darling Daisy.'

The old grief for Daisy clogged Iris's throat, and she swallowed down the tears as she watched Amelia try to grasp the blue flash. 'I wonder where Lily and Rose are right now,' she murmured to herself, remembering how the four of them had sat on the fallen stones at Rubha Clachan the night before she left for Ceylon.

Like the stones in their rings, the sisters had been meant to stay together. Now they were scattered around the world, Iris thought sadly. She kissed Amelia's head. 'Perhaps you will go there,' she told her. 'Perhaps Rose and Lily will have daughters too, and you can take the rings back to Skara, where they belong. Together.'

50

Roz

Skara, present day

Over the next few days, Roz's nerves settled, perhaps because the weather was so atrocious that she couldn't leave the castle. Even Bonnie was reluctant to go for a walk. The rain was relentless, sweeping in great curtains across the sea, or being tossed in fistfuls at the windows by winds that prowled and howled around Dundonan's towers and turrets.

Just when she thought she couldn't bear another day of relentless rain, the sky cleared. The temperature dropped overnight and she woke to a landscape glittering with frost. From the other headland, Rubha Clachan beckoned.

It felt so good to be out again that she shook off her earlier jitters and took a thermos of coffee with her. 'Want me to come with you?' Drew asked, but she shook her head.

'You're busy. I'll be fine.'

Impossible to believe that Richard could be here, in Skara, on this bright morning. The sea was a gleaming rippled metallic sheet and across the water the mountains were topped with snow. Roz could have sworn that they were close enough to touch.

She walked along the beach, enjoying the crunch of her boots on the frigid sand, remembering how she had avoided it once, frightened by the rushing tide and that dense swirling mist. It held no fear for her now. The voices that echoed on the wind, the sense of other women, long, long dead – they were part of the landscape, just as she was. She had no reason to be afraid.

She had feared so much and for so long, she realised, and so many of those fears had turned out to be baseless. She had been scared of love, and look how foolish she had been, she thought, her mouth curving with remembered pleasure as she thought about the night before, of Drew's persuasive hands, of the shivery delight of his skin on her skin, his lips on hers.

When she reached Rubha Clachan, the stones themselves glittered in the cold, as if they were embedded with chips of diamonds. Roz perched on the edge of the one she always thought of as hers and winced at the chill through her jeans. She wished she'd thought to bring a mat of some kind. Unscrewing the top of the thermos, she poured out the coffee and warmed her hands around the cup.

She was watching the steam curling into the air. She was thinking of Drew, of his mouth and his hands and the way he smiled against her skin. She was thinking how good it felt to belong. She was thinking that this was how it felt to be happy.

So when Richard's voice spoke above her, Roz's heart jolted in shock and coffee splashed over her jacket as she swung round.

'I had a feeling you'd be here today.'

She hadn't been thinking about him at all, and now here he

was, jumping lightly down into the hollow where the stones rested, his eyes cold and watchful. A predator's eyes.

In one hand, he held a gun.

Knowing that he wanted her to be afraid, Roz ignored the terror balling in her stomach and made a show of brushing at the coffee stain on her jacket, trying not to let her hands tremble.

'Is that Kenny Patterson's gun?' she asked.

Richard hoisted it in his hand. 'I don't know his name.' He shrugged. 'I just know he's careless. Lucky for me, though. I might have struggled to get a gun here otherwise.'

Roz wasn't going to ask what he wanted it for. She was afraid she knew. 'You've been watching me,' she said instead.

'I have,' Richard agreed. 'I've been looking for you for a long time, Rose. Anyone would think you didn't want to keep in touch with your own stepfather. In the end, I got a mate of mine who's into facial recognition to put out an alert for you.'

As casually as she could, Roz screwed the top onto the thermos and got to her feet. 'That's how you found me in Paris.'

Her mind was whirring frantically. How was she going to get away and back to Drew? The gun in Richard's hand looked huge. He was a police officer. He would know how to load it. How to use it.

'You disappeared again for a while, but then there you were, arriving in Adelaide.' He laughed at the memory. 'It was almost like you wanted me to know you were coming.'

All Roz could think of was to keep him talking. 'I'm surprised you didn't come and find me then,' she said.

'I was planning to separate you from that friend of yours in Ridgewell, but you disappeared before I could arrange anything.

I didn't think you'd leave so quickly.' Richard sounded aggrieved. 'Where did you go?'

'To the outback.' With a lift of her heart, Roz noticed that the tide had turned. Out of the corner of her eye, she could see the mist starting to creep onto the beach.

'Luckily a mate of mine saw you'd booked a last-minute ticket to London. I managed to get on the same flight,' he remembered, pleased with himself. 'You didn't even notice me.'

She had been too distressed about Hugo to notice anything.

'It was easy enough to follow you after that,' Richard went on. 'You seemed to be attached to that bloke who met you at the airport. I picked his pocket at Edinburgh to find his address on his driving licence, and he never knew a thing.' He snorted at his own cleverness. 'Once I knew where you'd be, I made my plans, and then I came to find you.'

He was standing between her and the track. The only other way back to Dundonan was across the treacherous bog, and Richard would catch her easily if she tried to run that way.

He followed her yearning look at the castle. 'No help from there, Rose. It's just you and me, and I've a score to settle.'

But there was the beach. The mist was coming, silently, steadily, smothering the sand, reaching out to the dunes.

Roz shifted casually, inching closer to the path through the dunes. She would have to keep him talking. The mist wasn't thick enough yet.

'You seem to have gone to a lot of trouble, Richard,' she said, forcing her voice not to quaver. 'Flying all this way, renting a house, pretending to be a writer. What do you want?'

'Do you have any idea what it's like for a police officer to be in prison?' His voice was light, almost toneless, but more chilling than anger.

'You killed my mother.'

'She was asking for it,' he snarled. 'Contradicting me, planning to go away with you on some trip. I couldn't have that. A wife belongs with her husband.'

In spite of her fear, Roz felt her heart lift. 'So she *was* thinking about coming away with me?'

'Said she was going to insist.' Richard gave a yelp of laughter. '*Insist!* I was just trying to teach her a lesson. Maybe I hit her a bit too hard,' he acknowledged. 'If you hadn't meddled, I could have dealt with it. I could have got rid of her body. It would have been fine, but no, you had to come over and make a fuss and stand up in court and accuse your own stepfather of murder.'

There was a faint tremble in his voice now, and Roz realised that his control was precarious.

'You need to be taught a lesson too,' he warned her. 'Nobody treats me the way you did and gets away with it. You sold my house and swanned around Europe while I was in prison, and now you're living in a castle like Lady Muck. You don't get away with that, Rose. Not this time.'

Swallowing, Roz inched towards the dunes. 'What exactly do you want of me?'

'I've had plenty of time to think about that.' Richard weighed the gun in his hand, his smile cold. 'Why do you think I rented that dump of a house? It's nice and isolated. There won't be anyone to hear you scream for forgiveness.'

Dread curdled in her veins. This wasn't a nightmare, it was really happening. He was going to kill her. *Come on*, she willed the fog that had once terrified her. It was almost at the height of the dunes. *Come closer.*

'I'm a methodical man, as you know,' he went on, almost pleasantly. 'I've made my preparations and I'm going to enjoy punishing you the way you deserve, you bitch,' he finished with a terrifying swerve into venom.

Roz stared at him, horrified. He had always been controlling, vicious, but now it seemed his time in prison had tipped him over the edge into insanity. She would not be able to reason with him.

'I saw you, you know,' he said. 'You and lover boy, poking around the house, him with his gun. I knew you were getting suspicious, so it was time to move at last. I've been watching you, and I knew this is where you come on your own, God only knows why,' he added, glancing disparagingly around him. 'I just had to wait for the bloody weather to clear, and now, sure enough, here you are, just like I knew you would be.'

With another terrifying swing of tone, he smiled and lifted the gun. 'Well, time we got on.'

Higher, higher came the mist, like a living thing, creeping silently up the dunes, gobbling up the sunlight as it advanced.

Keep talking. Keep talking. 'How are we going to get to the house?' Roz asked.

'I drove the car down earlier and hid it behind this dump that you seem so obsessed by. So better say goodbye,' he added, with a chuckle that knotted her throat.

The blue opal on Roz's finger seemed to be flashing her a message in the weak sunlight. Without thinking, she fumbled it off.

'I can give you money,' she said unsteadily. 'This ring is worth a lot.'

'What do I want with a crappy ring?' he jeered. 'I'll be getting Millie's money, one way or the other, when you don't return to Australia. I've found just the spot on the cliffs to get rid of you once and for all, but first I want you on your knees, snivelling for forgive—'

She didn't wait for him to finish. She had only one chance. She threw the ring straight at him. The blue flash distracted him, and he put a hand up instinctively to stop it hitting his face. That meant he couldn't bring up the gun, and off balance, he stumbled on the uneven surface while Roz turned and ran, dodging desperately down the path through the dunes until she could plunge into the mist.

It swallowed her, gobbling her up as she stumbled blindly along the beach. Richard was swearing, coming after her. The mist was a living thing, pressing against her mouth, choking her, plucking at her hair, just as it had before. It poked chill fingers down her neck and curled around her ankles like a hand, but it had saved her.

She heaved to a halt, disorientated again. It was impossible to tell which way was the sea.

Her ears strained to hear above the sound of Richard's blundering progress behind her. Was that the shushing of waves against the sand or were those sobs? Was that a gull wheeling on the wind or a scream?

'Who's there?' Richard's voice came sharp and terrifyingly near. He could hear the noises too. She could tell by the fear in his voice.

This way. A cold breath in her ear, no more than that, but insistent. *Run now. Run.*

Roz put her hands out before her and set off, with no idea if she was running straight for Richard, for the sea or for the rocks.

The mist was gluey now. It stuck to her skin. Fear and distress swirled around her. Had the four sisters tried to run too? Had they been caught in the fret, struggling to get away from their pursuers? Had their hearts boomed in panic as Roz's was doing?

It was so loud in her ears that she was sure Richard must hear it, but he was yelling, thrashing against the mist, firing the gun in blind panic.

Roz froze. The shots sounded so close, so terribly close. But so loud. Would Drew hear them at Dundonan? Would he come and find her?

Richard was still shouting. 'Get off! Who are you? Leave me alone! Rose, get back here, you bitch!'

Run.

She ran once more, putting her trust in the mist, in the four sisters who had run in terror too.

When she stumbled to a halt again, she could smell seaweed. The rocks! She was by the rocks! It was such a relief to realise that she knew where she was that she felt quite dizzy.

This way.

She remembered how she had climbed up onto the boggy grass before, how she had burst at last into the clear air and found Drew there. Richard would see her, but she had to get out of this cloying mist. She had to be able to see what she was running to.

Or from.

She groped her way over the rocks. She kept slipping on seaweed, and bit back a cry as her palms scraped on the shells that were fused to the stones.

Behind her, she could hear Richard stumbling and swearing, and when she made it at last to a tussock of grass, she crouched there to catch her breath.

There was someone beside her, just out of sight behind the dense veil of mist. They urged her on, guiding her along the edge of the grass, the edge of the rocks, until she realised that she couldn't hear Richard any longer.

Where was he? Had he found the grass too?

Shh. She couldn't be sure that she had heard the voice, but the lightest of touches on her arm, no more than a breath, made her stop.

The bog was shivering. He was coming.

A sob of fear rose in her throat, and she tensed to run on, but that whisper of a touch held her in place.

Too late, she realised that the mist was thinning. Without warning, Richard loomed out of it, wild-eyed, twisting his head from side to side in confusion, Kenny Patterson's gun waving precariously. 'Where are they?' he demanded. Then his gaze fell on Roz, crouched on the very edge of the rocks. His eyes cleared and he lifted the gun, but before he could pull the trigger, the mist swirled up and around him like a living thing and he jerked with a yell of alarm.

Roz didn't see what happened next. She heard a hiss, a shout, a sickening crack.

Then silence.

The sea fret was dissolving, receding, shivering away into the cold air. 'Thank you,' she whispered. She fell forward onto her knees, her heart racing with reaction. 'Thank you.'

'Roz!' Drew was running towards her, calling for her, but she couldn't move. She could only kneel on the frozen grass and stare down at where Richard lay on the rocks, his head bent at almost exactly the same angle as her mother's had been.

It was spring before the formalities of dealing with Richard's death were settled. Accidental death, the Procurator Fiscal had ruled. Drew had found Roz's ring where Richard had dropped it, and Kenny Patterson had his gun back, with a warning to be more careful with it.

The first tightly furled shoots of bracken were poking up, a bright, fresh green through the slumped brown clumps of the previous year. The raw edge had gone from the wind. At Dundonan, the hotel was gearing up for another busy season.

In the office, Roz's phone rang. 'It's Finn,' she said to Drew, who was perched on the edge of the desk. 'I'll put it on speaker.'

Finn had become a good friend. He often spent weekends at Dundonan when he didn't have to be with his parents. Henrietta was fond of him too, and the four of them speculated endlessly together about what had happened to the other three Blackmore girls, bouncing ideas around about how to trace any of their descendants.

'I've just heard from someone who thinks she has the moonstone ring!' Finn couldn't contain himself, and started talking the moment Roz picked up the call.

'No!' said Roz. 'What's her name? Where is she? What did she say?'

Drew rolled his eyes at her excitement. 'Give the man a chance to answer!'

'I don't mind.' Finn laughed. 'I feel the same. Ridiculously excited. Her name's Clara, but that's all I know. She sent a photo of her ring, and it certainly *looks* like the one from Amelia's necklace. Of course we'd have to establish provenance,' he added, summoning some lawyerly caution. 'I haven't even replied yet. I wanted to let you know straight away.'

'I know this sounds mad,' Roz said to Drew, when Finn had ended the call with promises to let her know the moment he had any more information, 'but I need to go and tell the Four Sisters.'

She almost ran over to Rubha Clachan, where she sat on the stone she secretly thought of as hers, resting her palms on its smooth surface. On her finger the opal glowed, and the stone beneath her seemed to be thrumming too, almost as if they already knew.

The rings were meant to be together, with the stones.

'There's another one coming,' she told the stones around her. 'I'm sure of it. We'll find the others too.'

She sat there on the subtly humming stones, thinking about the four sisters of legend, torn from their home and from each other. They had not been able to save themselves, but they had saved her, Roz was sure of it.

She hadn't told anyone, not even Drew, about that terrible day, smothered in sea fret and running for her life. He would find a rational explanation: the noises were birds, the sense of not being alone simply Roz drawing on her own strength. And maybe he would be right, she acknowledged, but she preferred to think of the sisters coming to her aid when she needed it most.

She thought, too, of the other sisters: of Iris, her grandmother's grandmother; of courageous Rose, clever Lily, Daisy the drama queen. She and Finn had wondered so much about what had happened to them and to their rings, and now, at last, it seemed they might discover another story.

The sky was purple and lilac, streaked with orange and red as the sun slid behind the mountains. It was time to go. Roz gave the stone a pat as she got to her feet. 'The rings are coming home,' she promised.

She ran lightly down through the dunes and onto the beach. On the sand, she paused, cocking her head to listen for the echo of ancient laughter blowing on the wind through the seagrass, and then she turned, smiling, and walked home, back to Dundonan, and to Drew.

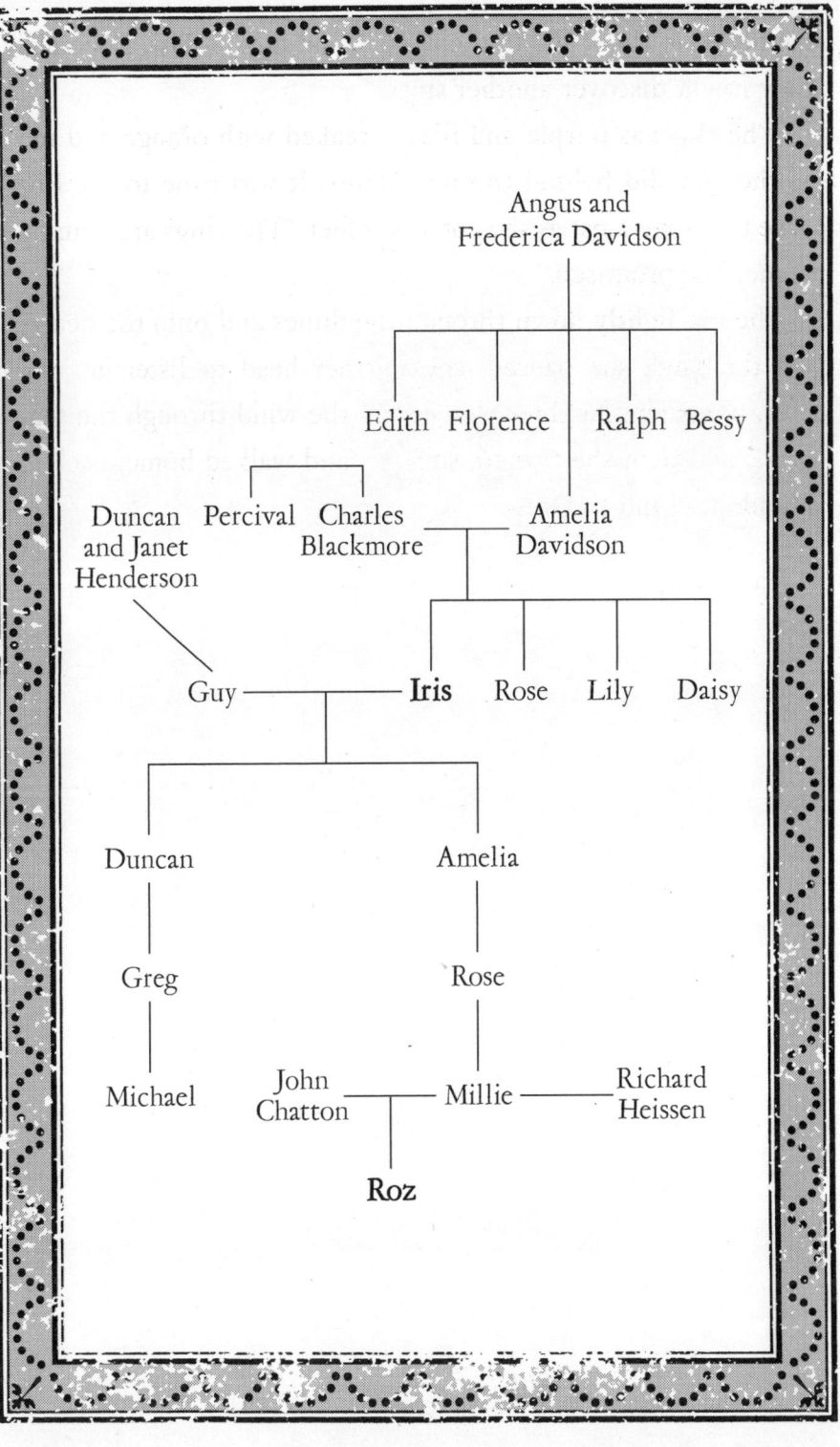

ACKNOWLEDGEMENTS

This book is dedicated to my agent, Caroline Sheldon, with thanks for her unwavering support over the years. Sadly, *The Sea Stone Sisters* will be the last book we will work on together, but I wish her a long, happy and very well-deserved retirement. I will miss her terribly, but am looking forward to working with Safae El-Ouahabi in the future, and am grateful to them both for everything they have done to help bring *The Sea Stone Sisters* to life.

When I was first published, I thought that an author wrote a book and that was that. I know better now. The writing is only the start of a shared enterprise that involves a whole team of people – publishers, editors, copyeditors, designers, proof-readers, publicists, the rights teams, lawyers and many more – and it is a pleasure now to be able to thank the exceptional team at Headline, who have made *The Sea Stone Sisters* the book it is. I am so grateful to them all, with a special mention for Jane Selley and her thoughtful copyediting, for publisher Sherise Hobbs for her enthusiasm for the project from the very start, and most particularly for my editor, Sophie Keefe, whose excitement has been so infectious, whose feedback has been so valuable, and whose encouragement has meant more than I say.

In the 1870s my great-grandfather was posted to the Civil Service in Ceylon, from where he wrote regular letters home to his mother and three sisters. I still have his letters, which were transcribed by my late father, and self-published as *Grandfather's Snakebite*, after his account of being bitten by a snake. Happily, he survived, unlike the fictional Bertie. He was a terrible snob and would doubtless have been appalled to find himself in a novel, but his accounts of colonial life in Ceylon and vivid descriptions of the country have been more useful and inspiring than he could ever have guessed.

While my father's grandfather was in Ceylon, my great-grandmother on my mother's side was on her way to Australia, starting a family tradition of back and forth between Australia and Scotland that I have been very happy to continue. I never met either of my great-grandparents, but I am indebted to them both for unwittingly providing so much inspiration for Iris's story.

But my greatest thanks go to John Harding for his patience, often tried, for feeding me and watering me and for keeping me steady. He might think I don't know what he does quietly in the background, but I do. I couldn't have written this book without him.

**Escape to the French Riviera
and discover Lily's story...**

The MOON STONE SISTER

Coming January 2027 from

REVIEW

RAISING READERS
Books Build Bright Futures

Dear Reader,

We'd love your attention for one more page to tell you about the crisis in children's reading, and what we can all do.

Studies have shown that reading for fun is the **single biggest predictor of a child's future life chances** – more than family circumstance, parents' educational background or income. It improves academic results, mental health, wealth, communication skills, ambition and happiness.[1]

The number of children reading for fun is in rapid decline. Young people have a lot of competition for their time. In 2024, 1 in 10 children and young people in the UK aged 5 to 18 did not own a single book at home.[2]

Hachette works extensively with schools, libraries and literacy charities, but here are some ways we can all raise more readers:

- Reading to children for just 10 minutes a day makes a difference
- Don't give up if children aren't regular readers – there will be books for them!
- Visit bookshops and libraries to get recommendations
- Encourage them to listen to audiobooks
- Support school libraries
- Give books as gifts

There's a lot more information about how to encourage children to read on our website: **www.RaisingReaders.co.uk**

Thank you for reading.

hachette UK

---

[1] OECD, '21st-Century Readers: Developing Literacy Skills in a Digital World', 2021, https://www.oecd.org/en/publications/21st-century-readers_a83d84cb-en.html

[2] National Literacy Trust, 'Book Ownership in 2024', November 2024, https://literacytrust.org.uk/research-services/research-reports/book-ownership-in-2024